Journey
Part II of III

When you step on it…

…sometimes, it pushes back

Continuing
The Love Story of the Century

For more information about Journey, to order bulk copies, or to have comments directed to the author, send an email to:

catlansamuels@gmail.com

About our books, visit: www.treborarthurpublishing.com

Journey Part II, Paper Version - ISBN: 978-0-9884957-2-2

Covers by David Schoeffler
Edited by Suzanne Driscoll

To find more about Journey:
- Google Search: Journey Catlan Samuels
- Amazon: Amazon.com/dp/B009WBJAO0
- Barnes & Noble: Shows up in Google search – Nook version
- Web site & video: TreborArthurPublishing.com
- Facebook: Catlan Samuels
- Twitter: @CatlanSamuels

For

brother Mark

and

sister Carol

When we needed each other

we were always there.

When we didn't,

we were still there -

that's when it mattered just as much...

Dear Journey Traveler,

We start the excitement again in Journey Part II right where you and I left each other in Part I (well, almost). Frankly I was exhausted at the end of Part I and although the ending is pretty disturbing and profound, when I went back to it, the ending needed and deserved a little more description. There is so much more to the story; the loss, the frail hope that they all had clung to, now so unexpectedly threatened. Therefore, the beginning in this book is a little longer than the original end of Part I where you read what I had planned for Part II.

And a big thanks to Journey fans. What I mean is, based on feedback and some prodding, Part II is written assuming you know the vicarious and colored background history of our friends. However, for you, some time may have passed since you ventured through Part I, or you may be new to the adventures, romance and antics of Journey and our friends. If so help is here – and this is where the fans prodded me to burn a number of evenings to help keep this story together for everyone: Early readers and friendly editors of the Part II manuscript received a "character map." They loved it. So I have taken their advice and included character synopses (who belongs to whom and so on) and short overviews at the beginning of this adventure. Also, readers asked for more background on Torrin; if you are looking to know more about him, you shall not be disappointed.

Thank you for the success of the Journey series. It seems that our friends herein have become the topic of many a "fireside" conversation (hopefully with a hearty mug of beverage). We find Journey fans to be an eclectic bunch – fitting it is. Very!

Also, early readers have told me Part II starts darkly. Yes, you are right to say it does, but keeping what is dear and precious is we find, harder sometimes than just accepting it. Once we lose something, or it's on the verge of being taken from us, we certainly learn to appreciate it. But what if we try to hold on, fight for it and then lose it? That starts the dangerous theatrics. There are many surprises in store, not only for you, but for our friends as they press on.

Journey Part II takes you along the rocky and wonderful path of getting what you thought you wanted without seeing it there, but then wondering what you asked for. Isn't that so true in much of life?

As you read, imagine thunderous music playing deep in the background. Sometimes you hear it, sometimes you don't, but it's always there. And as with really great music, you never know what's next; we just look forward to that wonderful conclusion that our hearts so richly desire and deserve.

And now, an early appeal for some technical forgiveness. A

sweet and dear friend let me stay at her cabin in the seclusion of a very large and wonderful forest. Being progressive, I took my tablet to the woods and had many enjoyable hours writing while sitting on a rock in the sun. Alas, the quotation marks that transferred over are different than the regular ones. Blasted technology! Well really, blasted user. Anyway, you may see changes in the quotation marks. I have left it as is, because it's the way it just naturally occurred. Forgive me.

Finally, I leave you with this thought as you venture into Journey Part II: strange as it may seem, as we gain experience, we need more.

Alas, as this story wraps up, I am watching the chipmunks that live under the deck venture out for early morning snacks. The creek is flowing just over its banks from torrential rains that included intense lightening and monstrous tree shaking thunder. My forest, washed fresh from the storm, awaits my early morning trek.

Dark black coffee is required for this morning's trek. Your story was finished very early one morning, as the brightly lit moon succumbed to the sunshine...

Catlan Samuels

Imagination is everything.
It is the preview of life's coming attractions.
Albert Einstein

Find more information visit our website:
www.treborarthurpublishing.com

Email the author at:
catlansamuels@gmail.com

Facebook
https://www.facebook.com/JourneyPartII
On Facebook look for: Catlan Samuels

Twitter -   @CatlanSamuels,   #JourneyLoveStoryoftheCentury

Acknowledgements

Peg, oh my gosh; boulders of huge adventure, woody trails that lead to sprytes and strange surprises, starlit adventures on firelit trails, ice hiking in the dark woods, sweet icy shots by candlelight and so much more? You are truly a Viking wench or warrior by heart (or maybe a Viking warrior of life?), and you not only let the thoughts wander, you stoke them in many heated ways!

For Buzz, you kept pushing every time I saw you, so here you go. And there is a special part just for you and that wonderfully whimsical little granddaughter of yours!

Marilyn, your feedback was always wonderful. It kept me honest. You may never know how much you kept me going at times.

Millie, my childhood Sunday school teacher, your love for life, music and family inspired me all throughout life. Although you are gone, you live on in the rest of us and reminded us to always smile.

To the unknown author of "To those I love and those who love me," thank you, whoever you are; I took some liberties with your work, but as I did, I wept.

Betsy, it takes courage to give frank feedback to a writer (although teaching 2nd grade takes courage too!). Thanks for the feedback, encouragement and careful tending; may your ever faithful spirit always flourish for it has brought the joy of the future to many.

Herb, your family research on our clan from the old world made the geography more real since our ancestors trod across the cold stony paths of this story. Pay attention to the details of the cabin. Good place to raise eight young Vikings?

Camille, thank you for the inspiration that goes back to such pure simplicity; it bowled me over.

Karen, what's there to say? You did it well and will be remembered for many good things, character being a big one. Rest in peace my friend, we all miss you and we are better for you having touched our souls.

To Sue, you always had something nice to say, even when you didn't necessarily understand where I was going, or maybe you did?

Holly, she found it. Yes she did.

Deb, you will never know how much of you is in this story. A world in need of you, lost you way too soon, but the spirit you grew up to, and shared with so many adults and children brings light to a path of darkness. Rest in peace my friend.

Bernabe, just as you are a stark contrast to a crazy world, you inspired a contrast that added so much that was missing. Just the way you do in such a warm and graceful way, you are an inspiration.

To that little group that moved me (and you know who you are), your honest love is not only appreciated, it moved me. Watch for it!

Ross, what's there to say? Your inspirational words rang true!

Josie, your unpretentious grace is about, 'your you' is powerful.

Mary Lee, you may never know the sparkle you put on the story, but you delivered to it a clean energy that will carry forth for generations. Blessings on your adventures.

Peter, maybe it's the hat or the smile, but anyway, your pressing and witty encouragement always came at the right time.

Tammy, now you will know and you don't have to keep asking. Love your energy! And, yes, you will ask again, just differently.

Will, your smile always got brighter as you heard about the chapters coming together. Your smile lights the world for many.

Andrea and company, your caring and generosity made all the difference on a tough day.

Linda, as a reminder back to you, "Yes you can!"

Barb, it is a great word and you will recognize your chapter. Thanks for the inspiration, smiles and sharing of your adventures!

Becky S., the nobleness you bring to the most cherished gift we all share is remarkable. I have witnessed first-hand the smiles in the lives you have brought to the world. Thanks for a special POV to something bigger than any of us.

Suzanne and Dave, your patience, creativity and support are as always, very much appreciated and you are a wonderful gift!

And to you, Dear Reader...

...Without you, there is no Journey, and remember,

you are verra much part of the story...

...'Tis time to trod forth

Journey

Part II of III, The Love Story of the Century

When you step in it...

Sometimes, it pushes back

Prologue

As we amble the worn and frosty path,

We look,

We see,

We feel;

We dream.

Who keeps putting those rocks in our way?

Background and Origins...

So very often readers, friends and family (who are very supportive – for which I am grateful) ask me about the origins of the Journey trilogy. And after having told the tale below a number of times, many told me (and they were quite frank about it), that the origin of this trilogy should be told to you, the faithful reader. These friends have implored to me that this little background adds something because the underpinnings of Journey come from real life experience and drama. Yes, mixed with more than a little anguish, but nonetheless, 'tis real.

So here it is for you if you are interested in a bit of real life romantic drama.

Here goes (deep breath on my part)...

...At a very difficult, yet very telling time in my life, I was in a new and intensely dynamic (very passionate) relationship with an extremely energetic, very smart and incredibly beautiful lady. Things were quite exciting as they often are early in relationships, but there was something nagging at me. The nag was deep in my head, and it was not a good one, but I was blinded as many men are by the events that were taking place. Anyway, it was, I would find much later, a tiny yet very accurate little voice that was giving me a warning – and it was quite some time before I really learned to listen to that voice (foolish me).

OK, back to this rather exotic (oh my, VERY exotic) and compelling relationship – as I had said, things were very exciting and I had sat down to compose a "love letter" to this lady (yes, I am a bit of a romantic). This letter would tell her from the bottom of my happily beating heart how I felt about her, and about our connection. It was important for her to know how she made me sparkle, how special she was and how much her meaningful friendship mattered to me. Please understand, it was a deep and personal letter, and my plan was to write it as a short adventure/romance story – it was to be something different. In my head the plan was to read it aloud over candles and wine with all sorts of flourish and panache to truly express the depth of the feelings I had at the time.

Alas, it did not work out. The letter (a.k.a. story) was about half written when she told me, and quite nicely too, that our relationship was over. It was not working for her and she needed to move on. At least she had the strength of character to do it in person and with real tears.

To be honest with you, I was devastated.

So, that night, while rain soaked the world outside and grief poured from my heart, I was but one small step away from turning that love letter into a forever gone shredded pile of mostly worthless trash. Most likely destined as blown-in brown recycled insulation for some cold northern attic with nothing left but the memory and a little dust.

Instead, I decided to bid her and the fond and rather hot memories of our now lost relationship a final farewell. This small act was to reread what I had written, and see if after the "fall" I still felt the same way about her and us as I had when I started this little adventuresome love letter.

The rest, as they say, "is now history."

That night, after I read the story I did not sleep. Instead, I sat and wrote. I wrote with my head, my heart and through my tears. That night Dessa, Quillan, Torrin and all the characters were born of love and loss, of fear and courage; of anger and justice – all of what we face in life. The whole thing just poured out, and continues to do so.

You see, Journey is not just a story – it's real… And, so with a little research, a long grasp back to my ancestors (thanks to some thoughtful digging on the part of my cousin in Paris) from the old northland and a dash of faith, I let the characters go, and go they do on the Journey.

A Journey that is the "Love Story of the Century."

Some Choice Words

The language you will find as you make your way through Journey is an eclectic mix of (very) old and new. In addition to the highly distinct local vernaculars and dialects you will encounter, many of the more interesting words come from ancient Gaelic and Celtic cultures as well as some very colorful, yet old-fashioned street slang. Some of the more obscure words are listed below (there are a few that I just made up to fit the story, because it seemed right at the time and it caused Suzanne, my dear and wonderful editor, a fair amount of aridujunculation):

Word	Description
alpenhorn	The alphorn or alpenhorn or alpine horn is a labrophone, consisting of a wooden natural horn of conical bore, having a wooden cup-shaped mouthpiece, used by mountain dwellers to communicate before the advent of church bells.
ancient herbals, healing plants	Many of the healings in the story come from topics such as this: http://glmorrisbda.hubpages.com/hub/Healing-Herbs-of-the-Ancient-Celts
aquavit	A northern climate potato based liquor flavored generally with caraway seeds; however dill or other spices are often used, depending on the traditions of the area.
aridujun-culation	A word I made up to keep my editor on her toes. Meant to imply stress and nothing more ☺.
báltaí	A woman's genital area.
blowdown	Area in the forest where strong winds push down many trees. Makes for a wide open space, full of logs that lose their bark and turn bright white to the elements. A great place for animals to find sunshine and play. Any hiker knows of such things. They are

	places both full of beauty and vivid reminders of nature's ability to be wildly destructive.
bràmair	Affectionate word for girlfriend or boyfriend. Can be used in the feminine or masculine sense.
cairn	Is a term used to describe an arrangement of stones. Cairns were used for centuries as trail and road markers (before signs). They can be specific (such as "turn left" or "danger ahead") or used to mark a place of importance, such as where a battle or accident took place.
chac	Shit. Used a fair amount by folks as an angry slang term. Favorite of my grandmother.
chéile	The Irish Gaelic term for wife.
chinking	Material that goes between logs of a cabin to keep the wind, snow, rain and small animals from getting inside. Most often just clay, but historians have found evidence of crude concrete and mortar in ancient dwellings.
chippering and twerping	Words of my own creation. When you have a woods full of animals, they make noise. This was the noise I could hear. Consider it the music of nature as heard by Catlan.
chirplings	Of course the sounds of many birds celebrating the onset of spring.
clach	A man's balls or scrotum, whichever you prefer.
consumption	Generally referred to as a disease that "consumes the person" and was probably the old term for a variety of cancers.
convictive	A word to describe a low down, dirty, cheating miserable scoundrel.
damnú	Damn – see also *mac an donais!*
deartháir	The Irish Gaelic term for brother
dlòtha stew	A standard meal, more than likely contains corn since 'dlo' is the Gaelic term for corn.
dubisary	A thing-a-ma-gig. Just a "watcha call it." No particular meaning.
fash	To worry
flens	Dick-cheese, a really gross substance that smells bad, also used in the context of "balls" or "does he have

	the 'brass ones' to do it?"
flintering	A term to describe something light and fun, such as, "Flintering fingers upon his chest."
galla	Gaelic street slang term for bitch.
gibbet cage	A gibbet cage was used as a form of deadly torture and punishment. It was built around the victim, holding them tight, often in a stooped over position so they could not stand or sit. Very nasty, very cruel. The victims often hung in public places to deter crime.
helvete	A term generally used to tell someone to "go to hell," however is of very strong language and is more along the lines of "Go to join the suffering of the damned."
kauppasaksa	A form of master traveling salesperson selling finer goods (sakas is a term for "master"). A name given to early Norse tradesmen. Also, a peddler.
knarfing	Not really a word, it's made up. When I went to see Katie's horse one day, I listened carefully to his chewing; needed to describe horse chewing in part of the story (to honor Samoot who eats like I wish I could). The sound was amazing, the best way to describe it was with the word "knarfing."
knull, knullare	Gaelic slang for non-romantic intercourse (as in "just doing it," but not rape), or a nasty (almost savage) and demeaning insult.
kuk, crann	Penis.
Mac an donais!	Damn it! – see also *damnú*.
mionntas	Gaelic word for peppermint.
miswak stick	Is a tooth cleaning twig made from the Salvadora persica tree. A traditional alternative to the modern toothbrush, it has a long, well-documented history and is reputed for its medicinal benefits.
plucsh	After having spent years in the woods listening to the leaves fall in autumn, this is the best word I could come up with to describe the sound of millions of leaves landing all around.
pontiferance	Partially made up, means to hear someone pontificate (generally like preaching).

rhodiola	Rhodiola rosea, (commonly golden root, roseroot) a plant in the Crassulaceae family, grows in cold regions. Rhodiola rosea may be effective for improving mood and alleviating depression.
rowan	A type of tree like the mountain ash, are thicker shrubs. Native throughout cool temperate regions of the Northern Hemisphere, with the highest species diversity in the mountains. Some are fruit bearing.
scruvuling	A derogatory term to describe a person or group who are of a lower position and overall intelligence than yourself – such as "a scruvuling lot."
sláinte	"God bless you," such as in after a person sneezes.
snappling	The sound a fire makes when it's just a quiet fire. Not loud crackling. Just snappling.
snarfling	The sound wolves make when talking quietly amongst themselves (yes, I made it up).
snow snogs	Snow shoes. Bent branches tied with rawhide strips.
soilent	When you talk to someone in a wry or nasty tone. Like a "dirty" tone of voice.
spryte	A spryte would be akin to a forest fairy; however, they are much more playful and tend to drink a lot.
teasach	A fever, such as with the flu.
tuilli	A bastard.
thóin	Generally a term used to describe someone's butt.
tiadhan	Gaelic for a man's testicle. Not sure or bothered by whether it's plural or not, since times to use such a word are painful or filled with negative emotion.
verra	Very
whipped rope	Whipped rope has its ends tied carefully with stout thread or twine so the ends do not fray. A very old practice used with older style rope made of sisal or hemp.
whiskerwhill	A simple term of endearment, is a word of Ol' Dogger's creation.

The Time...
and
The Land...

The story of Journey begins, as Part I states, *"a long time ago, before the mountains were fully tall and the seas very salty."* The place is actually a northern hemisphere environment with a very ancient Celtic/Gaelic flavor to it. Probably not too far from the Arctic Circle. The time? Well, it will become more evident as you read; just suffice to say it was an extremely long time ago (before mathematics, before writing, before clocks, before lots of things...).

This tale is built on what is currently a commonly held truth, or could be myth (but the author feels after considerable research and conjecture, the story is of probable reality). It is a story of such vast proportions and long term dire consequences that the very roots of our cultural ideologies as we know it would change if it became common knowledge.

As it is told, a great civilization grew up in the far north of what we now know as Europe; one that built and held dear, many centuries before, the kind of culture and freedoms we enjoy as leading free societies of today. The people lived and protected the same ideologies as our hard working modern society today. These folks had the same passion for what is right in the due course of what we see as the natural right to the pursuit of happiness.

Their story however, ends on a sad note. As it is told today, these smart and advanced people did everything right except develop the written word. So in the end, they could never really spread their ideas, save or archive their history for the future and share their ideology. They are, as is the common thought amongst historians on much of a worldwide basis, "lost." Their whole way of thinking was lost with the demise of their society when they were conquered sometime during the dark ages.

Well maybe that's true, and maybe, just maybe, they had some other way to spread their political theories, passion for life and version of truth? There are some who say their ideas and way of life were crushed and lost. There are others who feel differently. You may find the truth lies here in this marvelous tale of love and deceit.

Maybe something else happened?

And it may cause you to rethink history as we know it.

Most definitely, you should rethink the future!

Exploring
Places & Characters

For early readers of Part II's manuscripts, a character synopsis was added and they loved it; so here is a quick overview of each of our friends (the order of the introductions is on purpose, since each of the characters builds on the other). You may want to read the descriptions now, or wait until you run into each of them somewhere interesting, and then read up on them. It's your choice, really – it's your Journey now and you are in control! The little table to the right of each character is meant to give you a quick review should you need to come back and remind yourself of them.

For you new Journeyists, this will put some perspective on the folk you are about to meet (I do suggest you read Part I; they got into and out of so much trouble, you will really want their background to understand their true feelings and perspectives). For those of you who have ventured this far after reading Part I, what follows may put to rest some of the mystery surrounding our friends; for others, it deepens…

The Journey Inn

Journey is a very robust, large log cabin style inn located in the middle of a vast deep forest. Nestled at the base of a large valley, it is visited by many a travelling stranger.

The place itself is monstrously old. You will see in some areas where the steps of stairways are worn to a smooth finish and sport valleys in the center where so many feet have trod. Over time, rooms, additions, changes and variations have happened to the place.

In some places, Journey is two stories tall with a few special rooms upstairs (some are not open to the public, especially the proprietor's bedroom – more on that later). The antics and experiences in those rooms have filled us with love, fright and some questions. There is much more to the second floor that we shall discover as we trod along.

The horses and animals appreciate the attached stables,

especially during the long and snow filled winter. An enormous woodshed full of the dried timber to heat the Inn during the angry winters that befall the area is attached. It is the requirement of all visitors to assist in the hard labor of firewood collection. Many storms keep everyone inside for days at a time.

During those days of captivity due to the weather flexing its might, the great room is where much of the life of the Journey Inn takes place. The great room sports a huge stone hearth and fireplace (part of the lore of Journey in Part I) for heat and the constant drying of wet clothes. It is full of large tables and many folks sleep there in the winter on the tables to stay off the cold floor. Dances are held in the great room and it's a cozy place for many people to congregate. For your mind to form a picture, figure the room large enough to seat 50 people at the tables. There are many old artifacts on the walls of the great room and the ceiling is fairly high.

To one side is the very innovative and large kitchen that produces enormous quantities of food and treats. Karina runs the place like a well tuned clock. The kitchen is adorned with a fruit cellar, running water, a large stove and baking hearth. You will discover much more about the magic of this place and how it holds dear many treasures and surprises for everyone.

The Journey Inn is the center of the world for all the people of the valley. They meet there, have their festivals there in its broad clearings and find refuge from life's storms amongst their friends who live there.

The Journey Inn is very special to a great many people. It is the social and commercial center of the valley. Festivals are held on the fields around the Journey Inn. Also, just down the path is a modest creek and waterfall for summer enjoyment and cleaning up. Some folks have been known to have some fun at the waterfall. The soft falling water, warm rocks and solitude of the place often inspire intimacy and romantic fun.

Higher up in the valley are fields where various crops are grown that are used in the great kitchen of the Journey Inn. Most everyone helps in the farming process. It's a short growing season, and all efforts are expended to bring in a good crop.

Let's meet some of the characters...

Some key characters:

We periodically get to interact with the mostly transient and interesting folk who make the Journey Inn their home. Some will come and bring with them interesting stories (all true we are told) or deeds of both wisdom and folly. Most are on their way to somewhere, or back from whence they had come. The travelers who grace the Journey Inn are full of colorful long tales to fill the evening and the wanderlust attitudes of the tough and mostly virtuous traveler of that time. There are a few folks who seem to be permanent structures of the place – others come by, leave their mark and continue on their way. For both, you will learn more about them as you wander through the tale.

Some will go and we are sorry to see them leave, some we usher out, some we, well, we play with, because they need to be played with (not always in nice ways you see...).

There are some children about, some of the others are old, some young, some with various sorts of ailments or issues. But mostly a vigorous and happy lot of folk.

Old Dogger (most always Ol' Dogger) is the oldest. He has one good eye and one that wanders (makes for great fun for everyone about half way through a barrel of strong brew!) that makes himself and everybody laugh. No one knows how long he has been at Journey, or what he is up to, but nevertheless, he is a fixture of the place.

Valterra & Kaitlyn

These two passionate and stalwart lovers built the Journey Inn a very very long time ago. What Harold and Karina did not know was that Valterra and Kaitlyn were special in their own land.

A land that was unfortunately brutally conquered and the two had to escape. Staying as captives was not an option because if their true powers had been discovered, they most surely would have been forced to use them to hurt others.

Valterra & Kaitlyn
Valterra: Big man. Silver sword. Redhead like Quillan.
Kaitlyn: Sturdy Nordic blond.
Coronado: Valterra's horse, 18 hand tall (usual is 14 – 16)
No known children.

You see, Valterra and Kaitlyn were of the city of Troy. Their flaming power was the secret weapon that kept the Greeks at bay for ten long years of war. Just as Torrin and Dessa throw off sparks and heat when they are kissing, so did Valterra and Kaitlyn. Not until the Greeks used the Trojan Horse to sneak into the city was anyone in real danger. So when the great city was overrun, Valterra and Kaitlyn escaped via a secret water tunnel to a ship they had standing by and sailed north with as many of their fellow Trojans as possible. The story is told that the Trojans were not only mostly blond and redheaded, but were by nature extremely fierce warriors, great engineers and a people of deep passion for justice. So, as the legend goes, they predated the Vikings (and very likely were their predecessors) and built that adventuresome if somewhat brutal culture, so many years later.

You will meet (in a fashion) both Valterra and Kaitlyn and how they began the Journey Inn. Maybe they were a different sort of Viking? Read on!

Harold and Karina

Harold and Karina are the second set of caretakers for the Journey Inn. Harold and Karina are truly a perfect match in every way for each other. They have been the proprietors of Journey for many, many winters. Harold is a kind, hard working honest and caring man. Karina runs the kitchen and keeps all who are about the place fed and in rightful and necessary order (when necessary she will use whatever is needed to keep order). Both Harold and Karina have been

Harold & Karina
Harold: Can sense danger and threats when they are present, for himself and for people he cares about.
Karina: Sees the future and knows what people want, a Seer of sorts. Very kind and loving lady. Runs the kitchen at the Journey Inn.
No known children.

waiting for a new couple to arrive who are blessed with the "gift" to take over, so they can retire. As to the question of how long they have been at Journey, that will be revealed in due time (you won't have to wait long).

Normadia

A quiet hardworking lass who has been Karina's ever faithful assistant for oh so many a winter in the bustling kitchen of the Journey Inn. A quiet lass yes, a wallflower no – she is wily and smart, as well as possessing a robust sense of humor. Normadia guided Dessa to the waterfall and swimming pond not

Normadia
Key help in the kitchen at Journey. Single, bright, friendly and helpful. Tall young woman, long brown hair.

long after Dessa's tempestuous arrival to the Journey Inn and proved her protective mettle with the boys. She is not a woman men would stare at, mostly because the natural beauty of her thick and shiny long brown flowing hair, large warm brown eyes and dramatically well formed fetching curves have long been hidden by clothes one wears to protect themselves in a busy hot kitchen. As we carry forth, you might just feel that Normadia is ready for something just a little on the edge. Keep your eye on this one.

Dessa

A true princess, she is the daughter of King Tarmon and Queen Gersemi (sister to the late Prince Kael). Dessa is a tall young woman in her late teens with flowing waves of sturdy red hair, deep blue eyes and a dead on shot with a bow and arrow (even atop a moving horse!); she is very smart, nimble and bold (sometimes a little too bold).

Dessa
Daughter of King Tarmon and Queen Gersemi
Grandfather is Gale. Her blue eyes change to turquoise at danger, flaming red hair. Talks with and has an interesting relationship with the animals of the forest, dead on shot with bow and arrow. First marriage to Darius (all bad). Killed Haphethus (Darius' twin) in self defense. Enabled Chadus to kill himself (Chadus was brother to Darius & Haphethus).
Favorite horse is Uta who is the older brother to the mare, Calandra.

Dessa married a real miserable and nasty crum by the name of Darius at the start of Part I. Darius was an awful dirty brute and had the bad manners to fall out of bed the third night of their very short and incredibly miserable marriage and impale himself on his knife (although he was such a rotten sod, no one really missed him). Though not clear at this time, the writer expects there might have been foul play involved. Dessa, although fast asleep when he fell, was however charged with his murder and sentenced to be burned at the stake (ouch!). It is an old law in Tarmon's kingdom that anyone convicted of murder is burned at the stake – it helps to keep the peace. And in Tarmon's kingdom, no one is above the law (even the daughter of the king).

With the help of Sanura, (Dessa's personal maid) and her father (King Tarmon), Dessa was able to pull off a very spectacular and sneaky escape. The residents of Tarmon's kingdom thought she had burned; instead it was a miserable leach named Valdemar who had tried to rape her while she was under house arrest. And, when you consider it, at a very sensitive time of her incredibly young life. The escape meant she had to go far away, final destination the Journey Inn. Dessa was outfitted at the kingdom's hunting lodge by the head stable master, Gale, for the trip. While at the lodge, although she received orders never to return, she was told to let them know she was OK. Dessa also discovered that Gale was actually her biological grandfather, since her named grandfather Keegan was unable to sire children. Quite the triangle of lovers and carrying on preceded her birth.

Dessa learned much about herself on her way to the Journey Inn. She discovered her inner strength and actually had to kill Haphethus, the twin brother of Darius when he beat her and intended to rape her in the woods. She was tutored in the ways of self-defense by the wicked teacher Tallon, who in the end turned out to be a pretty good guy and is, as it turns out, brother to her half brother Quillan (so he is her half brother too).

Dessa arrived at the Journey Inn perched upon her horse (Uta) almost dead. In fact, she fell off Uta in a dead faint, neatly into the arms of Quillan (who at the time was quite taken by this ravishing, yet very filthy girl. He had no idea who she was until a bit later.).

In time, Dessa found she was very attracted to the affable and kind young prince Torrin (it was a slow burn though, both of them were pretty unsure for a while). Her other suitor for a while was Quillan – until they discovered they were half brother and sister. Maybe the red hair on both should have been an early clue?

It seems Torrin and Dessa were meant for each other from a higher order. Once they found their love, strange and wonderful things began to happen to both of them. Dessa can talk to animals and many of them serve her needs in times of trouble (Although there are some wicked animals of the wood who want her dead – as in the case of the old gray wolf Ahriman whose brother died trying to kill her at shepherd Phlial's cottage. He almost succeeded and she has the scars to prove it.).

The other wonderful thing is that when she and Torrin kiss each other, blue sparks of fire erupt in mad wild abandon and they create tremendous amounts of heat. It's quite entertaining, but also very dangerous.

King Tarmon and Queen Gersemi

A wise man, King Tarmon is the father of Dessa. Tarmon inherited the throne from his father, Keegan. In Part I, Dessa discovers Keegan was sterile, so Tarmon is really the son of Gale. To keep Gale around, he was appointed the stable master of the kingdom and tutored Dessa in riding and hunting. It seems that Dessa's grandmother (Tarmon's mother) Saoirse was not going to move on to the next life without leaving an heir. More on Gale below.

King Tarmon and Queen Gersemi
Son Kael (dead), daughter Dessa.
Tarmon's mother was Saoirse. Saoirse needed a fertile man to create an heir; she utilized the young Gale to produce Tarmon. Tarmon then made Gale stable master to be close to his granddaughter Dessa.

Tarmon's wife Queen Gersemi was killed by a pack of wolves early in Tarmon's rein; we don't know much about her. He was devastated by his loss, but through the urging and understanding of Gale and Sanura, he recovered to lead his people through a time of peace and relative prosperity.

Tarmon is a fair and good ruler, although he is aging and the issues with Dessa and Darius seemed to sap his strength. He misses his only daughter (really the only child he can publicly claim) and is looking forward to hearing from somewhere that she has successfully become ensconced in the relative safety of the Journey Inn.

Sanura

Personal maid to Dessa. Sanura is a wise woman from a distant land; she is actually of Greek descent and is part of the family of the Greek hero Odysseus who is purported to have developed the idea of the Trojan Horse. Anyway, we come to

Sanura
Mother to Quillan and Tallon. Father is Tarmon. Personal maid to Dessa.

find she is the mother of Quillan by King Tarmon (although this happened before Queen Gersemi's time; he was no philanderer). Sanura is a judicious and strong woman who is once again King Tarmon's lover and friend since Gersemi was murdered by the wolves. She loves Dessa as her own and Dessa has with time come to find how valuable that love can be.

It was Sanura and Tarmon who schemed up the ruse to free Dessa after she was wrongly sentenced to die for the death (murder?) of Darius. How they dreamed up the twisted scheme is a mystery, but they pulled it off. Their only loss now is that Dessa is gone and she cannot return (for Tarmon and Sanura would be convicted of harboring a murderer). Both Sanura and Tarmon have to assume Dessa is safe, although Gale told Dessa to get word back to Tarmon and Sanura after two summers of her whereabouts and situation. It will be interesting to see how, and if Dessa can send word – if she manages to stay alive now that King Gaerwn is after her and all the people who live in the valley of the Journey Inn.

Quillan
(full name Quillan GianFrachesco)

A big man with red flaming hair. Quiet and steely deep down, he was sent by forces of nature to Journey to guide Dessa and Torrin to their destiny. We did get a glimpse of Quillan's wild side early

Quillan
Big man. Red hair. Son of Sanura and Tarmon. Half brother to Dessa.

on in Part I as he is quite the romantic party animal with the young lasses.

Quillan was an important role model for Torrin during his first summer at Journey. In Part I Quillan feels he has already done his job. With the catastrophe that ended Part I, he is discovering that his role may not yet be over. Indeed! There may be a future for Quillan that he has yet to discover. Quillan is the son of Tarmon and Sanura.

Torrin

Torrin the prince, the eldest son of King Trebor and Ethelda. As a vibrant and growing young man in his mid teens, he is kind, but a little headstrong (imagine that of a teenage boy?). Part I starts with Torrin escaping from the inside of a dragon (now before you go thinking that so very odd, the story of Journey is that Valterra corralled a dragon and used the heat to build the great fireplace – there is a story that comes from this, stay tuned).

Torrin
Prince, son or Trebor and Ethelda. Long thick black hair, good with hands, tends to be an explorer of things. His hair stands on end and head hurts when danger is about. Akin to Harold's gift.

Torrin, having been ripped somewhat unexpectedly from his family misses them terribly. During his summer at Journey, Torrin discovered in himself a deep strength. A strength that he learned was very much beyond his expectations.

Torrin is a very industrious and hard working young man who is completely in love with Dessa. It is a true love that has a power beyond comprehension. It will have to carry him for a long time and through adventures he cannot even imagine.

Unfortunately for Torrin, being a little headstrong, he had to learn the hard way to believe and accept his destiny, and follow the path he is bound for. Readers of Part I may remember Gwendolyn. The very surprising and violent end to her life was a truly hard lesson for Torrin. One which we pretty much figure he will never forget.

Torrin has a special gift that erupts when danger is around. His head hurts in direct proportion to the level of danger and the hair on the back of his neck stands up in attention.

Above all things Torrin wants to go home.

King Trebor and Queen Ethelda

Torrin's mother and father. Living high in the hills, this small kingdom is still a bit of a mystery to Journey readers. However, it is Torrin's home. He longs to return.

Even though Torrin is the oldest son, for some reason he is not heir to the throne; his sister Gretatia is heir. Torrin would like to find out the real story behind this strange twist from normal royal tradition. Really, it haunts him. Torrin's short stories of his home intrigue us, and the people there seem content and friendly.

Torrin's Family
King Trebor and Queen Ethelda
Sister – Gretatia
Rules a small kingdom. Very kind people.

In Part I, we were treated to the wise ways of King Trebor and the loving kindness of Queen Ethelda through the thoughts and actions of Torrin.

Rebecca and Bartoly

These two are intensely in love and make for a picture perfect romantic and creative couple. They live in a well crafted bungalow deep in the woods, hidden from most other living creatures (or so they thought until Chadus raided them). Chadus, for his cruel efforts

Rebecca & Bartoly
Bartoly is a smithy. Rebecca a potter. Very much in love. Live in the woods.

though, left dead on his own horse. This was due to Dessa's creative treatment of his convictive self where she helped him to remember his own fear of spiders and he not reluctantly did himself in with a hatchet. And yes, I am sorry; the spider too expired during the event.

Bartoly is a smithy and a very good one at that. Rebecca is a very artistic and accomplished potter. One thing that became evident later in the summer in Part I is that Rebecca is with child, her first.

King Gaerwn

If you had to define evil with one word, it would be Gaerwn. He is the father of the twins Darius and Haphethus as well as the evil leech Chadus. All three sons are now dead (and for most intents and purposes, rightly so), by the direct or indirect hand of Dessa. This fact is somewhat known by Gaerwn; however the torrid details are not known to him, yet. For power and control reasons, Gaerwn has a desire to conquer the valley and all its inhabitants. He sent Chadus on a scouting mission to the valley that resulted in the demise of Chadus.

King Gaerwn
Father to: Darius and Haphethus (twins), Chadus
Gaerwn and sons are evil personified. Complete lack of respect for self and others. Gaerwn rules a large kingdom with a large army.

There is a link between Torrin and Gaerwn that we have yet to understand. Gaerwn is a troubled man with issues; and unfortunately for the rest of us, he has a brutal army at his disposal.

Scraddius

The right hand man and most senior advisor to King Gaerwn. He is an incredibly smart and cunning scoundrel. Scraddius has something in mind for Gaerwn; however, what it is, is not quite yet clear. Good to remember though, Scraddius is not the kind of person you would want to turn your back on. An interesting point about Scraddius to remember is that he is rather young, probably late 20s and is very good looking.

Scraddius
Senior advisor to King Gaerwn. Smart, cunning.

Ol' Dogger

A fixture character at the Journey Inn. He seems to be very old, and sometimes shows his age. However, he often acts as if he is just a young man. Kind, friendly, funny and often has a sense of wisdom that is not understood by many. Ol' Dogger has one good eye and one that wanders. Selfless sense of humor.

Ol' Dogger
A fixture of a character at Journey. Old guy, one good eye. Very funny.

The Animals

The animals in the story play a significant role in many areas. Is good to remember that Dessa can communicate with the animals in a sixth sense sort of way.

Uta	Dessa's best horse, a stallion. Uta is the alpha horse at Journey.
Unhem	Gale the stable master's horse at the stables in Tarmon's stables.
Calandra	Uta's sister. Somewhat quiet, but firm in her ways. Keeps Uta in line (as many sisters do for their brothers).
Happy	Haphethus' horse who survived his deserved murder in the woods. Very gentle and young colt.
Dalmonda	Strong stallion, part of Tarmon's stable. Dessa rode to freedom on the back of Dalmonda through the night amongst the threat of wolves.
Samoot	The horse Torrin rides from the Journey stables.
Zoltha	Chadus' horse. Part of Gaerwn's stables.
Praritor	The good alpha wolf of all alpha wolves. Tasked to watch over the fates of Dessa.
Ahriman	Evil wolf. His brother died in an attack on Dessa.
Ailis the Fergal	Large good cougar who watches over Dessa.
Sgail	Large cougar who is bad, evil and would like to see Dessa gone. Preys upon many people and animals.

You will no doubt meet some other interesting characters
in the pages ahead.

And now

Continuing Journey Part II

The Love Story of the Century

hold on tight...!

0.
Where We Left Off...

From the very end of Journey Part I of III...

Harold said, "Valterra was da first person and founder of the Journey Inn. He built this place." Harold was talking low and steady. "He 'ad such crude tools, he worked hard, and he made a wonderful start. What now with steel and iron and bronze, we have such tools, and so, Karina and I were able to add quite a bit to the building and make it a much nicer place, especially for da winters."

Karina interjected, "But Kaitlyn and Valterra made this place what it is in name, lore and tradition."

"Kaitlyn?" asked Torrin.

"Yes, Kaitlyn was Valterra's love," sighed Karina. "They were so very much in love." A dreamy look had settled in her eyes. "For the longest time, they worked to build a place of dreams and safety where people would be of their own, and of their best." Karina could sense Harold itching to talk, so she just looked at him, smiled lightly and let him kick in; she loved it when he got excited about something.

And Harold did just that, he excitedly picked up the story. "When Karina and I arrived at Journey, we, like you two, were verra much strangers. But Kaitlyn and Valterra treated us well, and when we got to know each other, something happened and we fell madly and deeply in love. I canna really explain it. It wasn't anything either of us planned. It happened and we embraced it," Harold smiled at Karina, who returned the favor, giving his bushy cheek a nip.

"Valterra and Kaitlyn told us they had been waiting for the right couple to come along. They told us the couple had to have the gift to take Journey, and we just assumed we would run it with them if they liked. Goodness knows, it always needs work, and willing helping hands are forever welcome," said Karina, now holding Harold's big hand in hers.

"But in the end, and it only took a few days, they gave us the place and walked off into the woods, hand in hand and happy as can be," said Harold. "And we had the whole lot of the Journey Inn. Not only did we have it, we had the awful responsibility to keep up the promise, which when they told us what that was, all made sense."

"So what is this gift and promise?" asked Torrin, getting a sense that all this talk of change was not foreboding well for them.

"Well, you sense danger and evil, when you are paying attention. Right?" inquired Karina of Torrin. "It comes from deep inside you. Very deep."

"Yes," he said rubbing his neck. That harsh burning sensation when he sensed Rebecca being attacked returned to haunt him for a moment.

"And does anyone else do that?" she asked him quietly.

"No, not that I know of," he replied slowly, "except for Harold. I seem to be unique, in more ways than one I guess." He had a twinkle in his eye as he looked a bit longingly at Dessa.

"And you my dear, there is a bit of the wild thing in you, you have something special going on with the animals, right?"

"Yes, but how did you know?"

"You see," continued Karina, "I can see the future and see someone's past. Like yours, our gifts are different, but they are connected in some magical way. And when we connect," she winked at Harold, "something completely new happens."

Harold blushed.

"Just like you Torrin, Harold senses danger, when it's around. Sometimes it can be far away and he feels it. He sensed Chadus the other day," Karina finished.

"Oh?" uttered Quillan from the far end of the table.

Somewhat formally, Torrin began; he sensed also, he needed to take control. Something was smirching at his sense of danger, different, but there. "You have done a great service for Dessa and me to let us discover each other, and we have never been happier. And yes, we will take over Journey, we have much to learn." Torrin bowed his head, "You have taught me so much, let me learn so much about myself. I don't know how I can repay you."

Karina patted his hand and smiled at him. Harold just arched a bushy eyebrow and grinned.

"I lost everything, only to find it all again, twofold," said Dessa. "I always wanted a prince; I didn't think I would find the real thing in a prince turned commoner." Torrin felt a warm squeeze on his hand and then on his thigh under the table, which stirred him in all the right places.

Torrin interjected, "And the promise, this is new? What is this promise? I can understand the animals and you will have to explain to us the fire when we kiss, but what is the promise?" Speeding up his words, the energy in him growing.

"My, you are so much like Harold," said Karina. "Well, you see, the four of us have our own special gifts, but we all share one gift along with having to guard the promise. It all started back in Valterra's boyhood…"

Karina had begun in earnest, talking steadily as one would talk to a close friend when delivering important news. But a commotion at the big front door stopped her short.

"Help! They're all dead. Burned to the ground. I have run this many days to warn you!" the little boy cried holding up three fingers as mud stained tears dripped down his sad pitiful face before he fainted dead away on the broad wooden floor of the Journey Inn.

1.
Expectations

For the inhabitants of Journey, the little boy's news left them all startled and in an immensely agitated sudden state of shock. Not so much sad as it were; it was more of a deepening anger that threatened to boil. A blood red anger that spreads in slow fluctuating waves, alternating between hate, fear and rage; igniting in cruel sparks at the very base of their souls.

All the Haradins dead? It seemed so and was, with any degree of thought, completely unfair. They had just built their second cabin and their youngest boy Stratus had decided to stay and work the farm. All had been so right. All had been so good. They had found happiness.

They had found peace and a way to grow as a family; they had set up a fine future.

Now it was all gone, destroyed, and had been brutally stolen from their hard working hands. They had been robbed of happiness earned and justly deserved. Their work, their dreams, and an ever promising future had been torn unfairly from them. And really, unfairly was not a powerful enough word, but for the moment, it had to do. In the middle of all this anger, wordsmithing was at a lull – because at the core of this travesty, it was not only the Haradins who had been robbed, it was every free person in the valley.

It only took a few moments for Dessa to figure out it must have been Chadus and his nasty raiding party who were responsible for this unspeakable and low life evil. The little boy, once he'd settled down some, told them the fire was cold and the bodies torn up by wolves when he had arrived. It was a gruesome tale that his young high voice wove in quivering tones of terror and anguish. He would talk some, cry some, eat some and then throw up again and again. It was a terrible, terrible cycle of terror and fear.

"He must have tortured them to get the directions to Bartoly and Rebecca's place," said Quillan. "Stratus' soul must be in absolute torment. I can only imagine the great intolerable injustices done to his body to make him give away the location of the cabin."

Quillan was quite anguished. He did not do well with terrorized children. The fact that he, Torrin and Dessa had decimated Chadus and the scouting party and sent Chadus back to his evil home on his horse with his face split open did nothing to really calm him. He had a steely look on his face. His crimson jaw was set as if in stone. His generally warm and caring deep green eyes were blazing in anguish. You could sense not so much his anger, as the helplessness and underlying hopelessness. But you knew the rage was building.

"I have come so far, brought ye to the doorstep of the future only to have this befall on us," he said in a low and tormented voice. "It breaks my heart, but it also inflames me soul!" Quillan sat down hard on a bench and groaned.

Dessa watched him and made a note to talk with him later. His fury was bothersome to her, not that he was mad, but that he was holding something in. That kind of anger always came back to bite you, and for someone as big and powerful as Quillan that could be dangerous. Or all that energy could be useful, depending on whose side you were on and what was happening at the time.

She was right, but she had no idea how deep it went or where it would take them. This, she would discover, could keep her at odds with not only herself but with her brother at the most unfortunate moments.

Dessa walked over and softly settled herself next to the young boy on a long wooden bench. Whether he had voluntarily or involuntarily taken on this gruesome task of messenger, they might never know. He was dirty, smelt of terror and completely wet with fear soaked sweat from the dread that had driven him for these past three days. She could not imagine how his overwhelmed senses must feel. She could not imagine how his poor little mind was screaming for love and some state of normalness. At his young age, he was not just hopelessly lost; he was struggling to face a situation that even the most steeled of grown adults would find terrifying and soul drenching.

Dessa put her arm around his thin and shaking shoulders. Heat poured off of his little body in great waves. He felt like a quivering bag of tormented bones from the effort of talking, vomiting and running. He was doddering from his very core. She attached herself to his little body and hoped to spread some comfort to him. As she clutched him, she felt weak, insecure, scared and a little lost herself, remembering what it was like to be alone and so afraid.

"Chadus told me they were on a scouting mission to get information about the valley so they could raid it next summer," said Dessa to anyone listening. Few at the Journey Inn heard her speak. They were all engrossed in their own arguments about how to deal with the marauders who had laid this cruel crime at their feet.

"Why here?" asked Torrin; he had been listening.

"I don't know, but one of the reasons was you," she said looking at Torrin with that quizzical sort of expression that longs for an answer.

"Me? Why?"

"I'm sure when we find out; we'll find we might already know. But for now we need to slow down and think," said Dessa, looking like she was struggling to maintain control of her own mind.

However, just then, the boy snuggled close to her and laid his head on her warm bosom. She watched as large cleansing tears trailed clear thin lines of fear down his dirt caked face. She knew it was good for him to cry. He needed to let the emotions run out. He needed to purge whatever evil torment was caught in his young soul; let it vent away and let the softness of her breast and the safety of the Journey Inn wick into him and bring him peace.

Torrin's gaze ran across the large timbers that made up the great room of the Journey Inn. Suddenly it occurred to him, in an icy reality, that even in their seeming immensity, they were so very fragile. To an advancing army of murdering marauders, Journey would not last a morning. He shuddered at the thought.

Torrin's gaze settled on Dessa and something in his heart stirred. Something deep, something more than special – its intensity only now beginning to rise. An important point was forming, forming as a black and hot thought. It was not complete, but it was strong.

The young lad had finally fallen fast asleep, fully ensconced in the softness of her ample bosom. His sobbing and sniffling had given way to that glorious even tempered breathing of a happily slumbering child – a slumber that should be carefree and lighthearted. He knew this lad would be forced to live in torment for a long while until his mind could sort out the unhappy events he had faced and let them slide into his past. But with time, he would be a wonderful man. No person faint of character could have done what he did. And they all owed him a great debt. Fortunately, now they knew more of the truth behind the brutality Gaerwn planned for the valley. And, upon reflection, without this terrible news, they might have been caught somewhat unaware with the onset of the next summer. Even though Dessa knew the raiding party was scouting the valley, they had not really understood the timing until now, and now it was sinking in.

Torrin's mind imagined terrible things. The residents of the valley bound roughly in chains; they walked through cold mud in a forced march. Now prisoners and slaves forced to serve a tyrant. All of them and their offspring facing an unbearable existence of cruelty and torture. Their lives, their family's life, their children and futures, hopes and dreams rent asunder. He saw comfortable homes and buildings burnt to ground level in smoky ruins with shattered lives strewn around. The great round rocks of Journey's fireplace falling to the ground as the building slowly melted back to earth and Valterra's very soul in tears as he watched his dream die all too soon.

He followed Dessa's hand as she stroked the lad's matted and greasy hair. Her affection was evident. Her caring even more so. His heart gladdened at the sight, and the caring allowed him to start the process of pushing away the evil and focusing on the good. She was as pure of heart as he felt she was.

Suddenly he became painfully aware that he did not want to leave Journey or the valley or the people. He did not want to lose something more precious than the air itself. And at this very moment it was obvious that all this goodness and wonder of a grand future seemed to stand in fragile peril. And all at once, he began to understand that the black thought emerging from the base of his brain was that they were counting on him to protect it.

It was not fair. But he knew, if he stood by and did not act, he was placing himself as a victim to this uncertain future. It was time for action or decide to let them be robbed by the unfolding treachery.

Torrin ambled slowly over to where Karina and Harold were standing. He was trying to breathe slowly and had been chewing his lip so hard it now bled. He could taste the coppery tang of his own blood and it smeared the back of his hand as he wiped it away.

The two were standing at the heavy front door. It was wide open to the afternoon sun. The lush but tired green of the late valley summer behind them awash in the glorious warm light of a sun ready to retire once again after a good day's work. They stood hand in hand, a small package of food hanging from one of Karina's wrists. They both looked tired, but at the same time, very much at peace. And, he noticed, they also looked so very old. So much older than just this spring when he had limped cold, wet and bleeding into the great room of the Journey Inn and found refuge from a disaster that still made no sense. He smiled at the words he had heard, "He's here."

But refuge it was, and the summer he had spent here changed him in so many ways. He knew now he counted on them for so much. So much more than he understood. So much more that it frightened him. He shuddered at the thought of Harold and Karina leaving them all here, vulnerable and alone.

He could sense they were well prepared to go. He was not ready for this, and he knew it. Knew it in his head and in his heart. The tenseness of its importance made his hands feel cold.

Something told him they were not going on a picnic; they were bidding farewell now for forever. Just as they had said they would. They had always been true to their word. Always!

Karina looked at Harold with a pleading sort of gaze. Torrin could see their hands were now clenched together hard, one upon the other. Their knuckles wound tight. White against the old and experienced bones that he needed so badly to help him and all at Journey to survive this threat.

They looked fragile. They looked worn. They looked at peace. It was quite confusing.

"If you want us to take this," Torrin said walking to them and gesturing to the big room that so defined the Journey Inn, "and the promise, I need to ask one thing of you." Torrin gulped hard, tears rapidly welling in his dark and usually inquisitive eyes, as he fought to say what he needed to say. "It looks like we really need your help. Will you stay until next fall?"

2.
Promise Made,
Promise Kept

Harold raised his free hand to Torrin's pleading face and wiped away the tears. His touch felt sincere in its delicate firmness, warm and loving. The caring there presented itself to Torrin's soul as an elixir would appeal to a sick man.

"Aye, ye have yer ands full ere," began Harold, and he said no more. It seemed he was somewhat choked up; Torrin could see him breathing deep and slow. His big Adams apple bobbed up and down as he struggled to find words. He looked past Torrin at the beautiful Dessa with the sleeping child. His gaze turned warm seeing the tormented boy finally at peace. He twisted his mouth into an uneven grin or grimace, Torrin was not sure, as he then fixed his stare on Quillan. The big red man had his head in his hands and was moaning low in tones that sounded almost musical.

Torrin followed Harold's gaze as the old man wound his thoughts systematically throughout the big room. The timbers seemed to reach out and caress him. The oneness Harold shared with the place was evident. The air fairly swirled around him as if he himself held the great beams aloft with his very soul; there was a tension and a oneness with the place and the man.

Harold's eyes closed and he permitted himself a great sigh. After a moment he looked back up at the tormented young man standing there. He let a long slow smile wash across his face; a deep sense of charity seemed to rise from him.

"Torrin, ye are right," he said. Ye do need our elp. Ye needed it when ye came lumpn up in ere that cold night in the spring and ye need it now. There is no telln' what orrible and nasty dangers ye'll be facn. I figure tho, it'll be more wicked and beastly than anythin Karina and I ave faced afore!"

Harold looked lovingly at Karina and smiled. She smiled back to him. The enormousness of the peace and trueness of love they shared was indescribable. It was something to experience it and when you were there, your heart was in awe. What they shared was what the human race would strive to explain in written books, poetry and on the live stage for thousands of years to come (once writing of course was invented). Yet, the greatness of what they shared was far beyond those feeble attempts and could only be explained by someone who had met them or experienced the peace that radiated from their togetherness. So of course, their story would be lost forever when they left, besides the telling that might take place around the fire at night. They knew that, you could tell; it was part of the weariness upon their faces.

Or would it?

They had enjoyed their togetherness. They had merged as one soul. And when one spoke, they spoke for each other and they spoke as one without doubt or question.

Harold turned back to Torrin and completed his thought, "That elp is far beyond the feeble and old washed out power we have. If'n ye ave us ere meddlin' in yer ways, you will not discover or tap into the power of your own that ye ave. A power I sorely guess ye is gonna need, and one that is stronger than ye know." Harold took a deep breath, "So understand, that by going, we give you our greatest elp." His big burly hand came down on Torrin's shoulder. Torrin felt as though he was going to fall over. He felt weak and without breath. Harold was about to graciously embrace his destiny with the woman he loved; he was going to accept and create the legacy he had been handed, and turn their life's work over to another. It took courage and faith, and they had it. But inside, Torrin was screaming, on the outside his vision was blurring. His hopes were being dashed like a ship being smashed on the rocks in stormy seas. He felt completely out of control.

Harold leaned close, rising up on his toes, his bushy face moved slowly as he whispered into Torrin's ear. An ear that was standing out of a hot and flushed red neck. He spoke in a low tone and had Torrin's shoulder firmly in his grasp.

"Son, this place, this valley, has somethn both men and women everywhere will die for, an it's worth protectin."

"Huh?" answered a very distraught Torrin, not at all in the mood for any games of guessing or riddles.

"It's somethn that if ye never knew it, you could live without, but ye would yearn for it always." Taking a deep breath, Harold carefully continued, "But once you ave it, you never ever are willn to live whitout et. You see, we bow down to no king. We here in the valley, we are free people."

Torrin had grown up the son of a king. He lived free, or so he thought. His father, King Trebor, was a kind and benevolent king. His subjects were able to do pretty much as they pleased, as long as the king approved. It was not a bad life. As his thoughts swung around the room, searching for some clue to make sense of this, as this vital news crept in, the enormity of it swept over him.

This freedom message that Harold was delivering into Torrin's very red ear was the reason for the feeling of the valley. The lack of edginess. He had felt it at the games. Felt it at Journey. But also felt it very much at Bartoly and Rebecca's. There was a carefree feeling about. No one was trying to please a ruler. They were here of their own accord, doing what they wanted, making the most of the life they had been given. Everyone here was here purely by choice. Because they wanted to be here. Not at the behest of a ruler or king or anything but their own free will.

They were a free people, and now all of that was in jeopardy. And not the least of which, was that protecting this special way of life was on his shoulders. Glassy eyed, he looked at Harold with his mouth half open.

"So don't lose it. Once gone, it is 'ell to get it back," Harold said with firmness that certainly Torrin did not need to hear.

"An one more thing?" It was stated as a question, but really was not a question at all. "Just so ye know," Harold smiled a long toothy grin. "As long as ye truly love the lass, or more importantly, as long as ye love each other, unless ye get yerself speared through and die riht away, ye'll live forever, or at least as long as ye choose. This is your special part of the gift. Never dying along with sensing danger and the lass having her say with the animals. Ye will be a might surprised findn' things ta elp ye when ye needs it. Just relax and pay attention te what's bein around ye."

His gaze did not waver as he delivered the rest of his words. Words that you could tell poured from his soul, "But remember, the promise is fragile," he paused to refocus his stare on Torrin's face. "The promise is freedom. Protect that the most, because it's worth more than living forever. And when ye protect the freedom, the world will rise up ta elp ye. I jus wishn we had not been so busy an could ave a taken it further than the valley."

Harold turned and smiled at Karina, she smiled back at him with a warmth you could almost feel. Their mutual look was as warm as the sun itself.

After a few more heartbeats, the old man slowly rocked back on his heels, tilted his head and just gave off the sense that there were now no more words. Torrin's face was awash in an almost rabid bewildering astonishment. His eyes looked to be as big as Uta's after a good scare.

And with that, Harold and Karina, the two who had been known as not only the proprietors of Journey, but as the bastions of this free land, walked hand in hand into the deep forest and disappeared. The forest appeared to swallow them in one graceful sweeping motion; or they swallowed themselves into the land.

It was hard to tell.

* * *

Leaves fell with the gentle breeze in a steady stream. It was as if there was a soft hurricane swirl of brown, red and orange rain. The whirling colors matched the whirling in Torrin's mind. The ending of summer with the ending of Karina and Harold was not a welcome event. Both of which frustrated Torrin in his powerlessness to control. And with the threat that loomed upon the next spring, his current hope for the future was not at all clear.

Times like this can drain a man's soul. The weight of uncertain yet heavy responsibility faced with an uncertain future makes it feel like the air itself is heavy. He suddenly felt very alone. And mixed with the news Harold had just left him, he suddenly had trouble breathing.

The empty doorway loomed as a vacuum in space. He just stared at it hoping that it would all change. The weak feeling in his knees was real. The vast emptiness seemed like a cruel joke. As much as his tormented brain screamed the wish for the two of them to reappear – to hope it was just a nightmare – it dawned upon him how real it all was. How terribly real it was. And the intense might of Harold's words began to gain strength and speed in his mind.

He heard nothing of the breeze, he felt nothing of the sun, and he could think nothing of the moment. It all at once seemed crushing. It was a moment that would define him. He would come to understand that later, for accepting your reality is a corpulent moment. But right now, he felt weak.

A gentle cough to his side broke his thoughts. As he turned, he sensed more than felt a presence next to him; that presence was Dessa and her shoulder touched his.

As his vision cleared, he noticed the boy now lay in a small bundled pile on the table, a warm blanket over his passive frame, a few kind women watching him and keeping his small frail self safe.

The cough had come from Ol' Dogger. He stood in a group with the unlikely lot of Journey patrons, most of whom Torrin did not recognize. They were probably on their own journeys and were here for a short break before probably heading south. He thought them smart, with them heading away from the evil approach of the cold, snowy winter.

Torrin felt a now familiar warm hand that offered reassurance slip into his still cold and damp one as Ol' Dogger spoke. Dogger's one good eye fixed on him, the other skipping around untethered from an ancient accident. "Mr. Torrin, we here is ready to do what it takes to make it right for ye." Ol' Dogger looked left and right and was given the go ahead by the nods of those clustered around him. "We can fight whatever evil comes our way. We just need some guidance from ye."

If it was not for the total immensity and gravity of the current occasion Torrin would have laughed, for Dogger had feigned burying a large knife into an invisible opponent. Those around him egged him on.

"Well maybe you are, but I don't think Mr. Torrin here has the flens to make happen, whatever it is that needs to happens, to protect this place!" These words leapt smoothly from a tall, well dressed light haired young man at the side of the group. He had one well embroidered boot perched upon a bench and a coarse smile on his fair face. He was for the moment very out of place. However he seemed very confident in his speech.

The crowd began to shimmy and murmur. They had, on the word of a stranger, changed their tune. Torrin could instantly sense the push against the back of his neck. It was not the danger sign he had come to know. It was different. Yet its pestering bothered him.

"And...," Torrin discovered his regular voice had left him.

"An...," began Dessa, but it came out as a suddenly strangled gurgle from the sudden harsh grip by Torrin on her hand. It startled her enough to stop her in mid word. She looked at him sideways with an unpleasant curiosity.

Regaining his composure, at least from outward impressions, Torrin said, "And whom sir, may I ask questions my ability?"

"You certainly may ask sir," said the tall character. "May I present myself, I am Etworth of Kalmar. I have been here studying all of you for a fortnight. My family comprises the largest trading company ever known along the great coast. I have been here searching to see if there is market for our goods that come by ship next spring. I daresay, you are a ruddy and worthless lot. There is no one here of any great value."

The crowd instantly seemed to turn back to their roots. The mutterings increased in volume at being designated "worthless." To that label, they had no quarrel, but not from an outsider. If they were to be deemed worthless, it would be of their own choosing.

Etworth stood tall. His manner of speech was not only foreign, it was cumbersome. He was very much an outsider. And so it seemed a very haughty one at that.

Torrin spoke, sounding as if in charge for now, "I will not respect nor deny your thoughts."

Quillan looked up at this pontiferance emanating from his protégé, and squinched his eyes together in question. He looked at Dessa who just shrugged her shoulders and threw him an odd questioning look, as if to say "Don't ask me."

Torrin continued, "As with anyone here, you are welcome to stay as long as you help with the daily activities and pull your own weight. And, as with any of us here, you may quarrel with our opinions. But sir, you may not hold us in judgment. Nor we you. It is not our place."

"Oh, but Sir Torrin," exclaimed Etworth. "I do not plan to hold any of you in judgment. For these fine people shall be my customers and my laborers. And this fine building shall be my place of trade. For it seems to me, that the owner just left and whoever wants this hovel may have it for the taking. You all here may not fetch much of a market, but the vast array of people in this valley, and those who pass through will."

As he peered at the double talking enigma before him, Torrin's mind went into a type of steamy overload. One where too much stuff, stress and threat pile up and a man goes into survival mode.

With what Harold had just told him, and with being given the responsibility of Journey, he now faced a man who wanted to take it from him. And to top it off, the patrons of Journey were easily swayed. He was feeling somewhat alone, somewhat scared and more confused. But mostly, getting angry.

"How do you plan to take the Journey Inn?" queried Torrin, hoping for some moments the fool would back down.

But alas, Etworth was certainly a fool, and meant to prove it. For he drew his sword and proceeded to assume a stance that made Torrin laugh. His right arm was protruded out, his left held to his back. His feet were angled and apart and seemed to be dancing about in resonant flight.

Torrin saw Quillan reach down toward his boot. Torrin looked at his freckled friend and shook his head in a decided "No." Quillan pursed his lips, frowned and sat back. His arms folded in either a clear display of anger or he was making ready to watch entertainment.

Torrin reached down and unensconced his grandfather's blade from its well worn sheath. Thoughts of the dragon filled his mind. The putrid dark and fumy hell he had encountered was not to be outdone by this bit of overdressed, self appointed bully. Torrin had not survived this long to be cheated by a trader who had the social graces of a well hungered goat.

"On guarde," said Etworth. He suddenly seemed to prance like a young girl dances, thought Torrin.

3.
Future Course # 1

Come the evening, Torrin would talk long with Dessa. He would try to describe the feelings and thoughts that seemed to encapsulate his mind and body. He would struggle to make sense of it. He would try to figure out something where there was no figuring out.

It just was.

Torrin had taken flight. In reality, he did not, but the speed and agility of his adrenaline charged movements made it look like he was flying. All who watched would have sworn he took flight.

And this time, unlike other moments of great importance, like when he was shanghaied by the dragon, he remembered every detail. He just did not remember thinking too clearly.

Deep within his soul, something took over. Was it instinct, was it training? He will never know, or most likely ever care. But whatever it was, it did and it was all encompassing, compelling and upon reflection exhilarating. Because, he was not just back in control again, he gained the upper hand in an instant.

The sword seemed to lead him to his movements. He could feel the thin tooling of the finely woven hilt under the dense and callused skin of his hand. The thick metal felt light, without its normal weight.

In a flash, he swung around in a tight fast circle. His feet alighted on one table and then another. The fast swing of the blade brought movement to the tepid air that was caught in the momentarily stressful confines in the big room of the Journey Inn. To those watching, he seemed nothing but a blur. This was a blur of focused power and determination.

The sparks that came from Torrin's blade as it sliced into Etworth's were tremendous. They were so very hot and large, that if a pile of dried hay had been about, it would instantly have caught fire. As it was, the dark burn spots on the floor would be the subject of stories for the long winter days!

Etworth's sword sailed up into the ceiling of the Journey Inn and stuck itself firmly into a thick rafter. Everyone looked at Etworth to see his reaction, and were surprised at what they discovered.

Torrin had one hand well wrapped around Etworth's throat. The other hand held not his sword, but his grandfather's sharply honed and brightly polished knife. Its blade pressing firmly and most likely uncomfortably into the taller man's neck.

Torrin could feel a heartbeat bumping against the steel. He could taste the mangled fear and surprise in the now very astonished Etworth. He could only briefly sense the astonishment he himself felt at all that was happening so fast. He did not so much see, as feel the trickle of blood oozing from around the edge of the knife. That ooze firmed in his mind that this deciding moment would forever set his future course. He had to set his example of leadership now, or all would be lost. Lost forever to despots, demons and despicably unworthy creatures who would wrench freedom, love and family away from people whose pursuit of life and happiness was pure and untethered. It would not happen on his watch.

And he knew he would die protecting it! But there were so many questions to answer, and he was not sure where to start.

4.
Candles Are Talking

Gaerwn could hear as well as feel the rapid shuffling of what seemed the entire kingdom's population of feet. Added to this rapid shuffling was an underlying terrified yelling and shouting all about the place that seemed crazed and fearful. This was ever so confusing because he had no idea what was going on.

And when one is a tyrannical despot, over controlling terrorist of a king, not knowing is a bit traumatic. Gaerwn was no fan of his own trauma.

The whole madness had started as a single hushed whisper, some furtive glances and a few folks exiting the big throne room in a hurry. At first he had taken no heed of what was going on; there were always comings and goings and people in some stage of hurry and pretense. However, whatever was going on had turned to wild screeching and a thunderous exit that consumed the entire castle. He sat suddenly alone upon his thickly padded throne in a now empty room and said coarsely under a puzzled breath, "What in bloody hell?"

Were they under attack? Certainly not; someone would have told him about that! Every time any marauding band of miscreants or even what one would call a notable army approached, the castle had had plenty of time and warning. And, oh what fun they had with attackers! The underground exits from caverns allowed his men to ambush from the back during the night. Sometimes they would dress as ghosts and throw cow and goat hearts into the crowds of frightened warriors. The stories of the dead walking and ghosts at his castle kept most attackers away. It was a wonderful deception to keep growing for all the countryside and other kingdoms to hear about.

Most often, attackers, being scared out of their wits, left rapidly. Fear seemed to loosen their wits and they left behind massive amounts of equipment and supplies. It just added to the storehouse of the kingdom and the terrible might of his army. He termed it plunder by fright, and thoughts of it made him smile. His trademark was fear, and he liked owning it.

But no – this was different, and the underlying fearful mood made his heart hammer in his chest. The secrecy of it bothered him the most. This was most unusual! He was always the one in charge of things, the one in charge of fear. But not this time! Something else was in control. He was getting angry.

He slowly slid his vision around the massive room with his large bloodshot eyes. It was a very eerie quiet and actually, it was just a little chilling. All this aloneness, all this silence, just him alone in the great room? How mysteriously odd?

Gaerwn's memory could not recollect ever being in the great throne room alone. Even when he was entertained by one or two of the kitchen wenches, naked and playful, there was generally some sort of crowd about watching in a startled, yet haunted voyeuristic glee. The squealing, laughter and moaning from the naked bodies adding life to the stone room – but not now.

No, even the noises from the kitchen were gone. The clanking of pans, the ordering about by the cooks and the regular noises of cooking were gone too.

Very odd!

The candles still burned with their warm yellow glow, sending muted shadows to the corners. Yet the usually filled corners were empty of people. Normally various globs of drably dressed peasants and nobles stood about vying for his attention and gifts. The fireplace blazed warmly, sending heat to all the heavy stone walls, but it felt cold sitting here all alone. The heat seemed to carry no warmth with no one about to share it.

Damn, something was wrong. Very wrong! And, he decided, no one had the flens to tell him what was going on, so in a panicked frenzy, they had all disappeared. They had deserted him. Did they think he would punish them all at once? Even Gaerwn knew there were limits to his reach of power. If something was wrong, he might gut one or two, but never the whole room! Just ask Scraddius!

Speaking of Scraddius, where the devil was he?

Even Scraddius gone? He figured that wretch was strong enough not to desert him. Scraddius was always around to support him, even when he got mad and needed to carve someone's heart from their undeserving chest. Scraddius was always there making sure the full effect was made known to the low life animals that he had command of here. Oh how he loathed the commoners; they were such a wretched lot. Yet, they were so required if he was to continue to live the kingly life he deserved. He sighed; it was a frightful pity that he had to work so hard just to keep order.

If you wanted to know the truth, Scraddius scared him some. Yet Gaerwn would never admit it out loud to anyone. The man's eyes burned into your face like an eagle's that were on fire. You just expected a beak to emerge from his dark mouth and gore your tongue from your lips while you stood in shocked terror and did nothing besides crap yourself from fear. And the women seemed to be speechless around him. They just would stare and gape at his good looks. All very disturbing since Gaerwn was the most important person in the room!

No, even with his good looks and terrifying presence, Scraddius would not desert him too, would he? He was too evil and lived too well to walk away from his King and benefactor.

Would he?

Suddenly, Gaerwn noticed, now everything was all very quiet and still. The yelling and screaming had stopped. The running had disappeared. The only sound came from the sizzle of the great logs in the fireplace and the gentle whine from the candles.

Always, candles had seemed possessed to him. They sputtered and popped all on their own. How the thin blue flame turned yellow was a mystery, and the low whine that emanated from the wick as they burned seemed like devil music.

He remembered as a young boy putting his ear close to the flame and listening to that ever present and regular whine. He was convinced the flame was a spirit trying to talk. It seemed to be saying something, or at least trying to say something. Always trying to say something, just almost there, almost.

The low blue, yellow and white flames that moved together but always apart were never quite able to catch their breath enough to get the words out. He would listen very quietly. He would hardly breathe on his own so as to not disturb the spirits in the candle. He did not want to miss that all important time when they would finally be able to speak to him. To tell him the important dark and mysterious secrets they held.

Of course, he would fall asleep and wake in the morning forgetting about his little spirit friends until the night again brought them together in his boyhood room. And he would then lay there and listen.

Now, the candles in the big room were all whining to him. There were a great many of them. What were they saying? What did all this mean? Did all the people leave so he could finally hear what the candles had to say? Was this finally the moment he had been waiting for all these long cold winters since he was just a little boy?

Shhhhh!

He stood up from the big throne and padded around the room, hardly making a sound. He held his robes close so they would not swish and disturb the message of the candles.

He ended up in the middle of the great room. His head bowed, his arms tightly wrapped around his chest. He hardly breathed. Oh, but for the beating sound of his heart in his ears, he could hear the candles murmur. He could hear the message. A message that was looming to him.

Finally the candles were talking.

And it was a message of death.

*   *   *

"Sire?"

This quietly and softly spoken single word was obviously aimed towards the pensive king standing in the middle of the room. This delicately whispered question came sneaking up on Gaerwn's ears from behind him like a black phantom attack in the middle of the dark night.

Even with the obvious great effort to be subtle, the delivery of that single word startled Gaerwn out of his boots. He jumped and turned to see Scraddius, one arm crossed decidedly across his chest with his other hand scratching his chin and looking quizzically at his master. Black eyes boring into the face of his king.

"What?" the rapid shout from Gaerwn's startled face was loud and immediate. It occurred to him that he had been holding his robes so tightly his hands hurt. He forced himself to relax. Someone was watching him and he needed to look as if he was in charge and not at all frightened.

Scraddius' head was cocked to one side. He crossed his arms in a thinking and un-defiant manner; more questioning than anything. His legs were apart and relaxed. His whole demeanor was at ease and oddly inquisitive. Yet the easiness about him was somehow disingenuous. It was as if Scraddius had steeled himself to look as if he were at ease. He alone in the kingdom, in a wonderful calm; but beneath him burned a fire of a fear. It was obvious.

Gaerwn instantly knew many things. He knew that Scraddius had not deserted him. He also knew Scraddius was intimate with some news. And, he suddenly realized; there was deep trouble.

"Scraddius, my friend and trusted advisor," began Gaerwn, in a very kingly and overdone welcome. "Please, come forward and tell me the news."

Scraddius' eyebrows arched at that fiendish word "friend." He knew he was as much a friend of this terrible monster as the souls that had left the dismembered bodies of all those Gaerwn had murdered. Those bodies that lay decaying as they hung on the walls of the ramparts under the cold of the gray moon each night, just high enough that the wolves could not reach them. Dead bodies that were a sign to any traveler or army to beware of this place.

"News?" Scraddius said inquisitively.

Gaerwn continued, "Pray, tell me what is forthwith? For all my dear loyal and dutiful subjects have left the warmth and comfort of my company. They have left the warmth of the great fire and the splendor of the throne room. It saddens me to think that fear would drive them so far from my compassion."

Scraddius really loved it when Gaerwn got into the "royal" language. It meant he was either scared or in over his head. The latter was often. The brute actually thought the words he used mattered. He was such a dried up old fitter. No one paid any attention to what he said anymore. He shouted and snarled and spit in all directions. It was only his position and thick vicious cruelty that kept him alive, and that it seemed, was unraveling. Scraddius was looking forward to the events of the oncoming days and season. He could not have planned this better even if he had had the chance to work on it for a lifetime of winters. Nature was taking its course and he knew better than to deny her, her way.

Scraddius breathed the theatrical heavy sigh that a troubled caring and trusted advisor should breathe in times of great issue. It was as great a performance as he could conjure. He had to play the part of the thoughtful friend, trusted companion and caring advisor in need of help from the great and mighty king. It would matter greatly to many of the people he needed. And most of all, it mattered greatly to himself. But these next few moments could lose Scraddius his head in a slow and painful way (which he had witnessed) if he were not careful.

"Sire," he began, with a deep (and well practiced) level of sincerity that had his own self almost convinced. "Your people have left you in quiet somber solitude to give you time to think and ponder as their great king must do in troubled times like these. They are, I say, to our detriment, all afraid and have run away out of unworthy fear. Yes, they are very afraid. They do not know what evil besets the kingdom. They want you to think clearly. Nay, they need you to think clearly for they do know that their happiness and very lives so depend upon your deep and wonderful wisdom (the emphasis was on the word "need"). So they have departed to let your great mind apply its full wisdom to the issue at hand." He bowed low, his black robes swirling aloft in mighty reverence to this idiot standing in front of him.

"Aye, they have left. The fools are shallow, they are ignorant. They do not fathom what it takes to consort such a grand and glorious realm," Gaerwn was impressed with himself. His eyes were swimming in self agreement.

"Yes sire," Scraddius began the most important sentence of his very life. And if he did it wrong, it very well could be his last. "I do pray that you are strong and can help us through this terrible time. For we long for your guidance, compassion and great truth of your wisdom." Scraddius was almost throwing up on his own words.

Gaerwn was suddenly cautious. Something was wrong. Even Scraddius was hesitant to spell it out for him. It was not an enemy at the gates. Certainly, that had happened before and all hell would break loose, but they had been repelled. It was not an outbreak of syphilis, for that too had cleared itself out by natural selection.

No. This was insidious. This was grave. This he decided was personal... his own personal. And he very rarely had to deal with any sort of personal issues at all. He really did not care for or almost like anyone. So whatever was going on was an enigma.

Suddenly, Gaerwn was alight with an inner sort of terror.

His terror was ripped deeper by Scraddius saying, "You need to go to the courtyard sire," and then after a heavy breath, "and I pray do tell you, you probably want to be alone. Your son has…"

But Scraddius never got to finish the sentence. Gaerwn was running past him bellowing something about "Owning the scruvuling lot of them."

5.
Future Course #2

Torrin was beside himself with doubt. It was one thing to tear the guts from a warrior who was attacking you and your friends. It was another to cut the throat of a stupidly rude and misguided trader who thought he could fight. And was so misguided that he had the bad manners and lack of wisdom to choose a really, really bad moment to pick a fight with the wrong person.

As he contemplated cutting Etworth's unworthy throat it occurred to him that the simple act of it would feel no different than slicing a nice steak for dinner. The knife would glide through the fat and meat with very little effort, neatly parting the layers, maybe touching bone, maybe not; yes some blood, but that cleans up later. It was a surreal thought; one that was interrupted by a warm, yet firm hand upon his wrist.

Torrin blinked the sweat from his eyes to see Dessa's intent look gazing up at him. The depth of blue in her eyes bordered on that of fiery emeralds mixed with a blaze of turquoise color. He could tell she was furious; yet, he sensed she was fighting for control of herself. She as most often though, was winning the battle.

"Torrin," she said in a hushed and dark voice, "As much, or as little," and her voice deepened as she talked, "as this worm deserves to live, we should probably let him go, at least for now. I'll explain later."

Torrin gave Etworth a mighty heave, and sent the mouthy and slightly bleeding trader sprawling across the floor.

With a hand to his bloodied throat, Etworth looked up at the man who had just spared his life and said, "Not that I am unappreciative of your charity, but do you always take orders from a woman?"

Torrin glared down at the weasel and then at Dessa and smiled. His desire to spit was enormous (but unfortunately his mouth was so dry he figured he would embarrass himself), but his desire to make the future work with Dessa was stronger. "No you impudent little man. I don't take orders from anyone. I work with people I trust." Torrin clearly emphasized the words "with" and "trust." "My guess is you've not ever had to deal with that type of situation. Maybe, just maybe, you should think about that."

Turning to the crowd of people who stood looking at him Torrin firmly announced, "We work together. We live together. We die together. If that arrangement does not suit ye, leave in the morning. The future for all yet to come, for all to be born hangs in our hands. That is a hefty load to carry; I don't expect anyone to bear it other than by their own free choice."

Torrin now spun around to face Etworth, who by now was standing on his own two feet. Some semblance of regular color was returning to his face, Torrin pointed his gleaming knife at him and said rather convincingly, "Except you! You stay until we tell you to leave. If you go, I will convince Dessa to have the wolves tear you down from your horse and eat you alive on the trail. Understood?"

Etworth nodded grimly. Somehow he knew Torrin was not kidding. He did not understand how wolves could be summoned to tear him up at will, but he was beginning to get the impression that this place was like no other, and minding his business for now might be smart.

Torrin stomped up the stairs breathing heavily and muttering the entire way. It wasn't until he got to the top that he noticed how hard he had been holding the knife in his hand. He was gripping it so tight, his knuckles were a ghastly white and it hurt.

6.
Homecoming

Gaerwn ran out of the main part of the castle into the courtyard and looked around. Even the sheep were gone. He always enjoyed their low bahhs and bleatings. All stupid and friendly with thick scraggy coats, rough and soft at the same time. He really liked the sheep because they reminded him of the dullard low life ratter he had to deal with to run the kingdom. Except the sheep did not complain. Sometimes he felt like most everyone here had married their sister (doing that got you children with issues, that much everyone knew and he had forbade it – unless the proper bribe could be made, of course).

But now even the sheep were gone.

All the people, the livestock, the soldiers, all of them gone. The ruddy yard was just naked of its usual business save for one stray horse standing idly by in the shadow of the gallows. There was a load of some sort across the horse's broad back.

No, it could not be – it was Chadus' horse!

"You are home," Gaerwn said under his breath. And then started shouting it over and over as he ran toward the laden animal. "You are home! You are home!"

He ran to the side of the horse and noticed that it indeed was Chadus' horse, yet the load that lay across the strong back, nay tied and trussed across the back, was hardly a load.

It was his son.

The body was a mess. Large holes where vultures and crows had torn at him lay gaping on his back and legs. His hands were puffed and black. And the smell was vicious.

With trembling hands, Gaerwn untied the cover on Chadus' face. The hatchet that at one time been securely embedded now wobbled unsteadily amongst ropes, twine and rotted body parts. Gaerwn noticed the small dead body of a spider fall slowly to the ground. Its dried out remains hardly mattering at all. Yet, Chadus had been terrified of the nasty little creatures, mused Gaerwn; they had scared him deeply (later

Gaerwn would marvel at the odd thoughts he had at terrible times and he would wonder why).

With growing alarm and astonishment Gaerwn took in the gruesome scene before him. His mind tried to deal with the strangeness of it, the wrongness of and then he snapped.

Pulling a long knife from its royal scabbard, he raised his hand above the horse to do at least the minor justice that presented itself. In Gaerwn's mind, the messenger was always guilty and must pay for the sins they carried. Hence, Chadus' horse would suffer the same fate as his son. It was only fitting and proper in Gaerwn's now muddled brain that had all but been rent asunder by the gruesome theater presented to him.

As he raised his arm to dispatch the horse he was startled by a low and menacing growl at his back. Thinking it was Scraddius coming to halt what must be done, Gaerwn turned to tell his friend and advisor there was no changing his mind this time, but he saw nothing. There was no one standing there.

Gaerwn blinked hard attempting to clear the tears from his eyes and make sense of the noise. The lack of seeing anything that would cause the growl befuddled him even more.

Then a high pitched and throaty wet "screeching growl" coursed through his ears. Looking down, Gaerwn saw that the noise emanated from a large brown cougar who sat low on the ground just beyond his reach. It made him jump. Gaerwn could feel his heart pounding in his throat. He breathed rapidly through his nose in short, terrified noisy bursts that caused snot to spray upon his chest.

The cat was as big as a small horse. Its claws, even though retracted, extended beyond his massive paws, their sharp ends clean and gleaming white. Two long and arched yellow teeth protruded longer than all the rest from a darkly outlined mouth. And when he growled, all his teeth showed wet with colorful spittle and his eyes scrunched up indicating his lack of joy at being in this hateful place. The cat then lay gracefully down upon the ground as cats are prone to do when finished growling or announcing their presence (no one but Dessa ever really knew what they were thinking). He was finished delivering his warning to Gaerwn that the horse should not be harmed and now he seemed to be idly cleaning his nails with his long pink tongue.

Gaerwn made small "Huh? Huh? Huh?" noises trying to get his brain working. Yet he was frozen in his boots.

Although he did not know it, nor appreciate it. Gaerwn had just met Ailis the Fergal. A cat of great proportions and one of great honor among the beasts of the forest. If he had desired, Ailis could have dispatched Gaerwn with one single swipe of a sharply well clawed paw. However the cat, being an honorable one had promised Dessa that he would do no harm on this adventure.

Fortunately for Gaerwn, Ailis was good to his honor.

After a few moments, Gaerwn felt his knife leave his hand and noticed Scraddius had removed it. Working carefully, Scraddius cut the bonds that held the body of Chadus to the horse.

Once Chadus was on the ground, Scraddius backed away from all of it. The horse, a bloody stinking body and a quaking king.

The cougar gracefully stood up and walked out of the courtyard, horse in close pursuit behind him. Neither in a hurry, but neither hanging back; they seemed to know what they were doing. They were certainly an odd couple. All Scraddius and Gaerwn could do was watch and stare as the two exited away.

However, once that spectacle was gone from sight, Gaerwn's mind returned to the crisis at hand.

Falling down to the ground next to the sad form of Chadus, Gaerwn cried out in a loud voice that seemed aimed to the sky, "You will pay. You will wish you had never ever been born!"

Scraddius' entire face smiled. He knew the day was approaching when this kingdom and all in it, would be his.

7.
Here Quite Awhile

Torrin was now on the second floor of Journey and stood tensely in the small yet comfortable room he and Dessa had talked about sharing while on the trip back from Rebecca and Bartoly's cabin. This was where she had convalesced from her run-in with Haphethus.

For Torrin just now though, blood was still pumping in his ears from his run in with Etworth and he saw red. He wanted to scream, he wanted to run. He wanted to relieve the pressure that this world had thrust upon him without his permission. Having to take care of the sudden and unexpected issues of Etworth combined with the completely unnecessary departure of Harold and Karina had just about taken him over the edge.

The sound of the door behind him closing startled his already taught and jumbled thoughts. Twirling quickly about, his nerves on edge, he collided with the mugs Dessa held. She had two large wooden ones filled with strong malted whisky, and the amber liquid had splashed and flowed over her pale smooth skin giving it a glisten, wetting the front of her gown, making it translucent in spots.

She looked at him and smiled a crooked and tempestuous smile. How could she smile? Journey was theirs? He did not know what to do! Did they together know what to do? Gaerwn was going to attack. Etworth and his family wanted to take over and turn this into a trading post? It was all too much. And besides, she was wet from the collision and the material from her wet dress clung to her soft curves in a way that made him suddenly feel a need for stress relief that bent his brain in a strange angle.

Yet, her smile melted him. She looked at him with what was as sincere and caring look as he could ever remember, yet there was a certain tenseness in that smile he could not put his finger on. It bothered him.

"Here," she said, handing him one of the mugs. "Here is to our future." And with that she took a good hefty swig. Her hair flowed back upon her shoulders in graceful waves of amber and the skin on her neck moved in fast rhythms of purpose as she drank a large gulp of the harsh liquid.

Torrin tilted his head to the side and looked a little lost. He finally pushed aside his angst, smiled and shared the moment with her. The coarse dark liquid burned as it traveled quickly down his throat. And fortunately for all involved at the moment, it did its intended job. All of a sudden, he realized that Dessa with the whisky was just what he needed. The fog started to lift and he said, "We need to..."

As he spoke, Dessa smiled even more brightly, and then at first biting her lip and arching those radiant eyebrows he found so tantalizing, she moved quickly closer. Her free hand reached across and firmly grabbed him between the legs. Rubbing her hand hard against him, she breathlessly said slowly into his ear while she nibbled his earlobe, "We need to what?"

Torrin, being a man, had stopped contemplating the issues of culture, society, politics and war swirling around in his brain. You see, it is one thing to have a woman come up to you and grab you by the crotch. It is entirely different to have a woman you care deeply about do it. For when a woman you care about does it, your focus is entirely on her and whatever plan she is hatching. And suddenly focusing on her and satisfying the needs of her plan were all that mattered for the moment.

And focused he was!

Putting down her mug, Dessa's other arm encircled his waist, and she brought her warm lips up to his. Her tongue thrust into his mouth and the heat of their passion exploded into bright, hot blue sparks that spread about the room.

Torrin pulled back. "Chac," he muttered. "We don't have to worry about Gaerwn and his bullies; we'll burn the damnú place down ourselves."

Dessa smiled, slithered her arm across his chest and took Torrin's hand. "Follow me," she said. There seemed to be a skip to her walk as she led him out the door of their room and down the long length of the hall.

He knew where she was going and the thought of it made him almost giddy amongst the stress that had been controlling him. She was entering Harold and Karina's room. A room that was always and forever off limits to everyone but the famed pair that ran the Journey Inn. No one, not one person he had ever spoken with had ever seen one hand's width of the place or ever been inside.

As Dessa pulled open the big door at the end of hallway, Torrin was taken aback by what he saw. A large room well decorated with furniture and interesting art met his gaze. Two large beds greeted his eyes. It was one of the beds that made him smile in wonder and awe.

It was a brutish iron monster that looked like a large cantaloupe. The top was a large iron cover that hung by ropes from the ceiling. Its rounded shape covered the entire bottom of the bed like a cover to a large Dutch oven. The workings were brought down by an intricate and marvelous system of pulleys and ropes. The bottom mirrored the top and inside, the large rounded bottom was covered by a smoothly raked layer of fine crystalline white sand.

"What is this place?" Torrin asked as his gaze revolved slowly around the mammoth chamber, trying to take it in (which was somewhat difficult considering most of the blood had left his brain and had proceeded to service other parts of himself).

As his eyes wandered, he began to see that the room was more than a room; it was a place of preservation. Some might call it a museum of sorts, but it was so much more than that. Full of artifacts, full of lore, full of memories and stories that began long ago. He sucked in his breath. He felt the sheer magnitude of the presence of the place push upon his chest. He felt the intensity of the history that surrounded him. A history steeped in something so much bigger than himself, but now he was becoming a part of that history that destined his future in ways that he could not control.

On one wall, a rusty and dilapidated set of armor hung from a peg. The man who wore it must have been very tall, and also very big around. Hammered pits upon the chest slowly drew themselves together into a rough picture. Torrin squinted and looked; something familiar was coming to him, and then his brain was able to make out the image. It was a dragon. Fire breathing, wings extended and madly attacking something on a horse. Surreal as it was, Torrin felt a kinship with the owner, long since disappeared he was sure, but nonetheless, this was the armor of a dragon slayer! Could this have been worn by Valterra, the builder of Journey? A long heavy iron broadsword lay across the wall near the armor. Thick rust belying the hard forging it had taken to hammer out its heavy measure so many winters before. Yet here it was on display, albeit a very private display. But why here, why in a private room?

As he looked around, as many "whys" as the stars in the sky encircled his thoughts and twirled through his fascinated eyes.

Odd tools, a throwing hammer, an old bucket and a leather hat adorned the walls along with colorful bits of cloth, and old worn kitchen accessories. Torrin's fingers graced the ancient used textures of the items. Some were so old as to be very fragile; pieces broke off at the slightest touch. Most items were dusty, not in disrepair, just so very old. And things made more sense now.

With his mouth open in awe, Torrin asked again, to no one in particular, "What is this place?"

He looked down and suddenly realized he had not been paying attention.

Dessa had lit a few candles and had then retired to the sandy bottom of the iron bed. Actually, not really retired; if he was to be accurate, she was seductively reclining. Dessa was head to toe naked, leaning on one elbow; her clear pink skin gleamed bright in competition with the gleaming sand. The candlelight flitting shadows across her graceful curves added heat and depth to the picture. The mug of malt rested in her one hand and a long smile of anticipation painted across her face. Her nipples were clearly excited by the prospect of what she expected and the toes of one foot idly made small circles in the sand. Her arched eyebrows told Torrin it was time to pay attention.

To her.

And she to him.

And thus, for now, he forgot the room and he decided (quite smartly) to pay her the attention they now both desired.

"Come here," she purred smoothing some of the soft sand next to her with the open palm of an awaiting hand. Uncoiling herself from the chamber bed, she set the mug on a low end table and reached out for Torrin, working his clothes off in what seemed like one long graceful, yet incredibly fast motion.

Turning sideways, and showing Torrin a view of her that he loved to see, she said, "Get in."

Coaxing was not necessary.

As he crawled upon the sand he was amazed at its softness. It barely clung to his skin. It was like finely spun wool. He had never felt anything like it.

Dessa crawled in next to him; one warm hand pushed his now warm body firmly onto the cool sand. Then her hand reached down and she gently traced a nail up and down his very firm parts. This elicited a long deep moan from the man of her desires.

She smiled.

Reaching up, she pulled the rope that let the cover down so that they were completely ensconced within this strange iron shell. The cover slid into place, counterweighted by some large stone off to the side. Later Torrin would marvel at the engineering of it. He would marvel at many things as time wore on.

"What is going on? What is this place?" he asked again, his concern evident, the echoes of his voice bouncing around inside the iron like a big kettle drum. It took him a few words to realize that when speaking in here, one only had to whisper, and he did so with a warm bit of her ear nibbled between his lips.

"What's going on?" she asked him quizzically in a sarcastic and sultry tone. A wide smirk across her face. "You know what's going on mister."

"OK, but where are we?"

This last question he had asked as she had started to nibble his ear. The heat that little favor created sent shivers of warmth through his neck, traveling down his spine and sent waves of delight toward toes that sat at the end of his large and now very arched feet.

Whispering breathlessly, Dessa began to tell her story (at the same time her hands were playing with different body parts). "This is, actually was, Karina and Harold's room. When you asked them to stay, I knew they weren't going to. Karina had showed me the room and told me they would miss it. But it was time for them to go."

"That's it?"

"No."

"Well?"

Dessa sighed. She had been in need of some intense play, not intense questions. But she knew that the questions had to be answered. After the scene downstairs and all they had been through, Torrin's head was looking for some sense of his world. She knew that trying to play when the object of your affection is distracted is futile, so with a long low sigh she rested her head on his chest and explained what she knew.

"Harold and Karina have lived here for many, many winters. Over on the far wall is a recording of how many. Harold chiseled a small mark on the wall boards on the day the snow was gone from each winter. There are a lot of marks," Dessa swallowed hard, the word "lot" had been said with a certain intensity. This truth seemed to bother her some, and he would understand more later.

Torrin, sometimes being of a practical nature, gently clasped her chin with one hand and said, "Harold whispered in my ear something about living for as long as we want, as long we are good to each other, or love each other. So are ye going to let me see how many marks there are on yonder wall or do ye leave me in suspense?"

"Wait a moment you silly boy," Dessa brought her warm body snug against Torrin and flowed over him like rich butter on warm bread. Her lips searched out his mouth and began to nibble in a meaningful way upon his upper lip. Her tongue darted in rapturous movement engulfing him in the most wonderful and strange sensation of losing himself with her. Suddenly the air was blue with sparks. With the speed of hot lightning these now all too familiar sparks snapped off the sides and top of the iron dome. And then for the first time since that small stream at Bartoly and Rebecca's place, the two lovers were able to lose themselves selflessly and carelessly in each other's desire without worrying about starting a fire.

Neither had to say much for a while. At least in words. It had been a while since their coupling in the stream. They had been afraid of fire and just the newness of it all, so for the last couple of days they had flitted with casual kisses and holding hands. Not the kind of passion new lovers really need. So for a long time, they touched, caressed and explored each other in all sorts of fashion. Finally, when neither could stand it anymore, Dessa whispered in his ear, "Take me now or I shall die of need." And she rotated her hips back, put her heels firmly against his tight bum and after he was firmly engulfed by her, she held him deep inside for a long while as she internally caressed his crann with her inner muscles that were finally again full of what she desired.

She then grabbed his hair, pulled him into a deep kiss and let him take control of movement. She responded with an internal fire that burned her to her core and could only be quenched by him unleashing himself into her.

Neither was disappointed.

After a time, they lay back and rested. The sand was hot, the metal around them hot and they were just spent. Spent from the long trip. Spent from the change, and happily spent with each other.

After a fashion, Dessa started to speak. She started slowly at first, as she was curled up against Torrin; the results from their passion were sliding back and forth between them, caressing their souls and helping to evaporate the stress of the day. A day they had not been prepared for. It was quite the stress relief to spend serious sensuous intimate time together, searching, exploring and finding the heat of each other's passions. It was just what they needed.

But now was the best part, cuddling and talking.

"Karina explained it to me, a little hastily, and she was some nervous. I'll do my best to tell you what she went on about," Dessa said a little tenuously. "I'm not sure I understand it all yet, but yes, let's go ahead and look at the marks on the wall. I have not even looked carefully yet."

"Ye seem nervous about it," Torrin asked quietly. "I mean, ye seem nervous about lookn."

A heavy sign escaped from her lips as she pushed the top of the clamshell up. The ropes slid around the rafters noiselessly on well worn tracks made by many repetitions of that same move. The large counter weight stone made a low thunk as it settled into its place on the floor just off the foot of their fire safe haven.

Torrin slid out of the big steel bed and Dessa followed. Each of them firmly holding onto the other's hand, each a little afraid to let go.

Torrin picked up a candle, handed it to Dessa, procured one for himself, and they padded quietly to the back wall. A broad expanse of wood greeted them, maybe twenty paces wide. Long boards, sawed from massive trees ran from floor to ceiling. Each one a pace wide. The size of the wall and the immensity of the boards were not what caused Torrin's chest to tighten.

The wall was covered in neat rows of carefully chiseled, shallow slash marks. Each one the length of Torrin's little finger.

"Oh," they both said at once.

Dropping Dessa's hand, Torrin walked slowly to the left side of the wall where the marks started and ran his fingers over their shallow length. Hundreds of marks filled the first board. The second board was the same, as was the third.

Torrin continued slowly walking down the width of the wall; it seemed to go on forever in the flicker of the yellow light. As he reached the end of the marks he marveled at how the last few were light in color. The older ones had darkened to the color of the outer wood. The only evidence of their existence was the fact that they were so smooth, symmetrical and even. Bending down, he traced his finger over the last slash. It was sideways, just perpendicular to all the rest.

For both Dessa and Torrin, the idea of record keeping was new. Especially on this scale. They had a sense for counting some limited things; fingers and toes, that sort of thing. But writing had not yet come into the world. Often, using small stones in a cloth satchel was how people counted. If you had ten sheep in the evening, you would put ten stones in your satchel. In the morning, you would see if your sheep count still matched your stone count. If it did, all was good. If not, then a wolf may have taken one, or maybe one ran off in the night. So for these two young people, grasping the largeness and meaning of the record of years before them was overwhelming.

All in all, if they could count, they would have counted two thousand, three hundred and forty-nine marks on the wall.

Torrin came back over to Dessa; he gently grasped her chin and tilted her head up towards his face. He could see the incredulous look in her eyes; eyes that were wet. He could feel the incredulous look upon his own face.

And then he said, "I must admit, it is much more than I could ever imagine, but it occurs to me that if we get to spend this much time together, it's not only a gift, it is nothing short of a miracle. I canna think of a better way to spend eternity, than to spend it wi you."

She smiled at him and said, "From the looks of it, they were here quite awhile. I could say that I hope we get to do the same, but something tells me we have our work cut out for us or it's all going to change."

Suddenly he held her close as she cried. He knew she was crying some out of happiness. But also some out of the frustration and impending terror of knowing that the home she had found was threatened. She cried from the weight of it and the sheer magnitude of what faced them.

He wanted to keep her safe, but he knew they could only be safe together. He knew in his heart and soul he was not alone, but he felt for the moment somewhat powerless. And, so very overwhelmed.

Finally they slept well.

They needed it!

And yes, starting even just the very next day, they were going to earn it.

8.
Getting On With It

With a long heavy sigh, Torrin sat on the long wooden bench outside Journey. This same bench had held his distraught frame with Karina tautly next to him after Gwendolyn's untimely, yet seemingly required demise. From here he had sat with his heart in hand and watched her aching parents toil away with her very dead body. Their strength a somber resilience born of long winters of hard work.

Now he ached all over with great runlets of sweat stinging his eyes. It seemed that today might turn out to be one of the last big firewood gathering days of the season. Dark storm clouds sailed angrily over the far hills, their black interiors reminding him of the foreboding heavy snow that would confine them all during the cold nights; trapping them to the warmth and comfort of the big fireplace, kitchen and well built rooms of the Journey Inn.

It had been a fruitful day. Even Etworth had pulled his own weight with surprisingly little whining and moaning (But did carry every armload like it weighed of the earth. Quillan had muttered with great oaths to Torrin that the little wench boy was just begging for wanted attention). The supply of massive heavy logs was enormous. All this wood was necessary for the slow, all be it hot, burning fires essential for survival during the long dark nights. They all agreed that what they had was adequate for whatever Mother Nature's winter plans were for the valley. The life saving pile was now tucked securely away in the wood room, as well as piled high along the walls inside the great room and a good supply in Torrin and Dessa's private loft. They had discovered a small hearth tied into the main chimney flue of the big fireplace in the main room. Mostly they would be heating large stones to put under the great iron bed to warm it before retiring. They figured, and rightly so, that on the coldest of nights, they would be joining the rest of Journey in the big room.

Or, as Dessa had whispered into Torrin's ear; they could just wake up every so often and create their own heat.

He had smiled and proceeded to run his hands over her in a slow and firmly gentle manner. For a few moments, in the clearing of the woods, they created sparks. Not many, enough to remember just how much they enjoyed the warmth of each other's lips.

But just now, as Torrin sat on the bench, a fuzzy brown and yellow honey bee circled near him a few times and then lazily floated down and landed on his arm. He could feel the tickle of its tiny mouth as it carefully searched for the tiniest ever bits of life giving moisture on his sweat covered skin. As the little tyke's small body moved slowly around the dark damp hairs, Torrin could sense its tiredness. He could tell it was the true fall for this small creature and that his end was as near as the end of the warm weather for a good while. The little guy looked as weak and old just as Torrin felt right now.

Seemingly satiated, the bee took flight. It was a slow rise from Torrin's sweaty arm. The buzz of his little wings was low and soft. The flight was slow yet determined as he made his way into the air, enjoying the afternoon. Torrin wondered if the little fella knew his days were short. Or was he just enjoying the sunshine that had blessed them all this day without bother for a future? Maybe knowing that you had a future was not all it was cracked up to be?

As Torrin wondered where the hive was and how these little creatures survived the coming onslaught of winter, a large black crow swooped down and the little bee disappeared, becoming nothing more than a quick snack. In a few moments, the crow had landed in the top of a nearby tree with nary a second thought and was back to making that terrible loud awking sound crows curse the world with daily.

Well, thought Torrin. Just when ye think yer tired and need to relax, nature reminds ye to watch over yer shoulder. He shook his head, got up and started his feet toward the waterfall and pool. He felt grimy and in need of a bath.

As he walked toward his much needed respite, he replayed Karina's story as told by Dessa over and over in his mind. He could not decide if he was amazed or enthralled or both.

He looked up towards the lowering sun and decided it just did not matter too much right now. They had what they had, and they would do what they needed to do as they could.

When they could. But most of all, they had each other.

9.
Plans

After the very dead and nasty body of Chadus had been delivered to Gaerwn by the horse and cougar, it took not long for action to begin. As you can imagine, Gaerwn's need for revenge and vengeance was powerful and overwhelming to his sense of kindness (of which he had verra little). He began barking orders at everyone and forming plans of evil before he was even back in the throne room.

So now, in the dark confines of the dirty gritty castle, the pace of preparation in every corner was frantic. Gut wrenching fear drove the frenzied activity; a fear of certain cruelties Gaerwn would sweep upon them if they were not ready soon. Day and night the entire sweating, dirty and fearful range of people slaved away at the gruesome tasks before them.

"Sire, it is time for you to inspect the army. They are ready to go," announced a tired and worn Scraddius, eyes red and watery with wear, voice scratchy from yelling orders and keeping dead tired people on tasks that they would have generally painfully avoided.

"Just send them on," sneered Gaerwn sitting hunched over on his throne, a mean and pithy look on his dirty face. His eyes were black with hate. His voice deep and slow with loathing, "I'm sure they are ready and able. The commanders have their orders, they know what to do."

Gaerwn had hardly left the throne room since burying Chadus. He was up all hours of the day and night, pacing, shouting orders.

Angrily eating as he paced, tossing frothy chunks of partially mangled food from his dirty mouth. It was not lost on his subjects that he wasted more food in one day from his angry hands while screaming at people than most of them saw in a full season. Once, Scraddius had brought two mugs of stout (Gaerwn's favorite) to try and talk and calm the raging monarch's nerves. That effort had found Scraddius covered with foamy beer and the snarling Gaerwn had almost decapitated him on the spot.

Gaerwn had announced that there was no time for sitting, sleeping or knulling until vengeance had been had. This coming from a man who most often time and again seemed to lose interest in most things. However, this time he seemed to mean it. He was not to be dissuaded of his goal.

In another effort to distract Gaerwn, Scraddius had sent out the fair kitchen maid Paroish with her top undone and the side ties of her dress removed. Scraddius had marveled at the soft pink skin of her breasts; how they always seemed ready to burst. He stared without abandon where her nipples created little mountains of excitement through the fabric. When she walked, her long smooth legs peeked out in subtle temptation and then hid quickly behind the thick fabric of her skirts. Her smile adorned an angelic face of happiness and grace. He had undone her thick golden hair and combed it so it flowed over her shoulders and had even endeared her to consume a large tankard of barley drink to loosen up her spirit and play the willing part of the wantful, playful wench just a bit better.

Paroish was actually the king's favorite. He would ask for her by name and then take her wantonly on either the padded seat of the oversize throne or the large bear carpet that lay in state on the floor. Most in the big throne room would turn away, but some would watch in horrid fascination, spellbound by the writhing and thrashing as the two seemed to insatiably have at each other. What seemed most troubling, or interesting, depending on your point of view, was the fact that the tall fair and beautiful Paroish seemed to enjoy the public treatment she received.

Most times, after satisfying the nasty king, she would rise up, and turn to the watchful crowd. Wordlessly, she gathered her strewn garments and then standing tall would curtsy gracefully before departing. A thin smile on her face.

However, this time Gaerwn grabbed her long golden blond hair in his large, greasy dirty hand and twisted savagely. The poor girl fell to her knees with a terrified scream, tears instantly streaming down her face from fear and pain,

"Vengeance is all I care about, you little galla. Cover yourself up and get to work. If you weren't so good at what you do best, I would gut you here and now as an example to the rest of you freaks. What does it take to make you understand that I mean business? We have work to do; this is not a time for knulling around."

When Gaerwn pushed her down and away, Paroish went sprawling on the cold stone floor and broke her nose on the edge of a stone step. Blood gushed from the wound on her face. The blood mixed with the tears of fear and rejection that poured forth from her beautiful sad face. She would never feel pretty again from the nasty bump the gash and break would leave. She would never be the same.

Gaerwn did not even notice she was bleeding; he did not seem to notice much right now (and maybe that was a good thing). He just turned and was going to begin terrifying someone else. It did not matter to him that another soul was now tormented from his actions.

"Sire," Scraddius said carefully trying to regain Gaerwn's attention. The brutish scene he had just witnessed made him think that maybe Gaerwn's foul mood could not be broken; maybe he was crazed forever? "Your men would like to show you what they have built to lay cruelty and suffering on the whores of the valley. Their desire is that you see the tools of hurt, pain and destruction they have built and carefully invented to do the vengeance you so deserve."

"Very well," Gaerwn replied, looking up through bloodshot eyes. Eyes that glimmered wet with what looked like a caustic glaze of hate.

As they marched without an entourage (very unlike Gaerwn) toward the waiting army in the courtyard, Gaerwn's mood and step seemed to improve with each turn. Scraddius hoped this would work. If it didn't, they were all going to have to endure the wrath of this putrid ruler until vengeance had been wrought. And until that happened, it seemed that Gaerwn was on the verge of needing to wreck vicious pain and death on those he found in his way or just even within eyesight.

Dying was not the problem, mused Scraddius. It was the possibility of the slow, cold, hungry and anguished death they all faced that had him a little unnerved. And it was the slow, cold, hungry parts that bothered him most.

As Gaerwn and Scraddius entered the courtyard any unorganized milling immediately stopped as the commander called the troops to attention. It was plain to see they were not such an organized lot, but they were fearsome as they endeavored to form a straight line.

As soldiers, as an army, as a conquering force, they had more than everything at stake.

It was widely recognized that if you did not come back with the blood of your enemies on your weapons, Gaerwn might either do you in, or at the least take your wife as a slave (generally for just a few nights) to teach you to be just a little stronger in battle.

But that was the easy one.

If you had the bad fortune to not even come back he would put your family in chains and work them to death. And of course, it was a slow death. Gaerwn had figured out how to work his slaves just enough to keep living, and feed them just enough to keep just barely living.

You see, Gaerwn had no use for a family without a man in it. He saw such a group as excess baggage. The woman would chase other men and enrage existing wives (and Gaerwn had no patience for angry women). The children would beg and bother other families that caused hunger and complaining from the intact units. Again, just issues.

No, a family without a man was baggage that needed to be thrown away when used up.

Of course he did enjoy watching the using up part. He would sometimes go down to watch the chain gangs work and hand out bits of food. He loved to watch them all struggle with every last ounce of energy they had in their being to get to his feet and grovel for a morsel.

Just plain, good old fashioned fun!

10.
Unfolding

Torrin remembered every little part, every little nuance and word of that conversation when Dessa told him about what Karina had told her.

Every little thing. Yes, every little thing, because he was in awe, and just a little scared.

After peering at the wall with all the hash marks, they had lain down in the regular bed that was along the wall and they had snuggled warm and close under the blankets. With the top of Dessa's head forming the softest place he had ever laid his cheek, Torrin had urged Dessa to slowly and carefully tell him the details of Karina's story.

"Only after you tell me what Harold whispered in your ear," she mused.

He told her, again, as cautiously and cleanly as he could. He whispered more than spoke the words of freedom because the immensity of their message was still sinking in with him (mostly because he was raised in a kingdom, and the idea of a free people was so contrary to all he knew). The part of living forever was still beyond his mental grasp. But nonetheless, he slowly and carefully told her everything.

Shifting herself to the side, she reached across and ran her fingers through the thick hair of his chest, occasionally stopping to toy with one of his nipples. He loved it when she did that, and she loved to do it. If you asked her why, she would just tell you "because I do."

As she stroked the short curls she said, "Now the whole story makes sense, well mostly."

"Well, go on," he said somewhat thickly. He was warm and comfortable; he was finally relaxed, the stress of the day had worn him out and he was now at long last getting away from it. "Go on until there is no more to say."

"Karina said she loved Harold slowly. When she first met him, she thought nothing of him. She was traveling with traders and they were traversing through the valley. After they had stopped at Journey to trade and rest, something inside her told her to stay. She never figured out what really made her stay, but she did, and never regretted it."

"Yes, but what about her falling for Harold?"

"Well, as I said, she did not think anything of him at first. But when she got to know him, he seemed different. He seemed special in a way. She told Kaitlyn that she thought Harold was a really nice young man and wondered if there would be a dance or festival where she could meet him and chat without seeming too forward."

"So dances are a good place to meet girls here it seems," said Torrin remembering that wild night of dancing with Gwendolyn – it gave him a slight shiver.

"It is?" queried Dessa, sensing something amiss.

"Yes," answered Torrin, a little too quickly, "Just ask Quillan about it."

Dessa sighed and continued, "It seems that Karina had caught

Kaitlyn off guard. Neither she nor Valterra had expected a replacement to show up. It was not in their plans. They had been so busy building Journey they had forgotten completely about it."

"Replacement?" asked Torrin.

"You see, as Harold said, as long as we are in love, we can live forever, if we choose to. But if we want to end it, we cannot just fall out of love or walk off. That won't work. We have to have a replacement. That was why, when you 'came lumpn in ere,'" Dessa mimicked Harold so well, Torrin laughed, "Karina told you they had been expecting you. You see, Harold and Karina were ready to go."

"Go where?"

"To die."

Torrin let the words sink in before responding. "They chose to go die? They willingly walked off into the cold wet forest to just up and go? That makes no sense at all. Why, even if this is true (he was still in denial), why would two people who are living with the person they love, in a place they built, choose to go off and just die?" Torrin was getting heated. He threw the coverings back with one foot to cool down.

Dessa laid her head closer to the man she loved. She felt the sinews of his shoulders. She could hear the air rush in and out of his lungs, and she seemed to time her thoughts to the thump thump thump of his caring heart.

"Because Torrin," she said softly, "they were tired."

"You mean I will get tired of you? Or you will get tired of me? That's not going to ever happen! When I am with you, there is nothing that can stop me. Everything is possible. There are no rules. This is beyond me, it's just not normal! Of course," he added, "What here is normal?" waving a hand through the air, taking in the whole room, the whole of Journey for that matter.

"Remember how many hash marks there are back there?" Dessa moved her head toward the back wall.

"Lots. There are so very many," a light began to dawn in Torrin's mind. A light that shed a bit of wisdom on his brain that had not been there before.

"Harold and Karina lived longer than anyone ever has. They loved each other very much, but at some point, it's enough. They had not been thinking about ending it until a couple of winters ago, when Harold found Valterra's sword again. And then it dawned on him what must happen."

"Again?"

"Yes, it's the old one on the wall by Valterra's armor. Harold had been using it many winters before to chop firewood since there were no dragons about any more."

"Don't be so sure of that," Torrin interrupted, rubbing the scar on his leg. The long line of hardened tissue had healed well, but the pain and terror of that hike was still fresh in his mind.

"Anyway, Valterra had told Harold that his greatest gift was to pass on the sword to the next ones."

"Harold sure didn't take very good care of his greatest gift then," remarked Torrin.

"No silly," said Dessa as she idly circled a sharp fingernail around the soft hairs of his chest. "The actual sword was only a reminder. The gift that Valterra and Kaitlyn had was that of true love and they protected the valley's promise of freedom together. And so Harold and Karina had the same things. And they lived for as long as they chose. But then it occurred to Harold that there was only one thing greater than to share your love with your lover."

"Oh?" Torrin asked.

Dessa held her head up and looked him in the eyes before softly pressing her smooth face back into the place that had been warmly holding her while they talked. Then she said quietly, "Pass that love on to someone else."

Torrin felt a little small. A little afraid, and a little more thankful.

11.
Departure Forth

In the courtyard of the dark castle Gaerwn's army stood quietly at attention. The families of the soldiers stood to one side and they, as the soldiers, made nary a sound.

They all as a people hoped that Gaerwn would be happy with the inspection and send the men on their way. The people were all tired from the preparations. The families needed to rest and attend to the vagaries of life. The soldiers needed to move out and engage in the terrible activities they were trained to accomplish.

Gaerwn ran his fingers slowly over the rusted blades. Their coarsely notched edges almost burned his skin as he thought of the jagged pain they would inflict. The initial pain would be excruciating, and if the victim lived, which was the hope, then the slow onslaught of infection would be even more horrible. He almost wished he were going along to feel the tender flesh and bones crushing and tearing under the onslaught of this wretched iron. The raw brute power and intensity of conquest that surrounded him almost made him smile. But he was still in no mood for smiling. Only in a mood for vengeance.

They stood in line, holding the most gruesome weapons of destruction they could invent. Grown men wanted him to inspect, bless and comment on their tools of war. Each hoping in some way to please their ruler.

As Gaerwn and Scraddius had neared the front of the long line, Gaerwn was growing tired of this parade. He had looked at spiked balls, long truncheons, iron tipped poles, arrowheads that flamed in flight and exploded on impact. It was all very interesting, but he wanted them on their way.

Finally he turned to Scraddius and said, "Enough, send them."

And with that the whole barrage of men, horses, wagons and assorted animals began to move. The creaking, groaning and dirty lot of them started out of the courtyard that was for the moment teaming with people.

As Gaerwn watched this exhibit of gruesome might make its way across the drawbridge and down the main path into the valley, he noticed something strange and a nag sprang up in his thoughts, troubling him.

"Scraddius?"

"Yes sire?"

"Why so many goats, sheep and cattle going with the men?"

"Your orders were to give the army whatever they needed. Commander Spreth ordered all the animals along with the army. He decided they could make much better time taking their meat with them instead of stopping to hunt along the way."

"How many are left for us to eat this winter as well as milk?"

"None."

The last shepherd of the army had passed by the gate urging his charges along, paying no attention to their low-full bleating, baying and mooing. Dark clouds of angry dust rolled above the long line of organized hate and destruction that shimmered and swayed along the dusty road that disappeared into the colorful forest in the valley below the black castle. Those clouds above in the sky would in a few days certainly begin to drive snow into the world. And Gaerwn also knew that in not so long a time, the cold and snow would leave them trapped in the castle for days on end.

Gaerwn sighed, "I guess we will need to organize a hunting party then to gain meat. Have all the men come to the courtyard in the morning for a hunt!" He turned to walk away, the thought of rekindling his fun with Paroish already on his mind.

"Sire, we are the only men left," Scraddius informed his king. "There are boys, but none of them even approach the age of growing a beard let alone draw back an arrow with enough strength to kill game. All the rest are with the army. It would give me most pleasure to hunt with you sire."

Gaerwn turned and his gaze took in the large crowd of women surrounding him and lined along the ratty hovels that stood just inside the main wall of the castle. Most were weeping at the loss of their husbands. Many had babies in their arms and wretched dirty children crowded at their feet. It seemed to him they were all dirty; or could it be evil in their eyes? He was not sure. But he did know one thing, the lot of them alone, without the sturdy men of the castle forebode a long cold hungry winter. And he knew that their incessant hungry whining would be impossible to live with for long.

A ponderous look spread across Gaerwn's droopy and sad face; and then for the first time in days he smiled. It was not a smile of glee; it was a leering smile of grim satisfaction. It was the sort of smile where a person's lips curl up instead of rise up. A smile that would not only scare a child, but make an adult cringe in grim fear and cause cats to hiss.

"Fetch me Commander Spreth. He is getting new orders. And bring back the damn sheep and goats and the lot of our walking winter meals." After a moment of pondering, he cocked his head and continued, "Bring back all but a handful. I have decided on a change in course. The army is not going as far, but they are going to wrench a higher level of vengeance than I had previous planned. I am surprised I had not thought of this before." And with that order Gaerwn, reapplied his evil smile, turned and trod purposefully back toward the throne room.

12.
Inventive?

"What are those?" Dessa asked of the strange contraptions Quillan had displayed on the table.

"Well m' lady," Quillan said smartly, obviously ready to show off, "These here are snow snogs."

"Snow snogs?" she asked, quite interested.

"Yes. You strap them over yer boots and with the webbing, you walk on top of the snow instead of falling down up to your crotch with each step."

Quillan demonstrated strapping on the device and then walking like a duck in mud around the floor of the great room at Journey, much to the delightful chuckles of all present. He almost fell over upon his big backside a couple of times. This caused great guffaws of belly laughs to erupt from the team he had assembled at the table.

Quillan continued, "This way the scouting party can easily hike, even with the nastiest of snows, and get to Gaerwn's castle alive to spy and make plans."

"I see," said Dessa, quite unimpressed. "And who may I ask is going to the castle and when?" She had her hands firmly planted on her hips and her head cocked to one side. It was hard to tell if she was angry, inquisitive or annoyed. Maybe all three?

Quillan looked around at the men, both young and old, gathered at the big table. They looked back at him, not providing any answers or obvious support.

"We had not decided yet, at least about who is going. We did figure we would leave right after the fall festival though."

"How many snow snogs do you have?" asked Dessa.

"They are all lined along the wall," and Quillan swung his hand to show about twenty pairs of what one day would be known as snowshoes.

"You have been busy," replied his redheaded sister, now

showing some color in her cheeks.

"It seems we are motivated some," said Quillan. "We are not looking to easily let Gaerwn's army attack. We need to know what is going on, what he is thinking and what he plans in his treacherous and nasty evil mind."

Quillan was not too sure what Dessa was up to, but he could tell from the questions that there was something on her mind.

And then a fearful thought struck Quillan and he blurted out with a passion only a brother could muster for a sister, "You are not going. This is far too life-threatening; I will not allow my sister to put herself in such danger!"

Dessa glared at Quillan. Her blood was boiling. How dare he order her around like some child? How dare he decide what she could and could not do? She could feel her hands clenching her sides as she fought for self control.

Dessa looked at him as straight in the eye as possible (since he was somewhat taller, it was difficult) and said, "I am not a child, nor am I some defenseless whim that you can order around. If I choose to go, I choose to go. You have no say in the matter." Her eyes blazed that turquoise green that rose up when she was fashing about something important.

"Yes I do!" snarled the big red man, now more crimson than usual and standing up with his own hands clenched. "Do you have any idea what Gaerwn's men would do to you if you were captured? Do you have any thought as to the depth of his cruelty? Especially if he finds out through torturing us that you were the one to cause Chadus to split his very own miserable foul head open?"

Quillan seemed almost to be frothing at the mouth. He looked scared and mad all at once. The others at the table were slowly sliding back out of range. This only being a passive defense lest Quillan become unnecessarily enraged and he engaged in blindly grabbing one of them or his throwing sharp objects like his knife or a jagged edged snow snog.

"You seem ready to be captured and tortured before you start, brother," taunted Dessa now without a trace of anger, frosted with mirth.

She had not flinched once during the storm that had loosed from her brother's mouth. In fact, she looked utterly calm and comfortable. Only someone who had known her for a very long time would have been able to assess the level of anger boiling up inside her. Somewhere in the back of her mind the calm teachings of Sanura had been taking hold. Even though her insides wanted to reach out and draw long sharp nails across Quillan's face and teach him of her strength, she held her tongue and talked calmly.

Dessa remembered that frightful night; that night that seemed so very long ago and far away when Sanura had stripped her down to her shift and tossed her mercilessly into the swirling snow and cold. She remembered all too well her attitude, foul language and disrespectful mouthiness that had gotten her into that trouble. She shivered deep in her bones with the memory of her hair freezing to her face and scratching her eyes. She squeezed her hands as the memory of her fingers so cold they hurt right back to her wrists, and then the pain in her frozen feet hurt all the way up to her knees. That had been the worst of it, the gnawing ache that finally led to her falling down into the freshly fallen frozen snow. The bone chilling grip and fear that she would most surely slowly die just outside of the big doors that had provided her safety and security all her life. The doors to her home.

No, she would never be that cold again, nor would she speak before thinking. It had been a hard lesson, and right now, it would prove to be invaluable.

"No!" sputtered Quillan. "We do not plan to be captured and tortured. Not at all." He looked around at his compatriots for support and could sense the mix of surprise, questioning and laughter on their faces. It dawned on him that he had been done in by his little sister and now he was going to pay the price. He did not know what to say, so he said the next best thing, "We'll talk about it tomorrow."

"Have it your way dear brother," said Dessa. "Everyone from the valley arrives in this many days for the fall festival (she held up two fingers). You better have a plan to present by then, or your snogs will go into the fire."

With that, she turned and tromped off.

Quillan and his men stayed up most of the night planning their quest. They knew it had to be well thought out or it would fail the test of review by the folk of the valley. None wanted to put the valley in danger. Nor did they want themselves to end up hanging from a meat hook swaying in the frozen bluster of winter winds against the cold stones of Gaerwn's castle. They were not sure which danger was worse, but they did know they did not want either to take place.

And most of all, Quillan wanted Dessa's approval of a plan that included her staying right here within the warm safe walls of the Journey Inn!

13.
Hope

"What's eating you, you sulking old bum?" asked Quillan.

Torrin was sitting in the big room at Journey at a large table off to the side of the fire. Normadia and Dessa along with the rest of the kitchen had put on a marvelous dinner. A happy yet unexpected duo of Ol' Dogger and Etworth had spent a fruitful day hunting and the demise of a pair of large hogs had given the kitchen all they needed for this splendiferous dinner and substantial additions to the winter storage of meat in the larder. And, it was just in time for the gathering of the fall festival that would start on the morrow.

Generally Torrin would have been sitting right in front of the fire with the rest of the men joyfully participating in the telling and retelling of today's story of hunt and adventure. But he just sat there alone with a long face by himself. Eyes cast down, shoulders slumped with his hand holding his face.

And, as Quillan had mused, the capture of the hogs was quite the story to be told and retold. The two hunters had left early in the morning full of hope and cheer (as most hunters are when they set out upon a quest). Quillan was initially surprised that Etworth would spend time with Ol' Dogger, him being quite the old man, until it dawned on him that Etworth was probably trying to regain some sense of status since his run-in with Torrin. And anyway was forever looking for pats on the back and strokes to his narrow and shallow ego. Nevertheless, he had proved his mettle in the hunt; or it seems they might have lost Ol' Dogger.

Even as successful as they were, Ol' Dogger had gashed his arm on a sharp stick. Dessa and Torrin had amazed everyone with a trick they had learned a while back. After covering the wound with Karina's yellow salve, the two of them meshed their cheeks together and then while holding each other's hands seemed to magically repair the wound. A fair amount of heat got generated over the spot, but it did the trick and Ol' Dogger was good as he ever was.

The hunting story was now embellished with the help of a healthy consumption of ales. It had gone from a normal quality hunt with the regular level of danger that one faces when dealing with wild things to one of almost mythical qualities and superhuman feats.

At the time Quillan had risen to check on his friend Torrin who was moping along the side; Ol' Dogger had again, and of course with great theatrical determination, proclaimed that he had been carefully lying in wait to catch the hog that he had skillfully smelled and tracked. He most definitely had not been taking a nap!

"Nothin's wrong," Torrin replied. Although the word came out sounding like "moothins roung," since Torrin's face was deeply pressed into his hand.

"Ye look like a lad who just found out he had ta shave his head for lice," joked Quillan. "This is jus not like ye, te set around moping and lookn all sullen an out of sorts, especially with the fall festival starting morrow."

Torrin looked up at the red man, and now, beside the pain in his heart he felt a little stupid. "Quillan, tell me, how have ye done it all these winters and summers?" he asked.

"Whatever are ye blastn' about?" asked Quillan gently and seriously all at the same time.

"Well, you had to leave home and of course you understood why, and it all made sense. But it doesn't seem to bother you?" It was more of a question than a statement. "I mean, don't you miss, or wonder about...?" He never really finished the sentence; he seemed not quite able to do so.

"Oh, yer missin yer parents, are ye?" asked Quillan, now instantly sober. His overly cheery and somewhat alcohol enhanced giddiness was quickly replaced by a heartfelt understanding of what was eating at his friend's mind, and generally tranquil mood.

"Not just only them. It's everything. Sure, my parents, but my friends, my home, my world." Torrin let out a great sigh.

"I know it's not easy," agreed Quillan. "Sanura and I are usually able to see each other at least every other summer, mostly up at Tallon's place. I remember the first summer I didn't get to spend some time with her. I was a mess.

"Oh?"

"Yes, I cut more wood, hunted more game and was quite the philandering fool with the ladies as I tried to blot out my misery."

Torrin sighed, "I guess I should throw myself at building a stone wall or something then?"

As Quillan chewed over an answer, across the room Etworth was again exonerating Ol' Dogger on his uncanny ability to climb a tree straight up like a cat after a squirrel. He proclaimed that he had seen Ol' Dogger grow claws right there and scurry up that old tree when the hog had so ungraciously woken him from his slumber, ere, or was it sly waiting?

Ol' Dogger was on his feet showing the crowd how he had accomplished the speedy tree ascension and was carefully (with some slurring involved) explaining he had decided to climb and keep the hog occupied so "Ethworthyer" would be able to claim a clear and glorious victory on the hunt. He was only, as the wise and duty bound old man he was, trying to teach the boy self-confidence, according to his story. He stated it was a worthy goal and one that deserved a toast (which of course everyone obliged).

"Thank ye, ye old cusser," quipped Etworth, "but I have learned how to hunt the hard way. Had the same thing happen to me once. Got treed by a crazy pig. Nasty old bugger with long crusty colored horns. He took off back into the woods after a while, which was a good thing because he was getting close to becoming bacon, and I don't even like bacon. It would have seemed like such a waste. I was on my way here from King Trebor's castle."

Torrin looked up at Quillan; his hand dropped down with a dull thud on the table. Eyes wide, he mouthed the words that slowly left his brain as his eyes found Etworth across the room, "You? You were at my home?"

* * *

Bartoly looked at Rebecca with a gleam in his eye and a patter in his heart and he asked "How are you feeling?"

"Fat!"

"Really?" Bartoly asked as he looked genuinely surprised. He really did not understand that pregnant women feel fat. And that pregnant women did not truly understand that their man saw not fat. Only warm beauty, a radiance and a blessing to their union.

"Well, a little. Do I look fat to you?" asked a somewhat serious Rebecca.

"Not one bit. You are more beautiful than ever. You used to

glow; now you radiate."

"Oh?" she asked, not really sure what he meant.

"Especially in bed, it's like sleeping in the fire. I hope you keep this up all winter; my toes will be warm like never before!"

Rebecca playfully bit Bartoly on his nose. They had been lying in bed, enjoying the golden sunshine of a glorious fall morning. Bartoly had with the sunrise, milked Jacqualde the cow. Now she and her calf Gantor were peacefully grazing the thick rich end of summer grasses, dark green amongst the falling leaves. The fact that a few of those fluttering golden signatures of fall would get stuck on her head between those pink ears didn't seem to bother her; in fact she wore it well. Bartoly mused it was as if nature herself was adorning her children with a crown of color. It made him smile. When the cow was happy, Jacqualde's milk was sweeter.

Bartoly ran his hand slowly along the fair smooth skin of the woman he loved. He marveled at how his fingers rose and fell as they traced the graceful curves of her long body. He traced a small circle around her swollen belly button and watched the tender fine silken hairs stand at attention as his fingers danced. He smiled as her now darkening nipples gave a rise in avid anticipation when his fingers danced over them. The gentle breathy sigh that escaped from her lips gave credence to the flinterings of his fingers.

Deep down they knew these peaceful mornings were now at a premium. The little one growing inside her would command as much attention as it would add love to their happy union. They were both ready for the change though and it gladdened their hearts.

Bartoly stroked the soft and tender underside of Rebecca's left breast. The supple softness that he had always remembered was still there, but signs of increasing heaviness were evident; a heaviness he both marveled at and enjoyed the sight of.

As he stroked her, she snaked one warm hand down between his legs and performed her magical dance with exploring fingers; alternating both gentleness and firmness as only she could. She explored the various round and growing shapes that she was fond of enjoying. He had always admired at how she knew just exactly to do what she was doing! The deep groan that escaped him was like steaming contentment escaping to the air.

At the same time she gracefully but firmly grabbed a handful of his hair and pulled his face to hers. With a cat like purr she thrust her tongue deeply into waiting mouth. Now she moaned deeply and pulled the rest of his warm and tingling body to be closer and on her.

She wanted him.

She needed him.

She was going to have him and give herself to him. Now!

Without much more preparation, she opened herself up and deftly guided him to where she wanted him. And as her body engulfed him in warm wet folds of wonder, he wrapped his arms around her shoulders and held the silky heavy softness of her head in his broad hand. Their kiss never parted, and as one they worked the kiss deeper, passing exotic explorations of their tongues and hot breath back and forth as if they were one.

Now, as he was inside her and she around him they did not move. Just for now, no movement besides the passing of a firm kiss. They clung together, their loving passion working as one to climb into each other's skin. Together they lay still, clinging onto that special and glorious feeling that doubles your soul and enriches life as no other thing can when you are close and warm with your lover and soul mate.

But as one might expect, after a while, the need for closeness and quiet sharing burned off. That internal fire they had been kindling for the morning took over. It didn't matter who started the movement since in effect, they both did. Slow and grinding at first, then long powerful strokes, ensuring maximum pleasure and depth almost all at once.

And it was boiling hot for both of them. Their passions exploded together as real lovers often do. Hot powerful waves of joy and pleasure passing through and between them. The coupling they shared was an equal giving and taking, as it most always was, and left both satiated and breathless.

Afterward, as they lay consumed by each other they held tightly to body, soul and passion; one in and around the other for a long time. As the warm thin sheen of perspiration slowly evaporated from their intertwined bodies they cooled and snuggled closer, trapping heat and affection.

That is, until they suddenly heard someone clear their throat from the front of the cabin.

14.
Home?

"When?"

"When what?"

"Etworth, when were you at my father's castle?" Torrin was standing now. Most of the color that had drained from his face had returned and was rising in his cheeks.

"Father?" inquired Etworth. He was interested in this conversation but suddenly wary. And from his experience with Torrin he decided he should pay attention, and think about his answers carefully before speaking. Torrin was no fool and was too fast on his feet to toy with.

"Yes, King Trebor is my father! When were you there? How are they? What is going on? Was there talk of me gone missing? How is Queen Ethelda?" For Torrin, the questions were blasting out at a rapid and steady pace. A large hand descended on Torrin's shoulder.

"Slow down there big guy. Yer like a squirrel chasing a flyn' nut," said Quillan.

Etworth sat down across the table from Torrin. "How long have you been away from King Trebor's kingdom?" he asked with surprising sincerity.

"I arrived at Journey quite by surprise late in the spring as the last of the winter storms thundered over the mountains. I've wanted to go home all summer yet I've been stuck here. Now, it's too late to go, we would perish in the cold of the winter storms if we attempted the long trek back."

"Why? It's only this many days' hard ride," answered Etworth, idly looking at the mug of ale in his hand (holding up three fingers).

"What?" cried Torrin.

"Really?" asked Quillan. They had been under the impression all along that it was a long and difficult ride to get to Trebor's castle from the Journey Inn.

Torrin was instantly standing and announced, "We leave before sunrise!"

"I don't think so fella," said Dessa with a calm that belied her true feelings. "The festival starts tomorrow and you are in charge."

Torrin sat down with a thump that sounded like a sack of flour hitting the floor.

Quillan smiled and patted Torrin on the shoulder and said, "Teachn' you patience is like gettn' rocks to sprout wings."

15.
Celebration?

Just as they had in the warm sunny days of spring, the residents of the valley, generally hidden deeply in the forest, again descended upon the floor of the sprawling valley. From far and wide, near and yonder they came. It was a marvelous sight: wagons and horses, hikers and dancers. They came to celebrate the end of summer, the gathering of the harvest and their mutual blessings as a free people.

The warm golden sunshine blessed them and they were thankful for the heat of the sun as well as the golden memories and times they shared. Just a few days before the air had been cold and bespoke of an early snow that could have easily cancelled the fall festival. But as is the way of weather, it had changed its course and was now blessing them with warm bright goodness.

Unlike the summer festival, the fall festivities are more tame and serene. Oh, the dancing and partying and carrying on were sincere and thorough, but at this time of the year, everyone is usually somewhat tired. The harvesting and firewood gathering, hunting and work of the summer had taken its toll. It was the beginning of a long rest for tired hands.

So there were no games, except some that were the result of casual pickup and practice (the younger boys had to learn how to throw the hammer if they were to participate in the spring). No real competition except for dating partners. Just what some might term a relaxing vacation.

On the evening of the second day Torrin called a meeting. It was a meeting for all to attend. But the seriousness of his summons somehow told the families to keep their children in camp. So for the first time, the people of the valley met in the great room of the Journey Inn in a more formal fashion than normal. And together, for the first time in any of their memories they had to hear bad news.

"As you can see, Harold and Karina have left us," began Torrin, standing on a large stump Quillan had situated in front of the great fireplace. "We tried mightily to have them stay to carry on, but they decided to go."

Gentle huzzas and murmurs emerged from the seated crowd. It dawned on Torrin that no one was surprised. He looked at Dessa and she just shrugged.

"So it is with great honor that we fulfill the wishes of Harold and Karina. They asked that Dessa and I assume the Journey Inn," and as Torrin extended his hand to Dessa, she climbed up next to him on the large stump.

The loud applause that followed was sincere enough and long enough to let them both know that everyone there appreciated them. But word and rumor had spread, and it was time to get down to the business at hand.

And so Torrin spent the rest of the evening telling the story of Chadus and the murders and the threat the valley faced. It was a somber speech and one that he wished he could avoid delivering. But he did what he needed to do.

As he talked, he looked at each face, at each set of eyes, each life, each set of hopes and dreams; and the conversation at the back of his head was loud and clear. Whatever it took to beat back the foe, must be done. Each face there represented a family; each represented hope and a future. Everyone there had the right to their peace, to their home and freedom.

When he was done, he felt exhausted. He was drained. The news he had delivered was not only bad, it was harsh, raw and very new, even for him.

       *   *   *

As Torrin finished his somber speech and his shoulders slumped, a heavy hush fell over the room. Not a muscle stirred; it seemed as if no one was even breathing. Then, from the back of the room came the scraping of a bench along the planked floor as a large man with strong flowing red hair stood up and looked around. Seeing no one else wanting to take the floor, he straightened himself up and began to talk.

"Mr. Torrin, my name is Kamale. My family has been in this valley as long as Journey has been around. Yes, it has been many generations, but my family arrived the same summer as Valterra and Kaitlyn. The story in our family is that they shared the same ship."

Nods and quiet agreements came in hoarse whispers from around the room at this statement.

Kamale continued, "You need not worry. When you blow that horn, and you'll know the time to do it, we will be there. Every blasted one of us will be armed to the teeth and ready to destroy anything that gets in the way of who we are: our families, our children, our farms and our future."

Again, nods and this time, much louder agreement.

"You see Torrin, you are not in this alone. We are together. We are one. We live as one, we die as one, we fight as one. And together, we can do anything." Kamale looked around the room and shouted the question, "Who of ye bloody scags is with us?"

As one they rose to their feet. As one they changed before his eyes. Torrin did not see the gentle farmers of the valley he had met this summer. He did not see the humble winners and losers from the games; he did not see the happy drinking friends he had come to know.

What stood before him was suddenly the fiercest lot of tall muscular red and blond haired, angry and menacing men and women that he ever could have imagined. Their dander was up and as a group, they were more than angry. They were not ready to fight; they were ready to protect their homes, their families and each other. Protect what was more than important. Protect what they cherished.

Suddenly, he felt much better and not so lonely at all.

"Torrin," Kamale said, "You just blow that horn when the time is right and we will all be here."

And with those words ringing in his ears, Torrin's mind went to the next adventure he faced – going home!

Nothing was going to stop him.

Nothing!

16.
Final Farewell

"Who's there?" said an instantly tense Bartoly. The heat from their passion was passing quickly. But the intensity of his alert was raised since being surprised right after making love with Rebecca was just somehow indescribably annoying and startling.

In one graceful movement both he and Rebecca had grasped long thin tapers from under the bed and were moving toward the kitchen. Both were naked and did not care. They were not about to become victims of another raid.

As Bartoly turned the corner to the kitchen he froze in his tracks. The blade in his hand was suddenly powerless, and he knew it. Especially when he heard the giggle.

"What is it?" asked Rebecca, a long-bow now in her hand with a quiver of arrows slung loosely under her left arm. The taper having been tossed on the bed should it be needed later.

"We have company," he said with a grin.

"What?" exclaimed an incredulous Rebecca as she too turned the corner and fell suddenly within full view of the enquiring eyes of Harold and Karina.

Harold's mouth opened to say something and Karina smacked him on the top of the head and shushed him up. He returned to the large chunk of bread he was munching on. Karina looked back toward Bartoly and Rebecca and said, "Why don't you two finish up what you need to finish up. When yer ready, get dressed and come out for a visit?"

Both Bartoly and Rebecca turned and walked away to find something to wear, shaking their heads and smiling.

       *   *   *

"Can't you just stay here with us?" asked Rebecca.

"No child," Karina said graciously. She knew this question would come up. "We must be on our way, but we wanted to see you before we left. Anyway, our path is the trail down into your beautiful valley, so we were coming right by and figured we would stop to see some of our favorite people. And anyway, we wanted to wish you the best of luck with the babe."

Rebecca was speechless and Bartoly was stoically quiet. It occurred to him, as it often did, you could not change someone's mind once it was made up.

"Let us pack you some food," said Rebecca as she rose to start putting together a picnic of grand proportions (at least that is what she saw in her mind).

Karina replied, "Thank you dear, but just some bread and wine. It's all we would be grateful for; we have all that we pretty much need."

Rebecca pulled a fresh golden loaf from the pantry. It was soft having been coated with butter right from the oven and its aroma filled the room with pleasantries that words fail to adequately describe. Then came along a large ornate ceramic flask of dark red wine. She put them both on the table in a manner that any good hostess would follow.

Both Harold and Karina rose and tears started to form in Rebecca's eyes.

Karina turned to her, wiping the tears from her face and said, "One last thing – stand up on the bench please."

Rebecca looked at Harold and he just smiled. She looked at Bartoly and he shrugged his shoulders in a way that said "go ahead," and finally she looked at Karina who just smiled at her and gestured toward the bench.

Finally Rebecca did as she had been asked, feeling altogether foolish. With the weight of the babe in her front, she was not as graceful as she usually was. Bartoly offered a hand.

"Go ahead Harold, you promised," said Karina, "And just tell the truth, no matter what the news."

Harold blushed as only he could and walked over to the girl he had known since a young baby now standing on the bench. Very gently he laid his head on her swelling belly and closed his eyes. He reached out, grasped her hand and put it over his exposed ear. After a few moments he sighed deeply and then backed away. There were tears in his eyes and he was very unable to speak.

All the eyes in the room were focused on Harold. It was obvious that a great weight was on his shoulders. He nodded a thanks to Bartoly who handed him a mug of the red wine. Harold kept breathing gently and then studied the artistic virtues of the mug. He knew Rebecca had crafted it. She never performed her art in a common manner. There was always some hint of love and caring built into all her work. This mug was a soft green and she had pressed red berries into the clay before firing the piece. The berries had left their marks of color before being consumed by the fire. The shape she had arranged them into was that of a small pointed pine tree. It was a figure of beauty, just as much as the love in her heart.

Harold signed and bit his lip. Finally, after a good gulp of wine, he was able to compose himself enough to talk. His speech was somewhat ragged, but he said through his tears in that calm and caring voice Rebecca knew and loved, "It is hard to tell. I do feel that all will be well. As far as I can tell there is no danger with the babe or yerself. But ye best take care and be careful." He looked balefully at Karina and then at Bartoly. He gulped and said. "Usually I can tell if all will be well or if there will be trouble. But this is the first time it is not clear."

He shook his head sadly and walked over to a bench. Slowly he heaved what seemed to be an all of a sudden very heavy body down with a loud grunt. Harold put his head in one hand and closed his eyes. He seemed very weary.

Karina looked at both of the prospective young parents and slowly shook her head too, then said in a soft voice, "I am so sorry."

17.
Going Home

An interestingly strange party of four ventured out on the excursion to Torrin's home. Dessa, Quillan and the enigma Etworth.

As they rode, what was a reoccurring theme of the entire foray was Torrin urging Samoot on. Dessa sighed as Uta kept up with little effort. Torrin's need to be home did not diminish whatsoever as they pushed onward through another long day.

Quillan rode steadily at the back of the foursome, but was keeping an eye on Etworth. He had confided to Dessa before they left Journey about his concern of the slight chance Etworth may be lying to them about the location of Trebor's castle.

"This could be a ruse," he had said, "To get the leaders away from Journey and do them in. The valley would be much easier to conquer or take over and turn into his blasted trading post with us all dead, gone or missing." So Quillan had his guard up, as did Dessa. The horses could tell as they always did. However, Torrin was clueless; he was focused on one thing and one thing only, getting to the castle as soon as possible.

As it ended up, it was not really a very hard ride and Etworth was no trouble at all. They traversed various tricky rocks and streams. Climbed a few long hills and had to endure pushing through dense valleys of thick growth. After three days, as Etworth had said, they came to a well worn trail and trotted along in a pleasant canter. The leaves skittered around them, swooshing in great waves and crunching underfoot as they pressed on toward their destination.

The shadows were growing longer and the sun was blazing orange against a dark navy blue sky, peppered with high wispy clouds. A cooling breeze flowed over the foursome from the back, washing away perspiration. Always a by-product of steady riding.

The horses could feel the gentle cooling too. If you really knew them, you might think they were smiling. In reality though, as they trotted along, they had their faces pulled back to feel the breeze against their wet lips. It was just like wiping a cool wet hand on your neck on a hot day, and they loved it. Of course Dessa could hear them chatting amongst themselves, and she marveled at how such a beast could figure out ways to enjoy themselves without so much as trying.

It occurred to her that since meeting Torrin, her ability to listen to the animals continued to grow. Most of all, she really liked it. This link to nature gave her a calming sense. And as she pondered this, she smiled and said aloud as much as to herself, "I wonder if they could someday listen to me in more ways than just commands."

"You have been able to for a while now, you just have not been aware of it," said Uta quietly.

Dessa almost fell off of her saddle. Breathing slowly through her nose she then said, "Oh. I." and stammered for a moment until she finally said, "Really?"

"Yes," said Uta. "It's new for me too, so don't think this is different only for you."

I wonder if they can hear my thoughts too? she pondered.

"Somewhat, but not as clear as your words," came the reply. She not so much as heard the comment, but felt it in her ears. Not as something out loud, more of a thought that crossed through her head.

"This could be interesting," she decided.

"Yes it will be," came a somewhat laughed reply.

*   *   *

Soon Torrin became aware that he knew where he was. The trees, the rocks and landmarks stirred familiar and homey thoughts in his soul. He could see it and sense it. He was almost home. His heart began to speed up, his head was full of the things he would say to everybody, he was tingling all over.

It was as if it was really true. He could sense the smell of fresh bread wafting from the grand kitchen of the castle. The thought of the sweet cakes and toasted treats made his mouth water in anticipation.

And then the words of his father struck him. He almost lost his breath as the memory came flushing back. He vividly remembered the moment; it was etched in his brain. He could recall in minute detail the cool night air, the sounds of the crickets and the smell of the dark red wine he and his father had shared.

It was around the birthday when he had first started shaving. He and his father stood outside on the battlements in the starry summer night. Somehow things were different. No longer did Torrin sit on his father's lap and bounce. Now he sat next to him and their discussions of late had seemed serious.

"Torrin?" began his father.

"Yes?"

"Torrin, you need to know, you are a good boy and you are turning into a fine young man and prince. You are not so headstrong as to be bothersome, but I need to tell, nay more ask of you, two things that are important not only to me, but I hope are important to you too."

"What are they?" asked the now quizzical young boy turning slowly into a man.

"First off, you are coming of an age where you might think you know more than most people. It is normal, it is common and it is a real pain in the ass for those of us who are somewhat older, but we tolerate it."

"Well I am pretty smart," replied Torrin, feeling good about this conversation.

"Yes you are. I just want you to know, that there may be times over the next few summers and winters that we may disagree. Please think before you question me too harshly, for if you don't, it could bode poorly for our relationship."

Torrin knew that this was sage advice and to make light of it or question further might be met with disdain. So he said, "I will keep that in mind. What was the second thought?"

"It also very important for you to know, that no matter what happens, no matter what you do or what anybody does, you can always come home. You are always, always welcome here." When Trebor looked at Torrin, he had tears in his eyes and Torrin had felt closer to his father at that moment than ever before.

The memory of that night was embedded upon Torrin. It stuck in his heart like fire. It was a good fire, the fire of compassion and caring. And having been away, having missed them all so much, and having been through what he had been through made those words his father had spoken mean ever so much more.

*   *   *

As he rode, Torrin was not sure how to tell the whole story of his adventures at Journey to his family. There was so much to tell! But he knew it would all come out, and in the end they would all laugh together and be happy like they always had been. He could feel the warm embrace of his mother and sister. He could almost feel their shining smiles. His father's strong arms would hug him, only the way a father can, and he could feel in his heart he was almost home.

All at once he spurred Samoot on and galloped fast ahead, disappearing around a bend in the trail with a wild whoop of joy.

When the three of them caught up with Torrin, they found him standing on a large rock. His legs were slightly apart and the setting sun blazed a silhouette of his tall squared form into their eyes. They dismounted to join him upon the rock and share in the view.

For some reason, Quillan noticed Samoot was walking around untethered and anxious. Torrin's jaw was set and the look that was swept upon his face was a mix of emotions that seemed so strong as to tear the skin from his cheeks.

As they climbed up on the rock, they followed his gaze toward the castle.

At least it used to be a castle.

18.
Duty

Ailis the Fergal finally returned to the thick grove of low rowan trees that served as his den. Out of the usually normal and natural way of living for cougars, Ailis lived with his family. Many times he had been forced to help others understand that even though he was a little different it did not take away any of his power. For Ailis, there was no particular reason for spending much of his life with a female near him that he could think of. There was no special logic to it.

He often mused about his special living arrangements, since no other males kept any long term female company. While waiting in the soft grass for an animal to make itself known, this arrangement gave his thoughts something to ponder. The pondering seemed to keep him quiet and less tense. A pondering that kept him patient and silent for game while on the hunt. He did not know if this at all made any difference. But he did know that he and the brood never went hungry.

Ailis often decided, when all was thought through, that he just liked it. And coming home was nice.

The journey he had taken to deliver Chadus with the horse Zoltha had been a long one and he was tired. He knew the fact that he was tired would not matter a wit. The cubs would want to play. That was never a problem and they were such simple fun.

The first time he had encountered offspring was a surprise. Three cubs had greeted him one warm spring morning when he returned with a large turkey (most cougars left their kill covered with brush and feed off it for days. Ailis completely enjoyed not having to guard his kills). When he had arrived, the cubs were still wet, covered in spots and had no sight.

His mate (she had no name, as most cougars) had eyed him warily. She had never let a male this close to her cubs. For that matter, no animal or human had ever gotten this close.

And lived.

Ailis had kept his distance and prepared this kill so he could share it with her when she was ready. He had no doubt that if she felt any kind of threat she would excise him from nose to tail.

These new cubs in Ailis's den had mewed and squeaked playfully as they searched for their mother's teats. A natural occurrence that Ailis never understood. It amazed him that such small blind critters could do so well. He bode his time at a safe and respectful distance and watched them grow.

Once, long ago, he had spied quietly from a hilltop as a stupid brown bear, huge in size made the mistake of underestimating a cougar mother. The bear was either hunting or trying to play with a cougar cub. Either way, the ferociousness of the attack from the mother made even Ailis jump in surprise. The bear was not caught off guard for long and went to make easy prey of the little cat.

The little cat had a purpose that seemed to give her strength and speed beyond her size and natural ability. She had tried to hold onto the bear's head from above and chew through its neck. But she was quickly shaken off and thrown into the trees.

But time and again she charged defending her offspring. She sprinted back so fast that the bear kept missing her with those massively fatal claws. And she struck blow after blow with long nails and sharp fangs.

Eventually the bear succumbed to her blows. Ailis never knew the details as of why and he was smart to never go near the site to investigate. Cougars, like most cats, are very territorial and Ailis did not want to violate the territory of a bear killer!

But now was now, and three little kittens attacked Ailis with all the ferocity they could muster. It was of course fun ferocity, and Ailis took the time they needed to wear out.

It was not long before the little guys were back fast asleep and Ailis could give attention to his mate.

After some nuzzling she looked at him with big questioning eyes. It took a moment for him to understand.

And shaking himself off, he slowly turned around and left the peace of the rowan trees.

He had forgotten to bring back spoils of a hunt.

And although neither could speak, her eyes told him all the story he needed to know.

His family was hungry and he needed to change that now.

19.
Poetry

The heavy glow of the sun shone harshly across the ruins. Lazy smoky tendrils of the dying conflagration struggled up toward the sky in the cool air of the approaching evening. The fires that fed the now diminishing smoke had mostly burned out. But the stench from the fading inferno was abrasive and had obviously been very hot. Putrid waves of nauseating stench invaded the now distraught homecoming party's noses as their eyes took in the catastrophe that lay in burnt shambles at their feet and all around them.

They walked slowly up to where the drawbridge had been. The well manicured moat had been lined with flowers and tall grasses. All that lay there now was a crushed mess of green, strewn with debris, wretched broken lifeless bodies and dead horses. The buzzing of the flies was a sharp pitched hum that filled their ears with the sad music of agony.

Dessa noticed no birds sang. No sounds of nature came to her ears. It was almost as if death fully enveloped the area.

The drawbridge was down and mostly burned away, except for enough board to carefully walk upon to keep from the grisly mess below. The heavy old steel that held it together groaned as each one of them gingerly stepped across. Dessa had to coax each of the horses in turn to make the crossing.

Inside the main courtyard the sight that they beheld caused Torrin to stop dead in his tracks. He doubled over and threw up.

After a while, Quillan's big hand grabbed Torrin's shoulder and helped the struggling lad regain his footing upon the earth. Quillan was steadily breathing in through his mouth and out through his nose in measured long deep breaths. It was the only way he could keep any measure of calm.

All around the courtyard lay the bodies of men, women, children and soldiers. It had obviously been a hard, but fast and furious battle.

There were no signs of a siege. No massive weapons outside the walls, no barrels of water on the inside as would have been the case during a siege. No places where the farming peasants from the outer areas had come to camp in the safety of the castle as was common during a long and usually hateful situation that attends to a siege. It was all just massive destruction. Burnt mayhem, chaotic death and brut force blasted upon the young and old. The innocent and the guilty. A final sentence for anyone who tried to stand in its path, or who was unlucky enough to just be there.

From what they could tell, not a soul amongst them was living. There were no sounds, save for a few crows. No groans. No cries for help. No sounds of life, no wounded.

Nothing.

The foursome walked up toward the main building. Torrin remembered the great blue flags with the long yellow crosses that hung on either side of the big doors; they had floated lazily upon the breezes as if waving to the teeming throng that lived a good life in this grand courtyard. They had always made him proud. Those flags had reminded him often he was part of something larger than himself, or his family for that matter. He was part of a kingdom of people. Good people who took care of each other.

Now those blue flags were mostly burned. Shreds of their former selves swayed dirtily in the breeze, the yellow was choked with black and it was as if they too had lost their life.

Dessa caught up with them. "Something is strange," she said.

"What?" asked a more than befuddled Torrin.

"There are no animals about. Not even a cat, and no bodies of animals either. None were killed as far as I can see, save for the dead cavalry mounts."

"So?"

"So, if this were an invasion, I would expect to see more than human carcasses," replied Dessa.

"Food," said Quillan. "They came here for the food for winter and took the animals. My guess is their soldiers had strict orders not to hurt the livestock. And of course the locals would not think of killing their own."

"Brutal, just outrageous," said a stunned Etworth. He had finally found his tongue.

"Just a short while ago, this was such a nice place," he stated to no one in particular and anybody who was listening.

"Musicians and kauppasaksa selling all sorts of things and children playing. I remember the laughter and I remember thinking it was such a happy place. At the time my only other thoughts were that these people would really be the perfect market for next year's tea and spices. This is so..." he just shrugged his shoulders and held out his hands in a disparaging pose. He was once again speechless.

Slowly they ventured inside the main hall and they found more of the same. All a shambles, all in destructed disarray. It was like a bad, bad nightmare that would not stop. One of those dreams where you are so scared, you're even afraid to wake up, knowing you will be frightened awake too, and the rest of the day. None of this made any sense.

Torrin knew where he was going and he plodded on with purpose. His anger and loathing growing with every step, he was headed toward the main throne room.

Upon entering, at first the starkness of it bothered him more than anything. Stripped clean of its rugs and blankets, its banners and tapestries, it looked as if it had been skinned alive and left to bleach in the putrid air. What was strange though was that nothing had been harmed. All the glory had been taken, but nothing burned. Not even a scratch. No bodies, just a big empty room. Even the throne was gone.

"Verra strange," remarked Quillan. "What do you suppose made them treat this room so differently?"

"I don't ..." but before he could finish his sentence, Torrin's hand went up to the back of his neck. The hair was standing straight up; he was awash in that inner feeling of danger. That feeling that always told him something was wrong.

Unsheathing his sword he swung slowly and carefully around. The other three, as if on command slid out their weapons. Looks of worry and trepidation rising on their faces as they instinctively backed into a circle so that no part of the room was without the wary look of their eyes. They were deep inside the castle and none of them save Torrin knew their way around. It was not a good place to be on the receiving end of an attack.

"This way," whispered Torrin pointing toward a wide wooden door that was well worn from much use on the right side.

They trod quietly, but quickly through a small kitchen of sorts and then into a good sized room. The smell of the room was off. It was strange. It did not mix with the other putrid smells of the place.

Dessa wrinkled up her nose and muttered as a question, one word, "Babies?"

"Shhh," said Torrin in a hushed whisper. His hand was on the back of his neck. He was more mad than frightened, he could feel it, it was in this room; he just could not see whatever was setting off his internal alarms.

And then he saw her. The old woman was lying on the cold stone floor. The blood from a nasty gash on her head mingled angrily with her sallow skin and thick grey hair. One arm was twisted in a grotesque way; broken no doubt by some savage monster. She was lying next to a long box. It looked as though she had been dumped out of the box; she lay there as though a sack of flour.

Torrin sheathed the sword in his hand and knelt gingerly next to the still form of this old gray haired lady who lay there without so much as any form of life. He picked her up and held her close. She was not tall, nor was she big. Just a bit of a thing, but you tell without looking hard she had a kindly face.

Etworth asked, "Is she your...?"

"No," Torrin explained, "Safon was...is the head of this room, this nursery. Any woman of the kingdom who had a child could come to the castle's nursery to learn how to care for her babe and just as importantly, learn to take care of herself. It was my mother's idea to take better care of the people. So verra often, many of the new mothers were just young girls themselves and they had not a clue what to do when a wee babe full of needs entered her life. Safon was their savior. She was a woman with the patience of a saint and knew everything about raising the wild needy little things."

"What happened?" he said to the still cold form of the woman laying in his arms. "What the hell happened here?"

As if his words had woken the dead, the old woman moaned and with a slow heaviness, fluttered open, just slightly, the eyelids of her thickly bloodshot eyes. Her head tilted a little and she looked at Torrin like you might look at something strange.

"Torrin, is that really you?" came the hoarsely whispered question. "Oh Torrin," the soft exclamation came from the old lady as though a thousand pound weight had been lifted from her soul. She ran her good hand across his cheek. And then as if on command a tear left her eye and trailed a long line of clean across the black soot that was on her cheek.

"Safon, what happened?" he asked again, urgency rising in his voice mingled with the surprise that she was alive. When he had said it before, he thought he was talking to a corpse. Now she was the only living thing connected to his family. As far as he knew, they might somewhere still be alive, judging from the lack of battle marks in the throne room.

Safon licked her lips and took a deep breath. Her jagged breathing rattled angrily in her chest. She seemed to struggle, even though she would only take in short shallow breaths. Torrin guessed she had broken ribs as well as a mangled arm.

As Dessa tucked a heavy blanket around the two on the floor, Quillan supplied some water.

Safon slowly and quietly began to speak, "Your mother took me aside as the castle was being overrun and told me that no matter what I did, I was to survive and find you and give you a message from them. From both your parents. So I ran and fought off three of them, not before they broke my arm," she grinned a painful grimace and looked at the swollen limb hanging uselessly to one side. "Anyway, I hid in that box until it was over. I really don't know how they missed me, they were so very thorough, and I have been in there for how long? I have no idea." She sighed, closed her eyes and rested for a moment. "I went to sleep and that's all I remember, until I woke up here in your arms. Oh you are so much like an angel, an answer to my prayers."

Quillan interrupted with more water from his skin, holding it carefully so the woman could drink and quench the thirst that stole so much from her. She drank some, slowly turned her head, breathed gently and then took some more. The look on her face eternally grateful. She did not utter any words of thanks; she just closed her eyes up to Quillan, smiled and nodded her head. He knew she was better for it.

"What happened?" asked Torrin again. "Who was it, how did they get in?"

"Torrin dear, I don't have much time, you will have to figure that all out by yourself, or ask someone else," she pulled in another tortured breath. He could feel the raggedness of her breath deepening. It sounded like she had gravel being flung about inside her. It made him wince.

"Then what is the message from my parents?" he asked pensively, but with a softness that came from his heart; not sure he was ready to hear it, but more importantly, he knew he needed to hear it.

After a few moments of rest, Safon began again to speak slowly, a look of true effort crawling creepily across her tired face. "Really it's a poem. You see, she knew they would not let either of them go. She knew their time had come." The old lady shivered from deep inside. Her blue lips seemed translucent and you could tell speaking was more an effort than she really wanted to expend at the moment. But she was full of purpose and nothing would stop her now.

As she spoke Torrin held her close with the thick blanket tightly wrapped around both of them, trying to share his warmth with her. She not only felt cold, she felt as heavy as a light bird, like brittle dry sticks. It was all so wrong. This woman had spent her life helping others, helping them deal with the wonder and challenges of new life. She had spread kindness and caring.

"Yes?" he said, his eyes full of tears.

Taking as deep a breath as possible that again rattled angrily within her bones, she closed her eyes and in a slow lyrical tone began:

> "Torrin we are gone,
> release us, let us go;
> We have so many things yet to see and do,
> but now they are to be done through you.
> Do not tie yourself to us with tears,
> just be happy we had each other.

We gave you our love, as best we could
and you can only guess
how much you gave us in happiness.
We thank you for the love you've shown."

Torrin began to sob, he could hear the words, just as his mother or father would have said them. Safon was tearing his heart with a brutal mix of love and grief.

"Boy, listen up!" said Safon, suddenly in her most commanding voice. "I do not have long." The strength of her bidding startled all of them. They were quiet and listened,

"So grieve a while for us,
if grieve you must.
Then let your grief be comforted by trust.
It's only for a while that we must part,
so bless the memories within your heart.
We won't be far away, for life goes on;
So if you need us, call, and we will come.
Though you can't see, or touch, we'll be near;
And if you listen with your heart, you'll hear;
All our love around you, soft and clear.
Now do the duty you were meant to do,
Stay clear and purposeful and true.
The path is long and dangerous,
So do not avenge your anger
Do not avenge our death.
Go forward to build, not to destroy,
But defend at all costs.
Your mission is to hold true the promise,
Keep it true, protect it, make it the future for all.

She had done her duty; he felt her relax. The tenseness left her completely. Her eyes were settled, her face was as if burned, but then she did the strangest thing – she smiled. As she did, her lips cracked and bled, but she smiled nonetheless. She slowly raised one hand again to caress his hair and then hoarsely whispered, "You did the right thing to come home; now you must live your destiny. You must live it for all of us. Please. Live it boldly, because that is the only way. It is the only way you may honor your destiny."

And with those words, the last link to Torrin's past; the last link to his mother, to his father, to his childhood and to his home faded on to an eternal rest. But she did it fulfilled and not so much happy as with a full and contented heart that had done what it needed to do.

Torrin stood and carried her prone form to a table in the middle of the room and laid her gently upon the place where she had lain countless babies, teaching mothers how to fix a clot of blanket to keep the babe dry. Showing how to gently wipe dry a sore bottom or apply a salve to a rash.

He turned to his little troupe and said, "In the morning we will gather up all the bodies we can and burn them together. They lived as one, they will go to nature as one."

Continuing on, he said to the confused and tired band of friends around him, "Until then, we will build a warm fire in my old bedroom, eat, drink and sleep."

"And how do you plan to eat and drink?" inquired Dessa. She looked at him. He was only a day older than yesterday. But suddenly many winters richer in wisdom. The boy was there, but gone now in the flash of a few moments. Gone for good until she could bring him back at the right time. To help him never forget the gentleness of his child, which would always be the foundation of him as a man. It would be a while she knew, and she had to let this all work through him. It would be a test of her. A test for him. And largely a test for them. All at once, she did not relish the thought. But then, she decided, she had done the same on her trek to Journey. His would be the same, only different. His difference was that he would not be alone.

Torrin then answered her question, somewhat matter-of-factly, but also tired and resigned, "I know where my father kept the secret stockpile of wine, dried meat and cheese. And I bet it's safe."

It was.

* * *

How did she do that? I mean remember all those words?" asked Quillan. He had his back to the wall. Firelight danced on his face from the blazing wood.

"She was a natural," answered Torrin. "Safon would teach poems to mothers. She would recite them all day to the babes to settle them down. She said the poetry was a gift to the spirit and would settle stomachs as well as help a mother's milk flow so the babe would be well fed. To all of us, she worked the miracles that babies and mothers needed."

He continued, "She was a gift to me as a child, and she has given me a greater gift now." And then gritting his teeth he said, "And she will be avenged."

Quillan reached out his hand and gave his friend's leg a slap and said, "I may not be able to be a great man like you, having the gift and all. But I can stand for great things, and stand I will." Raising his jug, he said, "To the mighty, wise and steely strength of the good woman Safon!" The others raised their own jugs and bellowed a mighty "Huzza," in agreement.

So by the flickering firelight the four of them rode through the treachery around this night in Torrin's boyhood room. Most all of his room had been wrecked in the rampage, but they managed to salvage enough to bed down. To keep warm, the fire was fed with wreckage stuffed into the fireplace to ward off the ever encroaching cold damp deadly feeling that permeated the room. Nay, this feeling infested the entire castle.

The wine was good, the meat tangy with smoke flavor and salts, the dense cheese even better. Torrin harkened that this was a fine irony. His father had always kept the stash in case of a storm or famine. Torrin had helped him to maintain the stock, yet had never been allowed to touch anything in the precious little storeroom, cleverly hidden off his parents' bedroom. He would have given most anything, except Dessa, to enjoy this little feast with his parents.

Just one time, just one more time. These thoughts invaded his mind, and he dwelled upon them for a while.

He felt robbed.

Violated.

Beaten.

Then the words spoken in great wisdom from Safon returned to him. "Go forward to build, not to destroy, But defend at all costs." He could not, and would not let this stop him from doing what he needed to do to protect Journey. Or the valley, the people, or Dessa.

But as he closed his eyes to sleep that fateful evening, he knew in his head and in his heart that as much as he wanted, as much as he wished, and as much as it ought to be; all was different now.

He had tried to come home. And now he could never come home.

Ever.

        * * *

The gruesome task took two long days. But after much sweating and straining, they had as many of the dead as they could find piled in the main courtyard. Torrin had found two barrels of candle oil in the secret stockpile to help make the grisly deed more successful.

They all agreed that this was better than leaving the dead to the animals of the forest. Although Dessa knew that the critters lurking in the shadows did not share the same opinion.

Finally, Torrin, Dessa, Quillan and Etworth stood before the wretched pile. Torrin bowed his head. The work of the past two days had cleansed his spirit some. He had mourned, he had cried, he had lashed out, he had gotten very drunk. Now, he was mostly tired. Very dirty and very ready to move on.

This job of cleansing the castle of this wretchedness was about to be completed. However, deep in the back of his mind he kept reminding himself and knew the bigger job was to protect Journey. And not just the building, but all the people of the valley, who now were the only real family he had left.

Dessa swept away a tear, looked at him and said, "Be thankful."

"Well I am thankful for you," he replied in a husky and taut voice, questions emerging from his face. "There is not so much to be thankful for right now about this place, as I see it." His arm gesturing about.

"Maybe you need to look at things a little differently," she said in a kind yet firm tone. "If you had not ended up at Journey, there would be no one to avenge this cruel crime. No one to be here to clean up this wretchedness and put these poor souls to rest in a rightful sort of way."

He looked at her, he pondered, he was so very tired and his brain was not connecting the dots of her meaning.

She finished with one short sentence. "We have work to do, and now more reason to do it. This is a very sad reminder of what will happen if we don't protect what we need to protect."

The thick black smoke rose to the sky in a last tribute to the place and the people Torrin had called home and family.

It was getting on late in the afternoon, the coolness of the fall evening away from the pyre was descending along with crisp lengthening shadows all around. They decided to leave early with the sunrise. There was only one night's quantity of wine, meat and cheese left to finish and they had all agreed that sleeping in Torrin's old bedroom was better than sleeping on the ground in the woods.

Quillan and Etworth went off to attend to the horses. They told Torrin and Dessa they would meet back up in the room. The two of them should get a fire going so that it did not get too cold.

As Torrin and Dessa warmly clasped their hands and walked sadly back to get ready for one last night, Dessa stopped dead in her tracks and said, "Uh oh."

20.
Meeting a Friend

Gaerwn was excited. It wasn't often he got to do this sort of thing. He relished the thought of it and he had been planning this little party ever since he received word that the army was on its way back to the kingdom. Word had it that they had been not just enormously successful, but all had gone according to his wishes. And that was the best thing. The good news seemed to dash the black cruelty from his heart, and it was replaced by the sparkle of insane terrorism.

Soldiers led the special conquered prisoners from Trebor's castle through the big doorway. Their bloody feet were proof of the fast and furious march they had made across the rugged trails of the woods. The gags around their faces were covered with dried blood and mud from the constant chaffing and falling; a testament to their treatment during the forced march. The rags that bound their elbows behind them were thin and cutting. Their hair stuck to places all about their head and shoulders and their eyes looked for all intents and purposes, beaten.

The room was packed with onlookers waiting to see what would happen. The long shadows from the candles danced darkly on the walls as the setting sun left for the evening and let the darkness add its own special sadness to the misery.

The head of the garrison, deciding he needed to show how much in charge he was, pushed the two forward with a loud warning that they should bow before the great king and not stand until told to do so.

As weak as they were, they both fell to their faces on the cold stone floor. Unable to catch themselves because of the bonds around their elbows behind them, they both hit their heads and lay there, too weak to move.

What passed through their thoughts was not so much the pain, but the fact that they could now stop moving, for at least a moment, and catch their breath. They had been constantly on the move for the last few days, never stopping except to wait for the back of the army to periodically catch up with the captives and the head of the garrison. It had seemed like a race toward the end of the world. Little did they know that the commander was doing them some sort of favor; he knew if they were caught in a freakish snowstorm, the prisoners would most likely perish by freezing because the soldiers would not take care of them for any reason in the cold. It was just their way.

Gaerwn looked up at the soldier who was beaming at himself in pure unabashed power and growled, "You are not treating our guests with the dignity they deserve." Turning to Scraddius he ordered, "Lash him until he falls."

Lashings in Gaerwn's kingdom were cruel enough. Often Gaerwn would put small stones in a bag, indicating how many lashes a person was to have. This had an effect of dual cruelty and fed into Gaerwn's lust for control. Gaerwn was in charge of the number of lashes, but the victim of the cruelty had no idea how many stones were in the bag. So part of the terror was not knowing when it would end.

However, lashing someone until they fell was worse. The ego of the men in the army was very fragile and they generally had to prove how strong they were to each other on a regular basis. The goal when you were lashed was to never fall down. If you fell down, the taunting would go on for what seemed an eternity. Usually until the next poor bastard received a lashing and the forlorn maggots who had been taunting you, forgot about you. So even though you could feel chunks of your back being torn off, you would stand until you passed out. That way, your friends would tell you, you were strong, that you were worthy, you were a "real man" to stand up to the pain and torture. To the men of the army, considering the evil they lived with, it seemed worth it.

What was particularly cruel about Gaerwn's lashing order was not so much the lashing as the intent. You see, Gaerwn did not find anything distasteful about the way the prisoners had been treated. What he wanted was for the prisoners to think he was on their side and friendly toward them. The fact that some poor wretched overzealous commander was now going to be whipped for this little ruse did not bother Gaerwn one bit.

It did bother Trebor as he watched the man being led away shouting his innocence. It bothered him because he knew that Gaerwn was foul and could not be trusted for anything except evil.

He was right; he just did not know how right he was.

*   *   *

At just about the time King Trebor's sad eyes were watching the soldier's hunched shoulders being led away, Dessa and Torrin were quietly picking their way through the woods outside the ruins of the destroyed castle.

Praritor, the head of the wolves had called to Dessa. There was a spy in the woods and Praritor wanted to know if the spy was fair game for his brood to feast upon. Dessa had quietly told him to wait.

So now the two were cautiously and quietly sneaking up on a lone figure crouched low amongst the thick bushes that covered most of the floor of the forest. The soldier was keenly intent on watching what was going on in the main courtyard through a very large hole that had been broken in the main wall. His attention was focused on the smoke and fire, along with Quillan and Etworth leading the horses toward the dilapidated stables. He heard nothing and did not move until he felt the cold point of Torrin's sword against his neck.

Turning slowly around he leered a long evil smile at Torrin. What this large and well trained soldier's eyes saw was a young man; nearly a boy, holding him at bay. It was quite apparent that escaping this predicament would be easy. And, considering his orders were quite clear, that no one was allowed to live, he looked forward to carrying out the directive, since he would be able to brag about it later.

That was until the image of a tall redheaded girl with a bow standing a few paces to the left of the boy came into focus. He sensed that the tip of the long dead straight arrow nocked between her fingers was aimed right at his eye. He could see the tip flash in the firelight. He also noticed that the tip did not move or waver. It was steady and firm. Quite menacing, he surmised.

"Who are you?" asked the boy. He seemed rather agitated and something about him was cautiously familiar.

"More importantly, who are ye young laddie?" sneered the somewhat now wary soldier, working the conversation to his advantage, as he had been taught.

"I am Prince Torrin McKenna, son of King Trebor, and you are trespassing on my land," replied Torrin as strongly as he could. Even with Dessa behind him, and knowing she was a sure shot, this stinking, hulking dirty brute was menacing. And anyway, he was not yet convinced of the story Harold had told him about living forever. He decided he did not want to test the theory quite yet, at least not right now, here in the woods.

The soldier could not believe his ears. This was the one they had searched so thoroughly for! The one who must have escaped the castle as they so easily overran it. This was one of the key members of the family that Gaerwn so feverishly wanted. He knew if he played this right, he would be a hero for the king and the riches would be enormous.

The only problem now presenting itself was that this boy would have to stay alive. Damn. These things were never easy. Killing them both would have been so much fun. He hoped the boy wouldn't mind leaving his girlfriend here; she would just slow them down. Of course, they would leave her here after he was finished playing some fun games with her.

So as one of the soldier's hands began to scratch at his thick black and very mangy beard to distract both Dessa and Torrin's attention, the other hand slowly crept toward a long thin, carefully sharpened throwing knife snuggly secured in a hilt under his coat at his back.

"Weeel now Mr. Torrin, uh sire, your prince sir," stammered the soldier, playing the part of the bumbling idiot, as well as he could. "I guess we mus have an unfortunate difference of opinion here."

Torrin scrunched up his eyebrows and said, "Huh?" He was not expecting this sort of response from the man. He had prepared himself for something much more vulgar. Of course, upon reflection he was not sure what he was expecting, but this certainly was not it.

"You see, I am very sorry for the loss of yer home and hearth," he paused. "Really I am, and in fact I deserted the army to come back here to elp. But it occurred to me when I approached, any survivors might not take kindly to me, even if I were a deserter, since I am wearing the colors of the army that just destroyed ye."

Torrin cocked his head and said, "Go on."

"So I ave been sittn ere cogitatin on what to do, and then I felt the cold point of yer steel again my neck and ere we is."

As Torrin began to lower his sword, he remembered hearing a mournfully loud, "No" coming from somewhere.

The rest was a blur.

21.
Truth

"Untie my friends, whom for the rest of you, are your guests. We treat them as the royalty the are! Take them to my private quarters and attend to their issues and injuries," ordered Gaerwn in a loud and commanding voice. His glare circled the room and made all who had ventured in looking for sadistic entertainment worry that they may have made a mistake.

The needles that stung King Trebor's arms as the blood began to flow back into his veins felt like the onslaught of a million little biting red ants. As the gag came off, he found that his mouth would not move; so crusted with filth and blood it was. Plus his jaw muscles seemed frozen in place.

Looking at Queen Ethelda he slowly and very stiffly held out an arm for her and they arose as well as they could. Together they walked with as much dignity as they were able to muster behind the servant who led them through a narrow doorway just off the massive and over decorated throne. Both were in agony from the march and just as much from the tight material being removed.

It was not a big room, but it was well appointed, carpeted in thick furs and had its own private privy. Two wide windows let in sunlight and clean fresh air. The windows' heavy winter drapes were tied back, for the day had been sunny and pleasant. The servant returned with three others in tow. This little entourage was laden with items that seemed almost too good to be true. Warm and cool water, sweet smelling soaps, soft towels, stronger beverages, some plain yet comfortable clothing. To top it all off, the scent of warm, fresh from the oven, soft crustless bread filled the little room.

Deftly depositing these items on a large padded bench (which someday would become known as a sofa) and table, the other three scurried away as the main servant quietly informed the two captives to please knock on the back door if they needed anything. There was no rush. Mighty and merciful King Gaerwn had indicated without a doubt that they both should take whatever effort necessary to become more comfortable.

With that, the servant turned and left. Trebor noted the man made no noise when he walked. It was eerie, but yet just one more quizzical mystery about this place that seemed to be all wrong, all at once, so fast, and in so many ways.

Ethelda emerged from the privy and was visibly working to get her mouth moving. Trebor wet a small towel and handed it to her and she began to gently wash her face as he let himself into the privy.

A castle privy is generally not a very eloquent place. Usually they are small rooms (barely enough room to properly work yourself out of your clothes so you can do your business) with a bench for sitting, and if you are lucky, a small window for ventilation and natural light. Often a small oil lamp provides some degree of light for night visits and a little heat to keep the place from fully chilling your bones during the winter.

Not so in this place! Gaerwn however seemed to like his luxuries. A large window adorned one end of this privy. The place was huge and could easily fit 10 people. Heavy curtains were tied to one side for use in the winter. There was a seat carved out of stone and quite smooth. Two buckets of water and scented soaps sat nearby for washing up as well as a small pile of hand towels. A variety of large oil lamps lined the walls, obviously for winter heat since all but one was idle at this time.

As Trebor sat and relaxed for the first time in days, he pondered why such an oaf as Gaerwn would pay so much attention to his toilet.

* * *

It took Trebor and Ethelda a long, while but after scrubbing and scraping and washing all the worn, scrapped and damaged parts of their bodies a few times they felt human again. The clothes brought in by the servant fit rather well and they were finally clean and feeling dry and warm. Having been parched, they had consumed all the water in the large pitcher that had arrived and then drank carefully the malted beverage from the thick ceramic mugs. It occurred to Trebor that Gaerwn probably would not poison them – yet. He undoubtedly had more interesting ideas in mind.

Eventually, as they knew it would come to pass, the time came for them to return to the great hall and deal as they must with their conqueror. The main servant arrived back to the room and informed them, "Pardon me sire, but the king requests your presence in the throne room."

The man was large, obviously quite bright and capable, yet he looked glum and forlorn. It troubled Trebor to see such a wonderful man so downtrodden. Trebor hoped that he could maybe talk some sense into the beast he was about to meet. He could teach him his life could be better if his people were motivated out of desire instead of fear. It might work he thought. Play to the monster's obvious love for good living and his overwhelming need to be needed and important. Play to what mattered to him. A plan of a discussion began to arise in Trebor's mind. One that would leave Gaerwn thinking he was winning. Trebor almost smiled.

As they rose to leave, Trebor put an arm around Ethelda's slender shoulders. Her red rimmed eyes rose to his in a devout and pleading manner. He could tell she was scared, but she would never admit it. He could tell he could count on her to do the right thing, as always. And he would do the right thing by her.

Over many winters, their relationship more than the office of their marriage had worked well on a mix of mutual trust and faith. They had both played the part they needed to play when required and both had supported each other when necessary. It worked, they liked it, and they did it well and never took each other for granted. All in all, it was very nice.

Quietly he said, "I know your cousin is a monster. I know you loathe him and would rather spit on his grave than break bread with him. However, we are in a bad situation here, and I do not know what will happen. Please trust me and know that my intentions are good.

Whatever I do, I do for us. For our future, and for whomever he has here as a captive. And for whomever, if any, are alive back at the castle. Please trust me."

Tears filled both their eyes as they looked at each other and fought the emotions that cramped their throats and heaved heavy weights upon their shoulders.

At last she spoke to him. It was not the soft musical voice he had known for so many winters. It was not the carefree lilt of the woman he loved. It was the choked and scared words of a strong, capable, loving woman, and these words made him love her more. "Trebor, you have always been faithful and done right by me. I have always trusted you, and you have always taken the path that for us and the entire kingdom was best. That will never stop, especially now. You go and do what you must do, and do it boldly. That man is pure evil. He cannot be trusted. You must do what you can to defeat him. My faith, my hope, and my trust are in you. It always has been, it always will be. If I can help, I will. Forever I have always been there to be part of this adventure with you. That will not stop."

With that, their lips met; a long slow kiss, each other sharing their souls. Each other connecting at a level only true love can offer.

When their lips parted and the heat of their compassion was held between them, he knew he could deal with whatever Gaerwn had in store. He also understood that making the best of it was worth whatever he had to do.

So with those thoughts in his mind, and she knowing she was part of a team, they walked back through the narrow doorway. The many candles of the throne room beckoned. There was a solid hush that had descended over the many people gathered there. Trebor led, now with Ethelda a few paces behind. They walked tall and they walked in with all the dignity that Trebor's reign had built over the many winters of his rule. They walked with a pride and a faith, borne from a knowledge that told them they could depend on each other and they had a proud people to represent and defend.

As they walked by the heavy wood of the throne she never saw the heavy sharp blade that sliced through the air like a lightning bolt from the top of the throne. She did not even sense the impact. All she could remember was that it seemed wrong for Trebor's head to be rolling along the floor when his body was right in front of her.

Trebor's dead eyes looked at her from the floor as his torso crumpled.

She did remember screaming.

22.
I Get By...

Torrin did not move or mutter a sound as the world in front of him exploded in gray fur. The soldier's chin jumped up and his left shoulder darted backward in a flash. The blur behind the soldier was a mountain of moving gray fur.

All Torrin had heard after the shouted "No" was a crashing and breaking of sticks and underbrush as the largest gray wolf he had ever seen rolled over behind the startled soldier and then stood up as if he had practiced this move many times. As the wolf stood, holding a large log in his mouth, the soldier brought his hand up to look at it. Except, there was no hand! Just a bloody stump that was mangled and bleeding heavily. Torrin, Dessa and the soldier all turned to look at the wolf.

As if on cue, the wolf sat on his back haunches and opened his large mouth, dropping the log, which by now looked very much like an arm with an attached and unanimated hand. As the hand thumped to the ground, a long silver dagger rolled out from the now pasty looking and blood streaked fingers.

Standing up, the wolf looked at Dessa. He seemed to nod, and then turning, disappeared noiselessly into the woods.

The soldier looked up again at the stump, grabbed Torrin's sword with his good hand and wrenched it away from the startled young man.

In one deft flick of his wrist the soldier reversed the sword into his good hand and was pulling back to run Torrin through. He did not look scared or angry, he just was doing what many winters and summers of marauding campaigns and fighting had taught him to do in the heat of the moment. If this had been a lesson at Tallon's place, the old master would have been exhorting his student to take control of the situation and never let your opponent have an advantage.

Through all the theatrics, through the melee of the arm disengaging from the soldier and the entry and exit of the wolf, Dessa had not flinched one bit.

She shot him clean through the eye.

23.
Incentive

To Torrin, the massive logs that made up the tall walls of the Journey Inn had not looked this inviting since he had emerged from the frozen snow-threatened woods the spring before. The memory of standing at the threshold of this haven, cold, wet and bleeding was still taut in his mind. Now, it was as if sunshine was plucking at the strings of Torrin's heart making beautiful music when he once again laid his eyes upon it. High in majesty as ever, the big pile of stately logs stood in sturdy dark brown contrast to the colorful leaves of the late autumn.

The friendliness of the place helped to settle Torrin's ripped and sad soul some. For the past three days he had been troubled by that feeling of impending danger and they had ridden spread apart, ready for the ultimate attack that never came. Even though they were back safe, the steady prickling danger signal had been omnipresent. It worried him. But for now, it had dissipated and he could relax.

And, he was exhausted.

Walking through the big front door, he instantly felt at home. For a little while he forced himself to allow the evil he had encountered to run out of him. That feeling of danger melted away as he smelled the cooking Normadia was conjuring up in the kitchen. The omnipresent nagging of danger melted away more as his eyes and soul took in the big room.

All seemed normal. A well maintained low fire was burning in the hearth. The flames throwing off glimmers and light shimmies around the room. The glow and warmth keeping the omnipresent cool dampness of the forest at bay. Groups of men and women sat around a few of the tables, talking in a mix of low tones and of course the ever present passionate frivolous chats about nothing in particular and everything at all. Some children played in the corner. Other folk and families were outside conducting their business. People came and went.

It was, just like all the others for most of them, a typical day at the Journey Inn!

As Torrin sat wearily down in front of the fire, some of the men gathered around to hear of his adventure. They could tell he was not a happy man.

Soon, they all knew of the great tragedy; and to a person, extended condolences. For as deep, sad and tragic as the story was, it troubled Torrin that it could be told in such a short time. He felt that the unjust death of an entire kingdom of good people should warrant something like bells ringing or beating of the chest or loud wailing. But now, all were stoic in their thoughts and rippled with their own pain and anger.

It would occur to Torrin later, during quiet mindfulness, that as much as he felt the loss, the others were grappling with the danger it represented. The tragedy of Torrin's home was a foretaste of what could descend upon their peaceful valley.

Then for a time, Torrin sat quietly by himself and watched the flames. He wondered what to do next? What would happen? What would be the best course of action? What needed attending here? Should they stay? Should they all go? His thoughts were jumbled and scattered. His mind kept running around in circles with no firm conviction. He just could not focus.

That he had not found the bodies of his parents both bothered him and enthralled him at the same time. He wanted, nay needed, to know their fate. If their fate was bad, he could put it behind him. If it was not, that would be for rejoicing. But not knowing was the hardest. He wanted closure. He wanted to be sure.

Were they lost somewhere? Were they captives of that awful brute? Could he help them? The doubt plagued him like a broken foot on a good horse – it seemed deadly. These thoughts nagged him and would not depart his tired and overburdened mind.

It dawned on Torrin that he had spent the whole summer not knowing. Not really knowing where he was, not knowing how he got here and not knowing really what was going on. There was too much up in the air. He was in need of some certainty. Even Dessa, as certain as he was about her, about them as a couple; she was really new and that had to play out for a while.

He buried his face in his hands and tried to think. After a while the millions of thoughts colliding in his brain began to abate. Soon he could again smell the crisp smoke from the fire and hear the gentle hissing and spitting of the logs as they expanded and burned. The soothing crackling was good for him. He began to hear the talking of others. He could feel the movement of things about the room as he slowly came out of his funk.

And finally, as the pressure subsided and the thoughts in his head began to slow down to a pace that he could handle, he at last began to mourn.

He mourned the good times. He mourned the hard times. He mourned the childhood that was now forever lost and could not be shared with the people who had made it real. The memories rushed back like a river out of control. The places, the people, the sights, the sounds, the smells.

He ached of sadness and loss. A loss of what was, and a loss of what never would be. Even with all the people around him, for right now, he felt very alone and decided that it might be just best to pack up in the spring and go somewhere else.

*   *   *

The light small pressure on Torrin's hand startled him. It was foreign. Out of place. Not threatening, just strange. It seemed somehow warm and questioning all at once.

He looked up and peered into a pair of sparkling clean blue eyes. Soft, almost translucent and clear pale skin rested gently on slightly blushed cheeks. Long wafty strands of pure golden blonde hair blew gently as the air moved their light angelic forms. Small pink lips were pressed tightly together on a very young and innocent girl.

Too tightly. Unless you noticed the lips, you wouldn't have had a sense something was troubling such a creature so pure of heart and soul. Yet something was wrong. Something very important was obviously on her mind.

"So, who do we have here?" asked Torrin, shrugging off his current issues and paying attention to the picture of purity and innocence standing in front of him. Her hand still rested on his hand. Not moving, not changing, but somehow transmitting the fact that this was an important meeting and should not be taken lightly.

She looked down and then slowly up at him in that shy demure way little girls do when they meet an adult for the first time. You could tell that for her, this was going to be a very important discussion. She cocked her head to one side and said quietly, "My name is Alexia, Mr. Torrin."

"Alexia! My, what a pretty name" exclaimed Torrin. She looked somewhat familiar, he was sure he had seen her around. But he had never really noticed her before as he had gone about his business at Journey.

She did not say anything further, she just kept looking up at him with those big blue eyes and with her hand planted on his.

So Torrin kept things going to see what was up. "What may I do for you Alexia?"

Her eyes cast down again for a moment as she pondered what she needed to say. Torrin could feel her hand tighten a bit just before she spoke. This discussion was obviously of great importance to her. Torrin laughed a little inside himself. He marveled at the distraction. He marveled at how a young innocent girl could distract him from his troubles. And with her issues, help him to feel better.

"The other children said I had to ask you," she said somewhat pensively.

Now it was Torrin's turn to cock his head. "Ask me what Alexia?"

"Come here," said her tiny voice. She was quiet, yet she very much needed him to follow her as she was certainly sincere.

Standing with a low groan emerging from the setting of his over used riding muscles, Torrin followed. He felt stiff. He felt sore. He knew he needed a bath. Yet, he followed little Alexia as she had asked.

Alexia led him to the corner of the big room at the Journey Inn. She and a small knot of other young girls had obviously been playing for quite a while in this little corner, considering how all set up and organized their toys were.

They were like, well, little girls. Some small, some tall, some fat, some skinny. Some were shy, some mischievous looking, but all cute, as most little girls are, in most every way. Everything looked normal.

A number of corncob dolls adorned the corner on the floor. As a little team they were all lined up in a group, in a manner like children sitting in school for story time. Very neat orderly lines. Their little outfits were made of fur scraps, material scraps and some were knitted from ends of wool yarn. Their personas were varied in line with the imagination of this keen group of girls. Some were in long dresses, some looked like crafters, and some were dressed in new outfits to be hunters with little quivers on their backs. To one side stood a pile of various assorted materials for making more clothes.

All in all, this represented a very creative and well cared for group of dolls who were very much at the mercy of their caretakers. Much the same way most children felt about their lives. At the mercy of the adults who ruled over them.

"So what is your question?" asked Torrin, trying to figure out what was going on as he knelt down to their level and remembering that not so long ago, he looked up too at adults, with very inquisitive eyes.

Alexia reached to his shoulder and squeezed. Her blue eyes were level with his. Reaching over, she moved the hair out of her face and with some reverence bit her lip before she started to talk. She seemed too very grown up for her age.

All of a sudden, the words just spilled out of her, "Mr. Torrin, some of us want to make new clothes for our dolls. But, others figure we should kill them and bury them since the bad men are coming and so there is no sense in making new clothes. We just wanted to know what to do. If we are all going to die, there is no sense in making new clothes and we don't want the bad men to have our dolls. We need you to tell us what to do."

She looked at him as if searching his face with those round and admiring eyes, searching for an answer that she knew was not there. But being a little girl, she needed to hear from an older person. So he was duty bound to answer her, and he could not lie. It was against the rules to lie to a child, even when it came to real affairs of the world. This was the culture of the valley. Certainly, there were things that children did not need to know. However, when it came to the direct question, they adults all agreed that they shouldered the burden of truth telling. Just as the people who raised them shouldered that burden.

No, he could not lie.

Torrin just knelt there, and slowly took her hand from his shoulder, holding it as if it were a fragile piece of art. Her skin was cool and soft. Not yet worn from harsh soaps or the labors of a life fulfilled that would hopefully follow after a few more winters.

No, she was completely unscarred and of the purity only a child can possess. Yet, she was now facing life and death with the panache of a gracious old woman.

He looked at the dolls. He looked at each one of the girls. And then he said huskily, "You girls go ahead and make new clothes. You have my word, you and your dolls have nothing to worry about."

They all, almost as one, clapped and cheered and went straight to work.

As Torrin rose and turned to walk away, Alexia looked up at him and said, in that squeally pure little girl voice that only a little girl can possess, "Thank you Mr. Torrin, I really do want ta grow up and ave a happy family. I really wasn't ready to die yet."

And as he walked away, he was very aware of the high pitched pure giggly laughter coming from the little group as they worked on their projects. It also dawned on him, in a hideous way, that those squeals were lost in his kingdom and would never be found again. It saddened him, yet, in those thoughts, something sparked, something melted, something more changed.

Prodding across the room he decided he needed to find a drink. And yes, before finding a bath (although anyone within smelling distance of him might have disagreed). Torrin thought about the fact that he had not asked for this fight, but it had been thrust upon him; and he needed to attend to it. Just as coming to Journey had been thrust upon him – damn dragon! But he had decided during the summer to make the most of his being at Journey and now see what had happened?

Having retrieved a large cool chalice of wine that bode well of this year's harvest from the kitchen, Torrin stood with his back against a wall and watched all of Journey move about the place. He reflected...

In one summer he had fallen in lust, fallen in love, discovered more about life and himself than most men discover in a lifetime. And, was saddled with the unthinkable that if he was true to the smartest, most beautiful woman in the world he could live forever.

And now with all the hard and fateful questions at hand, it had taken a child, a person who represented the future to help him focus, but nonetheless, she had done it! All of the wonderful things he had done and discovered were for naught. Even living forever, unless he took action and persevered to preserve a new way of life and love that was as sparse as the quenching rain during the heat of summer.

This all was so much larger than just himself and Dessa. So much so.

                    *   *   *

Soon after Torrin's exchange with Alexia, Etworth entered the room followed by Dessa and Quillan. They looked as tired as Torrin felt. They smelled worse than Torrin, since they had brushed and attended to the requirements of the hard run and sweaty steeds. They were greeted by large mugs of ale and plates of hot food at a table (Normadia had been waiting for them), and then Quillan made an announcement before they were seated.

He said, "Well, it's snowin to no end. Guess winter has officially started."

A log popped in the fireplace as someone began adding more wood to fend off the oncoming cold. The girls squealed in the corner over some joke or another, and Dessa sat down slowly to a spot at the table giving out a little groan as she settled her bones upon a broad bench of well worn wood.

Torrin decided, with all the love he had lost, it was better to die fighting than to lose the love he had found here. So he joined the group, and the food, and the feelings of life at the table.

And in the far reaches of his mind, very slowly, the beginnings of a plan began to form.

24.
"Kitchen Work"

Snow.

It was a gnarly early snow.

Wet and heavy. Thick swirling flakes speeding down from laden gray clouds lined with black swirls. Pelting all who dared be outside with great large splotches of wet cold that stuck everywhere.

As usual for the valley of Journey, lots of snow.

Of course, the wind pushed the cold white stuff into various deep piles along the walls and tree line. Nature made due her planning and piled the snow where she liked; where she wanted, whatever worked for her. First filling the cracks and crevices where need be and then sculpting long sloping piles where the objects of the valley, stuck upon the earth, came together. It was surely the work of a God, since it was all so beautiful, so orderly and so much unnecessary.

For all intents and purposes, the residents of Journey were now snowbound.

Deeply snowbound. At least for a couple of days, for it was too early for a long snow.

So there was only one socially acceptable and civilized thing they all could do.

Have a party and celebrate the storm.

     *   *   *

And ohh what a party it would be… tonight they would plan, and tomorrow night, they would party…

Journey style!

*   *   *

The early morning light had not yet peeked over the horizon as Normadia pondered new and emerging thoughts. "Every year as fall melds itself so perfectly into winter, it just smoothes me into a wonder." This thinking flittered across her mind as warm dough squished slowly and tenderly between her long strong slender fingers.

The change is always welcome, always on time, always just right. Although not as right as spring. Ah spring – where all the gray and brown of winter explode away under the onslaught of nature re-emerging from an always too lengthy and cold frozen sleep. Spring, she mused, is almost violent. One day all is gray and dark and then seemingly without a flutter of one's eye, the green and all the pretty colors of the plants thrust themselves without warning or pretense in your face and into your sight, into your nostrils; it's all so fresh and exhilarating!

Oh, she breathed, the change of seasons are such a wonderful thing. I wonder if anyone else feels this way? She bit her bottom lip some at the thought and decided that this would be a great conversation later tonight after dancing. Well, maybe?

She swept a tassel of long silky chestnut brown hair out of her right eye. She used the inside of her elbow, neatly tucking it behind her ear in a well practiced motion. You would never have known that it took her many frustrated attempts to get that right. It was a proud thing in the kitchen at Journey to say "A hair has never been pulled from our baking."

After rolling the dough balls off her hands that had adhered to her fair skin, she reached up to the neat row of well crafted ceramic containers that held the bread "additions" and pulled them down one at a time. With the grace of a magician, she deftly spread nuts, coarse wheat, rye and a variety of rich grains onto the dough. Then with a sigh folded the additions into the smoothness of the batch. The dough succumbed to the grains and gained a texture that always made her smile.

Smooth plain bread was something that she thought just very boring and dull. The course grains and nuts and other additions added something. A bit of liveliness, some mystery, some fun to the very joy of chewing. A bit like people she thought. Too smooth, they just take up space. A little mystery, a little roughness and a little texture certainly spiced things up.

Goodness she pondered? Where are these thoughts coming from? I am being a mystery to myself!

And then still with practiced hands, strong and knowing from a lifetime of rehearsal, she scooped up great balls of the dough mix and skillfully plopped each one into well greased loaf pans. Each one landed with that sliding whisper dough makes when entering a pan.

She loved the large ceramic mixing bowl, the storage containers and loaf pans. A great matching set, all beautiful, all artistic, and all a very special part of the Journey kitchen. They were gifts from Bartoly and Rebecca at the planting celebration two summers ago. Rebecca had been beaming in love with that great beastly, strong and wonderfully handsome man. She had told all of them, with some embarrassment, with some shyness, and with a wicked smile on her face that she had been "practicing" her pottery and did not think this set worthy of sale. Although upon inspection it was perfect in every way. And her spirit that surrounded it made it even more special.

Such was the size of the bowl that six good sized loaves could be mixed at one time. Good thing too with all the hungry folks passing through Journey now.

The place always seemed to be so busy, like never before! What with Karina and Harold having left, it was all the same, yet all different. Nothing was right, yet really, nothing was wrong? Was it? She liked Dessa and Torrin. Torrin made her laugh. He was such a boy just this spring. But had grown up and his spirit had grown on her. She still chuckled to herself harkening back to the time she and Dessa were at the waterfall. The boys did not seem to know what to do with girls. Or did they?

Did she understand the details of dealing with boys? So far such life talks were just discussions between her and friends. And sometimes in hushed tones in small groups of girls. It seemed that they had talked about this long enough. It was time to put all this yearning to test and find if there was any truth to the seemingly taut stories that came from the likes of the Celsys twins.

That last night of the games in the spring, she had stayed up very late stealing sips of farmer Niall's tart apple cider listening in awe as the two girls told the tale of their time at the waterfall with two lads. The lads, seemingly about the same age as the girls, were very innocent. These boys had been swept away completely by the beauty and unabashed brazen frankness of the blond freckled twins.

It seems that the hired hand's wife had filled the girls in on what to do with boys. To Normadia this whole boy thing was rather exciting.

And she decided that more than exciting, long term success was just as much about staying in control.

The control part made sense, but too much control might do to take the fun out of it, she thought to herself. The twins had lured the boys to the waterfall for a picnic. Once there, they had frolicked in games of tag up and down the hills with the boys so that the lot of them were all hot and sweaty. Ashlin suggested they all cool down with their feet in the water. Which worked fine for the girls; however the boys in breeches were hesitant to get them wet. Wynn said she just walked up behind one of the boys and took off his breeches to solve the issue. Seeing as how the boy was altogether shy at being the only one displaying his birthday suit, Ashlin and Wynn deftly, as one, only as twins can, removed their dresses and plunged into the water.

From the details that followed, Normadia determined that the boys and girls would never be the same and the girls had found the experiences they had been seeking. Although they had all been innocent before the picnic, the words of education from the hired hand's wife had been very instrumental in some intense explorations.

Since that night, Normadia's mind had been hatching her own plan to explore the feelings that seared through her at times. Oh my, they did sear hot though! Especially after having a few long talks with some of the women folk during the evenings.

One night, she had been startled by the warm hand of Kneafsey upon her arm. Seems that Normadia had been staring at the target of her affections and Kneafsey had noticed.

"Ye is all flush up in the cheeks there ye fair maiden," said the strong and sturdy lady who was the midwife of Journey and the valley. "I would a guess ye got some mischievously devilish thoughts a cooking up in yer young head and they is a making ye all hot and swarmy inside in ways that ye don' understand."

Normadia looked at the lady and she nodded a resounding "yes," blushing so hot she thought her skin was burning.

Kneafsey sat down next to the fired up lass and quietly said, "Well let me tell ye the mechanics of what to expect, so ye aren't all flustered and anxious when the right time seems to a come about. An from the looks on yer face, that right time may not bein to a far off."

The thankful look on Normadia's face was all Kneafsey needed to keep the discussion going.

"Now here is the awful truth you must know: the boys, they will no care ifn ye get with child. Sure they will tell ye they care, but really, there is only one thing that is on their mind and all the blood in their brains rushes right out and is gone from them. They is only thinking a one thing, jus as en you was doin a little piece ago."

"This seems complicated," sighed Normadia, taking a sip of the tea in her mug.

"Yes dear, it is," said the older woman. "Come, let's go into yonder kitchen where we can talk without bein a heard over."

And with that, they went for a long chat that did nothing to tame Normadia's mind, except to steer her on a path toward a goal.

*   *   *

Now was the time to take action, so this morning, after thinking and planning and pondering all summer, Normadia set the loaf pans side by side on top of the brick shelf over the stove. They would rise until lunch and make for a good addition to the evening's snow party. She wondered why the simple rising of bread brought such joy? She did love the yeasty aromas that wafted about as the dough began to emerge from itself and grow puffy and large.

So many questions had been forming in her head of late. Not long ago, all in life went as planned; now, she had questions. Why were things not simple and straightforward like they used to be? For many winters she had worked side by side with Karina. She had learned well, she had been taught well, and they had both learned from experience to leave very little to chance in this busy kitchen.

Normadia was smart and could tackle most any job the big kitchen had to offer. She'd learned over time that the others who helped out were just not as flexible in their capabilities. Karina had been a master at delegating jobs to the help that they always seemed to be able to master with little training or coaching. This skill of delegation was one that Normadia had to master slowly. Karina helped her watch and pay attention to what people did naturally, and what they did not. Normadia mastered the skills of chatting with others to see what they were interested in.

By now, light was just beginning to show around the big window in the kitchen. Mostly, the big room was quiet. Just the snappling of the fire in the stove and cooking fireplace keeping her company.

She had found many winters ago she enjoyed this early morning time. The quiet, the thoughts, the smells of the kitchen. And the warm space all to herself. She could think. She was fresh from sleep and she could putter around without any distractions, make ready for the day, organize her thoughts and just be.

It was a morning like this that she discovered that just a touch of hot pepper in a dlòtha stew gave the meal a whole new zest. Many discoveries had come at this time of the day. She had tried new additions to breads that now gave her the varieties she and everyone so enjoyed. For a long time she had experimented with various methods trying to preserve all sorts of different foods. She had a whole shelf of containers in the root cellar with various mixtures in some form or another to test. To her joy, a few had worked over time (such as packing some summer fruits in vodka for use later in the winter when no fruit was about) and some had not (packing leafy vegetables in a scotch and salt mix had proven disastrous, with Quillan teasing her about ruining both).

These early kitchen mornings were her own time of play. Her personal time of discovery and centering. She enjoyed the warm room, the space, the smells, and the uncluttered time to think.

This morning though, she bit her lip. She now wanted more. And had decided during the fall that the first snow party of the season was the time for her to get it. The thought of it made her laugh aloud. It almost tickled.

Normadia looked one last time at the rising bread and considering the stories she had heard, and with what Kneafsey had told her, thought it most appropriate. Tonight was the first snow party of the year!

She bit her lip in anticipation and squeezed tight tender warm muscles that seemed to just appear the other day. They had either just appeared, or now had made themselves known, and they wanted some attention.

25.
Conquest

Gaerwn felt almost as proud as any winning king could. Trebor's detached head rolled around amusingly on the cold stone floor for a long while leaving wide warm red splotches of blood as it rolled. Finally, it came to a stop, dripping what little life was left into a bright crimson puddle of death.

No one moved. No one even dared blink.

It seemed not a soul was breathing. The air hung so heavily with fear that it was a good many moments before people even became aware of Ethelda's sobs.

Queen Ethelda was kneeling at the feet of her now very dead and decapitated husband. Her shock and horror palatable. Her face was ghastly white, arms outstretched with her hands balled into tight fists as her eyes kept darting about the room.

Gaerwn stood tall, the long broadsword set purposefully upon his shoulder. He was grinning from ear to ear. You could tell, he was just very content with himself.

After a little while, as the shock of the event began to flow into bewilderment and confusion, Gaerwn brought the sword down and held it out to one side. Instantly, a young and very powerfully built young man rushed over to retrieve the weapon.

"My goodness Accalon," said the now happy King to the wide eyed man now holding the weapon, "You certainly did fine work putting an edge on your well built implement of fun. Feel free to have any one of the kitchen maids as your roommate this night. My treat."

Accalon nodded his thanks and without a word backed out of the room holding the heavy steel in his hands, taking care not to touch the bloody streaks near the tip.

Little did Gaerwn know, suspect or even consider that Accalon and Paroish were lovers and had been so since an early age.

Gaerwn watched in total amusement while Queen Ethelda tried

to come to senses that would not come to her. After a few moments, he calmly ordered some soldiers nearby to bind her to a chair near the throne. He then instructed them to take Trebor out and hang him with the other bodies outside the castle walls, but let him hang low enough so the wolves could play.

*   *   *

Accalon returned to his smithy at the edge of the castle's courtyard with his heart intent on resurrecting this once beautiful sword. He walked with his heart as heavy in his chest as was the sturdy metal weapon in his hands. He was a very skilled blacksmith as well as the town's head armourer. His work was in high demand throughout the kingdom. It saddened him to know that his art was used so often in disgusting deeds as this. He had fashioned this great gleaming and gilded tool with thoughts in mind of great ceremony, knighting brave warriors, hunters and skillful craftsmen. Maybe soldiers defending themselves in battle so they could return to home and hearth. He had hoped its use would have been to honor those who made this miserable place safe and better for all the people around him.

Angrily he clamped the shining steel into a vise and with great care cleaned the blade with a thinned muskrat skin soaked in turpentine.

Briefly his mind went to the day last summer when he and Paroish had hiked through the woods gathering sap from notches he had carefully cut in the towering pine trees. As his father had taught him, he fastened oilcloth in a bag under each notch to catch the sap as it flowed out and down the trunk below the scar.

The trick of the day was to keep the sticky stuff off of his hands and in the bucket they carried. Soon he would boil the sap in his little still at the smithy and collect the strange and smelly material into glazed porcelain pots that he sealed tightly. He did not know what made the cleaner work on steel, but he did know he could wipe with the smelly solvent and no rust would appear.

They had hiked the bulk of the day. Birds had chirped and the bugs stayed away because of the smells from the bucket. Paroish's golden blonde hair had bounced happily in the sunshine, framed by the glow of her smile. They made love in the tall grasses of a clearing. The sun warming their naked bodies as they rolled over in the grass, coupled in romantic heat.

A time that seemed so long ago. On that day, he had prayed it would not end. But now, it all seemed so far away. The warmth, the love, the fresh cleansing breeze.

So very far away.

The muskrat skin exploded into flame as he angrily flung the mess into his forge fire. In just a few heartbeats the cleansing flames were gone. He turned his attention to the beautiful sword in the vise. With one savage slice he removed the tightly wound skins that had carefully encircled the hilt. They too went into the fire and disappeared quickly as the ash from the high heat was transported up the black flue and chimney. He tapped out the pin that held the pommel, slid off the guard and loosed the vise.

After adding fuel to his fire and pumping the bellows he thrust the sword into the flames and instantly felt better. Fire he mused was a very cleansing force. This steel that had robbed a man of his life in such a low hearted and cowardly way would never be the same again.

After a while his thoughts turned to Paroish. His heart burned as hot as the forge.

26.
Determined

Journey's kitchen had been cooking at a full force pace all day. There were a fair number of people in tonight taking refuge from the early snow. Most would leave at the first light in two days after the melt as they were on their way south to avoid the coming onslaught of bone numbing cold. The storm that had been so harsh just last night and morning had subsided and the trails would be passable again very soon.

Yes, it was the perfect time to have a snow party. There were always enough good musicians about, and with a good crowd around this made for interesting music. And since quite a few people would never see each other again, the need for decorum and trite behavior was low. It was replaced by a little bawdiness and frivolity. Mostly good dancing, drinking and storytelling.

Always better this way thought Normadia, and she shook her head trying to concentrate on not burning the hams that were roasting on the spits in the fireplace for tomorrow's meals. People looking to relax, have fun and not take the evening seriously at whatsoever. However, she had some serious thoughts running through her mind!

Normadia had been running hard since her morning reverie with the warm dough, which seemed like a long time ago. By now the kitchen had been scrubbed clean (the new dish boy really was good) and everyone had been fed a good supper.

She pulled the last tray of dough bites from the oven and deftly rolled them in butter and various tangy sweet spices. She loved treats like these. They went well with the beers, meads and whiskies that would be part of tonight's celebration. The variety of crunch and spice added something just right and she was proud of what she could bring to the party. She was sure Quillan and Torrin would take care of serving the beverages from the many casks that adorned the wall by the door of the woodshed (far from the fire).

She also loved the oven Torrin had built into the kitchen's cooking fireplace this summer. Long slabs of sandstone were placed on granite feet to the one side. Once the stones were hot she could cook most anything in the space. Rebecca had fashioned fine heavy clay fronts that she fired to a shiny finish. These fronts fit perfectly to hold the heat. It was a marvel and let Normadia create so many wonderful dishes. And even better, things cooked evenly without attention to turning so one side did not burn.

She finished up, carefully placing the dough bites into baskets, presenting them in piled circles. Looks counted, as her mother had said. She stepped back, admired her work for a moment and then turned on her heel towards the back of the grand kitchen.

After untying her apron and hanging it on a hook with the others Normadia went to her room to bathe and change into her favorite party dress. Tonight would be a fair party, but tonight would also be a little different. She was vaguely aware that she really had no idea what she was doing, or exactly how she was going to do it, and she liked it.

Of course she was no stranger to intimate encounters.

But tonight, she was a veritable stranger to the level of intimacy she had put her mind to.

*   *   *

Normadia's room was conveniently located behind the big cooking fireplace that covered the back of the large kitchen. The room wasn't large, but it was private and she knew she had the warmest, driest room in the valley. Her tidy warm little place had been her home for a number of winters and summers.

Next to her room was the bath. This was only used a few times during the winter. But it was entirely necessary for the group to stay healthy through the long winter. Friendly or not, after a number of days cooped up the Journey Inn, even the young children needed a good scrubbing.

Of course, the bath was used more often to clean clothes than ruddy naked skin. And it was a source of pride by Harold and Karina. They had fashioned a tub out of carefully hewn and finely finished pine wood. It was verra large; up to three people at a time could scrub and soak off the nastiness of winter confinement or for that matter summer grime (When hot water and soap were needed. If not, the creek and waterfall were just perfect). A pipe of sorts ran from the kitchen to the tub so there was a regular source of warmed water given a good fire and a determined crew staffing the boiling pots on bath days. A drain in the bottom had been fashioned out of stone and that pipe led outside.

Of course, during the dead cold of the darkest part of winter, the end of that pipe would always freeze up and someone would have to trudge out and chop away at the ice. But it was a minor price to pay for getting clean.

She had noticed that the skin of visitors often sported boils and unhealed wounds. Whereas the residents and long time visitors of Journey were of clean and undefiled skin. Maybe that was why some of them stayed?

Her thoughts returned to her room and the warmth and light of the three sconces that spread warm flickering light around the room. Two were oil burners, graceful handmade urns of fired blue porcelain firmly attached to the stone on the walls of the fireplace. Normadia had added a drop of cinnamon to the oil in each to freshen the room and keep it homey. She loved the smell; the room seemed to welcome her every time she walked in. This evening, the sharp scent of the oils seemed sassy in her nose.

The third sconce was on the wall by her door. A large fat candle with a very fine thin wick burned ever so slowly with a tiny pinprick of flame. As reliable as ever, the flame shed its little light all times of the day and night. The tiny light flittered along the ceiling from within its holder's deep recesses during the dark of night.

Normadia called it her "forever" candle. Not only did it burn for a very long time before needing replacement, but she and others were forever lighting fire from it. Whether to start the fire in the kitchen in the morning if it had gone out, or to light tapers for the other lamps adorning the walls and tables of the Journey Inn. And with the forever candle burning, she was never completely in the dark. Often someone would need help during the evening, and it was Normadia who came to the rescue.

The source of the forever candle had been an odd yet educational one. A plump and friendly old man with wizened fingers that seemed magical in their ability to work with thread was selling candles and lamps of all sorts. He had taught her as a little girl to make the special "forever" wicks. Patiently he let her learn with her long slender fingers how to unravel a normal wick and then braid just three strands of the fine material in a succession of never ending crossover knots. And then, at intervals the space of the nail on her little finger he showed her how to tie tiny loops around the braided material. This he had told her, "Kept the amount of wax going up the wick to a minimum, and keeps the candle burning longer."

She removed her work dress and cap, letting her long brown hair fall in a steady stream of wavelets across her shoulders and down her long strong back. Lighting the candles on her wash stand she admired for a moment the gentle yellow light that danced about the room.

The water from the pitcher she had carried from the kitchen was almost too hot to touch. Just the way she liked it. And then using soap embedded with flower petals, she slowly washed off the work of her day.

Once she was clean all over, she smiled as she grasped the most wonderful luxury in all the valley. Her towel. You see, her towel hung on a pair of hooks and was sprawled across the large warm stones of the back of the kitchen's fireplace, and so was always waiting for her, warm and dry and ready.

She knew she was blessed in so many ways. And it was time to find someone with whom to share those blessings.

* * *

These sorts of evenings made him restless in a way that riled his bones and made him want to dance. It was just so wonderful to be jumpy happy.

Quillan had been sitting with his back to the fire and tapping his boot to the music that had been warming up the spirit of everyone in the room.

He noticed that when people returned from the privy, they had to stomp off clomps of wet snow. He sighed and mentally prepared himself for a cold winter.

The music was livelier now and he made his way to the tap by the woodshed to fill his mug with a strong and probably too young a mix of whiskeys that had been the gracious donation of a trader this summer. The man had needed a place to keep himself and his family while his son's broken leg healed. And in the end, whiskey is whiskey and one should never look a gift askance. So he just held his tongue and knew that after a few sips, it would taste much better.

Quillan knew that if you let a whiskey sit in the cask for three summers, it was of a much finer quality. This whiskey could not be more than one summer in age and had a terrible bite on the tongue. Being this was his second mug though, the bite had lessened.

A young lass with golden braids winked at him and he knew it was time to get the party going. Taking a large and what he decided was an unfriendly assault on his taste buds gulp of the brew, he sturdied himself and sauntered over to her, trying hard not to look nervous. With a mighty bow, he asked her to dance.

She threw her friends a sideways smirky glance and graciously accepted. With this, they stepped to the dance floor and around the room, as if on cue, so did a number of others.

Journey was not a place of too many "regular" couples, so just about everyone danced with everyone. Even old Ol' Dogger got into the act, stompn' his feet at about 4/7 time off of the music's own rhythm. People kept him dancing, encouraging him on because if he stopped, he might start to sing. And seeing as how it was too cold outside to escape the noise and too cold to throw him out, letting him dance offbeat was better than listening to the caterwauling he called singing.

It was all in good fun. And after a while, hot, thirsty sweaty fun. Good fun during a snow.

As he quenched his thirst during a self imposed break from the dance floor, Quillan watched Torrin and Dessa glide together across the room. They turned and addressed each other in ways he could remember from a very young boyhood at the castle that seemed so verra long ago. He had gone away before he was old enough to have started the dance lessons that King Tarmon offered to all in his kingdom.

Smart man that Tarmon thought Quillan. If everyone knows how to dance and then all have a chance to dance, it gives more people something to do during the long cold winter. Better than just lubbing around, he pondered.

As he placed his mug upon the well worn plank of the table, a porcelain plate magically seemed to appear in front of him. Upon it were neat rows of various dough bites, all sorted by different spices and toppings. It was warm and the aroma lifting off the plate was tangy and instantly made his mouth water.

Quillan's eyes glided up the long slender arm that had deftly deposited the plate before him. He was deep down a well mannered man after all and had full intent of thanking the kind person who had graciously placed this plate of tasty morsels there, so pleasantly in front of him.

However, try as he might, words would not come from his mouth. He just sat there with his jaw moving up and down and his eyes growing wider.

He blinked.

He swallowed.

And he still was caught on his words.

He knew in his mind that the person standing there was Normadia. He knew also in his mind that she was just a young girl who was the stalwart force that kept the Journey kitchen running in fair and effective operation. Her knowledge, skill and constant energy driving the operation through hot summers and long cold winters was the talk of the valley. Many a family had sent people to learn from both her and Karina over the last few summers. He knew she was young, fierce, mostly plain and hard working.

He obviously had not been paying attention.

At all.

The plain part of her had certainly changed!

She had become tall from her very center out. From feet to forehead, she was just tall. She radiated soft confident warmth. Her hair glistened like finely spun silk threads in the yellow firelight. She had pulled the thick rich brown strands back into a thick braid tied with flowing yellow ribbon. Strong naked shoulders framed her long neck that led down to a well endowed bosom. Her dress sported a low and open neckline on a dress of deep forest green that in not a too distant future might prove to be too small for her. Her eyes sparkled in mischief and her smile of white teeth shown through partially parted full pink and smiling lips.

A ringlet of hair decorated with tiny yellow flowers cascaded near her right eye and mischievously added erotic tension to her long glowing face. Quillan's mind seemed to go off in small screaming bits of white hot surprise.

He gulped again, trying to get his mind back in focus to thank her but she beat him to it.

"Mr. Quillan," she said softly, with a bit of a smile, her head tilted just a little to one side. "I have brought you a little dessert, which if you like, please do me the favor of consumption?"

He looked at the plate. He looked at her. There seemed to be more to this than well toasted bits of dough, neatly arranged and aromatic on the table. He was, as you might imagine, caught off guard.

The Normadia he did not really know continued talking and therefore rescuing him from having to try and talk himself. She said "Oh, dear sir, I should request the enjoyment of your company on the dance floor. And I do promise, there are more warm tasty morsels to be had later."

By now, Quillan had reached a state of semi-composure. With the proper flourish he stood and answered, "Miss Normadia, it would be my honor."

"Good then," she replied with an unwavering smile. "After you fetch me some of whatever that horrible stuff is you are drinking. It is high time for me to be on this side of the table. So to speak."

Quillan pulled a chair out for her and she gracefully settled her long self into its frame. And then without a heartbeat of hesitation, he was off in search of a mug and something to add to its empty contents. As he walked, he could see a few small crowds of girls, young and old, pointing and whispering like blue jays on a sunny day, all excited and just gasping at the "new" arrival.

No one had ever seen Normadia like this. It was as if she had burst from a cocoon and floated into the world from on high.

* * *

And yes, Quillan and Normadia did, as the rest of the room, dance. And it was as if they had been practicing since a time far before the one they now occupied. She twirled, he led. He twirled, she led. They laughed. They talked. They smiled.

He wondered where she had been hiding? How he had not noticed such a lovely lass about the Journey Inn?

She explained that until now, she had been focused only on the kitchen. But with being a little more grown up, she knew, there was more to life and it was time to explore it. And that, kind sir, was what she was doing. "Care to join me in my adventures?" she purred into his warm ear as the music and laughter of the room raucoused around them.

She calmed his fears that she was leaving the kitchen. No, not at all. That was where she felt at home. It was just that now, she needed to explore the neighborhood so to speak. She needed to explore all the life that happened in the big room and outside the confines of the Inn. It was high time to not spend all her days and nights in the kitchen. There was always plenty of help. And the help was doing a fine job.

She had a desire now to explore life and all it had to offer. Tonight was the beginning of many an exploration!

And then the musicians announced that it was time for the last melody of the evening. And as was the custom at Journey, the last bit of music to adorn the ears of the revelers would be a slow and melodic tune of unknown but widely accepted ancient origin.

It seemed to set the mood for sleep and rest.

And so with the entire population of the room, Quillan and Normadia arose and attended to the square of wood that served as the place of dance. She placed her hand firmly on his back and he hesitated. She reached down and guided his hand to her warm back and then as the music filled the room, she moved in close to him and they let their bodies and spirits collide.

They could feel each other move. He could feel her softness that was part of her long sinewy muscles as she seemed to melt into him.

She seemed to enjoy his response. He heard her purr a little and felt her move in towards him just a little closer.

Some watched from around the room and marveled at how the big red man had been tamed in one well planned move by the stunning brown haired lass from the kitchen.

And when the music stopped, they just stood there, not wanting the moment to end. Slowly they parted to let some space come between them.

He looked into her eyes, he searched her slightly flushed yet clear face and long brown lashes. He searched for something to say. Yet his mouth was dry and his mind seemed a bit of swampy black blankness that was of no use at all.

Normadia brought her cheek alongside his face letting the soft red bristles of his well trimmed beard brush both her lips and well chiseled cheekbone, and she whispered, "Should you like that refreshment I promised you?" and then she playfully gave his ear a little nibble.

She did not wait for an answer, deftly turning on her heel, and with Quillan's hand guided by her own, she set them both on a course for the big kitchen door of the Journey Inn.

Every eye in the room followed them out.

* * *

Dessa turned to Torrin with a quizzical look.

He said to her questioning face, "Did you know she had that planned for tonight?"

Dessa thoughtfully replied, "No I would guess not. But come to think of it, maybe I am not really all that surprised. Considering the questions I have been getting since the beginning of the fall season from Normadia."

"Oh?" asked the ever inquisitive Torrin.

"Yes, never you mind you nosey lout," she playfully twisted his nose. "It's all girl talk."

Dessa looked back and saw the door to the kitchen close. And she just let a knowing smile cross her face. And then she let Torrin lead her upstairs to their own place of adventures.

27.
Calling

"Stop eating so much," muttered Uta, "You are going to become one fat bitch mare and not able to keep up."

"So what?" came Calandra's muffled reply through large mouthfuls of wet chewy hay. "We are getting into the season of the snow and I would rather lie here full fat and warm than lean and cold. Anyway, why are you so tense? It's the time of year to relax and enjoy the sounds of the wind."

"There will be time for that later," Uta replied tersely. "There is one more trip this year and I don't want you lumbering along behind me like a whiny whelp wheezing and slowing us down."

"How do you know there is another trip?"

"I just know."

"Hummph," and Calandra continued chewing; enjoying it even more since she knew it bothered "bossy boy."

And, then she asked, "Why don't ye just take Samoot? She is big, strong and can go anywhere."

"Because where we are going will require speed. A lot of it and you and I both know how to run together over long distances."

*   *   *

"What?" asked Dessa, somewhat bewildered. Uta did not often speak to her unless spoken to first and especially in such a direct way. Usually it was warm nurturing thoughts. Quiet sentiments. This was very unusual.

"Get Praritor," said the great large steed. "Call for him and he will come."

"But? What?" replied the still bewildered Dessa shaking her head, trying to understand. "How? Really, how do I call for a wild wolf? It's impossible."

"All you have to do is walk outside and the how to do it will come to you," replied the horse, taking on a very commanding attitude with some frustration growing in his voice. "When you get to the edge of the woods, you will know what to do. Trust me, and we have not a moment to lose; winter is fast approaching. Now go."

Dessa put down the brush she had been using and looked at Calandra with the question clear on her mind asking what was going on. Calandra snorted a wet whinnying snort and went back to slowly chewing a fist sized wad of hay. Dessa noted that the horse had been chewing this gooey mess for a while now. Usually Calandra was chowing down firmly with that ever interesting crunching noise horses make in the backs of their mouths. Like walking over small damp sticks. She was slowly chewing, very not like her.

Something was surely amiss?

Most of the leaves were off the trees and lay in windblown piles across the ground; having done their summer duty and now had graciously accepted their eternal rest. The view into the great forest from the periphery of the Journey Inn had changed. You could see further than before, and the majesty of the woods was evident. Thick trees with massive trunks stood at ease, ready for a long winter rest. Saplings, happy to have survived another summer, stood lonely and thin, almost submissive to the greatness surrounding them.

Dessa slowly walked toward the forest, the snows from just a few days before gone and a warm cycle, probably the last of the season, had descended upon the valley.

Within the group at Journey, they all discussed the weather incessantly. It was something they had no control over, and could not predict, but affected them all. But right now, the weather did not seem to matter.

Dessa's heart was thumping in her chest. She had conversed before with the great wolf, but had never summoned him. She was just unsure of what to do. So many new things so fast. In all the other encounters, the big gray beast had shown up when he seemed to want her or knew he was needed. Not the other way around.

At the edge of the clearing, where the long brown grass was to her knees, she turned her back to the woods and looked up at the imposing lodge that would serve as her winter home. It was the first time she had spent winter away from the comfortable confines of Tarmon's castle. She remembered the long winters at home. The parties, the games, dancing, baking contests and long stories around the huge warm fireplaces. She signed and turned around to face the tall stillness of the great forest.

"Praritor," she said firmly to no one, yet to everyone all at once, "I need you. Please. Please come."

        *   *   *

"Are you telling me what we are doing or do I have to guess?" said Calandra to Uta.

"For now, you are better off not knowing," said the larger horse. "Just be prepared to go when the time is right. Now get some sleep, but drink some water before you do; we won't have much time to rest considering the season of the year. I'm counting on you. I can't do this alone and I'd better come back with you, or Dessa will be very angry with me."

Calandra ambled over to the water and had some fun slurping and splashing. Usually drinking is serious business for a horse, considering the size of their mouth and the amount of water they suck up. For no reason she decided to splash around a little and have some fun. She looked up at Uta, who himself now was lazily chewing a large wad of wet hay and gave a wet whinny.

Samoot watched the other two and just shook her big head and continued to pay attention to sweet mouthfuls of hay from the flake in the corner of the stall. She admired the faster horses and wished she could keep up with them in a race. But she also knew that when it came to hauling Torrin around, she was the queen; she tolerated his bumpy riding. Samoot was always Torrin's first choice for a ride.

Calandra walked over to the warm pile of dry straw and lay down with a large heavy sigh. The wisps tickled her nose, the fresh smells of summer still held forth from the pile and inside she smiled remembering the adventures of the warmer days. Dessa had done well. She proved her mettle and had kept them all safe. Even when those nasty wolves had attacked the sheep at Phlail's place in that long valley. That was really the only time she had been a little afraid. Of course the trip to Torrin's castle had been burdensome. But humans had to deal with such matters and these were not things for her to fash about.

Calandra fell fast asleep nestled in the warm hay.

Uta looked at the sleeping mare and wondered with all the trouble about, how she could sleep so soundly.

Calandra just burped.

* * *

As Dessa stood there at the edge of the forest, almost at once the barking calls started after her summons. At first close and then it seemed to roll over the hills, echoes tinging back slower and softer as her heartbeats kept pace with the noise. The sharp staccato yelps seemed to travel across the tops of the hills. The sharp sounds did not last long. They had seemed somehow direct and strongly concise.

Then a set of answers, seemingly the same sounds, but coming from far away and then closer.

These too abruptly ended, and as if a knife had cut the air in a sharp slice, all was quiet. Not a bird chirped or squirrel scampered. It was as if not even the wind dared to move.

Dessa shuddered, and as she turned and walked back toward Journey a cool breeze ruffled the hair at the back of her neck. The day was already growing old and darkness was creeping over the hills, chasing the light into tomorrow. The shorter days were part of winter, and she already looked forward to spring!

As Dessa entered the stable area she encountered a strange sight. Normadia was brushing Uta. And Uta was very much enjoying it. His ears were relaxed, his shoulders slumped and his head moved slowly from side to side. Much the way she did to ease the tenseness in her own body.

"Well what have we here?" asked Dessa with a broad smile across her face.

"The snow went off and melted, so I decided to enjoy some fresh air and here I am," replied Normadia, her long arm running the brush along the length of Uta.

"I did notice it has been pretty warm around here," replied the now quizzical Dessa. Dashing a snarky smile and wink to Normadia.

"Yes, tis all the talk I am afraid," replied the slightly blushing brown haired girl.

Dessa put both arms up on Uta's back, turned her head in that way one turns their head when they are going to ask a question and said, "Well, are ye goin to tell me about it or do I 'ave ta make up some story? Its killing me to know."

And then Dessa leaned forward with a bit of smile on her face and asked, "How was it?"

Normadia giggled and then her face relaxed into a long happy sigh, "They say a way to a man's heart is through his stomach. I'm not so sure of that now. I daresay, it's how ye lead him on and then kiss him. But staying in control is rather mighty difficult, especially after a certain point."

"Control"? asked Dessa.

"Well, more self control," replied Normadia. "I mean I was for a time lost. Did not even know me own name!" she said with a bit of a hushed whisper that was framed with a smile.

"And always have food at the ready," giggled Dessa, "especially with the likes of Quillan."

"Aye, yes, I suppose, tis good to have the food, if 'e gets hungry, or ye need to take a break," agreed Normadia. "But I'll be honest with you," and she moved toward the back of Uta and began to brush the long course tail as she talked.

"Yes?" inquired Dessa, with her eyes wide.

"We did not take much of a break, other than to quench a thirst now and then."

"Well I must say, I have never thought of my dear brother Quillan in such a spicy manner," answered Dessa.

"He bein your brother, I would hope not," smiled Normadia. "He is quite the gentleman, and not the bit of a rogue I was half afraid he would be."

"Do tell now, you naughty girl!" came the breathy reply seasoned with a sly inquisitive smile.

"Well we went into the kitchen and he passed on the seasoned baked dough bites I had set aside," Normadia talked, beginning to relive the moment. "I led him to my room and he just engulfed me with those big arms of his."

"Hmmm?" was the only reply from Dessa. She did not want to interrupt, nor more importantly for Normadia to stop.

"He had one hand firmly pressed against me backside though, and he just lifted me to his lips. I remember getting lost in the heat of that kiss. It was my first kiss on my first real night with a man and oh my, but I must admit," she pressed her lips together in a thin red line as Dessa looked to her, cocking her head as if questioning, "I rather did like it, I can still feel its heat," her cheeks flushed red.

"Oh he is a bit of a romantic, and very strong," whispered Dessa, waiting for the next bit.

"And then he stood up verra straight, got completely serious and asked me 'Are ye sure lass?'" Normadia breathed in deeply, "and I told him, that if I had not been sure, he would not be here in my room all alone with me, the door secure and just the light of the wee oil lamp."

"Well it is good to know he truly is a gentleman," came Dessa's reply.

"And with that he deftly untied the knot in my dress, which did as I had planned, slid down in one piece completely to the floor," said a giggling Normadia.

"What now?" asked Dessa.

"Well," began Normadia, talking a little fast, "Ye get to romantic notions ye know, all that time kneading bread and stirring soup. And, I had heard from the other girls that boys just sometimes get all aflustered with worken off the clothes. So I had made up my mind that something like that was not going to spoil the moment, so I planned up a fetching idea."

"And this was a way to?" prompted Dessa.

"Eliminate the risk of fumblin' and makn' it all get awkward and just lose the heat of the moment," answered a smiling Normadia.

"So you crafted a dress that did what?" said Dessa

"I sewed all the parts together and then attached everything to a tie at the back of me neck. When he pulled the knot loose it all fell to a pile on the floor," giggled Normadia.

"You are but a crafty wench," said Dessa adding her own giggles. "I must try this myself."

"There was another reason too," said a now somewhat breathless Normadia.

"Yes?"

"I wanted to see his face when he saw me naked. I had to make sure that his gaze was good. If it was to be, I needed to be seen and he had to have a positive glow about him," she hesitated. "I wanted to feel like he saw me as pretty," gushed the girl.

Dessa said, "You are a fair maiden in so many ways, why would you even fear that?"

"I have never seen myself as pretty, nor even at all be'n of the sexy sort," came Normadia's careful reply.

"Oh my but I do think ye underestimate yourself," said Dessa.

"Well, from what I could tell there was no hesitation on Quillan's part," Normadia said with a bit of a sly smile. "His hands were warm and he did seem to smile a lot when I looked at his face. It relaxed me some and the whole evening was just wonderful."

"And then?" inquired Dessa, deciding it was time to find out whether or not all this planning and thinking had produced the desired outcome.

"Well, not having much experience with this, he seemed to take his loving good old sweet time to make sure, oh my!" said Normadia on a quick uptake of breath.

"Oh my?" said Dessa.

"My, my, my," said Normadia, but it came out more of a "muuyyyh" and very slowly she raised her arm and pointed toward the open door.

At about the same time a deep, deliberate, low voice thrummed through Dessa's head and she heard, "What may I do for you, my dear Dessa?"

*   *   *

Normadia had seen a wolf once before when travelling in the woods. But never this close and she had never in all her wildest dreams felt that one of these beasts could be so verra huge, so gray and shaggy and have such magnificent blue eyes that just saw through you to your inner soul.

These large piercing blue gray eyes were fixed on Dessa, and the breeze rippled the thick gray fur in little tufts as if the coat had a life of its own. The light gray fur inside his large ears cast light upon his long and almost handsome face. His cheeks were high and large and caused his eyes to squint like he was either thinking about something important or rather considering to eat you. A scar upon the right side of his wet nose seemed out of place and gave credibility to the caginess that lurked about his very being. His shoulders were wide and powerful.

He was not just there at the entrance to the stables. She could feel him commanding his presence and his aura took over the entire room. It was eerie; it was something she would never forget.

He glanced at Normadia, paid her no mind, cocked his head and then looked back at Dessa.

Normadia sucked in a short hot breath and felt almost like she was not there, which she decided very quickly was not such a bad thing. But she was there. This was real and her feet were not responding at all. The only sensations she was aware of was the sudden loud beating of her heart in her ears and she could feel the raspiness of her sharp shallow breathing. Breathing that to keep doing seemed to take a huge effort at the moment since there seemed to be a great weight upon her chest

Dessa moved slowly and deliberately off of where she had been leaning on Uta's back and turned around. And then she smiled and said to Normadia, without turning her head, "Excuse me dear, I need to speak with my friend Praritor."

Normadia's brain could consider no more of this and she sank to the floor in a dead faint as Dessa walked out of the stable. The great gray monster was to her right, walking along as if they were going for a swim or to just chat for a while.

Normadia would remember almost nothing.

*   *   *

Uta let out a little sigh and began chewing some nice dry hay that had some sweet thyme mixed in (for some odd reason); it was heavenly. This might even work he thought.

Samoot had not stopped chewing, but had slowed to a very slow and deliberate pace and was watching carefully.

Calandra continued to snore in blissful ignorance.

28.
Sharp

Accalon the smithy was in a rhythm. The kind of rhythm that a smithy enters not when building something of steel, but building something of steel from deep within the soul.

The long blade that had been the savage tool of Gaerwn to the detriment of Trebor had been fully fired, flattened and was now in the process of being folded in half. Accalon decided that the edge of the blade that had met evil would be buried forever, and the other side would now be exposed to the earth and have a chance to even the score with goodness and honor.

The sweat that poured off his face vanished in little puffs of steam when they alighted upon the steel. His skin was covered in dark flecks of coal bits and steel shavings. His lips were tightly stretched across firmly gritted teeth as he hammered his anger into the glowing rod.

Paroish stood in the doorway for a long time, watching her lover expel his frustration and anger out onto the hot metal. She could not help but admire the sheer madding smoothness of his taut skin that covered long sinewy muscles. He was such a powerful and wonderful man, yet he was a gentle as a willow-wisp on the breeze to all living creatures, including herself.

But now, she was worried. Her nose had swollen up and was black and blue with blood. Her eyes were red and wet from her weeping tears and the sound of her voice to herself was like she was talking inside a drum.

She felt ugly.

She was afraid he would find her repulsive.

She was feeling the sadness of overwhelming rejection and fear before he said anything.

She was afraid.

And yet at this time, she needed him more than ever to be at her side, to be close to her. To slowly stroke her hair with his big powerful hands and tell her she was still his special bràmair.

Finally, after a few final powerful strokes, he stopped the loud pounding and thrust the blade into the pile of hot as the sun coals in the forge. He was breathing hard from the task, almost gasping. Globs of wet hair stuck to his face and neck from the sweat. His hair bantered around him in wild strands of blond and red. Sweat steamed off his body into the air as warm pond vapors might on a cold summer morning.

She let the stiff hot anger melt out of him. She watched him catch not only his breath but let his mind catch up. He closed his eyes and released a heavy sigh.

She gently cleared her throat and waited, holding her breath. Pensive, scared and hoping.

Accalon instantly stood up straight as an arrow, head whipping around toward the sound. His hair flinging strands of dirty sweat into the room. His eyes were blazing as she had never seen them. His face was hard and menacing, the lips of his face, so often warm and loving, were grimaced into a teeth baring sneer.

And then through the dimness of the room and the faint haze of smoke, he recognized her. All at once, he was transformed from a fiery demon. Transformed back into the man she knew and loved.

With hesitation she slowly entered the space. Fearful not of the rage that might emerge, that she could quell for now. But fearful of his vision of her. His seeing her. His reaction.

In two strides he was at her lifting her up fully into his strong arms as if she was light as a feather. His face pressed upon her bosom and he breathed deeply of her scent and softness.

For a moment they stayed reconnecting their souls to each other; and then he set her gently as a rose petal upon the hard packed floor of the blacksmith shop. She contrasted so from the black hard tools that littered the place. Her pale skin almost gave light to the dim interior. He always marveled at how the sunshine followed her into the room.

Accalon gasped, "Your face?" he said questioning. His eyes narrowed as his strong leathery hand touched her bruise, but so gently she hardly felt it.

Quietly he asked, "Him?"

Paroish closed her eyes. The tears that had been welling up were now released and slid down her cheeks. The saltiness stung where the floor of the throne room had scraped her fair skin. "Yes," it came out as a timid frightened squeak.

"How?" was the only word he said, and it came out low and whispered, almost inaudible against the hiss of the forge.

"Scraddius had sent me into the throne room to try and cheer the bastard up and he just tossed me aside. Quite literally. I fell and bashed my face on the stone."

"If he had hit you I would go and remove his hand just right now," came his low and menacing reply. "But we must wait until we can do the deed right." Then after dipping his hands in a bucket to clean them, he reached them carefully to her face. His strong fingers traced the outlines of the bruise. He swept over the cut, and then he caressed her neck and ears while delicately holding a great handful of her soft hair in his other large hand.

Willingly, she melted into his arms for a second time. This time being as warm and wonderful as the first, or almost better, since her fear of rejection had dissipated.

But, she had to make sure. "You don't? I mean, my face?" she fairly sputtered into his ear, "You don't find me repulsive?"

With a slow deliberate movement, Accalon made a space between himself and the tear stained girl in his arms. His face took on a chiseled look, eyes serious and menacing. Strong hands held her at the shoulders firmly, but with no menace. She saw his Adam's apple move up and down his long throat as he swallowed slowly before speaking.

"Nary a day goes by that I do not count me blessings you are in my heart." His face remained stern and his eyes pierced her like lightening would pierce the sky during a hot summer storm. "It is not so much just yer beauty that has touched me heart, it is the beauty of yer soul that pleases me to my core."

She went to speak, but he applied a long hot finger to her lips, shushing her as he worked to find the words that were trying to spill so from his mind. As he removed his block to her speech, she could feel the fine residue of the grit of his work upon her lips. It tasted of salt and sweat and fire. It was gross and erotic, both at the same time. As she moved her tongue in her mouth, the sandpaper effect of the grit was almost pleasing to her, for it brought his world into her being. She could hear the breath of her lungs pulsing through her nostrils as she struggled to maintain composure.

"Ye know ye entrance the boys with yer stunnin' beauty. Your blonde hair and blue eyes plastered on china smooth skin are more than I could ever have hoped for in a fair maiden. Yer beauty makes me melt. Ye make all the other boys melt. Yet it is I who asks how you don't find me own self repulsive?"

He continued, again applying a finger softly to her lips, "I am but a smithy. I stink from smoke dripping sweat. I am covered in soot most of the day; I am but a bender of metal. And how does a maiden so fair find me to be secure and safe in her arms?" His statement ended in a question. He had finally said what was on his mind. He had so longed to find what she saw in him. Why she came to his side. Why she? Why?

Now it was her turn. Her hand moved the soot from next to his eye and made a clean spot on his young but weathered sweaty skin. Her eyes followed the contours of his face and flowed down his whole self. Down one side and up the other. Almost mindlessly, her forefinger and thumb pinched his lip and held on almost too tight, preventing him from speaking.

And then after a long exhale of the breath she had been holding, she began. "Yes," and she stopped, trying to find words. He waited, knowing this to be difficult for her.

"The maids and others tell me I am beautiful. Yes, I am grateful. But I guess it scares me to my bones that I would be pursued and wrongfully wooed by some knave who for the long term would treat me poorly. My mother was of great beauty and she was left for another when she entered her later winters."

Her eyes searched his face. She seemed to search the room for words; she closed them and tears pushed out again from under the soft lids and traveled in clean lines down her cheeks. Her hold on his lip never faltered, and then she continued, "Long ago, I decided to ignore the approaches and entreatments of the boys. I just did not trust them. Until you came along."

He reached up, and pried her hand from his lip, holding her clean slender fingers in his massive hand. "I did not come along to you. You came to me. Here in this room with warm bread and wine." His eyes almost pleaded for the truth, "You came time and again, almost every afternoon. Feeding me, watching me."

"Yes," she replied, "because you were just interested in me. You did not look at me like some prize. You talked with me. Not at me. You showed me things, you treated me like a lady, like a person," she said in a sturdy voice, almost sounding practiced. Later he would reflect that these thoughts must have been planted and well staked in her mind for some time, so he mused they must be honest.

"I…" he stammered.

"Yes," she interrupted. "You never thought a lovely lass would be interested in you. But you were wrong. I see a good man, I see a man worthy of my heart. And I see beyond the dirt and the smells you speak of, because they are just on the surface. I see that inside you is a fire of love and honesty that burns hot, and I want to lie next to that fire and be one with it. Because you are a real man and there are so few of you around, I feel lucky, blessed and calmly terrified."

"Terrified? he asked, nodding his head to one side.

"Yes, that you will decide that since I am a favorite of the king, that sullying your name and bed with me will become unbearable and I will be dashed out of your life like scrap from your work."

A low grin emerged from one corner of his face making his eyes gleam playfully in the flickering light of the forge. "Never in my whole sweaty and gritty life," he breathed, "did I ever fathom that such a wonderful lass as yourself would take a fancy to me."

"And the king's fancy of me?" she asked in a small voice that shook of tight fear.

Accalon looked steadily at the blond girl in his arms. He did not waver at all when he said, "It tis somthin' we both need to bear. You I fear, be bearing it more than meself. I can without shame be beyond it and without issue. Tis you I afear for more than me."

"It will pass soon. I feel it in my bones," said Paroish quietly.

And with that, she wiped the soot from his lips and pulled his hot sweaty face to hers and engulfed his lips in her deep passion.

* * *

Hmmm, thought Scraddius as he watched the scene unfold from the doorway. Somehow this issue needed to either be resolved or used to his advantage. It was not safe to have people who were important to the realm be both not afraid of the terror of Gaerwn and be supporting each other in such fervent honesty and passion. Happy people, in love and unafraid, were a threat to the reign of law that must be Gaerwn's.

He fingered the hilt of the knife in his belt and could almost see in his mind the terror of Paroish as her lover died while kissing her. And then the surprise on her face as he cleanly slit her throat and left them both for others to find in the morning. It certainly would be an easy solution to a very vexing problem.

No.

Accalon was the best smithy in the kingdom. He would be useful later. And the loss of Paroish could set Gaerwn off like a spoiled child without his candy.

Yet, he also knew that his day would come when he was to be with Paroish. And he would watch the simple man in her arms work himself to death trying to earn her back.

These thoughts made his eyes smile with black glee as he silently padded away from the two lovers embraced in the smoky air of the smithy.

29.
Charge of Duty

"So the horse summoned me?" said Praritor, the great gray wolf. One of his long and powerful front legs reached up and scratched behind an ear.

"Yes, however a greater truth would actually be, he more commanded me to summon you than asked me," said Dessa with the word "commanded" said very strong.

"Well, then, this had better be good since I was warm in my lair with my warm sweet mate Hexly, and new fresh pups all around me. They are alone and vulnerable now. What does he want?"

"To be honest, I really don't know; he just was rather stern and commanding that I summon you," she replied, somewhat hesitantly. "Guess I better fetch him so he can tell you himself and get this all out in the open."

The wolf just looked at her and she would swear he smiled as he cocked his head, raised one bushy eyebrow up and waited for her to do the obvious.

She turned and walked back into the stables. Uta was waiting. "What do you want with him?" Dessa asked.

"I need him to do something," said the horse, just a little too casually and quickly.

"What might that be?" she asked, like a mother requesting

information from her teenage son and sensing something amiss.

"There are times when we just need to trust each other," came the terse reply. "Now please loosen this rope and let me go speak with him before he gets a burr in his paw and disappears."

She released the tether and went to lead the great steed out.

"You should look after the kitchen lady there; I will be fine," said Uta, motioning his big head toward Normadia's prone body, still in a dead faint on the floor.

She just looked at him with scrunched eyebrows; Uta wondering if he knew what he was getting into.

"Don't worry," said Uta. "He would never hurt me or any of us here. It's not in his code. He is to protect you."

"Why?" she asked.

"Because it was put into motion long before us, and shall be long after we are gone, and we cannot control it. Just accept it," said the horse, quietly.

Dessa shuddered and let the animal go as she turned to help the quietly breathing and very still form of Normadia sprawled upon the hay.

*   *   *

Dessa had let Uta out to have his talk with the wolf. The two very unlikely comrades, a grand tall powerful steed and the head wolf of the forest were alone now in the field outside Journey.

"I do not serve your kind," said Praritor sternly to Uta. Praritor was sitting on his long back legs. His bushy multi-color tail twitching back and forth in jagged, almost rhythmic strokes that had no rhythm but did not seem random. Gray eyes carefully watched the horse with either a stern curiosity or veiled caution. Thin tendrils of vapor emerged from his long snout now and then into the cooling air when he took a deep breath. The steamy vapors a testament to the distance he had covered to arrive at Journey, when Dessa summoned him.

"That is why I had the girl call you," said Uta. "But this is not for me. This is all about her, and all she cares about."

"What then? growled the wolf.

Uta looked at Praritor as well as he could. He knew he only had one chance to ask his question. The odds of gaining a yes were quite low he thought. The wolf was pretty much focused on his family and protecting Dessa now that Harold and Karina were out of the valley. So he lowered his head and said quietly, yet sternly into the wolf's pointed gray ear, "Send me the cat; he needs to lead us to Gaerwn."

"You cannot take them all to Gaerwn at this part of the season," laughed Praritor. "You would be caught there behind his dirty walls for the winter. And furthermore, once that cagey bastard figured out who you were, you would become a barbeque for his unruly lot. Of course you being barbequed would be quite the waste, since I could not get my teeth into your soft fat belly myself."

Uta returned his big mouth to the great wolf's ear and whispered.

After a few moments, the horse backed up a few paces, stood tall and just looked down with all the might he himself could muster at the gray beast in front of him.

The wolf sighed and squinted up at the horse. Then, in a blue blur of gray fur, vanished into the forest like a summer breeze quiets before the sunrise.

*   *   *

Uta walked back to the stable and took his stall.

When Dessa returned, she looked around and asked, "So what was that all about?"

Uta said, "You must leave Calandra and myself untethered, no bridle and leave the door unlatched tonight. That is all I ask for now. We will let you know after we get back."

Dessa looked at the horse for a moment and it occurred to her that since spring, she had learned a new faith that sometimes she needed to believe in. She hugged his long neck and told him she would do as requested.

Uta was happy that there was no argument, no questions and no whining. It was almost like having Karina there.

Samoot finished chewing the wad of grass she had been savoring and looked at Uta before asking, "Why the cat? She gives me the creeps. At least the wolf is big and clumsy and you would have a fighting chance if things go bad."

"Simple," replied the big horse. "The cat is faster and won't slow down. We don't have many days of clear weather and we don't need a guide who is going to get lazy if the weather gets nasty. Once the cat decides to do something, he won't stop at anything. He is such a bonehead. Anyway, the cat will not bother Calandra, I will see to that."

"So remind me not to be around when you tell that gray monster the cat is faster," said Samoot, nosing back into the flake of hay in her stall, looking for the sweeter parts.

Uta laughed.

Calandra continued to snore calmly, not knowing what was in store for her.

30.
Into Hands

Rebecca stood holding her swollen belly in one hand, the other supporting her on the doorframe facing what would surely be one of the last sunny days of the season, and stared off to the distant horizon. Tears streamed down her face and the sour burn of vomit seemed to pour from every part of her. Finally, she was able to take some deep breaths as the pain abated slowly from her quaking body. She turned on her heel and trudged off to Bartoly's smithy where rhythmic sounds of ironwork shattered the air in steady strong clashes of cold steel upon hot steel.

She stood for a moment, watching Bartoly work. The bright hot yellow flames from the forge danced through the sweat that ran in clear streams down his face. She loved to watch him work. His pieces were fine and well crafted. His ethic of family and work would never betray her, not for love or want. But now, she needed something else.

"Bartoly," she said, hoping to sound normal, but her voice quavered as she said it.

"Yes, sweet?" He looked up and instantly was tense; she looked awful. He sensed malevolence about her, swirling like black sand around a daisy in the sunshine. Just not the Rebecca he loved and cared for with all his might, but the two of them – her and the baby. She had always radiated warmth and peace. Even when she had been sick each morning for a while this summer. She had fairly laughed about the daily routine of throwing up. This routine had ended about the time the leaves had started turning. But now the space about her was all turned about and wrong. He dropped his mallet and ran to her.

"What? he asked, not trying at all to hide his alarm.

"We must go to Journey, it is not good," she said in a hoarse whisper.

"What is it? What is wrong? Is it the babe?" The words hurried from his mouth in a jumbled mess of fear and helplessness.

"It makes not a bit of sense," she said. "Yesterday I was fine, just feeling somewhat bloated, and today I am with chills and fever and cannot stop my stomach from heaving and my bowels from running."

She suddenly collapsed into his strong dirty arms, the soot of his work smearing in the perspiration of her body.

"I'm so sorry, I don't want to disappoint you or lose the babe, I just have no idea what is wrong. I am so scared; we need to be near the midwife Kneafsey," she gasped through wet tears.

As tenderly as any mother, the strong smithy picked the sobbing girl up and carried her across the yard to the cabin and into the big bed. He busied himself alternately with stoking up the fire to take the chill off the room, encouraging sips of water by the woman he loved and packing a few things.

Finally he turned to Rebecca and said, "I will bed the forge, vent the kiln and make ready the barn. We will leave on the first light in the morning. My best guess is that no matter what happens, we will be spending the winter with our friends at Journey."

She turned a very pale face towards him and breathed out a whispered, "Yes," as she slowly nodded her head. "Thank you, I am so verra sorry."

Bartoly responded firmly, but with compassion, "That will be the last sorry ye say. Ye have no guilt in this but ye are bothered by it. Ye are not bothering me. We are in this together and together we will endeavor to be beyond it. Now lie ye down and rest some; after ye drink some more water, I will have tea for ye soon."

He tried to give her a reassuring nod, but his insides were afire with fright. After what Harold had said to them, he had been uneasy. He turned with the milking pail in hand and strode out toward the barn. Twilight was beginning to settle in and he worked at his daily chores to clear his mind.

Jacqualde the cow greeted him with a long moo that seemed to say he was a little late and she was more than ready for milking. He patted her on the head and sat on the low stool and began the chore of extracting the white liquid.

Of course the cats showed up to get their fair share. Sitting on their back legs they reminded Bartoly of fat hairy little stumps with paws as they mewed and waved excited arms in the air. He aimed as best he could and of course, just like every other time more milk splashed their face than went into their expectant mouths. But just as every other time that he was doing the milking, he laughed.

The laugh caught him short. He suddenly felt guilty. It was not right for him to be out here laughing when Rebecca and his first unborn child lay in their bed in such a state. He cursed himself and went on milking. After a moment, he looked back to where the cats had been, and they were still there, carefully and methodically licking each other clean from the happy splashing they had received. And it dawned on him that no matter what happened the world would go on. The sun would come up and go down. Spring would bear forth the green of the earth and summer would light its way to warm days and fall would...

He stopped thinking.

He stopped milking.

He just laid his head aside Jacqualde's large furry stomach and cried.

31.
Gesture

Dessa and Normadia were sitting on two sturdy stools in the kitchen. Around them the kitchen people performed the "kitchen dance" in preparation for the evening meal.

Normadia had never before had dry eyes like this. They burned, and the slow whirling dizziness that wallowed around her ears felt like she had been drinking far too much. For a strong and mostly reasonable girl, these were not comfortable feelings. Very foreign. Very odd.

She looked down at the large brown earthen mug of rhodiola and juniper berry tea in her finally almost still hands and slowly worked at another sip. This time with much more vigor and intention than the first one just moments before. The mix of bitter leaves with the tang of juniper seemed to wash sense into her head. It was happening slowly, yet going in the right direction.

Dessa smiled and said, "You are looking better. It's nice to have the situation reversed and I can finally be the one helping you, since it is usually the other way around. My guess is that with you carrying on with my brother and taking over the kitchen and all of the changes around here, the surprise of a wolf at the door was just a bit too much for ye?"

Normadia squeezed her eyes tight, working to put some moisture into the dryness and then smiled as she said, "Well I have never done that before. Just faint away! You would think I was some sort of helpless little girl. It was only a wolf for goodness sake and you know him!" Her long eyebrows arched as she pondered the thought.

As she was taking a large medicinal gulp of the tea, Quillan burst into the room. His face red with exertion and worry. His eyes were wild with fear and the rapid gaspings of his breath were evident that he had travelled quite far and quite fast to now be here.

Before anyone could even begin to explain what had happened, the big man was on his knees in front of Normadia, her face cupped in his dirt smeared sweating hands. His eyes were large with wonder as he exclaimed, "You. You look, just fine. They told me you had been attacked by a huge black wolf that dragged you from the stables and greatly damaged you all over! They told me the damage was ghastly and oh so horrible."

He was panting, his face torn in anguish and flushed with surprise as he first looked at Dessa, then at Normadia, then around the kitchen at everyone who had stopped in that moment to stare at him. He looked for answers. He looked for someone who could make sense of all this.

And then he heard it.

Yes, he heard giggles.

He heard it through his ears. He felt it through his bones. It cut him like a knife. Just wet snigglings at first. Then cha-chawing from the back of the throat. Unmistakable giggling that emanates from the core of a woman and is directed to the source of a man's very inner being. Actually not so much at his inner being (although most men feel that is the case) as to the situation at hand. And then loud snortings as the giggling turned to guffaws and belly laughs.

The rest of the staff smiled, many of them giggling too, and went back to work. And so for a time, the picture was the three of them, Dessa, Normadia and Quillan looking at each other and all of them beginning to make gallant attempts at controlling themselves.

Quillan stood up after a few breaths were made that seemed somewhat in control, and asked, "Are ye ok? Was there a wolf? What happened?"

Dessa looked at Normadia, and since the girl was out of control giggling, she decided to explain, "My guardian wolf Praritor came to see me. Actually he came to talk with Uta, who had asked me to summon Praritor..." at this point Normadia stood up, looked warmly into Quillan's torn and worried face and wrapped her arms around his neck, laying her head upon his broad chest. As she settled in, Dessa continued.

"Anyway, when Praritor arrived at the stable Normadia was not prepared for a very large wolf to saunter up to the door. Oh my but he is big and he is good looking," she said a bit dreamily. "And the shock of it sent Normadia into a dead faint. No teeth, no blood, just a bit of a surprising scare."

Quillan looked down at the thick silky brown hair splayed against his chest and lay a hand gently upon the nape of her neck and softly said with great relief in his voice, "You are ok?"

The head nodded yes.

His big hands grasped her strong shoulders; he pushed her back to half an arm's length, and asked her, "Then why are ye crying?

Normadia wound her fingers around Quillan's wrists and moved his hands down to her waist. She then slowly resumed her position with her head against his chest. However, this time he felt her hot wet face melt into his neck. After a long slow exhale of warm air, she swallowed hard. And then ever so slowly, quietly whispered into his ear. Her words soft and breathy (because her voice would not work yet), "Ye came ta me. No one. Not anyone. Ever. Ever. Ever, has come te me before. Not ever!"

And she quivered in joy as tears streamed down her face and spread a soft wetness of appreciation upon his already damp shirt.

Quillan gritted his teeth and it took all his strength to breathe as he held on tight to something he too had never really had before.

32.
Travel

Bartoly was awake before Rebecca. While barely moving a muscle he watched her in the early morning darkness of their cabin for a time. Her breathing was even and normal. Moving with the gentleness of a wisp of cotton on the air, he felt her skin and the heat seemed to have retreated for now. She was her normal warm self, soft and tender under his hand.

Last night she had radiated fire. He had decided that keeping water in her was worth the possible wrath he might endure upon disturbing her uneven slumber. So he had woken her when returning from milking in the barn with a warm mug of tea. She drank, seemed grateful and fell right back to sleep. This was so unlike her; usually she tossed and turned with all the thoughts of the world twirling in her creative and inventive mind.

Padding over to the big hearth and kitchen, he heated the fire in the hearth, not worrying about how much wood he was consuming. He wanted her to be able to dress in the warmth of the great fireplace. Once the flames had begun to lick at the long thin branches he had heaped at the back, he then stepped out into the chilled morning air.

This early morning time of the day was a true gift most days. He stood at the step of the cabin for a moment and listened to the quiet of the woods as it began to prepare itself for the daily set of chores. He marveled at how the woods just did its job each day. Locust trees grew tall and tossed leaves and small flowers in the spring and rained tiny leaves all through the fall. The plants stretched up to the sun each day and in the fall lay themselves to rest for winter. The animals, the huge ones and the wee ones, foraged and scampered as they needed. It all seemed to have such order.

This though would be a day where all would change for this corner of the woods for himself and the woman he cherished. A day where they would venture out to search for help. If she was worried, he would do what he could, no matter what. She must be very worried since she usually did not ask anyone or anything for help.

He sighed as he picked up the milk bucket and rinsed it with well water. He had had his fill last night as had Gantor (Jacqualde's calf). Gantor was off the teat, but did like an occasional treat of his mother's milk. Some said it was bad to give the animal milk, some said it was fine. Bartoly figured that if the steer liked it, just helvete to all the naysayers and move on. It was bad enough that Gantor would be the sole sire to Jacqualde's calves for the foreseeable future. Bartoly shuddered at the thought.

As he walked to the barn, he looked at the sky and was thankful. At least for today, they would have decent traveling weather. It was gray, yet no rain was about or seemed to threaten. Leaves fell, a few animals scurried about, but it was mostly peaceful. The way things were supposed to be in the early morning.

And so he milked the cow, and then one at a time walked the animals out and tethered the bunch at the cabin. Mattie the horse was excited. Somehow she knew a trip was at hand and she was ready. Both the summer and fall had been generally calm and this would prove to be more activity than she had experienced in a long while. He walked back to the barn to secure the door and rolled three large logs against it to fend against the harsh winds that would arrive for certain.

The cats would stay. They would be fine, and anyway, they needed to keep the rats at bay. There was hay in the barn for them to burrow into during the cold of winter and the shallow well at the bottom of the fruit cellar never froze. Cats were interesting creatures. He marveled at their independence and constant inquisitiveness. It was almost as if a cat forgot everything from the day before, and for them the world was all new each day.

He had never before herded a cow, a horse and a young steer for a two or three day trek, but figured it was time he could learn. Maybe Rebecca could ride ahead on Mattie the mare if she felt well enough and he could catch up later. Jacqualde the cow was big and lumbering and Gantor her calf was young and strong. The only problem with them would be to keep them moving since every clump of grass would seem like a good place to stop and feed for a while.

All these thoughts were running around deep in his head, as well as how the forge and kiln would fair without his careful keeping for the long cold winter. As he was heading for the cabin for the last time, the tenor of the air in the woods suddenly changed...

Pounding.

Steady.

Strong.

Fast!

Hooves!

Flying like the wind.

It sounded like a lot of them. Very fast. Very strong. These were not farm horses like Mattie. These were battle horses, coming here!

Now?

He looked at his hands. No weapon. He looked across the clearing and decided to run.

And then he just stopped and stared slack-jawed and amazed..

*   *   *

When he walked into the cabin, Rebecca was lacing up her boots. Her long arms were stretched out to accommodate the large front of her that made so many regular day-to-day tasks awkward.

He ambled over to her and said not a word. She looked quizzically at him and asked in a low tone that meant business, "What's wrong? Yer face looks as if ye have seen a hungry bear."

Bartoly was not one to mince words or hold back on a thought let alone an opinion. She could count on him to tell her what he was thinking. And when he was quiet, it worried her.

"What?" she said again, this time a little more sternly.

"The world is fallen to pieces and we ave been just a settn' ere not known it," he said, shaking his head.

Rebecca sat down on the big bench in the eating area outside of the hearth. He had piled on a lot of wood in the fireplace and the room was warm. She was a little winded from getting dressed. It distressed her that a regular daily routine like dressing should wear her out, but she hoped that this too would pass.

Yesterday, she might not have even noticed he was troubled. However the good sleep had seemed to help pass whatever demon had attacked her over the last couple of days. She still felt weak and wanted more people around. Especially the help of the midwife Kneafsey, the likes of who was always available at the Journey Inn.

"How do you mean?" said Rebecca. This time she added enough sternness to her voice that she hoped she would break through to him.

He seemed lost in his thoughts.

"While I was comin' back from the barn I heard heavy strong horses approachn' fast," he said, still seeming a little dazed.

"I thought I heard something," she said. "Is someone here?" she looked around, as if expecting company to appear.

He looked at her and shook his head in a long slow "no." "They did na stay," he said. "Actually, they did na even stop or slow down for that matter."

"Well who was it?" Rebecca said. It was very uncommon for anyone coming by to just ride through. Anyone who knew how to find the cabin would always stop for meal or a drink and most often a night or two and pass on news. This was something that had never happened before.

"You may think me daft," he said. "But Uta and Calandra were chasn' that cougar our lady friend Dessa seemed to have befriended."

She looked at him and decided that he was being as truthful as ever and that it was time to leave now.

Right now.

Obviously, the world was going mad!

* * *

Uta reared up at the stream and walked around for a moment to catch his breath before drinking. The cat was on his side, resting, his massive chest heaving as bits of foamy spittle blew from his open mouth. Calandra trotted up behind the two resting animals and likewise walked around slowly, catching her breath and drooling a mess of foamy heat from her swollen lips.

In a few moments they all seemed to have settled down and they shared the stream for a long while. Drinking the chilled liquid slowly, taking either a few licks or a short pull before going back to labored breathing.

Uta did not mind getting out of breath. It felt so good to get it back. And, he had not run with such abandon since leaving Tarmon's kingdom transporting Dessa on this magnificent adventure. All this summer he had felt he was just plodding, and had not realized how much he needed to run hard.

And they had been running hard for most of the day. He liked the sound of the pounding hooves. To him the sound was like thunder. A thunder that made a difference because he was making a difference and that mattered to him. His own thunder!

The big yellow cat had arrived just as morning light had begun to turn the black sky to an ashen gray. No questions, no attitude; just beckoned and they were off into the great forest at full speed in a steady and unwavering single file of determined beast and thunder.

The pace they had kept had been consistently relentless. Uta was sure the cat was trying to prove that the big horses could not keep up the pace. By the end of the morning, Uta noticed the cat kept turning his head back to make sure they were keeping up, and after each check seemed to pick up speed for a while. There were a few times when Uta had worried that Calandra had fallen behind, but no, there she was, just back far enough so the mud from Uta's hooves would not flick her in the face. She kept up with nary a whimper.

Uta liked running in the fall. The forest was less dense and he could see much more around him. The air was cooler and less heavy. This time of season just seemed to be a better time for a long run.

Now the three of them were settled in some to the cadence they needed as a team. They had grown a mutual respect that comes not so much of competition, but of a depth of commitment. When you are standing in the thick of a challenge next to a teammate who is willing to go the mile as strongly as you are, the relationship changes.

The three were different now.

Nothing would change that.

After a while the cat, having stopped inhaling long heaving lungfuls of air and settling down, said "At this pace we will arrive at the time the sun is highest in the sky on the morrow. Assuming you can keep up this pace?" He said it not so much with disdain or sanctimony, but Uta sensed he was giving them a chance to ask for a slower pace if they needed it

"Good," said Uta, "Then we can turn back and we shall not be caught in an early winter storm."

"We are not staying?" asked the cat, now rolling on his back in the leaves to scratch and then stretch long, the way only cats can do, and it always looks so fetching. And, as Uta watched, he noticed it was the only time the cat seemed to really smile.

"No, all we are doing is learning the path to the castle," said Uta. "We must travel there in the spring to deal with Gaerwn."

"No one 'deals' with Gaerwn," said the cat to his paw as he worked to extract pebbles and mud from between great brown pads.

"You did," answered Calandra to Uta's surprise. Calandra was usually quiet and did not attend to a conversation unless asked. "I heard you walked right into the castle with that nasty spoiled child dead on his horse and stared the bastard down."

"You heard right," answered the cat finally digging the miscreant pebble out of his paw and spitting it into the brown leaves. "But I tell you, I have never seen a place so miserable in all my days. Every man, woman and child was dirty, hungry and just empty of all emotion and energy. It was like I was looking at a kingdom of walking dead people. But come to think of it, dead people have more life than these folks did. Shame too, since I was hungry. but I was not eating any of that meat that was standing there within the walls of that castle. Those people looked rotten, but they certainly were alive, just not like anything I have ever seen before."

Uta and Calandra looked at each other and shrugged. It was not theirs to worry about the emotions or lack thereof in Gaerwn's castle. Uta had explained to Calandra that he was sure Dessa would need to go to the castle at first thaw. So it was their job to figure out how to get there. Simple as that.

Uta said, 'Let's go, we can cover a lot of ground before we need to bed down."

The cat said, "Watch yourself at the top of the next ridge. We go right and then down a long rocky trail. And remember, if you break a leg, I get to eat you."

"Sure," said Uta, glad to have the directions, not so keen on the reminder.

33.
A Memory

Rebecca's body posted up and down in close rhythm with Mattie the horse as Mattie walked along. She did not feel so sick, but was weak and just waiting for this little journey to be over. She had walked some, but it was just better to ride; it helped the aching and sharp occasional pains in her back.

They had been trodding along all this day, just like the day before, moving at a slow and steady regular pace. The camp they had made last night was not so bad. Bartoly had outdone himself in gathering wood, swearing that keeping her and the babe warm was all he cared about. Their campfire was almost like a signal fire: large, broad and hot.

Rebecca remembered that the moon had played hide and seek with the clouds all evening. She had lain there, enjoying the warm dryness the fire provided and played games with the moon. She watched its brightness and then she tried to keep her eyes open until it came out from a cloud. It was dumb, it was just fun, it kept her mind off her aching back and in the background the knowing fear for her unborn babe that held her for a time.

As they moved along the trail, Jacqualde and Gantor mooed almost to a rhythm that lulled her into a trance. It was all too often that Bartoly had to wander back and prod the bovines forward after they had discovered tall tasty clumps of fall grasses. More often than not, both were walking with their cud full of a wet wad and Rebecca periodically marveled at how they could walk, chew and continue their lowly mooing all at once. It was decidedly unknown whether or not the two bovines were complaining, happy or just mooing. My she thought, I have not had all this much space to think in a long while and my mind is just conjuring up all sorts of mumble.

Their pace was steady as Mattie ambled her long legs over the rocky path, a sheer cliff on one side and a long drop down on the other.

She knew that at this pace they would arrive at Journey by midday tomorrow. The sun was steady and no black snow clouds threatened them, yet. The surprises that the weather could offer was what worried her most. At this point of the year the snow could be waist deep just overnight. But today they had the blessing of sun and crisp fall air. She allowed herself to relax and let the quiet unanxious part of her mind take control.

Peace invaded her thoughts.

Rebecca closed her eyes and smiled inwardly as she felt a foot or some appendage inside her slide across her front. It felt somewhat like stomach rumbling after some bad food, but also was entirely different. Bartoly had asked her what it was like as he had rested his head on the tops of her thighs and gently ran his hand over her swollen belly. She had liked the feel of his cheek on top of her mons; it was warm and comforting. His head was where all this had started on a cold winter night that had included all the right pieces for a romantic evening just before the solstice.

Her mind now harkened back to that wonderful evening. They had roasted the last thick venison steak of a buck she had surprised a few days before while hunting in the woods. The rest of the buck was smoking with the other meats, but this steak had taken both their breaths away and they agreed that they were blessed. They had noshed together on the last of the summer greens as the steak sizzled and sputtered over the hot coals of a well tended and perfect cooking brazier in their great fireplace.

The cabin had been cozy and snug that night. She had cleaned up and put away all the summer plants and pots. Stored the seeds for spring and had scrubbed til smooth all the water jugs that were so important through the long cold winter.

She had lain that evening with her head on his lap as he fed her greens. She fed him too, reaching up with a wad of crispy fodder and he would nibble her knuckles and kiss her fingers as she tried to find his mouth.

The wine they shared had been robust and presented itself in a remarkable peppery red. The dark liquid was from a large cask they had opened, one that she had found at the back of the root cellar, hidden there for many summers and winters. Half empty when they tapped it, they had been dramatically surprised at the boldness of the blood amber liquid, but also at the smoothness and overwhelming flavor. To say it was a heady smooth and bold wine would have been an understatement. They had decided that letting some wine age some for a few seasons would be smart, if not difficult. Much had evaporated, but what was left was as if sent from heaven.

As they prepared to sit and feast on the steak, something overtook Rebecca's senses. Maybe it was the wine, maybe the licking of her fingers, the snugness of the cabin, or just all of it together. She did not know, did not care, and to this day just accepted it as fate and relished in the serendipity of it.

Bartoly had set the well seasoned and sizzling meat upon the table in the smooth brown platter she had formed and fired that summer. Rebecca had put both wine goblets down and then said to him, "Me-thinks this wonderful supper deserves just a little more." And with that she motioned him toward her and deftly undressed him down to his very own self. She took care to avoid touching his very tender and sensitive parts. Something smoldering inside of her was at a sharp point of a teasing and she was in a wanting mood. She was looking to let their personal fire take hold of both of them.

Without taking her eyes off him she erotically peeled off her own long dress and then sat next to him on the eating bench. She remembered the heat of the fire on her back as they fed each other, naked and lovingly. However, with the wine and meat and the fire, it was now completely different. Succulent and tender morsels of steak were shared and consumed. But the dishes were not cleaned that evening.

He had carried her to the bed, her head was hanging down as she stretched her long lithe body over his arms and had arched herself toward him. She enjoyed watching his eyes as they scanned her nakedness and drank in the view of her wanting flesh.

As he carried her, she ached so pleasantly with a burning desire that needed stoking and quenching. And just in that order.

She remembered wanting to tease him. To play with him. She wanted him to slowly explore all the warm damp parts of her and she of his. From head to foot, hand to hand. She wanted him to bathe all her skin, which tingled in need, in attentive kisses and touch. She desired calloused hands to caress her and mold her heat into a narrow volcano of the utmost tempest.

She herself wanted to start nibbling at his ear and move her mouth down one side and then the other. She wanted to feel the firmness of his heat and make him want her and need her more and more and more! She had decided to tease him to the edge and then turn away and change it all and do something silly like ask for her feet to be rubbed. She wanted this glowing, full, luxurious feeling to go on and on all night.

This desire in her had never before been to such this degree; she could almost taste her need. She remembered biting her tongue because she wanted all of herself to feel. The roughness of the edge of his teeth as he ran them across her tongue was spectacular.

And so with all these plans in her head, she laid him down on the bed, looked at his expectant face and then at his swollen glans, and kissed him deeply. And, for lack of a better way of describing, dismissed all the plans, climbed on top of him and impaled herself.

All the planning in her head, the long labor of foreplay and building toward the erotic climax that would last all night went away in an instant. And this was most unlike her. One of the things he and she were fond of was the long tender and teasing foreplay they enjoyed.

However, for some reason, for some deep seated need, just now, she needed him. She wanted him, and she took him.

It was just perfect.

Now, much later, and with a baby all inside her, anytime she wanted, she could replay that evening in her mind and it was glorious.

He would ask her sometimes, "Was something wrong?" after they had made love. She always looked at him and smiled and then whispered, as her hand found some tender erotic part of him to caress and would say, "Sweet boy, nothing is wrong, I just enjoy climbing inside your head when you are inside of me."

And he would see in her face that all was good, and would lay back and sigh, because he did not understand. And that was ok, because he knew; he did not need to understand.

*   *   *

Mattie's cadenced ambled on. The clomp of each hoof. The rise and fall of her back and the rhythmic motion of her steady breathing added to Rebecca's quiet trance. The memories of that steamy evening lolled in her head. The rise and fall of her extended belly reassured her that all was well.

Jacqualde stopped mooing.

The one small corner of her mind that was paying attention leapt to full alert and screamed loudly at her to wake up.

Now!

As she worked to open her dreamy weighted eyes and looked ahead, they opened wide in surprise as her brain tried to really register what was going on. As she did this, Mattie saw too and reared up so high that she was standing on her two hind legs. Her large front hooves clawing at the air.

Rebecca could only hold on as she tried to scream.

34.
Oh, Those Voices

Torrin was carrying the last of many armloads of old damp straw to the side of the stable that faced out towards the big clearing. He was using it to create a barrier and insulate the outer walls from the coming onslaught of cold and snow.

Dessa had decided to give Uta and Calandra's stalls a good cleaning for winter. And there was no better occasion than while the two horses were on their little scouting excursion.

"So how do you do it?" he asked, spreading the straw against the wall as another barrier to the oncoming cold of winter.

"Do what?" she asked, not really paying attention as she tamped down a corner with a flat rock, making sure there were no low areas where water would pool and turn to ice on the coldest of nights. She knew that a slip on ice could mean sure death for these great creatures.

"Talk to the animals," he replied. "You seem to carry on quite the conversation, but no words come out. There is some sighing and hissing and moaning, but nothing that ever makes sense to me." He stood up and admired his handiwork, noting that no light seeped through the tightly piled mass. This would keep the snow from piling up in the stables from the cracks that were ever present in the old wood.

"It's as much a mystery to me as it is to you," she said. "Maybe more to me, because I am doing it, without knowing how it really happens."

"Do they all speak the same?" he asked, his curiosity still piqued as he began to tie a new rope handle on one of the many handsome wooden drinking buckets.

"To me it all sounds like words, just as thoughts though in my head, so very little real sound. The words seem to appear in my mind. The language is all the same, but they each have their own peculiarities," said the girl as she moved red hair out of her face.

"Oh, such as?" he asked, as he deftly whipped the rope ends tightly with thin stout twine.

She marveled at how good he was with his hands at tying such small knots as she answered, "Uta is very commanding, yet on the other hand Calandra is quiet and gentle. Now Praritor, I could just listen to that voice all the day!" and she giggled and sighed at the same time.

Torrin looked at her with one eyebrow raised and a bit of a nasty squint on his face, but he said nothing other than, "Why for?"

Dessa looked at him and saw the worried jealousy written on his face, but for what? She thought, "He's a wolf." So she answered a bit slowly, letting her mind catch up, "He talks in almost hypnotic rhythm. A very measured pace, quiet yet firm, and it's such a soothing bass, almost like music. Or," and she flashed a smile at him, "Like when you whisper in my ear after having your way with me."

Dessa smiled inside, knowing that her witty response would soothe his worried heart and he would forget his discomfort.

She was more than right.

Torrin put down the bucket he was attending to and walked over to Dessa. He could feel the heat of her body from the efforts of the manual labor seeping out from all around her. Looking into her eyes, he slid one hand under her thick red hair and the other low around her waist, his fingers rubbing that sensitive spot very low on her back as he whispered into her ear, "Well for sure, it's good to know that you are listening…"

And his head banged hard into her temple, knocking her down as he staggered forward, pitching face first into the fresh straw. Head held between both hands with a shrill moan escaping from his lips.

Dessa rolled up from where she had tumbled; she ran to him and rolled him over. His eyes were shut tight, tears leaking out of the sides, squeaks and groans were loosed from between clenched teeth. He was breathing hard and fast through his nose and bits of foamy suds sprayed out from between clenched teeth.

And then, as suddenly as it had all started, it stopped. His body relaxed, his breathing slowed and slowly his hands released from this head.

As she held him close, pressing her warmth into his shaking body, it dawned on her what this must mean.

Tears started to stream down her face as she began to mourn, for Uta and Calandra. She had no reason, but in her heart, a tear as wide as any bad frown had formed that clutched fear into her very soul.

Torrin's breathing had slowed down to normal and he said, "OK, give me some air." And she lowly laid him back on the straw.

"Any ideas as to the source. To the where?" she asked pensively, almost not wanting to know the answer.

Tears filled his eyes as he looked up at her.

Torrin choked on words that hurt to say, "Nothing specific, but I could hear a baby screamn'."

35.
A Destination
of Much

The three stood side by side at the top of the rise. Well, almost side by side. The cat's back just reached the horse's underbelly, but yet, they were there side by side. They would be forever different. As different as any group that makes a hard journey and ends up at the finish, safe and victorious.

As they knew at the outset, any group that travels the distance and stands at the finish becomes more than a team. They don't often think about it until many years later, when that moment reappears in the mind, and something clicks about the magic. The magic of doing something that just was not supposed to be, not supposed to happen. Yet there they were, the vapor of their collective sweat retreating up into the air as they stared down at the place that had become their nemesis.

Their holy grail.

The dirty brown walls of the palisades clung to the earth before their eyes and the tallness of the walls seemed not to matter. The horses knew that their job was to guide and play the part of the Sherpa. The humans would take up the delicate task of conquering the evil.

Something in Uta made him sigh. He looked around to get his bearings and then looked at Calandra who was just staring. For once not making some snide comment, not looking for a wee morsel of grass to eat, not really herself.

"You OK?" he asked tentatively.

Calandra did not look at him or turn her gaze. She did not change her features or admit on her face any emotion. She just said, "Is that where we all die?"

The question and its stark cold reality startled him; this had not been a trip where he had at all worried about bad endings. All he wanted to know was the route they would take in the spring. Simple as that. No more, no less.

He looked down again at the dirty brown structure. It was wide, it was long, and smoke emitted from various places around the walls. As he kept watching and studying, more parts of the picture took shape and what he saw was disturbing.

A large gate with a narrow drawbridge seemed to be the only way in or out. A green speckled and slimy moat protected the entrance making an attack at the drawbridge difficult unless you lay siege, drained the moat and let it dry. The mud there would stop even the most determined force.

Well protected archer platforms were situated across the top of the main wall about the length of a horse apart, making access deadly from any direction.

And as his eyes adjusted to the light that kept changing in the panorama before him, he could see bags hanging on the walls and wondered what kind of defense that could portend.

So he asked the big yellow cat, "What are the bags for? They are hanging on the outside walls."

The cat had finally cooled and was now sitting as cats do, his long legs wound under him and mindlessly arranging his fur to the way it should be with his large pink rough tongue. Without looking up, he answered between the great strokes of his fur arranging, "They are not bags. They are bodies. Human bodies".

Uta looked back at the scene. A new knot forming in his belly. It is one thing to deal with a formidable enemy; it is another to deal with a madman. He said quietly, "I would guess to send a message to any invader?"

"Seems to be," said the cat, now lying on his stomach and cleaning his ears. After running for two days, all his parts were in dire need of attention and he was making the most of this opportunity.

Uta sighed and turned toward Calandra and said, "Death there in that dark mournful place would not be good; let's hope for a better ending."

Calandra said, "Sure." And with that she turned her attention toward the ground to find grasses and greens to eat.

Uta was not convinced that she did not really care and just sighed. Yet he was a little jealous that she could just let it go and find morsels for munching.

"Well," said the cat. "I am assuming you can find your way back to that nice warm stable where the humans feed you and attend to your every need?" The irony and sarcasm in his voice was plain and simple.

"Yes," said Uta, somewhat discouraged, a little scared and clearly not understanding all the thoughts flitting through his horse brain at the moment. "Just answer for me if you would, some curiosities," said Uta.

"Yes?" said the cat, cocking his head. He had never known a horse with such veracity. Usually they were just stupid, big, scared lumps of edible meat. This one was actually interesting and seemed to be able to think.

So Uta began, "Why did you come, why did you bring us here?"

The cat licked his right paw and deftly arranged the fur above his eye. Uta looked and actually could see how the thick brown mass, with wisps of thin yellow intermixed, was now arranged in perfect order. This set off his handsome face just so and Uta understood all the licking. It was just to make it right.

"Praritor and I are certainly not friends, but we are not true enemies. That, in the great view of all this, is somewhat important and I guess good to know. But it does not really matter." He sighed, and went on, "Long ago, his father's father and mine met when another great evil began to stand strong in this land. They met to decide if they could make a difference or should they just run."

"Why did they care if the humans slaughtered each other?"

quizzed the now curious horse.

The cat stared hard at the brown walls for a bit, and then slowly started to explain himself, but did not stop until he was very done with what burned in his belly. "Real evil, like the evil behind those walls adorned with the decaying bodies of tortured souls, does not stop at killing just other humans. The evil spreads to other people who turn to fear and that eventually turns not only to hatred but a hatred that hates the hatred and then does nothing but destroy. The armies do not hunt to eat, they hunt to kill and maim. Stories of entire litters slaughtered just for the sport of it still ring our evening family times, lest we forget the value of supporting the side of good. The memories of burned forests and whole prides turned to dust keep us on edge. And most of all, the evil that eventually invades our own kind as they learn to hate the evil. It becomes a vicious circle of death and destruction. Fear and loathing. Dejection and despair."

The cat looked up at Uta, his face stern, the corners of his usually smiling mouth set firm, and his eyes were blazing.

Uta said nothing but "Oh, I did not know." He had not ever thought that the woods would hold such a story.

The cat breathed a heavy sigh and finished, "So when good comes along, you do what you need to do to give it strength. To help it engage. To help it not so much fight, but to win. And win is all that matters with good and evil. For if we don't fight evil, it wins."

"I see," said the somewhat startled horse.

"Anything else before I return to my warm attentive wife and wonderfully energetic brood?"

Uta asked the question that had been on his mind ever since they had set off on this adventure, "By what name are you known?"

"Why do you care?" came the terse reply, that sounded almost like a threat.

"Only because it would be nice to refer to you as something besides the cat!" said Uta a little strongly, sensing that this brown cougar was getting just a little full of himself. Long sharp fangs backed up by razor sharp claws were only weapons of the flesh, not the soul, and Uta knew that this cat had a soul. He could sense it, and figured that having a deeper relationship might prove to be good – for everyone.

The big cat continued, deep from the soul, "My father took me to this very spot when I was just a cub. He told me of evil, he told me of good. He told me I had a choice to entrust my soul to either direction, and after I left the litter, he would be expecting me to do great things.

And then he said that I shall be known as Ailis the Fergal. One of noble kindness and strength. And he left me here to think about what I would become as I grew older."

Uta was jealous. His father had never taken an interest in him, let alone laid down the gauntlet of greatness upon him. But without hesitation, he said, "Thank you. And your father would be proud to know that we all appreciate you."

"My pleasure" said Ails, standing a little taller, as he walked to the edge of the hill for one last look. And then he turned to walk away, stopped and said, "Remember, to watch out carefully for Sgail, he is an evil cat and will do whatever great damage he can everywhere."

As Uta began to ask "Who is...?" Ailis was gone in a flash of brown fir, one wisp of which Uta noted had stayed behind on the sharp outcrop of a rock. He suddenly longed for the warmth and safety of his stall, the knowledge that good humans were about and that he trusted his care to them. It made the trip all the more important.

So he turned his attention to Calandra and saw that she had found long tendrils of fall grass in a low damp area and was knarfing on a large ball of wet succulence. The wet munching sound that came from deep within her mouth sounded good. The crushed stems smelled good and the relaxed eyes of contentment on her face looked good. So he acquiesced.

With a sigh that could have been mistaken as a moan, Uta walked over to where Calandra was totally engrossed in the eating. He really wanted to say that they needed to be on their way, and then again looked at the grass and decided a little knarfing might be good just now.

Calandra watched a little amazed at Uta, tearing into the long green stems and wondered what the cat had said. Whatever it was, it must have been good to settle Uta down enough to relax and eat for a while. So she continued to happily chew and relax before they set off for home.

*   *   *

The best of the grasses around the horses had been consumed and a cloud flitted over, making the sunshine blink for them in their little place on the hill. They both looked at each other and had the same thought at once together. Each spitting out the ball of grass that had been entertaining their back teeth, they began.

They began their journey home.

Uta, being stronger and faster took the lead. He would keep Calandra at a faster pace. They had agreed to it before.

The trip so far was a success. They had found an ally in Ailis. They learned of Sgail. They knew the way to Gaerwn. There was now just one thing left to do.

Unlike their approach just a short while earlier where they had been quiet and careful (well as quiet as big horses can be), they thundered on in a full gallop.

They thundered with purpose and grace.

They thundered for home.

36.
Peril

On the quiet mountainside path they had been following, pandemonium had emerged in the time it takes to blink.

And Bartoly was suddenly faced with many obstacles.

The path was narrow, sheer cliffs on one side and a long fall on the other. Said path was blocked by both a frightened horse rearing full up on her hind legs and a screaming pregnant woman. This woman also happened to be his wife, who was pregnant with whom he supposed was his child! This made the situation even more frantic, terrible and meaningful.

The snarl that emanated from the trail in front of Mattie told him all he needed to know even before the large steed reared.

Cougar! And it sounded very angry!

And as if the situation could not get worse, it did. Bartoly watched helplessly as the big brown cat leapt at Mattie. Long powerful arms encircled Mattie's neck and massive teeth sunk into her big long neck.

In his mind he told himself that he should have been walking on point to guard against a frontal assault. But he had been actively engrossed in herding the bovine members of their little caravan, Jacqualde and Gantor. Neither of whom had been too keen on keeping up.

Bartoly grabbed Mattie's rear legs and vaulted around her to the cliff side of the trail. Rebecca was screaming and holding onto her belly. The area was too close to draw a sword so he decided to reach to his boot and grab his knife, until he saw Mattie's eyes.

Mattie looked at him as she desperately tried to shake the cougar from the death grip on her neck. His long teeth were firmly sunk to the gums and had her windpipe in a closing vise-like grip, blood beginning to spray in all directions.

Mattie's eyes said to him "Take Rebecca off my back."

And as Mattie put her head on the ground to give Bartoly room, Bartoly took Rebecca off the horse. He never had any recollection on how he did it. He just did. Both he and Rebecca ended up sitting on their butts on the trail.

And then Mattie pitched herself and the cat that was wrapped around her neck off the sheer side of the trail. It was over in a heartbeat.

All that was left was a sobbing Rebecca, a terrified Bartoly and two worried bovines. Two bovines who could not turn around, could not defend themselves and really had no idea what was going on.

Bartoly just sat there, holding Rebecca, listening to his breathing and thought he heard a noise from the hill above, but could not be sure, and did not bother to care.

37.
Mission

Dessa was rubbing her head where Torrin's head had banged into hers. "Rebecca?" Dessa asked Torrin, worried and alarmed. His head hurt when danger was about, but he had never been bowled over and completely out of control before.

"I dun know," he said, rubbing both temples with his hands. He was still breathing hard and trying to regain a sense of equilibrium.

"Was it their baby?" she quizzed a little frantically.

"Dunno, jus a baby screamn' and then it was over, but it was verra harsh." He rubbed the back of his neck, "Felt like I was on fire and there was white light in my eyes; I could not see, and oh…" his voice trailed away as he squeezed his eyes shut and she noticed a little blood seeping out where tears should have been.

Dessa straightened up, her face set to thinking. After a few heartbeats she said, "We need to go there. They might need help."

Torrin started to protest. He knew in his heart that a two and a half day journey would take far too long to be of any practical use. But he had learned to listen and look at people's eyes and he stopped. He decided that the practical aspect of this was unimportant. And if they arrived at a place where they could not help, then they could at least say they had tried. However, he was still a man, and therefore, without shame, usually overly practical…

"We have but just Samoot and Happy. They be just light horses and even on their best days, they are not meant for any speed or distance, just jaunting along. And my fear is that with these lighter animals, if we get caught in a storm, we are in real trouble. I am not saying that we do not go, I am just saying, we are left without any speedy or strong options."

Dessa looked left, she looked right and could hear the deep heavy breathing of Samoot and Happy. It was a breathing of just a light horse, not speed. There was nothing wrong with either of them, but these horses were not what Dessa and Torrin needed right now.

She lay Torrin down in the fresh straw, and then she lay her head on his chest and said, "Sometimes I just hate reality."

Winding his finger around her ear he said, "All will be good."

"Yes" she said, and her mind was a whirl and not believing for a minute any truth to what he had just said.

38.
Endings...

"Are ye hurt?" Bartoly said to Rebecca. He had asked it quietly, breathing it into her ear, almost fearing the answer.

"Not sure," she said tentatively. "Let me up; I am so big, sometimes I wonder if I know where my parts are."

They stood, helping each other, holding hands, and then exploring the damage.

Rebecca took a few tentative steps and then moved her arms about to see if everything worked. Satisfied that all her parts were intact, she interlaced her fingers under her swollen belly, closed her eyes and tried to quiet her racing mind and connect to the babe.

In the meantime, Bartoly attended to Jacqualde and Gantor. He talked softy to them, reassuring, and then aggressively scratched their heads and ears.

They answered with the customary, "Moo."

"Well?" Bartoly asked of Rebecca, wondering how she could tell if everything was ok with the baby, and not understanding at all how she might be able to do such a thing.

"I am intact, the babe is aflutter, but I would expect that after all the excitement." Rebecca sighed, "I canna tell if real damage has been done, but I can tell, you, he or she is mighty awake and kicking up a storm."

Bartoly placed a dirty, scratched and bloody hand on her swollen belly.

"Oh, and you. You mister tough guy, let's have a look at all your parts," said a very worried girl turning the bloody hand over, looking for the wound.

"I will be fine," said Bartoly pulling away the injured appendage, but not too quickly (she knew that he wanted the attention; he was just too proud to admit it).

She saw he was scraped and bruised, nothing of long term damage, but he was damaged. They would need to get to water soon and wash their injuries. They had learned a long time ago that small bits of dirt and debris would heal into a wound and be a cause for much discomfort later. Best to wash all that out as soon as feasible.

Together, as if one, they looked at the edge of the path. It fell off at a sharp edge. Slowly and carefully, hands together, they walked to the edge and peered over. The canyon below went on for what seemed forever. And together they shared the thought that this was poor Mattie's very own last forever.

Rebecca breathed and swallowed hard. She said in a pinched voice, squeaked through tears, "Did Mattie know what on earth she was a do'n?"

Bartoly, not used to such feelings, took some heartbeats to respond and said, "I saw er look back at ye. She knew. Oh my she knew. An then as soon as ye was free of her she flung that damnú cat over the cliff ta save ye!" He lowered his head and softly exclaimed, "I saw it, I saw it in her eyes, and knew the moment I saw her look at you. Yes, she knew, and there was nothing, not one donais thing I could do different. Poor Mattie just took it upon herself to keep ye safe from that blasted varmint."

Rebecca lay her dirty head upon his breast and let out low sobs. The quiet around them was strange, like the silence before a great thunderstorm. And as with all other thunderstorms, this thunderstorm too had passed.

With one hand supporting her belly and the other reaching for the ground, she knelt down. Grabbing a handful of the trail's torn up dirt from the mêlée, she said to the deep canyon, "Bless ye my dear Mattie. Bless yer loving heart, bless your loving and protectn' soul. Rest in peace; ye are now part of me earth, as I shall one day be, and join ye." She tossed the handful of dirt over the edge of the trail where Mattie had gone over.

Then Rebecca arranged nine stones in a cross of a traditional Celtic cairn. When she was done, she knelt down and put some blood from her cut lip on the top stone.

Bartoly breathed a heavy sigh of acknowledgement and helped her stand.

They looked around at the torn earth of the trail, the scattered rocks and disheveled trail. The contents of the pack that had been tied to Mattie were strewn about in a complete mess. Together they rescued what bits they needed to from the mess and tied it into a bundle. Pottery had been broken, the lamp holding their fire was put out, their water jugs smashed to bits and more damage than they cared to think about had been done to their meager belongings.

But soon they were finished, and as finished as they could be given the immensity of the disaster that had befallen upon them. So they prepared to continue on, as one must in times of difficulty. They bucked up as well as they could. Going back was not an option. Going forward without a horse would be difficult at best. Staying put where they were on this trail would find them dead in just a few days from the surety of the oncoming winter.

And then, the little troop, what was left of it, began to move forward.

After a while, even though the walking was painful, she playfully grabbed his nose and said, "Let's find a place to camp for the night. We both need some sleep."

He did not protest.

The others just said, "Moo."

* * *

"Enough," said Uta to Calandra, swallowing a last bit of grass after a much needed rest. We still can be a long way from those dark and scary walls and stinking filth before it gets too dark to travel. And ye know, if ye trip and break yer leg, that cat will come back and feast on ye, so I do not fancy a runnin in the dark.'

They had run hard for a long while. Stopping only for a moment to drink when water offered itself to them. But now they had found a field of nice grasses and the toll on their bodies and empty stomachs had overpowered even their sense of longing to be home.

Calandra looked at him and said, "I intend to be a wonderful feast someday. For I shall be dead and then nothing more is needed of this big body."

Uta did not understand, and started heading toward home.

Calandra bit off one last mouthful of now cool and juicy grass and followed.

They picked up speed until the trail became dark with the shadows of the forest. These shadows hid the gopher holes and roots that could trip them up, so they found a place for their evening rest.

*   *   *

Night fell.

And two camps were made far apart, deep in the great forest.

In one, the Rebecca and Bartoly were cheered and nurtured by a large warm fire of dry logs that had weathered in the summer heat. This of course after a time of blisters and swearing and broken twine to start a fire from scratch. The sleep that came quickly was from a day of complete exhaustion and the melting of terror at the cougar attack and loss of Mattie.

In the other, complete fatigue from a feeling of accomplishment after a hard run. Two large steeds lay in the tall brown grasses of fall. The trees that surrounded their little clearing stood tall and stretched up toward the stars. The stars were the only light on this cool black night that held no moon. Their backs to each other as their mothers had taught them.

In both camps, there was the hope that the new day would bring a better world to embrace them.

A better world that was safe, and warm and full of creatures that cared for them.

*   *   *

Funny how a relaxed mind tends toward the positive.

And how wrong those positive thoughts can be.

39.
Movement

"I still think we should head to their cabin," said a somewhat bedraggled Dessa to Torrin who was still relaxing as she sat on a low stool in the light of the cool morning. She was pulling a brush through her hair and noticed brushing required quite a bit more effort now. The red locks had mostly grown back from when Sanura had quickly cut them off for her escape, and she loved how it looked after a brushing. But this tangled morning reminder was a clear message she had not missed the maintenance of the longer thick mane that was thicker than most redheads (of which there were a fair amount in the valley).

Curling a ringlet around on a finger, she smiled and asked him, "When do you want to leave?"

She knew he would go. After what she had done to him this last evening, she had no doubt. Not that the long slow progression of her lips and fingers across all his skin and sensitive parts had only been for the purpose of getting her way. She would admit though that it had been just a wee part of the source of entertainment and her passion. She knew that her intentions, in the end were honorable, only to help their friends.

Torrin climbed out of the iron bed, brushed the bits of sand away that had clung to him and ambled over to where the red hair was flying around. He mused that taming that hair would be like trying to tame its owner.

He intended to do neither.

He reached down under her upraised and busy arms and cupped her breasts, one in each hand. He liked the full feeling of her in his hands. He liked how she leaned back into his nakedness as he gently caressed and teased her. He enjoyed the visible reaction she displayed at the tip of the softness in each of his hands.

She relished how she could feel his heat grow and press against her back, and she liked taking credit for it. Memories of some long explorations from last night flooded her mind and she pushed her back just a bit harder against him and moved from left to right in a firm gliding motion she knew he would appreciate.

"Let's have a good breakfast," said Torrin, "and then be gone by the midday sun. I still don't feel snow in the air, so we may be safe on the trail. Although it does feel like rain."

Her hand found his hand and squeezed it reassuringly.

"You know," she said, "if we get caught in the weather we might have to stay at the cabin all winter."

"I can think of worse things," he said, teasing her in a tender spot with his hand, which caused her to push against his hand in some erotic moves and moan.

"There is no iron bed though," whispered Dessa to his ear.

"Oh, I have not a worry at all about figuring something out," he said as he gave her a squeeze and then proceeded to dress and pack a few things with a smile.

40.
Exploring Options

Rebecca was now walking, almost in a daze. Her back hurt, her feet hurt, her arm hurt from something that must have happened, but she did not remember during the attack of yesterday. The other arm was tight around her swollen belly, trying her best to hold the weight up off her back, and to keep the whole big thing from swaying. Her eyes were open just enough to see where her feet were planting on each pain soaked weary step.

She felt quite miserable, very out of control and thirsty.

Behind her she could hear the heavy slogging of bovine hooves combined with labored and mostly unhappy breathing and the occasional "moo." She hoped Journey had facilities for two more cows. She did not want to have to commit them to the smoke shed. Although, as she was feeling about now, she was reluctant to care about most anything.

They stopped and rested. Bartoly searched some and found a small creek and he led them all to its smoothly running waters. As Rebecca drank, she became grateful for him taking such good care of her. Then she felt guilty about not caring about the bovines as she had walked. This then caused her to shed tears of guilt.

She decided that all this emotional turmoil was ridiculous and she hated it. She was haunting herself!

This revelation made her laugh out loud. The look from Bartoly made her laugh even harder.

And then she cried because it hurt to laugh.

The cows were undeterred by the brutal swing of her emotions and they munched away at the grasses fed by the little stream. And since walking was not even close to one of their favorite pastimes, they pretty much stood still and rested.

After a while, with prodding by Bartoly, the mostly very silent, yet determined party continued on.

Rebecca felt somewhat better now. While resting she had found a nice dry trivet of fall grass and lay on her side for a while to relax. It took the weight off.

As the afternoon wore on and the effects of the attack wore off, she enjoyed the crunch of the leaves underfoot. She looked around at the marvelous mosaic of colors that were the gift of the fall season and breathed in the cool dry air. After the heat of the summer, especially with being in her condition, she reveled at the lack of humidity and crisp freshness of the open breeze. Finally she thought to herself, I am able to say I am appreciative now of where I am. At least a little.

They had decided to be creative and had tried to have her ride Jacqualde. Even Gantor the calf seemed to watch and wonder at the odd attempt.

It was a minor disaster and all were fortunate neither mother-to-be or mother cow were injured. If she had felt that Mattie's back was bony, Jacqualde took the prize. And the cow was not amused at the thought of a whole entire person riding her (plus one almost ready to enter the world). Rebecca had been able to slip off quite gracefully as Jacqualde began to make vain attempts to buck.

After everyone had settled down, she and Bartoly had shared in a hearty laugh. And this helped them both to feel better.

He said what any man would say in a grave situation like this, "Guess we walk."

She had smiled at him with a twinkle, "I marvel at your genius."
He just blushed.

*   *   *

"We can make the creek by nightfall," said Torrin as he pushed
the soft sycamore cork into the ceramic water jug that was strapped to
the side of his backpack.

"Do you plan to run all afternoon?" inquired Dessa, somewhat
out of breath as she too sealed her water bottle.

"No, just a brisk walk," replied Torrin with a devilish grin.

They had said their goodbyes and left Journey in the capable
hands of Quillan, Normadia and the gang. The sun was directed
straight down on their heads as they bundled off up the trail, already
breaking into a rapid trot as they entered the woods.

Dessa had told Normadia she was going to take the lead and see
if Torrin could keep up. Normadia smiled and just shook her head at
the giggles they shared. Both knew that Dessa was stronger and just a
little bigger than Torrin, but no one ever flaunted that in public.

There was just no need.

As they disappeared into the forest, Normadia turned to Quillan
and said, "Can you imagine how Torrin felt as he watched Harold and
Karina walk up that trail, and disappear?"

"No, I quite cannot think about what that musta' felt like," said
the big red man, somewhat slowly and thoughtfully. "But I do know
that watchn' them there couple disappear is not scary at all. That is
cause you are here with me." He smiled and kissed her on the lips in
front of the crowd.

There were some mild murmurs of course from the folks
collected around, nothing else.

"Come on ye bloggers, we gots to get more wood or die a black
frozen death this winter," said a very smiling Quillan, determined to
take the focus off himself.

They all murmured their agreement, knowing that having warm
weather after a snow that had come was a gift not to squander.

41.
Befuddling

Something was amiss? Yes, very amiss, mused Scraddius as he trudged back toward the castle away from his hunting cabin (which most of the time served as his main place of entertainment and relaxation). It bothered him greatly, yet he did not, and could not, figure out why. Yet, it just bothered him.

What he had witnessed amongst the animals in the woods on the hill was more than unexplainably strange. And with the storm clouds gathering behind him, had removed the levity he had just not long ago felt. A levity that he knew had cost him a fair amount of good will and one that had ended up being politically dangerous. He also wondered if he was getting soft since the two of them were still alive?

Glenna trudged behind him. Their relationship was different now. He mourned the loss, yet he reveled in the fact that he, Scraddius, had not, was not, and would not, be compromised.

*   *   *

This adventure had begun just two nights ago when Scraddius had traveled quietly without an entourage to his hunting lodge. His only companion for the trip to the lodge had been Glenna. He desired a few days of rest and thoughtful relaxation. Scraddius had become tired, stressed and grumpy at the dirty mournful castle of late. After lying awake one night, his mind racing with turmoil and thoughts that he could not connect, nor understand, he figured it was time to break the monotony. He needed to leave the hustle, anger, fear and dirt of the kingdom behind for a while and let his mind clear.

Anyway, it had been a while since he had enjoyed fine company, good merriment and well tended food without a crowd around. And with the coming of the blasted cold, this seemed like it was a good way to end the season. Actually it had been perfect, until Glenna had popped her little surprise and with what he had just witnessed. Now he was amiss again and wondered if the outing would be for naught.

Glenna was the perfect mate for a small intimate getaway with the goal of losing yourself in something spectacular with no thoughts in mind. She too appreciated the break from the big operation of Gaerwn's muddy fortress. Even though she helped with much of the cooking and taking care of the cabin on these little jaunts, it was still a time to get away and enjoy things.

She was tall, fully a head taller than Scraddius. This he did not mind and it allowed him to rest his head on her in a soft comforting way that they both seemed to enjoy. Actually, there was nothing about her that he minded. His mind did wonder about some things, but nothing was so bothersome that he would wander around and take a chance on some other wench. He found it interesting that such a strong beautiful woman who was at least again as many winters as old as he, would take an interest in him.

Her hair was black as night, even though a few gray ones were starting to show. Her eyes though were a piercing crystal green and they flashed with a gaiety rarely seen in the depressing dark kingdom. What he liked most about her though was that she was smart. Really smart. That was the main reason he had her as his assistant when it came to playing the little games they played with visitors to the kingdom. She was smart enough to play the part well.

Also, they could carry on a conversation about anything. She asked good questions and had deep thoughts about a lot of topics that other women, as well as men he was acquainted with, would not dare even notice let alone think about. Sometimes he would say something and she would get a faraway look in her eyes, just get up and walk away for a while. Of course this was most fun when they were both naked, because he liked to watch her walk. But then she would come back, sit down or curl up next to him and deliver a new perspective on the way he saw something.

They had walked to the cabin together. It had been a clear day and the jaunt had only taken the part of the day between the midday meal and dinner.

As they turned the corner and could take in the full view of the cabin, Scraddius let out a long sigh. He loved this cabin. This place. He loved the simple yet sturdy structure. The low hanging trees in front that kept it private. He loved the clear deck off the back that let the sun's warm rays warm his skin.

The structure was simple and elegant all at once. Crafted by passionate and skilled labor, the wood and accents were almost like art. The place was small, but very comfortable. A compact kitchen served all the cooking needs. A separate living area was filled with warm and comfortable couches. And off to one side was the master bedroom.

The master bedroom was its own work of art. A huge bed sat in the middle of the room with long flowing thin curtains all around it, to keep the bugs out in the summer. A small corner fireplace provided heat when necessary. Two large windows allowed fresh air to flow through during the hot summer days. And heavy skins as well as ornately crafted shutters were in place to keep the cold out during the winter.

A few oil lamps and candles were scattered about as necessary. Other than that, the place was devoid of knickknacks and the typical treasures found in a hunting cabin.

As they walked up towards the cabin, Scraddius could feel the tension leaving his body. It had been a relaxing trek.

As he had expected, all had been made ready for them. Scraddius' private butler and caretaker, Peroxious, had the cabin humming and ready. The fire was warm, but not too big, the water was clear in the cistern, fresh meat was smoking and a plentiful stash of spirits was in the fruit cellar with an assortment of fresh fruits, sweet summer berries, and well-rounded root foods such as potato and rough brown celery. And of course, fresh cut meadow flowers adorned the main table.

Peroxious was an entirely talented cook and Scraddius appreciated his talents. Well pounded and sea salt seasoned venison steaks had been set aside for the evening. The steaks were covered with wet lettuce leaves to keep the flies off and Scraddius could almost feel the other spices in the air that had been carefully infused into the tender meats. Full bodied red wine trekked in from the south by the summer kauppasaksa was perched carefully on the steps to the cellar, not too cold, not too warm; just cool to the touch and opened long enough to encourage the flavors to emerge.

A flavorful mixed dish of seasoned, smoked and then sautéed vegetables in a heavy cheese sauce was sitting near the fire. Peroxious had baked the urn all day, letting the flavors mingle and allowing the smokiness of the fire to add thick rich flavor by letting the edges of the cheese turn crisp golden brown. When served, it would almost be like a pudding, yet smoky and warm.

Peroxious enjoyed playing the role of chef to this small audience. He was a master at taking care of things, and so much more. Most importantly though, he was completely reliable, creatively sneaky on Scraddius' behalf, as necessary. And most of all, he knew how to keep his mouth shut.

* * *

Peroxious had been Scraddius' private butler since both had come of age. They had met after a jousting tournament where Scraddius had been brutally upended from his horse by a man much larger and stronger than he. Scraddius had hated jousting, but he needed to be in the arena to earn time with the King's court. He had won every match in his life until that day, and he hurt both physically and mentally. He was in a terrible state of anguish and pain, more from the failure than anything else, but still physically beat.

As Scraddius had lain in the recovery tent with the nursemaids cleansing the wound in his shoulder, Peroxious walked in with a shattered chunk of wood in one hand. Scraddius had looked askance at the man and thought nothing of it until Peroxious had laid the wood on Scraddius' belly and pointed to the shaft of lead that had been cleverly implanted in the core. Of course the wood was from the tip of Scraddius' now unworthy opponent's lance.

Bleeding and full of rage, Scraddius had entered the King's dining hall bellowing hate and holding the guilty handful of wood aloft charging the large man with cheating. Of course the man denied knowledge of the deceitful act until an armorer stepped forward and claimed he had been paid handsomely to build the lance.

The only thing that kept Scraddius' knife from slashing the cheating knight's throat was the king's hand wrapped around Scraddius' wrist, with an evil sneer upon his face. The king turned to the big knight, seated before him and asked him his name.

"My name is Najjar, your highness," said the man without one hint of uneasiness about him. He was dark with a moustache cut thin like a scimitar. His eyes were cold and black. He was built like a mountain and around him, there was no smile or joy.

A rematch was set for the tournament day before the beginning of the next winter. This would give Scraddius enough time to heal and allow a fair fight that was more for honor than anything.

In order for it to stay interesting, the king had decided that the rematch would be been set for the last pass of the day at the tournament. Generally, each set of opponents are given four passes to determine the winner. Scraddius and his nemesis were allotted one pass; winner take all.

The tournament day arrived and the air was charged with excitement. Ladies were fanning themselves from the heat, and the horse flies were in abundance, eating flesh where they could and causing distress upon any open area of skin.

There was almost a hysteria of betting going on for the final match. Scraddius was known to be tough and now full of hate and furious anger. However, Najjar was large, strong and over the past month had shown how strong he was in many a tussle. Very few really believed Scraddius could win against such a man.

As the flag dropped, the tournament site went silent, except for the pounding of the big war horse hooves and the rattle of armor.

The king himself had inspected the lances and handed them to each of the men from his booth. They had been carefully carved, painted in bright colors and guarded well so that no mischief could become of them. These lances were just a little heavier and longer than usual. The king had hoped this would cause both men to be routed from the saddle and planted on the ground, where a good hand-to-hand battle would ensue.

Of course that is exactly what happened.

Najjar and Scraddius battled for a long while. Najjar was bigger and stronger; however, Scraddius was smaller, faster and just a little more cunning. Back and forth the fight went until Scraddius lunged himself down and under Najjar legs and thrust a short sword up into the man's midsection from down below.

Najjar looked down at Scraddius, up at the king and then without fanfare, drama or any oratory, died.

Scraddius cut out the dead man's tongue, bowed to the king and marched off the field of battle, thus securing his place at court for a long while. Scraddius became an advisor of strategy to the king. And he had enjoyed all of it. Except of course the overall idiocy of King Gaerwn.

It could all have been much worse for Scraddius! Very much worse.

For when Scraddius arrived at his tent, he collapsed and vomited in his own helmet. He had run completely out of energy and fight. Not much more time with Najjar, and Scraddius knew he would have been killed, and killed slowly by the Crimean creature. That was why Scraddius had taken the chance to avoid having his throat slit and slid under the man in a move that neither he nor anyone else had ever seen. It was just a matter of kill or be killed without any options. Scraddius knew he was good at making life or death decisions at the time of the final heartbeat. He also knew that at some point in his life, this might become a curse and catch up to him. But for now, he took what he could get and was glad in it.

*   *   *

After arrival at the hunting lodge and settling in, Scraddius, Glenna and Peroxious took their wine on the patio to enjoy the setting sun. The patio was on the southern exposure and faced the large wooded hill that dwarfed the castle from afar. The colors of the leaves were perfect. Even though there was not the slightest of breezes, the autumn descending of the leaves was in royal process with a parade of colors and whirling of the dying leaves all about.

Scraddius loved the fall season. The chilly nights made cuddling with warm soft skin so much more fun. And he also relished those few nights of peace, where the only sound was the plucsh, plusch, plusch of the leaves landing on the roof. It was a subtle reminder that in the grand spectacle of the nature of things, there would always be parts of the world in motion where there was nothing he could do about it. So he let those things in life that needed to be left alone, very alone.

However, some things were worthy of attention. And as the evening shadows slowly elongated toward a crisp black night glamoured brightly with stars, he smiled a broad smile. This smile covered all across the heavy sensuousness of the fine chalice of wine held in his hand. He smiled because this routine had played out before and he liked it. It was a little odd, but he liked it nonetheless.

Scraddius lay back, stroking the soft skin of Glenna with one hand, balancing his now almost empty chalice with the other and he finally was able to begin to decompress. It was a physical thing he noted in one corner of his mind. He could almost feel the stress run out of his body, like warm honey sliding out of an overturned bowl. He had the sticky ironic sensation of the stress just dripping out of him onto nothing at all, and all over everything. And then the stress was gone. He loved the feeling, and never ever even tried to explain it to anyone, because the words would never come to him.

He relished the feelings here at the lodge and knew that he would sleep well tonight. Three things were going to be at play, and the first (decompression) just made a magnificent entrance. He sighed deeply; it was almost a growl.

Presently, Peroxious bid them a brief slán to perform his magic in the kitchen. Scraddius knew it was nowhere near a farewell, but a gracious hello to an evening that no one else, even that slob Gaerwn, would experience.

Scraddius tipped his chalice in the direction of his faithful servant. Glancing at Glenna, she raised her eyebrows to Peroxious and said, "My dear Peroxious, from the work I have seen so far, we are in for a treat of wonderful proportions." And she too tipped her chalice in honor of his parting to create culinary delight.

After he was gone, Scraddius turned to Glenna and inquired with knitted eyebrows, "You always ask him if he wants help. Now we have this fine evening," he said sweeping his hand across the naturally chiseled scene before them, "and you have broken the normal routine of things. Care to share your thoughts?"

"Sweet Scraddius," she said, rising up and then laying herself smoothly across his lap, "I asked him in the kitchen if we were going to play that silly game again tonight, where I offer, and he denies me, and he was very ready with an answer." She took a long swig of wine and then whispered with wet red lips sliding down the soft warm part of Scraddius' cheek. "He told me to relax and let my mind open to the wonders of nature and to prepare myself for the most wonderful time ever tonight."

"Really now," said a somewhat perplexed Scraddius. "So you both seem ready to break the long traditions we are all accustomed to and comfortable with, now? For this evening?"

She placed his free hand upon her mostly uncovered breast, pushing his fingers into the soft flesh and said, "More than you know."

42.
Step Aside

Just tonight she kept thinking, just after this night in the woods and then I shall be under the big roof of Journey and with friends and shall be warm and have clear clean water and a bath and all shall be good and... Rebecca's mind was rambling. Rambling not so much for good thoughts, but rambling that kept her attention away from the numbing back pain, greasy grime that covered her body and oddly sweet smelling sweat she was enduring now.

Her mind rambled, and rambled, and rambled until she stubbed her toe and went sprawling with a yelp into the gritty stones mixed with the leaves that lay upon the path.

Rebecca could hear Bartoly yelling something, but the dirt and leaves crammed in her mouth were her main focus at the moment. The blasted mess from the trail was trying their hardest to make their way down her already parched throat. Rolling over on her side she continued to dig the mess out her mouth and then noticed the blood on her palms. Both were scraped raw and bleeding in large crimson rivulets that ran off her palms like heavy rain methodically drops off the eaves after a serious shower. She heaved a big sigh, knowing that soon both palms were going to hurt very badly.

Finally, with her mouth cleared enough that the leaves posed no threat to her lungs, she looked up directly into the face of a scared and shaking Bartoly. Tears streamed down his dirty face, leaving wet trails of clean skin in the dirt that had clung to his tired and loving cheeks. She almost laughed as she turned to work the rest of the mud and sandy grit from her mouth. She had wanted to laugh because the clean trails of tears reminded her of the wet lines the slugs would make on the rocks as they slipped out of the morning sun to their safe wet hiding places. But she was too miserable to laugh and so his tears of fright ran lonely and forlornly off his chin.

As Rebecca worked with her now throbbing hands and fingers to try and clean her mouth, Bartoly slowly cleaned the trail debris out of her hair. Then, as if things could not get worse, he felt the unmistakable sensation of rain on his neck.

He almost began to sob, thinking that this was just too much! The attack, losing Mattie, the trail, the pain in her eyes, the danger to the babe and now the weather was dealing a very rotten hand for them. Damnú rain!

And then he felt the rain again. However this time the rain slid down his neck and it was warm and slimy.

Huh?

His hand went up to the back of his neck. Yes, warm and wet? As he turned his head to try and understand, he looked into the big brown eyes of a heavily panting horse, none other than Uta.

Slowly he stood and began to consume the view of the great big horse. Then, he looked at Rebecca, back to Uta and started to cry.

"What's the matter? she asked while sputtering the last of the trail foliage from her mouth, "Now I can ride to Journey." She was instantly alight with promise and hope.

"Not with those hands," he gestured to the crimson blood dripping off her palms.

Rebecca closed her eyes and saw in her mind the miserable enormity of their issue. She was fading fast. She knew that since it was going to take all her strength to even rise, the idea of walking the rest of this day, and most all day tomorrow was next to impossible.

And so joining her love in the understanding of their terrible misery, finally Rebecca also began to cry. She decided that for the first time in her life she was going to just feel sorry for herself and give up in wanton despair.

It was a hollow feeling.

She felt ashamed.

Weak. Insufficient and completely undeserving of motherhood.

But all this loss and heartache and pain was all too much to bear. And she was scared, and seemed to have run out of options. She was just so tired.

Exhausted.

Dirty and spent.

Then his hand was on her shoulder and he said to her very matter of factly, "I think what you need right now is a riding partner."

The comment made sense to her.

Yes! With help she could ride. Alone, she could not hold on, but with a partner it would work. It was all so simple, she and Bartoly could ride Uta to safety and help.

But, as usual, Rebecca being the matter of fact woman she was, logic clicked over and informed her of logical reason! Even this thought of riding together would mean great loss.

The cows would be left to the slaughter of the wolves and great snarling cats because they would never be able to keep up. Jacqualde's big eyes instantly haunted her mind. It was a sacrifice they would have to make for the sake of the baby. Poor Jacqualde! Her poor calf!

But?

What?

All the parts of her brain stopped.

She was suddenly confused.

She truly knew now she was very much in trouble. She was going stark raving mad. Bartoly had said these words to her very dirty ear using Dessa's voice?

Her mind kept swirling.

With resignation.

With fear.

Finally, with confusion and tired bloodshot eyes; with despair written on her face, she looked up.

She looked up to see the slightly freckled porcelain skin, flaming red hair and eyes that resembled mountain almonds born of a storm in the sea. All this was framed in a large wide grin on the face of her friend Dessa, who was as real as the warmth of the sunshine.

Rescued!

And Rebecca fainted away right where she sat upon the trail as the wanton fear and desolate hopelessness ran from her heart.

43.
Giggles

The giggle almost startled Scraddius. Actually, it did startle him. Glenna was sitting smoothly across his lap; he had been winding her long black hair around in his hand, idly thinking of nothing for a while, with Peroxious banging away in the kitchen. And then came this foreign giggle?

Scraddius looked carefully at Glenna. His eyebrows arched at about the maximum and asked with not very kind inquisitiveness, "Who was that?"

Glenna snaked her arm up to his hair and played with the long curls that fell in tousled confusion behind his head before slowly answering, almost as a purr from a cat. "That my dear, is a close friend of mine who I call Leandra."

Scraddius smirked a dark smile. He decided that this could turn out well. Or poorly? But since it was already done, there was no use in getting angry. Not yet anyway. "So tell me about this lady whom you call the lioness? And why would you invite someone here during one of our little adventures without discussing it with me first?"

She licked her lips, the only sign that she was at all nervous now about her decision. The rest of her looked calm and cool, if not just a little on edge.

"She is fun. She is smart. She is adventurous," began Glenna. "I have known her since we were both little girls. And we have shared more than a little of our lives and hearts since I can remember."

"Go on," said a not yet convinced Scraddius. He was acutely aware that many people would do anything to be in his favor. He had great power over that idiot on the throne and the temptation to misuse and take carefree abandon of his position was often on his mind. But he avoided this, since obligations were a paradox he did not have the energy or desire to manage. This was why he appreciated the situation with Glenna and Peroxious. They never asked for anything, they were quite smart, and they kept the relationship uncomplicated. That was until just now with this little surprise.

"Sweet Scraddius, just trust me for now," frowned Glenna. She will make a handy addition to the evening's festivities and explorations. And if you do not like her, you may send her back to that stinking pile of rock in the morning with Peroxious."

"And?" he said, holding her chin just a touch too tight.

"And I shall never do anything without talking to you first," she said with a perplexed sigh.

Scraddius nodded, and then said, in a fatherly way, "Sweet Glenna, you know I am all for some adventure. However, we must be careful."

She looked puzzled; she was smart, but not politically savvy save for wanting to control Scraddius.

He continued, "I have a very comfortable station at that stinking pile of rock, which would not be so bad except, as we agree, that there is a stinking pile of chac on the throne. Anyway, I digress," he said as he playfully ran his fingers over her soft white skin at the frilled edge of her dress where her breasts pointed pleasantly toward him. "I am the only person in that joke of a throne room with any honor whatsoever. And," he said pointedly, with emphasis, "I want it to stay that way. So even a hint to that crowd who are regularly bowing and groveling to Gaerwn that I may be available to be favored, by any means, would sour my disposition greatly."

"Oh!" she declared, now somewhat quieter, with a look of concern on her face. Her plan was not going too well. She liked her relationship with Scraddius. He was young, virile and powerful in the kingdom. She was older and yes, in good shape, but she knew she could walk away from this relationship at any time because he could replace her in a moment. This kept things uncomplicated for her. It allowed her to be in control. As long as the male counterpart of the relationship was not relying on her, she was free to do what she wanted, when she wanted, without recourse. And that was why she endeared sweet Leandra to join them. It was all about control.

Sure, the intimate relations tonight would probably be just completely wonderful. Glenna and Leandra had occasionally met each other's needs when the men were just not available or they did not want the drama that seemed to always accompany a man. They were by no means lovers, but they were compatriots when they needed to be so. No, the control part was to give Scraddius the variety she thought he might crave, but on her terms.

"What does she want from me?" he asked quietly.

"Nothing more than a break from the drudgery, and to have some fun," she said with a little smile. "I told her that this would be a wide open, no holds barred evening, and she is very much in favor of some uncommon group delicacies."

Before Scraddius could reply, a woman of no remarkable consequence entered the room with a chalice in one hand and a wine decanter in the other. He noticed immediately that she exuded an air of quiet confidence. Physically, she was completely unassuming except for the fact that she had the strongest and most well defined arms he had ever seen on a woman. This he found surprisingly erotic.

She walked over to the both of them. Smiled politely, dipped a small respectful curtsy, introduced herself and then without saying another word, poured wine into both of their chalices. With that she set down her own chalice and the now mostly empty decanter on the sideboard and returned to where Scraddius and Glenna were lounging. She smiled once more at Scraddius and then proceeded to kiss Glenna full on the lips.

44.
Heading

Dessa had told the big horse in no uncertain terms to go as fast as he could manage without bouncing. Uta had looked at her like she had lost her mind but then proceeded to do the best he could with two women on his back.

The men had carefully set the barely conscious Rebecca on Uta, facing Dessa. Her head lay comfortably on Dessa's chest with her bottom slung low over Uta's neck, where the ride was the smoothest.

Dessa knew the men would be following as fast as the cows would amble on. Calandra would be bored, but she would also get over it when she was back in her stall with fresh hay and water.

On they plodded. Rebecca periodically woke up from the periods of unconsciousness that were haunting her mumbling. Sometimes she would come awake with a start, sometimes with a smile. And then she would fall back asleep with a long groan.

Dessa knew what it was like to be this tired. It did not matter what was happening to you. You just slept. She had experienced it on her trek to the Journey Inn. After ridding the world of Haphethus with her dagger, she had been tired. Nay, the word tired had not done justice to how she felt. She was fundamentally and totally exhausted. Her body would not respond. She could not think. She was a wreck.

So much so that she had fallen into the waiting arms of Quillan upon her arrival. She had been asleep on Uta. Riding on automatic. And fortunately, Uta knew the path to Journey (Sanura had visited Quillan a few times previously and had ridden Uta).

Dessa knew they needed to keep up the pace, not stop and get her into shelter soon. Black clouds had been skirting the horizon for the larger part of the morning and a fast and furious snowstorm would not do them any favors just now.

Uta plodded on, hardly moving his big broad shoulders. When it came to babies, he was going to do his best, even though he knew his back was going to ache for days.

In short snippets, Dessa was able to obtain the results of the scouting adventure Uta and Calandra had undertaken. She was not surprised by any of the news. She was happy to hear Ailis had behaved and had had the good sense to not have tried to take even a nibble of either horse. The news of Sgail troubled her. She wondered how or what was the cause of this ferocious evil in the animal.

The memory of her time at the hunting cabin flooded back to her. The long lean brown cougar, rolling off her head with her hat impaled on its long teeth made more sense now. She had known that Ailis was not that cat, but she did not know until now there was one that was wildly known as the keeper of evil.

These thoughts, along with the mysteries of the wolf attack haunted her mind as they traveled on. They stopped once to rest, relieve themselves and drink water. It had been tricky getting Rebecca off the tall steed, but they managed. Getting back on was relatively easy. Using a fallen tree to use as a step, off they went.

As they padded along, the obvious and widely common use of the trail by more and more people was evident by the wideness and smoothness of the path. The leaves were floating down in their twirling spiral in real earnest now. Dessa relaxed some, knowing they were getting closer. She was able to look around and take in the dense intertwining elements of the woods that surrounded them. She mused that she was often on such a mission when she passed this way that she missed the breathtaking splendor that was everywhere.

The thick green vines that wound around the great trees had turned to its dark brown winter color for hibernation. How dramatic she thought; a few days ago, you could have cut one of those vines and had your fill of water if you needed to. Now they were dry and brown. The previously dark green leaves of the vines were mostly lost to the ground forever, having done their work for the summer.

The swish and crunch of Uta's legs and hooves through the thick coat of fallen leaves was a constant cadence of pure natural music. The sounds lulled her into a low trance, letting the travel pass in gentleness.

As they rounded a curve, they surprised a large buck grazing on the last of the summer grass in a mostly sunny clearing. Uta missed not a step. The buck looked up, tipped his head in wonder at the sight of the big steed carrying two women and then bounded into the woods. He disappeared from sight in two heartbeats. Dessa knew that without Rebecca on the horse, that buck would have been dinner and more for the whole crew. But even with her bow and quiver of arrows on her back, she did not have the time or space to react.

It occurred to her that today was a day of life, and she looked at the face of Rebecca who grimaced on every other step. Knowing that deep in her was the need to create and build, and Dessa felt special to be able to help. And she smiled.

As they neared Journey, woodcutters spotted them and sent runners ahead to make ready for the arrival. Just knowing that hands would be there to help settled Dessa. Rebecca just groaned and kept breathing slowly and deeply. Wishing it would soon all be over.

Presently they arrived at the Journey Inn and the eager expected hands rescued Rebecca from the confines of Uta's neck. They carried her to one of the upstairs rooms while the kitchen was preparing soup and plenty of hot water to clean the young expectant mother up to the standards of the midwife Kneafsey.

Dessa took Uta to the stalls, brushed him down and fortified the stallion with plenty of dry hay, some oats and of course a few apples. She left two buckets of fresh water, knowing they would soon be dry.

Walking outside, she looked at the dark clouds racing across the sky and smiled. She knew they would not spend winter in the cabin, but here at Journey. Safe and warm with people she trusted.

*   *   *

The men, the bovines and Calandra arrived by the midday meal the next day. Tired, dirty and hungry, they frumped a bit at the lady's command to clean up at the falls before the snow descended but went anyway. No one was yet in the mood to heat water for the community tub and anyway, they knew this would be the last swim before snow.

So they built a fire, uncorked a cask and relaxed as men do. Torrin noted that Bartoly talked very fast and quite a lot for a while and then seemed to doze off with no warning. In fact he was in the middle of a sentence and then for no reason whatsoever went limp. Torrin just smiled and understood, because he too had been like this before. Where you work so hard, physically and mentally, and then your body just goes to sleep. It does not matter what you are doing; it just goes to sleep.

Back at Journey, Dessa sat talking with Rebecca, letting the stress of their adventure dissolve from her body. They talked of baby names. They talked of love. They talked of nature and how the future might be for them and their families.

And everyone felt a little better, a little less nervous and a little less rushed. Rebecca had slept from sundown to well after sun-up and was feeling refreshed with sleep, and from finally being clean.

All in all, they let out a collective breath.

That is, until Rebecca's water broke.

45.
Ending

The meal was not just good; it was, as Scraddius would explain later, "Something of a mix of great joy, beauty and art rolled into one experience that should last a lifetime." The venison that Peroxious had roasted cut like butter under a warm knife. The flavors of the wine were heady and added vigor to the meal. The vegetables and cheese that had baked to a golden hue crunched delightfully. Their strong essence was a celebration of the summer that had grown them.

And of course, there were very many chalices of good wine consumed with the meal. Then afterward, upon Scraddius' request, one special jug was brought up from the back of the cellar. A sweet wine pressed from the special grapes that endured a frost. It was as we know today, a dessert wine. Flavorful, sweet and just a little sticky, it was a perfect way to finish off a heavy meal that bordered on art. Perfect that is, especially before the evening's entertainment began.

Scraddius had indulged just to his limit, as usual. He knew exactly how many chalices of the rich red wine he could consume during the meal and still keep enough hold of his senses to stay out of real trouble. He always allowed himself one more chalice after the dessert wine, and this one he would let last the entire evening.

The others though, were not as keen on staying within control of their senses. Peroxious had been sipping at the grape all afternoon as he cooked. Fortunately, he had the good sense to keep drinking water as he cooked in the warm kitchen, or Scraddius was sure the man would lose a finger or two from the sharp knives he carried with him to his cooking adventures.

Glenna, for all her intelligence, loved to enjoy the fruits of the grape, and she consumed, as usual, a copious amount. Scraddius always wondered how she did it, and it amused him to see her go from someone who enjoyed serious discussion to a woman deliciously in charge of nothing but satisfying some well lubricated desires. She was wholly desirous as needed at any time back at the castle without the fortification of more than a casual chalice or two, but out here, she really let loose.

And it was grand fun to be with a woman whose libido was as hot as the sun.

The new and somewhat mysterious addition to their little party, Leandra, was getting quite drunk after trying not to do so for the better part of the evening. Scraddius had been very kind to her and Glenna. He had uncharacteristically gotten up from his repose and refilled their chalices a number of times. Scraddius knew that when you got a person good and drunk and they felt safe, you could get any question answered – which he planned to do later as the evening festivities and jovialness wore on.

After dinner, Glenna, Leandra and Peroxious had planned a little skit of sorts. Scraddius was somewhat amused and curious since this was usually the venue for just Glenna and Peroxious. They would make up some story about him rescuing her from the edge of a cliff and of course, to get her down, her clothes would tear off. Layer after layer would be lost to the clutches of his strong hands as he pulled her to safety. Then, when she was saved and owed him her life, she would deliciously remove the rest of her garments and offer her body in thanks to her savior. Peroxious being the gentleman he was would never deny the gracious lady her need to say thank you. And as Scraddius watched, they would give him a show that he could never see in the public rooms at the castle.

Tonight however was different.

Tonight, Peroxious was caught under a heavy rock, his foot trapped and bleeding (a large chair was overturned on his foot and some of the wine added color to his leg as blood). The ladies were all aflutter to help him, but were distressed to find the strength to move the heavy rock. Magically his kisses and true love for their beauty reinforced their strength and they were able to move the heavy stone. Peroxious was thankful beyond life and offered them anything within his power to them.

The ladies explained that a witch had taken from them their desires. This left them without needs for men or romance and they were now barren for many winters. Alas, this left their hearts broken and cold. They longed to be flush with feeling and cravings for what men offered. They missed satisfying the heady intense intimacy they had experienced with the field men before the witch. They missed the satisfaction of wanton lust that filled the cold nights with the twisted heat of satisfied desires. Their ears missed the moans of happiness that brought joy and pleasure to their otherwise miserable world.

Peroxious promised to conjure a spell that would remove the shackles the witch had laid upon them. With great fanfare he began to chant and mix his potions.

Into an urn went the various elements of passion and lust as were needed to conquer the spell. His laments were strong and ferocious to return these beautiful women to their rightful place as lovers and heartbreakers.

First cloves to stimulate the senses and reawaken dead feelings of lust and intimate cravings. Their twang exploded into the room as Peroxious pounded a portion of the pungent spice in his pestle and mortar (which he just happened to have with him – Scraddius loved theater!).

Next came dried orange blossom flowers; these precious petals were carried from afar to the kingdom by brave and now rich tradesmen. The sweet aromas of their power lay in the true love of the honey bee that pollinated the flower to give life to the fruit. It was like the man to a woman, but in a pure way. This he told them was his adding a layer of love and embrace to the potion.

By now these barren women were beginning to feel a heat that had escaped them for many a winter. And of course, their clothes were beginning to be discarded to enable the heat from their body to vent into the world.

The orange blossoms were followed by thinly slivered shards of dried bark of the elm tree. Made famous eons before by the forest elves, this exotic ingredient attracted men to serve the needs of the soon to be very needy women.

A four-leaf clover was rolled between his hands and added to the mix. This was to provide luck to their hearts so they would find not only passion but true love to end their terrible drought.

And finally the torn and shredded leaves of the peppermint plant. The scent attracted the nose of men without fail and the oil provides the soul the lubricant it needed to begin sliding to the lust it craved.

All this was added to a mix of honey and water, stirred slowly over a candle. Then to work, the potion had to be applied. Applied to the body of the woman in need, and in just the right ways. Peroxious was grinning from ear to ear as he played the part of love sorcerer.

He commanded the loveless lasses to disrobe and prepare to be healed. And he then proceeded to create an incredibly sticky mess upon two lovely bodies. And of course, the women were not just healed, they were cured of their misbegotten lack of lust. And Peroxious was the first man they saw and demanded he satiate them.

Being of a mind to serve whenever possible, Peroxious obliged in all the ways he could perceive. Scraddius noted that even though her demeanor prior to dinner was somewhat gentle and tame, Leandra had turned into a tigress and seemed to command their little troupe of actors. This was where her strong arms played a role. She not only commanded the others, but moved them to the positions that seemed to interest her.

And of course, with all the wine and play and then the body painting, they all got the giggles. And as the fun escalated, Peroxious himself was now naked and being painted by his new friends.

Scraddius roared with glee at the little impromptu play. He loved the mess, he loved the interaction, he loved the nudity and the passion. But most of all, he loved the fact that this was all for his enjoyment and he did not have to share it with the idiot at the castle.

Presently, the three were all laughed out and covered with a sticky mess. Scraddius sent them to the outside to clean off. He sat back in his chair and closed his eyes, letting the sweet sounds of the laughter slowly dissolve the stress in his mind. He relived the meal and the tastes that had entertained him before this foolish playfulness. He just sighed and let the relaxation that he knew he needed come to his body and flow through him like sunshine through the water.

Soon, two slightly damp and slightly drunk naked woman were on either side of him, paying attention to all his body parts. He opened his eyes, held out his hand and accepted the wine chalice that appeared in it. He just watched and said nothing as the two women methodically pushed and pulled and worked to get him rid of his clothes.

Peroxious continued to be perfect. He piled a goodly amount of large logs on the fire before retiring to finish his work in the kitchen. Scraddius knew that Glenna enjoyed a hot fire in so many ways. She loved just watching the flicker of the flames as well as the fact that she could keep her feet warm. She had told him once that as a child, her feet were always cold, and she really liked to keep them warm.

In the kitchen Peroxious was cleaning up. His duty outside the kitchen was complete and he would leave at first light. Scraddius could hear him whistling.

If he was to be honest, having both the women there was certainly different and he would not deny that it was fun. And then after a time Scraddius told Glenna to tie Leandra to the top of the big table. Truss her hands and feet, secure and stable.

Glenna took her time making Leandra fast to the table. She wound the soft sisal that was usually meant for playing games around each wrist a number of times so it formed a wide secure cover. Each wrist was secured to table legs opposite of each wrist. Glenna pushed Lenadra's head forward so that the lady bent at the waist and her head rested on her elbows where they crossed in front of her.

Arms unmoving and secure.

Each ankle received the same winding treatment as each wrist. Her ankles were made fast to corner legs.

Scraddius looked at the strong, muscular woman tied fast and helpless to the table in his lodge. She seemed unstressed, but not at all comfortable. Her muscles and parts moved and relocated as she tried to make herself comfortable.

He enjoyed watching her. Helpless and under his control.

Presently he told Glenna to bring him his favorite knife.

46.
For...

The midwife, Kneafsey was in her element. The alternating patterns of noise and stillness, joy and pain were all part of the rhythm of life for her. The beginnings of yet another saga of sweat, blood, and too often it seemed, the largest and hardest heartache ever.

She had seen on some sad occasions, and just once was all too many times; a young woman, with her first. Full of promise and life and dreams and hope. Full of the marvel of it all. Just full. And far too often all that hope that she carried, or often herself, ended up wrapped in a bloody blanket and buried in the woods.

It was a hard thing, this birthing. But for every one that died a screaming wretched death of burning pain, there were more babes that came quietly. The lucky mothers, where a few hard pushes popped that shoulder out and in a just the space of a handful of heartbeats, a babe was filling the room with joy for all its worth. And the smiles in the room would light up even the darkest of those frozen black winter nights. Of course the cryin would start, but it was most because the little one was not as warm as before or was feelin the first pangs of hunger. And that was an event, gettn the milk flown. But just now was the birthn time!

You never knew. You could never tell. She long ago had given up predicting. She was too often wrong and so often surprised. She lately had been so often sad with this line of work. It seemed that a dark evil had inhabited the land. Just too many gone. Women gone for good in their brightest moment. Babes with the promise of life's adventures cut short.

But no one would know of these fears that clutched Kneafsey's heart. They couldn't. They shouldn't. It would bring terror to the lasses. It would befuddle the men. So she arrived in the room with her regular big smile and took both command and control. Because it was the right thing to do, and having control now would make it all easier. Easier to keep order when that moment came when all the control was really in the hands of something larger than all of them.

Kneafsey firmly believed in a greater power. She had seen too much goodness and too many miracles occur to think that all this was just a random natural business. This business of having babies. Kneafsey had no idea or pretense about this higher power. Nor did she bow down to it. But she did respect it and she let it have its way. She had concluded a long time ago, that her job was to assist. Not make the laws.

And she had also decided that part of assisting was keeping all the onlookers busy. If for nothing, to keep them from just standing there gawking at the birthing process.

"Youha," she said to a young lass with long mousy brown hair. "Make sure there is plenty of clean water on to boil." The lass fairly bolted for the kitchen, never wanting to be the point of Kneafsey's wrath.

"Youha there," she pointed to an older woman with thinning blond hair, punctuated by a bright smile. "Make sure the swaddlings are clean and ready for a new one." And the woman shuffled off to fulfill the demand.

"And youha," she said to a middle aged mother whom she had known from both ends of this business many a time, "Fetch the spirits. It's almost time to put some atmosphere on this lass, now go." And off this mother went with a smile. She knew all too well the importance of a good few mouthfuls of spirits before the heavy lifting began. And she also knew that everyone in the room would be able to share in the joy of it all. It was a tradition here!

"Youha," she said sternly, with complete compassion, to an

eager, yet scared teenager, "fetch some drinking water and a mug of hot tea for myself. Now go, we haven't much longer to wait from what I can see, and I am thirsty."

And then she turned her attention to Rebecca. Finally with everyone duly charged, she could now concentrate on the woman of the moment. She sat next to the bed and looked Rebecca strongly in the face and asked, "How are you really feeling, and describe what all your parts are up to?" It was a no nonsense kind of question that needed a true response, not one that was shallow and every day.

Rebecca's eyes widened as a contraction coursed through her lower limbs and back. When it subsided, she began with, "Pretty much as I expected, based on what I have seen. It's not too bad. But..."

"But?"

"I am scared," and Rebecca began to cry.

A large calloused hand found her cheek and pressed in, taking over for the fear and taking over for her thoughts. Rebecca's eyes met the midwife's eyes and she heard, "My name is Kneafsey; it means to merge the new with the old. And here we are."

Rebecca closed her eyes, taking a deep breath, and for a moment lost herself in the thoughts of the ages. For all of time, women have been doing what she was about to do, including many of those in the room or attending to her needs. Suddenly she relaxed, knowing that there was not one blessed thing she could do about dying. But she could do her best at birthing and be like those around her. So she opened her eyes; lay them upon Kneafsey and said, "My family is in your care."

"Good, now tell me how all your parts feel."

"Hot, then cold. The pains feel like someone is twisting my insides the way you would wring a towel dry. My back hurts, my feet get numb and I am thirsty."

"Humph," said Kneafsey. "Get up, stretch yourself and wring out the kinks in your muscles. Drink some water and take care of yourself. I do proclaim, sometimes women in childbirth lose all sense of common sense. If ye are stiff, stretch; if you are thirsty, drink. It's not like anything has really changed. Just prop yerself right when those damned contractions sneak up on you."

As Rebecca moved about the room, feeling better almost instantly; then a contraction almost doubled her over.

"Breathe," said Kneafsey... "Deep hard breaths lass; they wash out the pain."

And Rebecca breathed hard, and the pain subsided as the

contraction went the way of the other ones.

And so it went. The towels arrived. The water arrived. The tea arrived (of course with some baked treats) and Kneafsey shooed the food away, knowing that right now, food was not on the agreeable list and should not be around Rebecca.

And then the ceramic jug arrived. Dessa noted that it was the very good whiskey and they all shared a good solid swig, especially Rebecca.

After another contraction, Kneafsey carefully explored and felt about in Rebecca and proclaimed that it would still be a while. And with that, she curled up on a chair and fell asleep.

Dessa held Rebecca's hand, gave her sips of water and wiped her forehead with a cool cloth. She seemed to do what she could while worrying for her friend, and was at the same time, she decided, just a mite envious.

After a time, Kneafsey awoke and after some exploring, now proclaimed that things were progressing and it was almost time so everyone should pay attention and attend to their duties.

As was the custom, as the towels and water and such were brought back to the room that she asked Rebecca, "if the man who was responsible for all of this should be present with them." After much discussion it was decided that having a weeping, worthless and worried Bartoly here would be of no help.

And now after another contraction, this time one of great magnitude, Kneafsey checked again all the vital parts. This time, she moved slower, was more thorough, more intimate. She seemed to go everywhere twice. She paused to ponder, her eyes closed as she pushed and held onto certain areas.

And then, with a face that was not grim, nor of joy, Kneafsey looked up at Rebecca and said slowly, "I am so very sorry."

47.
Consistency

"My dear," said a very naked yet tired and satiated Scraddius to Leandra. "You should not have come here."

Glenna was aghast. She looked at Scraddius. She looked at Leandra bound to the table and then at the knife held firmly in his hand. She knew of his fierce temper. She knew of his almost oppressive need for privacy. Yet, she could not for all herself fathom that he would now murder this lady with whom he had just engaged in lustful enjoyment. His head was low between his shoulders giving him a hunched over menacing look. A sneer pulsed at the top of his upper lip and his eyes were black as wet mud on a rainy winter night that brought sleet and wet, bone chilling dampness to all.

No, this could not turn out well, and Glenna was at a loss of what to do or say.

Leandra lay still upon the table. Her pale skin was luminous with moisture. Glenna did not know if that moisture was from the frolicking of just moments before, or from the shiny steel threat that lay just within her sight.

Glenna knew not to beg or plead. It would be useless. Yet she knew she had to do something. She well knew that any fervent plea would be rebuked. Any playful request could mean death. Her mind raced for a solution and none was to be found.

The sharp tip of Scraddius' knife now toyed with the flesh just to the side of Leandra's soft breast. He seemed to be looking for a space between her ribs. Lenadra's eyes were closed and she was gnawing her lip, yet she also seemed calm and almost at peace.

Finally Glenna, coming to stand in front of him blurted, "It was not her, I asked her to come. She is not guilty. If you must rid your life of a threat, it is I."

He looked at Glenna's tearful face, grabbed her hair and pulled her head back harshly. She lay half across Leandra's moist body with the other half of her fighting for control to stay up. Scraddius then pressed his knee against her hand. This pinned her hand to the table. He then quickly sliced her arm from her elbow to the very middle of her wrist. Scraddius then walked away, growling and muttering.

48.
...Soothe

"What?" asked a suddenly now startled and very scared Rebecca. "What do you mean you are sorry?" It was almost a shriek. A plea. A demand. But most of all, it was a question about her baby. This dear sweet impending baby that she had carried now for all this time and... what!?!

"It is breach. He, or she, is feet first. I can try to roll it for you, or you can push all night. Yet it might kill you, and/or the baby."

Rebecca's wild eyes turned to Dessa and then to all the women in the room. She searched their faces for a good answer.

Any answer.

But for something.

Anything!

"What do I do?" Rebecca pleaded with Dessa.

Dessa had watched this before. Sometimes it worked, sometimes it did not. No one knew why. There were no good or safe answers. There was nothing she could suggest. Tears fell across her freckled cheeks as she looked at Rebecca and then to the stern-faced midwife. Finally Dessa said plainly to Rebecca, "Just trust her."

And with that a piercing contraction consumed Rebecca. Her legs were stretched hard and far with her toes almost pointed flat against the front of her legs.

"Do it?" asked Kneafsey.

Dessa looked sternly at the woman and closed her eyes. She had gotten used to the powers that she and Torrin enjoyed. The calling of animals, the foretelling of danger and the loss of the threat of death. She suddenly appreciated again her immortal status and wished things were different and then said to Kneafsey, "Do yer best."

"Move," said a now animated Kneafsey. She rolled Rebecca to her side and began to manipulate Rebecca's front.

One of the younger girls started to protest and Dessa held her tight. Soothing her fearful sprit telling her that this is what women must endure and that she should have faith.

Kneafsey kneaded and prodded and pushed and manipulated Rebecca like she was a child's rag doll toy. During contractions, she backed off like an animal ready to attack. And as soon as the contraction subsided, she was at it again.

Sweat poured from Kneafsey's body like rain. Rebecca, usually the strong and powerful woman in a group, was reduced to a panting mass of sweat and sobs.

Presently Kneafsey ended her manipulation and knelt down between Rebecca's legs. Panting, she watched all of Rebecca and then in a voice that could not be ignored, shouted, "Push now woman. Push now or forever we'll be here for both of ye. Push."

Rebecca pushed with a great yaw of sound that shook the rafters and filled the room with weary and sweat soaked spirit.

The room held its collective breath.

"Stop," said Kneafsey. "Ye wait until the next contraction takes ye, and then ye push again. It may take a few tries."

The women in the room seemed to breathe as one. Not one word was muttered. Not one sound was made. You could have heard a tuft of wool hit the ground.

"Now!" Kneafsey almost screamed the forceful command. However, Dessa would remember later, that the mid-wife never even really raised her voice. She just held purposeful and strong command of what was needed.

Dessa saw that something had possessed this woman. Never before had Journey held such a wonderful midwife. And Dessa wondered how long she would stay. They had made a good deal for the woman. She did as she pleased, yet was there for any birth. The folks at Journey agreed to it.

The arrangement just worked for everyone.

And as she could never have imagined, Rebecca gritted her teeth so hard her face contorted. She grabbed the plank she was lying on so hard that her fingers turned white and her arms shook from the stress and she pushed with all her might. She pushed past pain. She pushed past the devil and she pushed to something so much greater than herself.

"Stop," said a breathless Kneafsey. "Now, gently on the next contraction, just push it all out. Take it easy, this might work; oh please don't let it win this time."

And Rebecca pushed, but not so hard. Her teeth were grit tight, but not so tight. Her eyes were shut against the light of the lanterns in the room, and her will was powerful against the threat that lay at her feet. Her hands held the table in a grip that could crush rock, but not to the depth of before.

That is until she heard the first gasping cry of her baby. And the world righted itself for a time as she smiled through tears of pure joy as a warm tiny body was gently laid into her waiting arms.

49.
A Troubling View

About a few days before Rebecca gave birth, Scraddius was enjoying his last time at the lodge. He had actually been plodding around naked, enjoying the freedom of it all. He now lounged upon the big southern facing bench without really seeing anything. He just let the enormity of the view consume him. It was a chilly afternoon, just around the mid-day sun, and the well polished wood should have been cold against his naked skin. Yet, the southern sun had been warm and he luxuriated in the warmth still radiating from deep within the well-carpentered fixture of his favorite patio.

It all just is, he mused; it just is, and it is so big and calm and wonderful. The trees, the leaves, the grasses, the animals...

And then he saw them.

Two large stately steeds standing on the hill where the forest broke just a bit. Well maintained horses. Strong and powerful. Not anything that looked even just one bit wild, these were obviously well kept. One began grazing about, almost playful. The other was standing tall and looking out across the valley – looking stern.

What the devil would a horse look at, wondered Scraddius? He followed the gaze of the animal and found himself looking directly at the big brown castle. The contrast was dynamic. This tall honorable steed, at one with nature, calm and in charge, looking intently upon the most wretched, dirty and miserable place you could imagine?

Scraddius slowly stretched, not wanting to make any sudden moves so as to become apparent to the animals, or the yet to be seen riders. He sat quietly and waited. He was certain the riders of these steeds would appear. Maybe a scout for a raiding party? These wonderful horses were too good for traders. War horses? Hmmmm?

And then a brown face appeared next to the bigger of the horses. This face was one that was completely in charge, very alpha, but was certainly out of place. A very large, muscular and tall cougar? Scraddius had hunted them before. They never were much taller than his knees. This one would have come up to his abdomen.

The cougar stepped forward, looked at the castle one last time, turned to the horse like they were talking, and then gracefully swung his large powerful body around. In a moment, he was gone. Scraddius would have sworn he saw a brown flash of blur through the trees a few moments later.

All wrong! Cougars ate horses.

After a short while, the large horse turned around and Scraddius could see the tails of both swishing at the flies and that was all, just two seemingly content horse butts. And then, just after a cloud rippled the sunshine over the crest of the hill, he heard them go. He had never heard a pair of horses break the stillness of the forest so completely before. The beating of their hooves was enormously fast and loud.

It was almost a thunder.

And then as quickly as the sound had started, it was gone. And the complex backwardness of it all struck him as almost amusing. Animals did not look at things with intent unless it was food. And animals that ate others did not spend idle time together as if having tea.

This made not one lick of sense. He was going to have to figure it out.

Presently, the birds and talkative animals chimed back in with their chippering and twerping, filling the forest with normal sounds. He thought it interesting that nature could come back to center so fast. Just so fast and without thought. Nature just is, he again mused. It just is, and does its job so very well.

Scraddius shook his head. Almost deciding that he had not seen what he had seen. And of course it was all wrong. Cougars eat horses whenever possible. Horses tend to avoid cougars because of the dinner thing and so they most often were not to be animals that you ever saw together. Yet, he just saw a pair of wonderful steeds with the biggest cougar imaginable. And they were obviously here with a purpose.

None of it made any sense and it was causing Scraddius' head to hurt. He uncoiled from the now overly cool wooden bench and padded into the cabin. He found Leandra tending to Glenna's arm and hand. He just glowered at the two and shrugged on his clothes.

Glenna seemed wrapped nicely and none the worse for her ordeal (and maybe a little smarter – he hoped). So he said to her, "You come with me. People are used to seeing us walk back together." To Leandra he said, "Go back a different way, use a different gate and come in close to dark. I don't care what lie you have to tell but just don't tell anyone you were with us. If you do, I shall hang you alive with the bodies on the wall to squelch thoughts by anyone that you are in my favor or that my favor is available."

Leandra nodded a complete and through "yes." Too afraid and confused to say anything that might have resembled words.

As Scraddius and Glenna walked out, he turned to Leandra and said, "Close things up, put out the lantern and never come near me." But with an afterthought added, "Unless of course I summon you."

As Scraddius and Glenna walked the trail back toward the castle, his mind was working hard. Horses? Cougars?

And then he stopped. He turned his face toward the hill, not really expecting to see anything, but needing to look. And then after a moment, the thought was clear to him.

Yes! He had seen that cougar before! That was the one who had come back with the body of Chadus on the horse. He could never forget that animal. Huge. Thick yellow fur. Long sharp yellowish curved fangs. Long legs made for running fast.

After a moment of pondering, he returned to hiking back toward the castle. Consumed in the thought that something was amiss and did not seem right.

Not right at all, because he did not like variables that he could not control.

50.
Dubisary

He was almost on it, he could feel as much as hear the heavy fast terrified gasping of air. The smell of defeat and fear filled the air as the big elk churned through the thick meadow at full gallop. Every time he leapt up and snapped at the neck he could taste the savory saltiness of the heated flesh. His stomach glowered in anticipation of this soon to be, oh so grand feast. It was only a matter of time and his own patience now before the great animal tired and became easy prey. This was how it worked, when they tired they eventually would fall and then all was finished. All was right and all in his family would eat their fill.

But for so long now he had had to keep running at full stride. Always on a clean and terribly fast path that provided no obstacle that would trip the beast up and send him to his doom. The massive elk body drove along at high speed over a clear trail through the meadow and just seemed to keep going; it was wrong. Now after all seemed so right, it was going wrong. Breathing hard but not slowing, Praritor wondered how long this would keep up. He began to wonder how long he could keep up. It was out of character for an elk to stay at full gallop for such a great distance. He reached up again and snapped at the bobbing heaving neck. His teeth just grazed the tender flesh beneath the thick coat and then he felt the rain.

But the sun was out. It was the perfect day? Then he felt it again. Rain on his nose and he was befuddled and now wondered what was going on. The rain now tickled and the elk looked at him with small close set dark blue beady eyes and smiled.

Smiled?

Yes, smiled. And then the beastly thing, all hundreds of pounds of him, all sweaty and smelling of fresh meat and stale sweat took flight and left the ground. His magic making Praritor's menacing jaws useless and flapping like dead dry leaves of autumn on the breeze that ushers in the cold nuisance of winter.

And then of course the best thing of all happened and he ran headfirst like a stupid goat into a large tree. He lay there, embarrassed and waiting for the pain to begin. Slowly, he opened his eyes expecting to see the other hunters laughing at him, but was confused to see three small excited pairs of blue eyes staring intently at him. The faces that held the eyes were muted and in control through training, yet they were very full of vigor and energy.

Praritor shook his large gray head, closed his eyes tight and opened them again. The six eyes were attached to three cubs who were sitting up straight and tall, fully at attention and sorely in need of his attention.

It took a moment and Praritor realized he had been dreaming again. The trip back from meeting Dessa had about worn him out. Getting to her had been easy for he had been just the other side of her mountain.

For the trip home though, he had only stopped for water and run straight through. But now he had slept for who knows how long. And he had slept hard. The stiffness of his body told him he loved it, because he was rested and ready to go.

It all made sense now. One of the three in front of him had been licking his nose, trying to get dad's attention and not get in trouble.

Praritor looked across the den to Hexly, his mate. She was laying against the wall, comfortable and smiling. Her long gray nose slender and moist at the end. Her eyes were relaxed, if not a little tired. He surmised that she had either had enough of taking care of the cubs or had decided he had slept long enough and given the OK to wake him. Whatever the reason, he was fine with it because he was rested, he was at home and he was where he belonged.

With all the masterly father figure he could muster, he slowly turned his alpha wolf gaze back to the attention of the brood in front of him. He rose elegantly to his feet and stretched every muscle in his body. There was some popping and cracking as he stretched. Just as his father said there would be in the later years.

As much as he could, and enjoying it all, he was waking up in a luxurious fashion and watching the pups very cautiously. He watched to see who would break rank first.

His goal was that one of these would be an alpha like him. He was growing older and needed to unleash the strength and might of a new alpha in the woods. For over thirty years now, he and Hexly had put over one hundred eighty cubs into the woods. Most all of them good, none of them the alpha that the woods needed. None was an alpha that would rule and keep the peace. He needed strength and cunning to deal with the likes of Ahriman who would try to ruin the party.

Nobody moved. Tanna, the only galla in the litter stood just a little straighter and taller than all the others. She so wanted to be number one. And for now she was. She was faster, smarter and more cunning than the other two combined. But she was a galla and the forest would not accept her as an alpha. She would do good things and carry good pups, but she could never be an alpha. And that was just the way it was.

Brice was the studious one. Always right, always perfect. Always needing one extra lick of encouragement and a nibble on the ear. A good boy thought Praritor. But not one who will lead. He will follow well, you will always be able to count on him, but he will never lead.

And then Faelan. He sat with his paws askance because he could not be bothered to stand fully at attention. His eyes were fixed straight ahead, until he thought Praritor was not looking. Then Faelan's fast, curious little mind was drinking in all that was around him. He was a rebel. He was not a rule follower. And he had big feet. Faelan had promise. Just not right now; he needed to grow, to run, to explore and learn. And just right now, he had a little foreign dubisary hanging from his nose. Obviously the result of snooping somewhere interesting. If Praritor could harness this curiosity, this growing cunningness, he might build an alpha worthy of the woods around them.

One last glance at the brood told Praritor all he needed to know. On the front, the pups were all at attention and in order. But they had telltale twitches at the end of their tails as they envisioned the fun that lay ahead with the routine romp dad usually offered upon return home. They almost bubbled over with excitement, and keeping it contained was hard for them.

One last look at Hexly and he knew that the time for his rest was over. She yawned and tilted her head toward the low stone hallway that led to the great outdoors.

Praritor led them out, but only after feigning a large growl and attacking all three at once. They rolled about in the den, raising a full cloud of dust and dirt. The whole yipping gray and black mass was playfully gnashing at anything they could find (at one point Praritor had Brice chasing his own tail).

All this lasted until Hexly gave a sharp motherly bark. The four of them hastily left the den. She was tired and needed some peace.

Down the stone hallway they went, a great gray mass of yipping and barking. They seemed to explode from the doorway of the den and went racing for the logs. And most any living creature within earshot ran smartly far away to let the brood play undisturbed. Most all creatures knew that they would be fair game to this playful but dangerous team.

Tanna led the way sprinting over the tops of the logs in the blowdown like a dragonfly touching the water. She headed straight for the pond. She both wanted water and something even better. She knew if she was the first to arrive she might get to chase some animal that had not been paying attention to the noise.

Brice and Faelan ran everywhere and nowhere all at once. First chasing and then being chased. They yipped and snarled (as well as pups can snarl; it sounded more like cats grousing than anything), rolled and tousled their way to the pond. Arriving to the big wet grins of both Praritor and Tanna.

Praritor got them both to take a big drink, for you never knew when the pond would dry up. And then Faelan froze. His eyes glued to a large black mass that the others could not see yet. And so he crouched low. The others followed instinctively, as a team. As they had been taught over and over.

Presently they saw it. Large, dark and foreboding.

Tanna went left, Brice went right, just as they had practiced time and again. Faelan stayed his course, straight on, drawing the attention of the enemy while the others pursued the flanking maneuver. As his siblings made distance and came around in support, Faelan stood taller, letting the enemy know that he was there and he was in charge.

He let a few more moments pass, letting his flank attackers set up good positions and then with as much of a menacing bark as he could muster he sprang to the now hapless victim.

From both sides came death, silent and fast, with no warning or sound. The three of them collided as one upon their target and ripped the large dark pile of leaves apart. The leaves never had a chance.

After a while of more yipping and snapping and playing, Praritor sauntered over and called for attention. Instantly, the line was formed and they discussed the attack in great detail. Again, learning from the master and learning that no matter how fast or strong you are, you need your flank if you are to win, eat or survive in the forest. Because the forest never forgave a mistake.

Not once.

Never.

And learning how to work together hunting a pile of leaves, although great sport, was just as everything in life. A time to learn how to work together.

It was just before dark, that time of restful twilight before the brood of four made their way through the doorway. They had played, learned, hunted and feasted. And now were off to a good night's sleep. Tired, happy and just a little wiser.

Except for Faelan.

Praritor noticed that when they returned to the warm safety of the den, Faelan was not there. Praritor returned to the entrance and then just stood there, looking for the mischievous devil boy.

Soon, in the gathering twilight two eyes glowed for a brief moment from the reflection of the setting sun. The wayward boy was sitting near the pile of leaves they had attacked as a team. He was perched on a large rock.

Praritor ambled over to where the young wolf thoughtfully sat on his haunches. Faelan's ears were back, and Praritor could tell he was deep in thought. Something Praritor had never before experienced with Faelan.

"Thoughts?" inquired Praritor.

After a time, the not yet full bodied voice of his boy said, "I attacked too fast and did not give Tanna and Brice time to better get into position. I was too hasty."

"And what of it?" asked Praritor, wondering where this was going. He had never before had a thoughtful conversation with the boy.

"If this had been real prey, it could have escaped to the rear. Tanna and Brice had come in too sharply from the front flanks," answered the still thoughtful young wolf.

Praritor nodded a yes before agreeing in his slow, full baritone voice, that was both at once mighty and reassuring. "Yes, you need to work on the threat part of the attack. When I move in too fast, my partners have not had a chance to position themselves for victory."

Faelan looked up at his father and said, "I'm sorry."

"Son, this is why we practice as a team," said Praritor giving the cub's ear a fatherly caress.

The two of them retreated now towards the warm, dry safety of the den hidden in the stones of the hill.

A son trotting along having learned a lesson and a father walking a little taller for it.

51.
Repeat?

Presently then, as the promise of winter is always true, the cold wrath of winter arrived. And as always to the valley of the Journey Inn, it came with a vengeance and lashing that reminded everyone why they cut so much wood, packed away so much food and learned to share so much song for the long dark days ahead.

All the day angry black clouds had formed upon the northern horizon. Immensely dark, tall and menacing. They built up tall and mighty like a fortress of cold against all humanity. They waited to unleash their fury that had all summer long been held at bay. And they lashed out with all the force they could muster from the pent up heat of summer and moisture of the autumn.

And so, as was the winter custom around the sturdy logs of the Journey Inn, the winds howled for days and nights. The angry dark northern snow clouds, very organized and vicious dumped layer after layer of cold crisp snow in fast succession upon the land. All hunting had been canceled. For good reason. All the animals were either frozen dead or buried warmly in the many natural escapes that these great northern woods provided.

The only trail in existence for now was the one to the privy. Covered fresh each night by the storms that continued on in succession, one after one, it was well worn by the time the day was fully light (well, as fully light as the days would get this time of year). One part of the trail went directly to the door; the other part branched off and circled behind. This trail was the one the men and boys used most often. And boys being boys (and yes all men are to an extent boys when it comes to peeing in the snow), there was a variety of snow art on the ground each day.

Of course then, as fast as the heavy snow had come, it abated. The wind still howled. The trees stood in silent defiance to the continuing onslaught, waiting in steadfast patience as they always did for spring, warmth and the life enabling light and sunshine. When the snow did stop coming down it swirled in great mosaics of crystalline art that formed large mounds of resistance against walls, tree trunks and anything immovable.

Inside Journey all the small, medium and large voids that naturally appeared between the logs that let in the icy wind had become a menace to all inside. These gaps had missed the chinking work of summer and were quickly filled with warm mud from the pot at the great fireplace. It took the better part of one morning for all the nasty frozen gaps to get filled. And once completed, it made a huge difference to the comfort of the great room!

Kitchen help was plentiful since the kitchen was the warmest place in the Inn (other than Normadia's tidy bedroom and the community bathing room when in use) and there was always a tasty extra morsel or two for anyone helping out in the kitchen. This was the time of the season that was most favored by the kitchen regulars. And they played their jokes upon the new helpers (such as "please taste this salt to see if it's salty") or not teaching someone to oil their hands before kneading dough.

After just a couple of nights Torrin announced that it was time for a dance. This was different than the first snow party. This was more of a regular thing since they were now in a form of hibernation. It would take place the following evening, to enliven the crowd and let them focus on how much fun they could have and not worry about the weather. Instantly the great room was alive with planning and anticipation since this was about all they could focus on, except for the rude living quarters they shared.

And the evening, as they all worked, wore on. The well prepared dinner was over with everyone having consumed what they needed. The great fireplace was blazing with big logs from the great wood room. It was a good thick fire that generated hot coals. Hot coals that would fill the heavy iron pots to place around the room helping to keep the heat even.

Serious discussions of party planning had droned on most of the night. Debates about the music and theme ideas were punctuated with belly shaking guffaws as fresh innovation and creativity were supported by the newly opened cask of scotches that was happily consumed.

Outside, the brief interlude of the winter weather was laid waste to another blow. Heavy snow pounded down, harsh wind whipped about and it was winter again as usual. An icy unforgiving environment.

Torrin and Dessa were engrossed in a long and large Tafl game with Normadia and Quillan (like four sided chess with a lesser army in the middle of the board, the goal is to capture the other person's king before your king loses its head). They had been at it for three days with no clear victor in sight. The situation had gotten to the point where, for each person's turn, there was muttering and walking around the table for a long while, trying to figure out the best move. The serious strategies were good exercise for the mind according to the old ladies. According to the boys, the serious strategies were good thinking for battle. To the girls, it was just fun (except for Dessa; you could see her watching how people played. She wanted to know who could think and who could not).

At this moment, Normadia had run her hand across the lower extremities of Quillan's tiadhan and he was completely not paying attention any longer to the game. This due to the fact that all the blood in his brain had left for his lower extremities. She liked being a distraction to him.

Torrin had started to playfully pinch the inside of Dessa's thigh, hinting at some ideas of warmth generation upstairs. He did not know why he was doing this; it just seemed like the right thing to do.

It was evident that the close quarters and blowing wind, combined with the warmth of the room was having a general effect on everyone. A few couples had already retired to the upstairs rooms and a few were also already bedded down on top of tables along the back wall just enjoying each other's proximity.

Rebecca and Bartoly were at the next table still cooing and fetching over little MacGowan. Bartoly was already talking about what a grand smithy the boy would surely make, and the other men had heard about enough. They were beginning to plot a snow planting to get the man's head back in order (this would be planting Bartoly head first in the snow). They had to explain to Bartoly that this was not the first or last baby to be born upon the world and he needed to get a grip on himself. This made everyone smile, since no one believed he would settle down for a long while, nor did they expect it.

A few women in one corner had become quite engrossed in making the snow snogs of Quillan's invention. These had proven quite the treat when walking on the snow. There was a heavy pent up demand for them. The sewing was tough and kept fingers nimble. This provided a perfect venue for a circle of chairs and good gossip.

The Journey Inn had, as it always had done, begun to settle down for the winter. It was a time for relaxing, creating and togetherness.

And then as if possessed, the great door to the outside swung open halfway and a tall, ice encrusted stranger fell through the narrow opening, followed by swirling crystals of icy white cold.

52.
Discovery

The residents of Journey picked up the frozen traveler and deposited the mostly ice covered body to a table near the door of the woodshed. Here is was not too warm, nor too cold. Experience had taught these folks that you had to thaw out a frozen traveler verra, verra slowly. Too fast and they seemed to go into a traumatic fit and their heart always seemed to stop.

This frozen traveler's hood had been wrapped in fur tight to his face to try and protect it from the cold and keep heat in. And of course his breath had now frozen all this and untying it was impossible. His coat was like a solid slab of ice and the ties were just a mass of frozen tails all stuck together in unusable disarray.

Torrin thought the dichotomy interesting. He had been caught by a fiery dragon, this one by the ice. Journey was a nice place, but somehow, there were threats that were just all around nasty.

Quillan had the presence of mind to go out onto the big porch at the front of Journey to make sure there was no one else about and found not a soul. But he did find a pack of substantial proportions that he figured belonged to this frozen victim of winter travel. This he carefully set upon a stool against the wall where it would slowly thaw and the water from the ice would drip away, hopefully not soaking the goods found in the interior.

Normadia emerged from the kitchen with two pots of warm water. She and two other young women, who had done this before, slowly poured water over the ties of the coat so it could be removed. By now the fur around the head was loosening and Torrin was able to make headway in removing what was still pretty much a solid ice helmet.

Once part of the face was exposed they had Kneafsey check to see if the frozen stranger was even still breathing. And she pronounced that cool shallow breaths were coming from the dry chapped lips and so they should continue. "But wi the utmost delicacy," said Kneafsey. "He seems verra, verra cold indeed."

Once the coat was open, Quillan brought over his big bear sleeping bag that he had been warming by the fire and they laid the warm monster over the prone body on the table. Lukewarm tea emerged from the kitchen, and after some time and gentle coaxing, wet thankful sips began to be accepted through those cold chapped lips.

As is the case in these events, suddenly all the ice and snow began to melt and slough off at once. Now the residents of Journey removed layer after layer of cold sticky wet clothing. Slushy balls of cold snow and ice littered the floor. Someone had ready a large, well warmed muslin nightshirt to wrap the ice traveler in to keep the warming going once they got him undressed.

The stranger had dressed in all sorts of odds and ends trying to cover and fend from the cold. Many small wraps emerged and were discarded to the floor until finally just a long brown shirt stood between them and this stranger.

Kneafsey stood tall and exclaimed, "That's no shirt, that's a dress."

And with that, the soft voice of a woman sputtered quietly, "Did I die and are you all angels?"

Quillan looked at Torrin and said, "This should be interestin."

53.
Something New

And so a new member was brought into the Journey Inn's fold for what would prove to be an intense and more than normal brutal winter. Her name was Ipi (pronounced Ip-ee). Her story was that she had been traveling south toward Kalmar to take a ship to warmer climates when she was sidetracked in a town teaching the ladies how to brew teas that would settle stomachs and perform other amazing feats of healing. She admitted with a sigh that as was not uncommon for her; she just lost track of time. Ipi confided proudly that she was a teacher of sorts. Not in any one thing, but of many things. Mostly anything interesting; which in her opinion, was just about anything that affected the spirit of anyone or assisted in them living a gentler life.

When Ipi would begin to talk, instantly, a crowd gathered around her. Hungry minds wanting to know what she knew. There was amongst these hearty souls of the valley a thirst for understanding and knowing. And, because you see, it was not so much just the words she used. It was also the variety of curiosities that emerged from the big pack she had almost lost to the weather outside. And Ipi seemed to like to share the mysteries of her curiosities.

Not the least of which was a small scroll of vellum on which bore small and very confusing lines that Ipi called written words. Also contained in its dark recesses were objects such as a magnifying glass. Small bits of metal with pictures on them called coins. Some writing ink in a glass bottle and a small abacus. And oh so many more very interesting curiosities. Unwrapping a thin oilcloth produced a gleaming pair of the sharpest scissors anyone had ever seen.

Such grand ideas as writing and counting were completely new. Well yes, counting had been going on, but not beyond the number of fingers most people had. The whole idea of math was foreign.

And writing? Never before had they seen the written word. As you can imagine, the mystery of this topic was very new, very confusing and somewhat odd. And thus, the people of Journey would not be wanting of things to keep their minds occupied for the winter.

Nature had produced Ipi for them, and they seemed ready for her.

* * *

Ipi's recovery from the cold seemed to be accomplished in record fashion. She commended her speedy recovery to the many layers she had attached to herself. Layers she said she kept adding as she trudged through the snow. She had gotten to the point in the storm that she really was not sure what would happen, except she knew that if she stopped, it would be the last time she did so. She hardly remembered finding Journey, only that the big building was instantly a blessing.

Torrin knew instantly how that felt!

"Anyway, that's an old story, let's build some new stories," Ipi said gaily as she deftly unrolled a good sized oilcloth that was surrounding a long length of canvas. The canvas rolled out onto a table and it was almost as long as a tall man. Sewn into its entire length were pockets of all sizes and shapes. These were sewn from all sorts of materials of varying sizes and origin. Some of these pockets had objects sticking out, some had rolls of material in them. No two the same. No real order to it. Just a lot of it.

"Oh yes," squealed Ipi in obvious delight. "I am so glad they stayed dry. It would have been a shame to start over."

"Whach ye got ther?" asked Quillan from his perch upon the bench, one leg, as usual up on something higher. He was intrigued but wary.

"Why Quillan, you big red silly, these are my herbals," Ipi said, still with obvious glee and delight. "Here, give your nose a bit of delight with this!" And she deftly rolled some damp leaves between her forefinger and thumb, wiped her fingers on her wrist and then held out her exposed arm for him to explore.

Quillan leaned forward and scowled once, and then smiled. He had smelled the gentle fragrance of the flowers before that had been pressed into the soaps they used. But never anything the likes of this. This was powerful. This left a lasting scent. This was clean and clear and seemed to cleanse the very inside of his face when he breathed it in.

It was the first time he had smelled peppermint and was the first time he had ever smelled anything so wonderful on a woman. He sat back, wondering if he could convince Normadia later on to apply some to various and sundry parts of herself. Or maybe he could apply them?

But more importantly, Ipi had won him over. She had piqued his curiosity and shown him that these new explorations could be fun.

And so that night, she went on, explaining the various mysteries of her herbal cache. The burdock roots made a wonderful tea to help digestion. Nettle plants could be used to heal a cut or sore. Mistletoe to reduce the pain of consumption. Boiled dandelion tea to toughen up a body when it turns a little yellow and needs help to get the urine flowing again. And willow bark; which when chewed, reduced the soreness of muscles and other aches.

"So ifn you don' mind me askn ye," inquired Quillan. "How

many winters do ye think it would take someone to understand all this and the mixn options ye have to be good with it all?"

Ipi said in her excited voice, hoping she had a willing pupil, "It depends on the person really. I have had some folk that just never understand the nuances of the art. And some who take to the herbs like gray to my hair." She put one long hand on a hip and said to him, "You just never know."

*   *   *

It also came to pass that the kitchen and root cellar of Journey was one very well stocked herbal store with many of the items Ipi carried or knew about. The little troupe had been harvesting and drying many herbs for many summers. Some they had used, some they thought they might use. And some, well they just got lucky.

So not wanting for fresh supplies to learn from, the residents of Journey began to experiment with a powerful variety of herbal concoctions as they had never done so before. The adventure of learning useful things during the long cold winter seemed to invigorate them all.

Ipi was in her element and for the folks of Journey, she had so much to offer.

54.
Welcome

As Dessa wiped the back of her hand across her mouth she could feel the slight tingle of the willow bark juice seeping from the corners of her lips on her skin.

Ipi was just brilliant.

Chewing on the willow bark from spring's new shoots took the edge off muscle pain, especially when she had overdone it. And she had definitely overdone it again. They had all overdone it. But when you have purpose, overdoing it is easy. You put in the enormous effort without thinking. Without effort at the time, the next day all your muscles tell you differently.

This part of the trail was dry. That was different. Very different and she was thankful for the southern exposure of the hill. They had been slogging through cold mud for the better part of two days now. They expected to reach Gaerwn's castle today and begin to put their plan into action.

The four of them had all enjoyed the relief the willow bark delivered. Dessa, Torrin, Quillan and Etworth had embarked on a hard ride. The wet ground and periodic piles of snow had made travel tricky. But none were strangers to a long ride that commanded attention and perseverance.

Dessa held up her gloved hand and counted one and then two days on the trail. Counting gave meaning to "this many fingers" and now just saying two days instead of "this many" made everything completely different. There was context to the thought. There were other concepts to bring to bear. You could add another number to it. Take one away. Compare it to something else, to another trip. To someone's thoughts. She had lain awake at night, just absorbing how different it all was.

So very different.

These thoughts and other teachings from Ipi during the winter had kept her occupied the entire way here. Why, just the memory of the whole event when they had tried the willow bark for the very first time was vivid and telling.

Ipi had extracted a number of small willow branches from her mysterious cache of curiosities. These, she explained, had been cut just two months before (yes, they had days of the week now and a calendar to follow) while she had been training the ladies in remedies at the town where she had been staying. The branches in question had been moist and green at the time and full of the secret of the willow.

They cut a few branches into lengths about as long as Quillan's thumb, shredded them into a pile of what almost looked like wooden hay and then made tea. Boiling water covered the pile in a pot and they took turns churning the lot for a full afternoon. It then steeped until dinner, after which they strained the mess through a cheesecloth. The smell of the concoction was woody, earthy, but sharp.

Normadia emerged from the kitchen with mugs and a large sticky vat of honey to take the edge off of the sharp taste of the concoction. Dessa had thought this just so regular, Normadia taking care of them. She did it so well, without thinking, without any stress. She again felt her brother to be a lucky man.

Dessa had tried some, but because she had no aches and pains at the time she left the larger portion to those who did. Ol' Dogger had himself quite a gulp or two, hoping that something would take the edge off the pain in his leg. He was almost hobbled by his leg on many of these winter days.

As usual that night they all slept well as the wind howled outside and the snow piled ever deeper. However, the morning brought something they did not expect to see.

Ol' Dogger was dancing. Now as you remember, Ol' Dogger was a good dancer of sorts, especially with a belly full of scotches. However, this morning he was dancing across the wide floor of Journey exclaiming the wonders of not achn' to beat the damned. His smile lit up the very room!

Dessa's chuckle around the memory was cut short as horsemen with steel tipped spears suddenly emerged from all sides of the woods. They were orderly and trained. Very determined and brisk in their movements. The lead one with the feathered helmet ordered them to put their arms up high and if anyone moved, it would be the last time they did.

55.
Entrance

The four horses with their Journey travelers and their captors plodded slowly in single file through what seemed to be the main courtyard of the dark castle. The mud here seemed thicker and blacker than what they had encountered on the trail. The typical assortment of short, tall and odd shaped people milled about, doing their business.

Dessa noticed though that not a soul looked up at them as they entered through the black stone entranceway. No eyes searching for recognition of a face come home. No glee in the approach of a stranger with news of other places. No interest in ideas to share from other lands. It was as if that intrinsic concept of curiosity had been swept away from the inner and outer minds of the entire community. These were what looked like hopelessly dreary people.

Even, impossibly so, the children were dull. Dressed in shabby rags, the children contributed their part to the almost instant monotonous drudgery of the place. Heads down, shoulders stooped, arms limp, showing no sign of life. Even their faces, which should have been full of shining curiosity and glee, were slack and forlorn. Not one of them ran, not one of them played. Not one of them looked up either.

So different from the experience anyone would have around Journey. Upon entrance to the little field around the great log building, any sort of traveler or visitor would be surrounded by a thronging group of wild eyed (yet polite) children spouting forth questions and wonders. "Where ye from mister? How long ye been ridin? What's yer horse's name? Want to see me do a summersault? Follow me to the stable, we'll take good care of ye. Make sure ye keep room to try Miss Normadia's desserts!" and it would just seem to carry on. When you arrived at Journey, you were not a stranger for very long.

Here, it looked like everyone was a stranger. Not only a stranger at arm's length, but a distance that could never be covered.

Torrin turned in his saddle to peer back from atop Happy and was about to say something to Dessa when a yelp arose from one of the guards who had rounded them up in the woods. "Hey there, no talkn.' Keep yer eyes forward, hands where we can see them and no one gets a sword though the heart. At least not yet," and all the guards laughed a dark chuckle.

It was a large area, full of trading stalls and plain activity. It's just that the activity was so very plain vanilla. Plain and dull. Not dead. But certainly not alive. Very little color at all. No bargaining, no noise. Just dull activity.

The guards guided them through a maze of dark alleys and narrow passages. Families obviously lived in small dark apartments built in long gray lines. Dirty rags and torn skins covered small windows. No fireplaces or stoves were in evidence and how these people stayed warm in the winter was an instant mystery. Periodically there were long rooms that they passed sporting combat equipment along the walls. These were obviously barracks for the soldiers who hovered about, idly pattering around in aimless activity. Torrin wondered aloud, but not so much to cause trouble with the guards, "How can any place need so many soldiers?"

After a time they came to be upon the entry to what were large and imposing stables. It was the first place they had seen with any color or sense of order and cleanliness about it. Quillan rightly so decided that the evil sot they were here to see must put great stock in the value of a horse.

Five young boys dressed mostly as the others, but arriving with some of the energy you would expect from a young boy, attached their hands to the reins of the entourage's animals. These fellows then stood quietly at attention as if waiting for orders.

"Get down, all ye," said the obvious leader of the soldiers. "Ye stay in a room over the stables until Scraddius sends for ye. Bernabe will take care of the steeds. If ye leave here alive, ye'll have 'em back." And with those words all but two of the guards left. The two left behind were obviously supposed to make sure this unruly lot of strangers to the kingdom followed orders and did not give rise to any mischief.

So the small troop dismounted onto some dry straw that had been flittered about across the mud. Torrin looked at Dessa, wondering if it would be OK to speak. Dessa looked at Quillan with a face that said "behave." Etworth just looked out of his element, never before having not been warmly greeted upon an entrance. They all stretched the stiffness that a long ride puts into your muscles.

They waited, attended to by boys and guarded by soldiers in front of the largest stables any of them had ever seen. A long sturdy building of logs with windows set evenly in a row for ventilation and light was in their sight. A sign with the image of a horse burned into the wood swung in the dirty breeze. The image was very elegant and whoever had done the art was a pure genius.

A few ropes and tools of stables were hung from pegs inserted into the big logs. Anything metal was shiny bright. Even the windows were held open, all at the same angle by an even row of sticks clean sturdy sticks, stripped of bark.

A movement at the stable door caused them to turn and set their gaze upon the most unusual man.

One of the guards spoke, "This'n ere be sa ead stable master. He go by Bernabe. He take care you now." Bernabe the stable master was fully a head taller than Quillan, and Quillan was the tallest among them. His very bald pate was as a wet smooth rock in a mountain stream. Powerful shoulders framed a massive hairless chest that seemed eager to burst from its solid resting place. The shoulders and chest together were not so much as broad, as they were the image of controlled power and might. His arms were the girth of young trees that grew freely in the forest amongst plenty of water and sun. The impressive arms were obviously for the sole purpose of supporting the will of two large and commanding hands that sported long strong nimble fingers.

He wore a stable master's apron adorned with tools, hooks and the trappings of stable life. Nothing else covered the big man other than a weathered leather vest that clung tightly to the rippled muscles of a torso that could have wrestled a horse to the ground in an instant if necessary. His massive feet were bare and pointed out slightly to each side, supported by legs that were just a breath shorter than they could have been. These legs however looked as if they could split wood, or worse yet, yer back if need be.

In one hand he carried a hammer with a massive iron head and then as he stood there, tossed it from hand to hand as if it were nothing but a spoon.

Strong eyes of steel gray looked at each one of the boys standing attention at the horses; each in careful turn, as if inspecting them. And after an almost imperceptible nod, these boys did wordlessly, in single file, lead the steeds into the stable. As Uta ambled past Dessa he gave a nod and quietly said, "I trust you will not be far from us; this place does not sit well with me."

Dessa's mind responded back, "We will do the best we can. Get some rest."

Bernabe's gaze now settled upon the four weary travelers. He, with obvious intent, inspected each one in turn, taking in all their parts and pieces. It was not an inspection for looks or money; no this was an inspection of character and virtue. Torrin felt like the man could somehow see right through them. And then the big stable master did the most unusual thing. He smiled. Those steel gray eyes smiled with his face and then he said with a kindly strong voice, "Welcome to the stables of King Gaerwn."

Dessa stepped forward, giving a small nod of respect followed with a mini curtsy, as much as she thought was appropriate for a woman in breeches. She then introduced the team accordingly, "Mr. Bernabe, my name is Gale. This is Etworth, Quillan and our leader Tarmon." Each one nodded a welcome and tipped their riding hat at the mention of their name. "We welcome your graciousness and hospitality."

Bernabe relaxed some and with a tilt of his head, he turned on his heel and said, "Follow me please, after handing your weapons over to the soldiers. They will be returned to you later. Never mind the horse droppings; they are part of the trade here."

*   *   *

Quillan marveled at the stables. Never before had he seen such an enormous and well kept stable. Everything was pristine, neat and orderly. Even each rope was wound the same exact way, and they hung on pegs at the same perfect angle. Each end whipped tightly with stout black twine. Each whipping was exactly the same.

As they walked, more order became apparent. All buckets were identical, clean and tilted the same way. Feedbags orderly. Piles of hay and straw almost as if created exactly the same. The stables themselves were filled with a full variety of great and small steeds; all colors and temperaments filled the wooden stalls as well as sounds and smells. You could feel the contentment of the horses though. In fact, the inside of this place, although rich in precise order, was calm and relaxing.

Etworth commented quietly, to no one in particular, "The change from out there to in here is amazing! I wonder how he does it? This place is alive, out there is just dead."

They climbed clean steps to a second floor and entered a large well appointed tack room. Again, order prevailed. But before any inspections could take place, Bernabe continued through a wide entry way and down a long hallway lined with doors and lit by oil lamp sconces. The two guards stayed in the tack room, obviously having been through this experience before. Opening a door at the end of the hall Bernabe motioned the four inside and then followed them in.

It was a comfortable room; a reasonably sized window at one end had hides on the outside and inside for security and to keep the cold out when necessary. Two bunk beds were tight against one wall for the four of them and a small table with two benches was set in the middle. Three small simple tables were scattered about in what seemed to be no thoughtful pattern. In one corner was a tiny fireplace made of iron. It was the size of a big man's boot and no larger with a long iron chimney running up the wall backed by round stones.

Torrin looked at this little fireplace and wondered almost aloud, how would ye get any heat from such a wee thing?

Bernabe, now seeming much more relaxed that they were away from prying ears and eyes said, "This is the way it's done here. All visitors are inspected by Scraddius. If you are deemed safe and not a threat, you may stay and perform your business. He seems completely without vice or consistency. I warn you now, he cannot be bought. He is the only one in this entire place who cannot be bought, besides me, but just remember, he will judge you on how he sees your merit. You may find yourself outside the walls before dinner. Or you could find yourself dining with the king by the time it is very dark tonight."

Quillan asked, "So what do we do now. Jus await ehre or do we need to be a doin something?"

Bernabe, never with a quick reply looked at Quillan and said after a few moments, "Scraddius is the chief advisor to the King. He will summon you presently, or tomorrow, or the next day to talk with ye and see if what ye have to offer is worthy of the kingdom. If he deems ye good for the common good, ye may stay. If he deems ye important, ye meet with the King. If he deems ye trouble or a threat, he makes one of two choices."

Dessa stood tall, her shoulders square and her chin pushing out just a bit and said, "Two choices?"

Bernabe looked at the lot of them and decided they were experienced enough to hear the truth, even if it was not what they wanted to know, "If the fair man Scraddius deems ye a threat, he leaves the room and the guards make sure ye do not walk out. If he deems ye as just a nuisance, he usually will just send ye on yer way in the morn."

Etworth piped in, "We are here to teach and trade. What trouble would that be?"

Bernabe, either true to form, or putting on the act of his life said presently, "Then ye really need to act and look the part. Because right now, ye look like a small lot of angry people on a mission."

And with that Bernabe walked out the door and left them all to their own thoughts and devices.

*   *   *

They all turned their heads to the knock on the door of their little sanctuary. Three of the stable boys appeared carrying an assortment of items. Warm water in a bucket, a handful of cloths, a pitcher of something to drink, four mugs and one black bar of soap. Waiting in the hall were two other boys, carrying the pack from Calandra with all their saddlebags carefully stacked on top. They hefted the load into the room after the other three had exited and set it down carefully.

As they were leaving, Dessa asked, "May we brush down and attend to our horses?"

The taller of the two boys looked at her and said, "No mam, you havin to a stay here. But we will be finshin up brushn' and then feedn' those grand steeds of yours soon. Pretty much have their feet all cleaned up and dry already. They are lookn' a mighty hungry though. They be gettn' sweet hay mixed with some nice oats and plenty of clean water. They is nice horses, they is. We be takn' good nuf care of 'em." And with that he smartly left the room and closed the door.

Dessa began to wash as the boys unpacked their belongings. Soon the room was full of clothing and hats and bedrolls and all the things that accompany a group on a trip.

And then presently, three smartly crafted cases with thick leather handles emerged wrapped carefully in oilcloth. These were lined up on the main table, ready to do their bidding. Each was about the size of a horse's head. One person could carry it, but it was better with two. They were not heavy.

Of course, all their knives, swords and Dessa's arrows and anything that could be used as a weapon were missing.

Quillan set to work with a small stick of wax, affixing a tiny seal to each case to indicate that it had not been tampered with.

As Torrin washed, Dessa combed her hair. The hat line crease that bent her curls formed from her riding and sweating all day in her hat was already fading. She swished her curls some and loved the feel of the locks falling and gliding across her back. Then she just closed her eyes, sat for a time letting her mind reset as Ipi had taught her. For a few moments, she let the rest of the world melt away.

*   *   *

Quillan looked at Torrin, about to ask what the devil was wrong with his sister, sitn' like that? Just havn' ere eyes closed and her arms sitn' on her legs like she was about to catch an egg?

Torrin gracefully brought his index finger to his lips to hush Quillan. He then moved his hand smoothly in a motion that said, just keep everything moving along normal, do not react. He did this and then he splashed warm water on his face and washed off the grime of the trail. The warm wet cloth felt good on his neck and face and the color of the water was testament to the need for a cleaning. The soap was dark yet smelled of deep purple grapes and the sweetness of its scent lingered on his skin.

Dessa was practicing what Ipi had described as a spiritual art. Ipi had thoughtfully, carefully and methodically delivered and taught it to the varied and interested folks of Journey. Ipi had spent some time trying to define it and had called it finding your midpoint. Torrin did not understand it, but he did know that every time Dessa practiced it, she smiled and was somehow different, in a good way. He could not describe what his midpoint was, or if he would know it if he saw it, but he did know that she liked doing this thing. What's more, this little detour from the world around her seemed to suit her just fine in a variety of ways. That was what mattered. And there were times that she would sit in the big wooden chair in their room and her body would just seem to float. Then after searching for a time for this far flung and mysterious midpoint, she would float softly into bed.

Often she was very warm and flushed after these little sessions. And always relaxed and very open to his touches. Actually more than that, she was desirous of his touch. She would just lie there and let his fingers slowly explore her pale pink skin with the tiny soft hairs standing at full attention. And mind you he had the presence of mind to be slow, gentle and actually tease around the really sensitive areas for a long while. She never moaned during these explorations after finding her midpoint, but she did breathe ever so deeply. She would inhale forever so slowly and just keep inhaling until he thought she would burst. This did make for a grand rise in her chest and paint looks on her face that were so intoxicating that he himself was inflated. But oh, the making of the best part was in the waiting.

For as he explored, her very skin seemed to grow in sensitivity. After a time, she would wind her hand into his hair and guide his now expectant and moist lips to play a little midpoint symphony upon some very fiery part of her now ready self. It was never the same place twice. She always seemed to be finding a release in a different area each time. It did not take him more than two times to discover that skirting around the area in question was much more fun than just diving in. If she pulled his face to her breasts, he would push himself up so that his lips started exploring just at the bottom of her chin and then wander in a circular and teasing path from there.

When he would finally attend to the expectant target, she was almost now savage in her need. By now he would have kissed her neck, earlobes, and shoulders. Even gently explored the edge of her fingernails for a time; never losing touch, never breaking the connection, and slowly heading toward the target of her intended intensity.

Once there, her explosion of energy and need was exhilarating. She was lost in lust and passion of her very self that was possessed of nothing more than just her whole and wonderful being. All her current needs, wants and desires exploded into a firestorm of engaging with him that was not only intoxicating, it was madding and wonderful.

His closed eyes were reliving the wonders of just a few nights before when she poked him in the ribs and said huskily, "Move over."

"Huh?"

"Move over," said Etworth. "Yer not the only one to ave gotten a head full of dirt and grim over the last two days. I would like to wash up and be presentable for the lout we are a seeing, Mr. Chief Scannius."

"Oh," said a now not as startled Torrin as he moved away from the warm water feeling the flush of the memory wash away the tension in all but one part of himself.

* * *

After everyone was suitably presentable and cleaned up, Quillan and Etworth walked to the end of the hall. No one else was about in the other rooms (they looked inside each one).

The two explorers sauntered into the large and neatly organized tack room. The two guards were sitting on large chairs and they just looked at the two men. Quillan and Etworth looked back, shrugged their shoulders and returned to their room.

"Well?" asked Dessa.

"No one but us on the hall," said Quillan lying down on one of the lower bunks, claiming it now for himself.

"Two guards in the tack room," added Etworth.

Quillan sighed, "It's pretty simple really."

"And how is that?" wondered Dessa.

"We are prisoners, at their behest," said Quillan with a slight yawn and stretch of the leg that was hanging over the side of the bunk.

"At least they have the manners to put us in a comfortable prison."

Etworth was not pleased at someone finally voicing the obvious. Clearing his throat and walking over to the window he moved the skins that blocked the view. Then he stretched himself long, standing on his toes and bent way over looking down. Turning to the members of the room he said, "We could get out this way; it's not too far to the ground. We could scale the stones easily and be on our way in just a few minutes."

"Go and do it," said Quillan.

"Really?" said Etworth, beginning to make his way toward a chair that would assist in climbing onto the sill; the thoughts of freedom and successful escape obvious on his face.

"Sure," said Quillan. "An let's just suppose ye reach the ground without slippn on a rock and ye don't break yer scrawny neck."

"Yes, we can do that. We could all do that!" cried a now more excited Etworth, obviously missing the dripping sweet sarcasm in Quillan's voice.

"Oh I am sure we could," answered Quillan, mischief gleaming in his eyes, knowing he was going to very much enjoy this little discussion.

"So get yer such a big mighty self over here and let's get going," whispered Etworth in a conspiratorial tone.

Quillan looked to Torrin and Dessa for support but found they had lain down on the bottom of the other bunk. Dessa's head rested on Torrin's chest. They were both either fast asleep or in some sort of mystic nap. Anyway, it was evident that they were not partaking of the fun in this little exchange. So now, Quillan tired of it since there was no audience said, "And when ye get to the ground which direction do ye go?"

Etworth started looking at his hands, trying to figure out which direction he would turn and Quillan continued.

"An of course, if ye pick the right way or the wrong way, did many of them folks we saw slogging round down there when we sauntered in look like they was itchin to elp ye?" Etworth looked a little forlorn at the truthfulness of Quillan's words. "Shades be a-mighty, I bet they would hardly know enough to get up out of the mud iffn' they fell down themselves let alone help a stranger with a clean face and in good clothes."

Torrin was listening with one ear and now looked at the bucket of warm water with interest. Was this hospitality or a wonderful ruse to make them all stick out in a crowd? Yes, if they escaped, they would just stand out! Clean faces, clean clothes. Energetic, excited, interested? He lay his head back down, enjoying the warmth of Dessa's head upon his chest and sighed. He wondered if some of the most diabolical plans were really so diabolical, or if some people just got lucky? The washn' could have just been the good graces of Bernabe, or it could be part of a grand scheme. It really did not matter now; they were here.

Quillan was continuing his tutoring of Etworth in the wily ways of the world. "And I bet those nasty brute soldiers at the drawbridge entrance just sit around and wait to help strangers leave this kingdom. Then he made a high quivery mocking voice that said, "Pack ye a lunch master? Ehe, let me shine yer boots for yer journey? Ha ha," chortled Quillan.

Etworth sat down, looking dejected.

Quillan said to him, "So ye got a lot to learn, and…"

There was but one sharp knock on the door and in walked a tall young man, adorned with black robes with a heavy silver gauntlet adorning his neck. Unless you were blind, you could not help but notice the large and furry black boots that adorned his feet, being so very different than anything they had seen on others. His hair was as black as his robes and he sported an odd white spot to one side, making it look like a bird had done him wrong on his way here. However, from the airs about him, he would not have been finding it amusing to point it out. Probably never, even if drunk with his friends (that is if he had any friends).

"Good evening. I am the squire for master Scraddius. He will see you at first light." And with that fast and definitive pronouncement, he turned on his heel and smartly strode out of the room.

It all happened so fast that the four of them wondered if what they had seen or heard was real. But it had broken the spell on Etworth and turned the relaxed mood for the rest of them into something a little more stressful. Anyway, before they could all rise to talk about the impending morning the stable boys returned.

One carried a tray of dinner that was a veritable feast. Salted pork, pickled vegetables, fresh warm bread, a large helping of butter and four enormous sweet rolls to pose as a dessert fit for royalty.

Another boy carried a large wooden flash of dark wine. And a third went to the miniature fireplace in the corner and busied himself arranging logs for a small fire lifted from a steel bucket that he carried. A bundle of short, yet stout wood, cleanly split for good burning was left to the side for use during the night.

Torrin and Quillan quickly cleared the table for the tray of foodstuffs and the other items that accompanied the meal.

After depositing the delectables on the table and ensuring the fire was working well they all left, sans one. He was older and obviously practiced at speaking with strangers. "We are delighted to have you stay at the stables tonight. Mr. Bernabe is sending his apologies for not being here to deliver to you this news; however, he says to inform you he is indisposed." He stopped to gain his thoughts before continuing, "We shall bring you a light breakfast before your meeting with sire Scraddius. In the morning, please eat if you like; however, be aware that Scraddius often offers a meal to the folk he is evaluating. He deems it very insulting if you do not partake. But there is no knowing what will happen. Bernabe would rather you not go hungry on his account."

He too turned on a well instructed and practiced heel and headed for the door. As he went to close it, he said, "Feel free to wander about the stables tonight, but please know there is a twilight curfew in the kingdom. Anyone but the guards found wandering the streets after dark is beheaded and their body hung outside the walls for the robbers to see. Sleep well."

He closed the door gently.

* * *

Quillan just growled low and then began pulling chairs around the table so they could feast. As it was getting quite dark Dessa lit the other candles and lamp in the room from the lights in the hallway with a taper that was hung next to the door. Etworth just sat, not yet recovered from having seemingly been ready to escape, only to find that others had plans for him that he had no choice but to follow.

Torrin went to investigate the wee fireplace. He noticed that the iron pipe was warming up nicely from the small fire and he could feel the heat from it filling the room. Verra wise he thought! At Journey they endeavored to make the large stones hot to radiate heat into the room. Someone here was quite the engineer to build such an installation and he figured that it saved greatly on wood too.

"Torrin, quit ruminating on things and eat," said Quillan.

Dessa just smiled and crunched on a very pickled section of carrot. It was tangy, almost seemed fresh, yet had been in storage all winter. She said, "For all the dreariness of this place, they seem to be good at doing some things."

Quillan agreed, saying, "Everrabody is good at something."

And as they ate, they rehearsed.

*   *   *

A while later, in the stalls, Dessa asked, "What have ye learned from the others?" She talked to Uta in that strange way she could communicate with the horses. Some sounds, mostly with her mind. She knew it worked, but still did not understand. Which she surmised really did not matter, especially now.

Uta replied, "This is a very nasty place. All the beasts here came with riders who never came back."

"Oh," replied Dessa, trying not to let the concern rise in her voice. "How are they treating you?"

"The stable boys here are well trained, gentle and take their time. It was a very nice brushing as well as their attention to my legs and hooves," replied Uta.

"Good," said Dessa. "We see some man named Scraddius tomorrow morning. I guess he decides everyone's fate."

"Just make him look good," replied Uta. "That is what I hear is important."

A stable boy walked by and cocked his head, almost like he was wondering why Dessa would be standing at the head of a horse, like they were talking. Dessa made like she was looking in Uta's ear. As she did so, she willed herself to relax, knowing that all would work out. Well, at least she could hope it would all work out.

As she pushed the stress from her head, murmurings began to form. Just soft murmurs. And then it struck her. All the horses in the stables were chatting. Like a large crowd of people talking in low tones. She could only catch a word here or there, no complete thoughts. But it was just an amazing thing, hearing it all going on. Something that she never in her wildest dreams would have thought possible.

She gave Uta a hug and they said good night. Calandra was fast asleep and Dessa did not want to disturb her. Samoot and Happy were slumbering quietly as well and looked kindly cared for.

As Dessa climbed the stairs she stopped and looked down across all the stalls, taking in the broad backs of the steeds, great and small. So many colors and kinds. Just like people she thought. No two are the same. And she decided that just as with people, this variety was in the end, a good thing.

Dessa returned to the room where the other three were already fast asleep.

She quickly and soundlessly joined them.

*   *   *

As promised, just as the sun was quenching the pinpricks of the stars in the eastern sky, a boy arrived with a light breakfast of tea and warm biscuits that Etworth thought wonderful. The others woke themselves some with the tea and no more.

The men had brushed their jackets and donned clean muslin shirts underneath, having removed their soiled riding shirts. One of the stable boys had appeared the evening before and collected laundry items, promising to return them the next day. Again the contrast between the stables and the greater lot of this kingdom was acute. Dessa had remarked that she would bet her hair the rest of the people had not washed their clothes but once a year, if ever.

The boots the men wore had been scrubbed clean and each had inserted matching turkey feathers in their hat to give them a sense of a team uniform. Dessa was the standout. Shedding her riding costume, she had donned her heavy blue velvet dress with only a thin chemise beneath. Attending to the plunging neckline in the front she had tied the laces in an orderly and fairly demure fashion. However not so much so as to make it uninteresting to any man she might want to distract. She wore no cap (which she knew would raise questions and the ire of some, but that was her intent, keep them questioning and wondering vs. thinking and attending to what was really going on). In her hair to one side, she had had Torrin tie a long and narrow turkey feather. She now shared the team item with the others.

Etworth had asked, "How do we explain the turkey feather? What is the meaning of it?"

Quillan piped in, "We mean to beat the black death. How does that work for ye?" The red man gave a sly look at his own joke.

Etworth nodded and the thought kept him occupied for a while.

Quillan just rolled his eyes, still smiling at his joke.

* * *

Presently a page of some sort arrived to escort them; they did not introduce themselves or say anything but, "Follow me."

This person was young and it was hard to tell if it was a woman or a man, girl or boy. It did not really matter, as this person of mystery was all business and proceeded at a steady and rapid gait.

Down the hall, past the still sleeping guards, they trod single file as if on a march to a very solemn event. Torrin was in front and between each of them, they had one of their grandly carved boxes.

Whoever it was in the lead, led them through the grand stables. The place was noiseless but for the sounds horses make when idle. Dessa heard nothing; it was an odd contrast to the evening before. The four were led out the back way, opposite of the side they had entered. They now walked on stone. No mud here.

Somewhere in the distance someone coughed. But nothing more. Not a sound. Dessa thought it strange, that a castle of this size be so quiet. She had remembered as a little girl getting up early on her riding days and the sounds coming from the kitchen and workrooms would be a part of the morning.

Here, nothing.

She decided it was the contrasts here that bothered her most. Contrasts of daily life not lived. Contrast of people on a gray existence. It bothered her and she was curious all at the same time.

They entered a massive building via an arched doorway made of ancient stones that sported moss and other assorted molds. The sounds their boots made echoed coldly off the stone walls. Bits of moisture danced along the walls and droplets littered the floor. An ever present issue in castles thought Dessa. She had always hoped there could be a way to save the heat of the summer and use it during the winter. This thought passed quickly and she focused on the task at hand.

Upstairs and down corridors they travelled. Past rooms, past other halls. Past doors, past windows. Past an occasional lamp that lit the hallway where dark. But they met not a person. Not even a stray cat was about.

Their guide opened a door and ushered them into a medium sized room that sported nothing. A window on one side let in air and light. Brown, black, rippled and gray stones made up the walls in no fashion other than to be walls. No tapestry. No furniture, no lamps, candles, scones or carpet. The doorway they entered through was at one end, and an unimposing door frame with a plain wooden door stood at the other.

Their guide said nothing; he just walked back through the door they had entered and closed it. They could hear something very heavy and sturdy thud into place and rightly supposed that the door had been barred. Now a quiet descended upon them that can only descend upon one within an empty cold stone room. It's a quiet that is so astoundingly without noise that it almost hurts the ears. But when amongst stone, the quiet is sharp. Almost tangy. The sounds of their breathing slowly came into focus, and the noise that made it to their ears was a chiseled echo.

Eventually Dessa could stand the waiting no longer and looked at Torrin and gently said, "Well?"

"What do ye mean? Well?" he said back, not making any sense of the question at all.

"How do you feel?" she asked, wondering if his warning signal was bothering him at all.

"Oh, yes," he replied now with understanding. "It's somethin ye just don't notice when it's gone. And right now, nothing." Setting down the case he had been sharing with Dessa, he released the handle and ran his hand across the back of his neck. After a long rub, he took it away and looked at it, like it was supposed to say something. He just looked up and shook his head left and right in a long quiet "no."

Dessa looked at them all, almost afraid to say it, but she did anyway. "So there seems to be no danger signal to Torrin; maybe it will all be good?"

Quillan did not seem amused nor in agreement. But did not say anything; he was intently listening and paying as close attention to anything and everything as well as he could. He was out of control which meant he was out of his element. He had no weapons with which to defend himself and could not even see a way out. He looked very stressed.

Etworth began to explore the room they were inhabiting and eventually walked over to the window. This, of course, seemed to be his normal thing to do.

This time though when he looked down, he said sharply, "We are very high now! Yes, very high. Oh my!"

"Oh good," said Quillan. "Oh just verra good."

56.
Possibility

"You look a fright," said Normadia to Ol' Dogger. She had just finished braiding her long silken brown hair into a neat plait and was tying the end with a length of rawhide to keep it neat.

"I jus thinkn I took on too much of the scotches las night," he replied, his head in his hands. "I avh a been feeling so good lately what with the willow bark tea and chewing some that I forgot and overdid it."

Normadia handed him a mug of this morning's communal herbal tea with no particular remedy in it besides warm and tasty and said, "Here, take this in and ye'll feel a might better. Maybe go outside and get some fresh air; it's a nice day and the sun will do ye good."

"Thank ye dear. Ye have always been awful good te me an I 'preciate it," he smiled at her, a few teeth missing, but nonetheless, it was a genuine smile.

Slowly he rose from the bench that had been supporting his stooped body. His long and bony fingers reached out and wrapped around the mug of tea, happily absorbing its warmth and he turned toward the big door to make an exit into the sunshine.

He slowed down when he passed the table where Ipi was teaching a few individuals how to peel and then carefully grind dried roots with a mortar and pestle. "Whatcha cookn up now Ipi?" he inquired.

"Why Dogger you old fool, I din't know ye cared," she said with a smile. "This is going to be a powder of Ginseng. Good for the mind when ye can't seem to think."

"Ah," he said smirking. "I don't think there is enough of that in the whole wide world to help me."

"Hmm, you never know," she said. "Say, what's in the mug?"

"Just some nice tea that Miss Normadia made," came his reply, still a little thick and slow.

"Well Dogger, said Ipi. "What ye say we have a nice quiet night tonight, build a good fire after supper and you finally tell all of us your story?"

Ol' Dogger stood a little taller for a minute. He seemed to be mulling over thoughts and whimsies in his brain. He scrunched his eyes tight and his old long gray bushy eyebrows almost touched each other. When he looked up, he yawned, cocked his head and said, "I suppose we could have a story time."

Ipi smiled up at him in that way she did when patiently teaching someone the same thing for the third time and said, "No Ol' Dogger. The real story. The whole thing. All of it."

"Why?" he just breathed quietly.

"Because it's time you told these good folks here, and it will make you feel better. Besides," she added, "You been wanting to tell it for a while now. It's written all over your face. And it will be good for you."

Ol' Dogger looked at her for a moment, shrugged his shoulders and said, "Yes, there be no denyn' it. Guess then it's time to get some air and get me memory in line. It has been a while since I was fully forthcomin with the group here."

Ipi smiled as he shuffled out of the room and she turned her attention to the young man who was peeling entirely too much of the good part of the root away.

57.
Parboiling Begun

Quillan was pacing around in the stone room where the four of them seemed to be gently jailed. It was not so much a prison, but there was certainly no obvious way to exit, and certainly no one to talk with about their present situation.

"Will you just relax?" Dessa said for the hundredth time to Quillan.

"Relax you say," came his hushed response. "We been coolin' our heels in this tomb of a room for what seems to be an eternity. There is not a way out that I can see, an I don't hear or feel anything going on. We is trapped like animals and you tell me to relax!"

"Do ye think that maybe making us wait is part of the act?" She looked at him calmly and continued, "When you get stressed, you will react. And don't you think that all this here, for us and for everybody in this dark damp place, is to keep everybody in reaction mode? Maybe everybody but that man Bernabe? And who knows, maybe he is just a setup too and the contrast of the man is part of the act.? A very well planned act for sure!"

"So what is ye suggestn' we do about this situation wee sister?" came Quillan's terse reply.

"Exactly as we had discussed," she said firmly. As she finished, the plain wooden door at the end of the room opened and a tall beauty of a woman with stunning green eyes entered the room. She said smartly, "He will see you now; please leave your cases here."

The four filed through the doorway in front of her and she secured the door behind them.

They entered an opulent room. Especially in contrast to the room they had just left. Torrin looked behind them and noticed two layers of heavy thick curtains now covering the door they had just come through. That explained why they had not heard anything from this side. It had been purposely muffled.

This room was as over-decorated as the other room was plain.

Thick tapestries hung from ceiling to floor upon every wall, some of them overlapping. There was no theme to them other than their rich thickness and purpose of insulation to the cold winter weather. Well-crafted tables, chairs and a large desk were scattered about in a fashion that led to the desk being the other center of the room, besides a great table for eating to one side. Two large windows with heavy skins rolled to the sides let light and fresh air into the room. A broad fireplace on the inside wall sported an enormous fire with logs four feet across engulfed in hot flames.

Torrin noted that the wood was not entirely dry so it would burn for a long time. This would allow for less tending and burn less wood. Again he thought, smart work.

As his eyes took in the rest of the room he continued to be amazed at the opulence. Large animal trophies hung on the walls. A few swords were stacked on pegs near a door and rugs of various sizes and shapes allowed for a much warmer feeling across the room. Art in the form of steel and iron as well as clay and carved wood sat upon tables and even in a window sill. This room had been attended to for a long time by someone who enjoyed their trinkets and trappings.

The tall green eyed lady said, "I am Glenna, assistant to Scraddius. Scraddius is the chief advisor to our great King Gaerwn. It is a pleasure to make your acquaintance."

Dessa noted that this woman choked some on the words "great King Gaerwn" and more importantly, she did not welcome them to this kingdom nor say it was "her" pleasure to make their acquaintance. It was subtle, but told mountains about what was going on. Dessa did not say anything or react, but she felt a distance that up until now was not real. So she did the best she could and just said with a curtsy, "We are pleased to be here and obviously blessed by your hospitality. These are my assistants." And she pointed them out, introducing them each in turn as Tarmon (Torrin's name for the event), Quillan and Etworth. She introduced herself as Gale.

Glenna bade them to sit at a large well carved wooden dining table where five broad chairs with wide ornately carved arms attended to the larder set before them. One chair was at the head of the table. A fine linen cloth was draped over its broad back. In the place in front of the chair at the table was a large plate with a linen napkin carefully folded across its top. A heavy tankard, filled to the brim with a dark liquid stood to the ready.

Upon the expanse of the table was placed in fine arrangement an assortment of smoked fish, carved ham, venison jerky, fresh aromatic crusty breads, toppings and a variety of hot boiled vegetables in wooden bowls. This feast filled the center of the table accompanied by four pitchers of various beverages.

Dessa turned to Glenna and asked. "How do you keep vegetables all winter?"

Glenna, somewhat proud of this little miracle said, "Just after they are harvested, we dip them in boiling water for the count of two hands," and she held up ten long well manicured fingers that held bright purple paint on the nails. "After which we pack them immediately in ice shavings held all summer in the ice caves. We keep them frozen solid until we need them and then back into the water they go and it's like magic."

"You must tell me the secrets of your cooking," exclaimed Dessa. "This is just, just wonderful! At this space of the year, it almost seems like magic."

Glenna beamed. She had perfected the process over many seasons. The kingdom had good stores of beans, carrots, peas, potatoes, roots and other items packed in the ice caves. "It would please me to show you the process," said Glenna, "after you have completed your business with Scraddius." And then she suddenly turned very somber. "He shall be here momentarily; please sit and begin to dine."

Dessa went to sit at the big table, cocked her head toward Glenna and asked, "What happened to your arm?"

Glenna blushed, trying and failing to cover the extensive winding of fabric along her arm that displayed a long line of wet where her wound was weeping. "Nothing, a run in with a jagged piece of stoneware in the kitchen." And she promptly left the room.

*   *   *

One after another in turn, each of them took a sampling from each of the delectables presented so nicely at the table. At each place they had a well carved oval shaped platter to use for their eating. The platters were well worn, finely made with careful tooling around the outside, but were smooth on the inside where no food could be caught and spoil. A spoon rested at the top of each place.

Quillan thought it again a dramatic dichotomy of the place. Here we go from a room as plain as dirt to overwhelming opulence. He figured it was all designed to keep you on your toes and on your guard.

So he did the thing he needed to do.

He ate.

* * *

Etworth was talking with his mouth full. Carrying on about how his parent's trading company was making great amounts of gold selling venison jerky to a king's army's to the south when one of many doors to the room swung open on what seemed its own power. Not immediately, but just a few seconds later, a man in black robes strode into the room with an air of authority about him.

Dessa could feel the tension release from Quillan as they shared the same thought. "Now we can move this party forward."

The man motioned for them to stay seated, already claiming control of the meeting and he sat down at what was obviously his place at the table.

A servant boy scurried into the room and exchanged the tankard that had been sitting at the head place for one he carried. He then left as quickly as he had come. Another whim of a person in this strange place on a breeze. Happening so fast and without as much as a sound. Some things seemed to happen here that were almost like a dream. They happened so fast your mind wondered if it was really true, wondered if it really happened.

Dessa decided that a place like this would get on her nerves in no time at all. So she smiled sweetly to the mystery man at the head of the table.

As was custom when meeting with royalty or persons of power, one waited until the royal one started the conversation. And so, for a while, no one spoke. The only sound was Etworth trying to finish chewing.

Scraddius looked at each one of them in turn with inquisitive black eyes. He then enjoyed an elegant sip of the beverage from his new tankard. Clearing his throat gently, he broke the silence and said, "I understand that the redheaded woman is your leader. I do not approve."

59.
Story

Normadia marveled at the change that just a few days could bring. The fall would come on gradually. The greens slowly fading to color and then brown. But spring was just an explosion of the world coming alive and it almost brought her to tears it was so wonderful.

As the snows finally melted off and headed down the stream beds, the tender grasses pushed up and emerged in the field around Journey. Each day she would go to the woods to look for edibles, but she knew that her real reason for going was to watch the daily progression of the buds on the trees. She marveled at how they just slowly swelled up. How their husks would fall off to litter the ground in a gentleness that was like a newborn baby. And then the soft green leaves would burst forth and stretch boldly to the waiting sun, reaching up to the brightness and warmth.

Today had been one of those days of the rushing beauty of spring. Warm sun, flitting clouds and the happy chirping of the birds celebrating the return of warm weather.

She had been able to venture forth during lunch to commune with nature and experience spring's progression thus far. The soft light green leaves high in the trees had now stretched forth into their fullness and were turning into that magical dark green that is such the color of summer.

It had been a happy walk and she returned with a basket, heavy and full of dark green leeks. Their leaves would make a wonderful salad. Their long white ends, light with onion flavor would boil with a ham and add sweet spring tenderness to a marvelous meal.

It was just such a gift to have fresh food again!

And so it was with a happy heart that she supervised the ending of another day in the kitchen at Journey and looked forward to the much talked about story that Ol' Dogger was about to tell.

*   *   *

The oncoming chills of the early spring evening at Journey were well chased away by the brisk fire the boys had stoked up in the big fireplace. They were now burning the wood that came from the bottom end of the winter pile. It was dryer and seemed full of more heat than the wood of the fall; however, it did burn faster. But no one cared. They were well now beyond the time when losing the fire could be fatal.

Candles and oil lamp flames burned in their friendly normal yellow flickers. They danced shadows upon the folks resting after a good day's work. It was just enlightening to see the smiles that a few days of sunshine could bring to everyone.

Today, the folks at Journey had gone to the fields to clear away the winter's debris and pull early spring weeds before they became a terrible nuisance with their roots sinking deep into the moist soil (and yes, some of those weeds would show up in tomorrow's salads on the tables at Journey). Some folks had gone hunting, but to no avail today. All they came back with were some scrapes and very wet feet. A few men had dug a pit for a badly needed new outhouse after a full winter with the one they had been using. The plan was that on the morrow they would move the privy to a better place and cover the old pit with enough dirt as to keep its smells at bay. The moving of the privy was a spring ritual that everyone appreciated.

And many a man and woman had been attending to the project of the grand plan, started by Dessa, Torrin and Quillan. They had searched and found many willing and able crafters to build the wagon train they needed to put their plan into action. It was hard, hard work as the frames of the sturdy, yet lightweight vehicles were pinned together. They had to be narrow and rugged, yet able to hide at least seven soldiers in each one.

Ipi had plied Ol' Dogger with some herbal brew that he said tasted like an old shirt more than tea. This brought a good laugh from everyone. But he drank it without fuss as the liquid seemed to do him good. He had asked for a mug of the scotches but she had persuaded him that he should tell his story mostly complete before the scotches would limit his words. However, she did promise that he would be well taken care of later. Ol' Dogger was amiable to the whole thing, much more than anyone expected.

Ipi's eyes had looked at him in a way that he could not refuse. As old as he was, he was still a man, and men are certainly of a nature to only resist so many things. So he held off on the scotches and had sat quietly in the corner, mulling over his thoughts and memories, getting ready for what looked like the very biggest evening of his long life.

And so, when Normadia came from the kitchen with a tray of dough bites and her mug of wine, the room quieted since now it would start. Ol' Dogger was perched upon a high stool with his tea in one hand and he looked about as regal as he could look. Normadia noticed he had cleaned up some, even shaved and had tied his hair back. As she sat down, she had a funny feeling that something important was about to take place. More important than just a story.

Ol' Dogger started.

"Well, ye mus remember, that the memories of wha I is about to be a telln' ya go verra far back in this wee little brain of mine, so it might get confuzzeled some and ave to backtrack. But I'll be a don' the bestn I can a manage."

Alexia came up to the man on the stool. She had her hands on her hips in a classic little girl stance and said to him firmly, "Mr. DogEars (she could never get his name quite right), you do what you can cause we love you anyway!" Then she hugged him and promptly sat down.

If you looked closely, you could see some tear glisten in the old man's eyes. With some obvious effort on his part and with a large, long and deep intake of breath, he began to tell a story that he had not told to anyone in that room.

Ever.

In fact, he could not remember when he had told this story before. The truth was, he never had told this story before. The time had never before been quite right. And for some reason, now it was.

"This starts back when this ere fireplace was only half as wide as it is now." His wizened hand swept a long gesture toward the huge hearth and every set of eyes in the room followed him.

When the eyes had returned, Ol' Dogger continued, "Ther whear no upstairs or big kitchen. Yesn' we had a stable, but only for this many steeds," and he held up four fingers. This was in great contrast to the large stables of now that could hold twenty head of whatever large animal seemed to show up.

He continued to talk to the now very hushed group, "The forest was just as big as it bein' today, but it was a much closer to the buildn' since it had not a been cleared yet away for eny festive or nothin. Only a few people were here now and a then, and ardly anyone stayed for a verra long. No, it was a verra lonely place and the Journey Inn was a verra young. But it was a start, an we was a proud of it."

"Who is we?" piped up Alexia, excited to understand!

Ol' Dogger looked at Alexia, and then at the crowd of friends, travelers and people whom he considered his family. This truth as his truth, and he had not let on about it for some reason or another, but now it was to be told.

Ol' Dogger said, "Well besides Coronado the big 'orse, myself and me parents, Valterra and Kaitlyn."

60.
Condition

Dessa smartly said nothing; however if you looked closely, or knew her well, you would sense just some color rising in her porcelain soft cheeks.

Quillan looked as if he was about to spit nails. And Etworth just picked venison from his teeth.

Torrin cleared his throat and picked up the conversation, playing his role of leader just as they had decided.

Sitting up tall, Torrin looked at Scraddius with the look your pet cat might give you saying, "I am interested in you, but not too much, and I might change my mind in a moment, and ask me if I really care, however, I do wish you would not ask me."

Cats they had all decided were impossible to understand.

And with a cleverly practiced set of words that impressed even Quillan, Torrin launched into the story. "We and our partners in Gotebörg have invested the last ten years developing a set of powerful healing medicinals that are now on the verge of being ready for wide distribution. Our coordinated system of producing key compounds for these incredibly powerful medicinals began production last summer. A limited number of the final products are now ready for use. As much as we would like to have these powerful healing products for all the petty kingdoms, our supply is limited as well as the number of wagons that can make the trek via the existing trails. Our mission is to find the best environments for our products so that we may direct the wagons once they reach the midlands during the early part of summer."

Scraddius' eyebrows went up just a shade, but not enough to prove to them he was convinced.

Torrin continued, "We have personally transported a few samples of the early medicinals that we will freely share with you over the next day to gauge your interest. If you are willing to guarantee purchase of a full wagon of products, your kingdom will be considered for early distribution."

At this Scraddius began to look angry. Never before in his life had a trader of any sort spoken to him in this manner. These people were usually groveling at his feet and licking his boots for the chance to trade here because all trade was controlled by Gaerwn and when a purchase was made, it was usually a large one. This group did not seem at all interested, unless Scraddius was willing to ask them to send a whole wagon of things he knew nothing about. The more he listened, the angrier he became, and the angrier he became, the more his interest was piqued. He found it maddening and enthralling at the same time. What he liked most was the fact that this was different and he had a chance to maybe be part of something interesting and valuable. However, he did not at all, not like not being in control.

Scraddius picked up his mug of whatever the servant boy had brought out and drank deeply. He was thinking. He placed the mug on the table and slowly wiped his lips with the delicate linen cloth.

Below the table, Torrin was pinching his palm very hard with the fingers of his other hand. The pain kept him focused on the story. He never wavered. He never flinched.

Scraddius looked down and considered the artistry on the side of his mug before asking, "Then why was the red-haired girl giving the introductions to Bernabe and the only one speaking to Glenna while you louts stood by silently?"

Torrin sighed, inclined his head to Scraddius in a conspiratorial way and said, "The girl is a rare beauty and we can often procure better lodging and favors if the right people are taken with her charms. As for your galla Glenna, we did not feel it necessary to waste our breath with the conversation when the two were discussing foodstuffs. Gale here is very good with the medicinals; however, she is really just a girl, but we let her take her lead when she desires or she gets angry and we have to put up with her pouting. "

Scraddius was finally relaxing. This man "Tarmon," seemed nonplussed by anything. It was refreshing to have to actually think during one of these conversations. He sighed a little, trying not to be too interested and said, "Tell me about your medicinals."

Torrin continued on with the story, keeping all the details just so, "Our cases in your hallway contain our samples; let us inspect each one in turn with you to give you a flavor for the power they may bring to you."

Scraddius waved his hand and said, "Go ahead." He had experience with groups like this before, full of promises and cures for the ailments of the people. Their promises were empty. He hated wasting time with people like this, but you never could know when a real one might come along, so he needed to be diligent. And anyway, if something of value was here, he did not want to take a chance that someone else might find out about it before he did or that he let it slip through the fingers of the kingdom.

They retrieved the cases from the hallway. As they had figured, the small wax seals had been broken. Scraddius already had helped himself to a view. But they were not surprised. However, nothing was out of sorts or damaged. For the rest of the morning, the four of them showed Scraddius the trappings of their art.

And their intense study all winter with Ipi began to pay off. And they knew that the preparations at home were going to pay off too. Things were looking up!

             *   *   *

"Return to the healing box," said Scraddius. "Show me again what you have that may be used to fix a person who has been injured or is sick."

Torrin led the way to the case Dessa had carried. Salves, ointments and tinctures were arranged neatly in front of the open case on a forest green cloth. He said, "De...Gale is our expert in healing compounds." He caught himself, almost slipping up on her name.

They had decided early on that both Torrin and Dessa's names were a liability. There could only be so many red-headed Dessas around, and that her name in this kingdom, for all they knew was forbidden. What with her name being the one tied to the demise of the king's three sons, just uttering it could be dangerous. And Torrin's name, although maybe not as dangerous as Dessa's, would certainly raise a question or two. So they decided to keep things just a little safer and adopted Tarmon for Torrin and Dessa's previous namesake of her grandfather, Gale.

Only Dessa had noticed the color rise some in Torrin's face at his almost fatal slip. To distract the dark man who was the focus of their ruse though, she slyly said, "This may be bold, but a man of your intentions should understand." She seductively arranged her red curls to one side and then unlaced the top set of laces of her blue velvet dress. This she did unhurriedly and hardly took her eyes off of Scraddius. She noted with delight his attention to her fingers as they slowly worked the laces. Bending over with a bit more sultriness than a true tradesperson might, she picked up a small brown jar that sported a green ribbon tied around its tapered top.

"As you are well aware," she began. "Your men in the field cannot fight effectively when they are fending off the feverish teasach or their nose is dripping with such ferociousness from an inflammation of the face that they cannot breathe well. Alas we have found a remedy that is so much more effective than wishing the infected person sláinte."

She then with a fluid motion wrapped her long fingers around the tall top of the jar, removed it and laid the top and bottom gently on the table. Deftly, and maybe a little more slowly than really necessary, she moved the fabric of her dress off her shoulder. She was revealing much more of herself to Scraddius than Quillan would have liked, but Quillan kept his ground, figuring she had good intentions.

Dessa gracefully ran her finger in small circles upon the top of the green paste, the contents of which filled the jar. She then slowly ran that paste laden finger in an even oval atop of her exposed pink shoulder. Once the compound had warmed on her skin, which took only a moment, she then slowly approached Scraddius and offered her now well anointed shoulder to him.

Without looking around, and certainly without taking his eyes off of her, he did, with as much authority as possible, bend over and smell the now oily wet oval atop her shoulder. His head jerked back with a start. "What is it?" he said, giving his nose a long wipe.

Torrin began speaking so as to not let Scraddius' fetid gaze be distracted from what he was looking at. Although this gaze bothered him some, he knew this was necessary. "It is an extraction of the mionntas plant carefully imbibed with essential oils and the wax of honeybees. It took us four years to obtain a mixture that met our intention of helping break the inflammation of a teasach and enable better breathing without causing harm to the nasal passages of the user."

Scraddius was pleased. These people actually might have something of value. In all his winters of looking, he had never before experienced something as strong as this, nor as pleasant. And of course, the fair haired wench with the very naked shoulder did help to frame the value of the goods offered. Still, he needed to push for more that would make an audience with that scruvuling scod Gaerwn more enjoyable. "Yes," he said, having gained his composure from his first experience with strong peppermint. That is very interesting. However, much of the same result may be had by holding a hot rag with steam over a person's face for a short while. The steam breaks up the evils in the face and helps the teasach to abate. So nothing different than what you have here." Turning slyly toward Torrin, he said, "Do you have anything else? Maybe something that can help that is not just a substitute for hot water?"

Torrin wanted to ask the silly arse standing here if he thought the men in his army, or for that matter the people living in this kach of a place often had access to hot water and a rag. But he decided that letting Scraddius continue to be right was the best path forward. So silence descended on the room for a moment and then Etworth nonchalantly said, "Do ye have anyone with an injury that refuses to heal on its own?"

Scraddius stood in thoughtful ponderance, one hand holding up a well chiseled chin. He knew of many people with cuts and scrapes and injuries that would not heal; it was a common problem in any kingdom. Infection killed more people than anything else. However there was not one of them he could think of whom he would want to sully this room for a demonstration. Furthermore, the fewer people who met this little band of medicine traders the better. What they had was on the border of powerful and he was not about to share it. Although he had not let on yet that he was enormously interested.

Dessa stood behind Scraddius and mouthed a word to Torrin.

Of course, Torrin could not understand her and stood dumbly with his mouth threatening to utter something ridiculous.

However, Quillan, being her half brother picked it up in an instant. "Did the fair maiden, yer assistant Glenna have an injury about her arm?"

Dessa smiled.

Scraddius thought for a moment and then remembered. Yes, the lesson he had given her last fall had lingered. It would not heal, no matter how she attended to it. The best doctors of the kingdom had worked on her long slender arm. To no avail.

"Yes," he said presently. "She does have an injury to her arm that does not want to acquiesce to healing. Would you care to attend to it? I am sure she would be a willing victim to your compounds. Mind you though, if you kill her, one of you must stay here and take her place as my assistant." At this joke, he smiled a low and treacherous smile while looking at Dessa, followed by a raised eyebrow.

None of the others in the room thought it a joke.

Torrin stood tall and delivered a strong question, "And if we can heal the maiden's wound, what good comes of it for us?"

Scraddius was not worried and saw this as an easy way to ferret out the claims of these people and move on. He was growing tired of the charade and was thinking he had more interesting business to attend to. Glenna's injury had held unhealable for an entire winter and so this would end things now. He did have to decide whether or not these people could leave though. He understood they had brought very well-tended steeds that would be useful to keep. If the only thing they had to offer was a nose clearing salve, then they were not of great use.

"Show me healing on the wench's arm, and you may have an audience with the king."

Dessa said firmly, "Have her come to us with warm clear water and two clean cloths."

Cocking his head at the impudent woman who had just spoken without permission, Scraddius lingered his eyes thoughtfully on her glistening shoulder, smiled and decided to play along, "As you command," he said whimsically and with a note of sarcasm.

*   *   *

Soon Glenna had arrived with the requested items in hand. Dessa explained what they were going to do and got to work under the thoughtful gaze of her team.

Scraddius was at his desk, meeting with a never ending stream of disparaging and always pleading people. Each one, one at a time at his own pace, which was never very speedy.

Most of them got sent away in tears.

61.
Tale

Besides the crackling of the fire there was not a bit of sound in the big room at the Journey Inn. It was as if everyone had stopped even breathing.

The news that they were sitting in the same room, at the same moment as the son of Valterra and Kaitlyn was astounding. Almost heart stopping astounding.

Everyone had known that Harold and Karina were very old and might have known Valterra and Kaitlyn. That was a myth anyway, and everyone enjoyed believing in the story.

However, this was now the real truth.

Many eyes searched out Ipi. They looked to her as the knowledge in the room. Her quiet and gentle smile told them that what they were hearing was the truth. It made the whole thing even more astonishing.

The feats of valor and heroic might of Valterra were not only legend among the people and travelers of the valley. They carried about them a mythical air of true nobleness and the highest form of goodness imaginable to any living human.

All eyes focused back on Ol' Dogger as he swallowed hard. He brought his lips tightly together to control his face as the memories had come flooding back from oh so long ago. The strong tea that Ipi had endeavored him to drink was a potent mix of ginseng and rhodiola. The concoction had made Ol' Dogger not only feel better, but had loosened the strings to his memory and now he wanted to share these intense wonderful emotions that were bubbling up.

"I remember gettn' rocks. All day long, everra day, collecting rocks for the fireplaces and to fortify the bottoms of the walls around the great room. The rocks along the walls would help keep the animals from tryin to burrow in towards the warm area. There were certainly a lot more of them critters back then. So much more than now."

"Valterra and me mother Kaitlyn was such in love. I would lie abed at night and watch them go about the evening chores. Stoking the fire, putting up the breads for risn. There is always works to be a done." Ol' Dogger breathed in the memory and continued.

"An always, every night, there would come a time when they astop workn', and would wash up. I mean, they would wash each other up. Me dad would put on smaller sticks to the fire to get up the flames, and ma would have a big pot of warm water awaitn.' An each time, it was the same. She would take off his boots and hang them on those pegs right there," and he pointed to two solid wooden pegs, high in the room, near the fireplace. Every eye in the room followed his finger to these pegs. And suddenly, something just so normal, just so regular linked them all to Valterra and Kaitlyn. And they all knew that over the course of the next few days, each one of them, by themselves would walk over and carefully touch one, or both of those pegs. They would close their eyes and relive the story being told and they would connect to the past of Journey.

"Me dad always told me that dry boots was ever so important, and ma supported that need." His gaze fell away from the pegs and back to the audience that he never had ever thought would be there. Just waiting for him to tell his story. He just marveled at the idea, them all caring.

"Of course by the time they got to the washn' part, I was fast asleep, so I dunno all the details, but they always awoke with a smile and nice words to start the day." He grinned a knowing smile and continued, "When I was but somewhat older, we had abuilt the first wing, which is now the kitchen and I had my own room for some privacy. They had their own room too, with warmth and safety. That ben' the room the kindly Miss Normadia uses, along with the bathn' room. Harold and Karina split that room in two ta make what we gots now. I thought it verra smart of 'em."

The group now looked upon Normadia. She knew what they were thinking and she could not believe it herself. She, just she? The common maiden was living in the same space these legends had used as a bedroom? It explained the feelings sometimes that she was not alone. That something lurked in the air. Something kind, yet she had felt at times, not alone. She blushed and brought the back of her hand to her mouth as the idea settled in and a warm glow settled upon her face and flushed fully through her body.

Ol' Dogger kept on, "And so the winters came and went. We added to the place, we kept a livn and word spread thast there was a safe place where ye could be if ye wanted ta be. Of course, father had to deal with a few folk who thought they could just come here and make this their home, free and clear. Most saw the light of wisdom by a good talkn' to. But there are three or four souls buried in the woods who would not listen and challenged that grand man to stand to a fight." Ol' Dogger shook his head slowly. The long gray pony tail swished and swashed gently across his back.

"He would try to deter them from such foolhardiness, but they would get up full right of themselves and figured him tryn to talk them out of it was his way of showing his cowardness." Ol' Dogger sighed and then sniggered a little. "These events, though few and far between, were the only time I would see me mother become at all disenchanted with the man." Everyone in the room was at the edge of his seat, wondering how Valterra, defending his honor, could somehow annoy the fair sweet lady Kaitlyn.

"I remember one time, a man as big as me father had been livin here for a time. This big lummox, he just sat by the fire or outside in the sun a feelin' sorry for imself. Seems his father had a run off and the mother was so distraught she found a ledge on a cliff and hurled herself to the great beyond. He was just a miserable mess and worthless to us," and Ol' Dogger smiled, "Other than given off heat and makn' shade, accordn to me father."

Everyone laughed a little; they all had known or met folk like this. People not pulling their weight, thinking the world owed something besides air and today's weather. So what Valterra did to solve this problem was of great interest to each and every one of them.

"So one last time, Valterra had asked the man to gather firewood, for the summer was a burnin up and soon we would be in snow so deep that any sort of reasonable firewood was not to be found. So later that day, as me father an myself came back from choppin logs for the new stables, we was greeted by a bundle o wood. Yes, that big self-imposed man had spent all afternoon and gathered all of one armload of winter heat. An he was a sweatn and a sighn like he was a tired out and would need some lass to massage his achen and abused muscles on the evening."

Murmurs of understanding swept through the group.

"An I was there, carryin the axe we had used to chopt down the logs for the stable. Father just said to the man, "Ye leave tomorrow so ye can find a shelter for the winter, but ye is not stayn' here." The man took hiself up to full height, looked down at us and informed my father that the only way he was a leavn was ifn he was dead." Ol' Dogger swallowed the last of his tea before continuing. "So father agreed and told him he would kill him in the morning if he was still here and then we walked away from the man. I remember the look on his face, his mouth sorta standin' open like he was catchin flies."

Alexia asked, "Did ye have to kill him in the morning?"

Ol' Dogger smiled and said, "Well the whole story seemed to go in many directions at once. Of course, the big guy, he was there, eatn our food and as father said, takn up space in the morning. So after the meal, we went outside to do a few things and I remember dad was in a fairly foul mood. He did not suffer takers well. So after a bit, we went back ta the inside and there was the man, just sittn by the fire, staring into the flames. So Valterra grabs his coat by the neck and drags the man a kickn and a cursn out the door and drops is sorry butt into the dirt. Well, as ye can a figure, the man takes off to me dad like a horse fly to a steak. An good old dad taught him a lesson or two. It was like a cat teasn a mouse before eatn it. The big man came time and again to Valterra. And dad, he just stepped aside or tripped him up, lettn' him wear hiself down to where he could not hardly stand no more."

Ol' Dogger looked around; he could see in their eyes they had the story going round in their heads. They could hear the thumpings and see the dust rising from the turmoil. They could feel the sweat upon the brow of the big sourful man, and the look of distain on Valterra's face as he let the big man beat himself into submission.

"Finally, the big man was so tired he could hardly stand up, and me dad just pushed him backwards and he fell like a sack of oats. As the man turned over to get up he was I am sure fully surprised to find a large boot stepping on the back of his neck. I will never forget it, because, this for me, cemented what Journey is all about." Ol' Dogger looked at Ipi and said, "I thinks it's about time for them scotches."

Ipi nodded a yes and replied, "Just finish this part of the story, because I am not moving until I hear the end. Then ye can enjoy all ye want."

Ol' Dogger fixed his feet into a new position around the legs of the stool and continued, "So me dad says, 'Where is your face?' and the man talks in the dirt, but it was of course sort of muffled since the man's mouth was really full of dirt and leaves. And so then dad asks him, very calmly, 'and who put it there?' Now the man was already to say it was me dad, or someone else, and then something took hold. Something clicked and all the blamin he had been doing to his own father seemed trite. An all it took was a mouthful of dirt." Ol' Dogger smiled.

"We packed him some food and sent him on his way. Of course invitn him back when he decided to pull his own weight and take responsibility for his own self."

Alexia asked the question everyone was thinking, "So he did not kill this man? And why was Kaitlyn, ere, your mum mad at Valterra?" Her eyes looked confused.

Ol' Dogger gave a good chuckle, "No we din no kill this one, me dad just killed his self pity was all. Me mum, well this a occasion, she thought Valterra had played with the man jus a mite too long and had enjoyed it too immensely much so."

"Well?" asked Alexia, "Was that true, did he?"

Ol' Dogger sighed this time and a look of seriousness crossed his face, "Me dad confessed to me years later that he had enjoyed that little round jus a wee too much, but it was all for the sake of good, so he was settled with it. An then he looked at me and said, "Never forget son, we all have a few issues that we must carry. All of us. You. Me. And even your dear mother.""

Ipi left to get the drinks.

Ol' Dogger climbed down from his perch upon the stool and stretched himself. Everyone else stood, it being a good time for a break. But now, they knew the summer would be different. It would be a summer of old stories that brought them back to their very roots. Stories that gave meaning to their history, to the people they knew and loved.

Ipi returned with a good mug for Ol' Dogger who accepted it with sincere gracefulness and set it down. Yes, he would consume it, but slowly tonight. There was so much more around him than the strong brew that was good. And he was looking forward to sharing with the people who all of a sudden seemed to matter to him just a bit more.

As the children prepared to sleep, the adults arranged themselves in a tight knot around Ol' Dogger. Each one in turn hoping the kindly old man would continue his tales for at least a while this evening.

* * *

Ipi walked over to Normadia and inquired, "You look deep in thought my dear, whatever is on your mind?"

Normadia looked up to the older woman and said, "My bedroom will never be the same. It's just so… it's such a …I cannot describe it."

Ipi agreed, "Yes, to be where great people have been, to walk their path is always something of an experience, because we often wonder if we are worthy of walking that trail. And to have slept where they slept all these winters? Well, when you think about it, it is sort of exciting! Is it not?"

"Why yes, but that is only the small part of it," agreed the beautiful brown haired girl.

"Oh?" said Ipi, her head tilted, waiting for the answer.

Normadia said slowly and quietly, "We had wondered, and," she drew a long breath, "now finding that Ol' Dogger is the son of Valterra and Kaitlyn, well, it would seem that there may be nothing stopping Torrin and Dessa from producing a babe."

Ipi smiled and said, "So the work Dessa and Torrin are endeavoring to accomplish in the field is even more important now!"

62.
A long thin line

Dessa slowly and gently washed the long red festering wound that ran the length of Glenna's arm with the warm wet rag. She took her time abrading and cleaning all the nastiness that comes from a weeping infected injury. Glenna was very stoic and hardly winced at all as Dessa invaded and cleaned the open sore. The entire length of the wound had not healed and ran with sticky odorous manifestations that were very unpleasant.

No one would know how or why the injury would not heal. Glenna had explained that she kept it clean and had no clue to the issue at hand. However, the pus and seepage would not stop and she had suffered with the idiocy of this all winter. It hurt on and off, sometimes much, and right now a lot since Dessa was messing with the entire injury.

Torrin had extracted some of the fresher willow bark for Glenna to chew upon, explaining to her not to swallow the wood, but to just let the juices from the chewing travel their natural path. She accepted without question and took her time, grinding the tough bark between her oddly white teeth. Torrin decided he would ask her sometime if he was afforded the chance, how she kept her teeth white.

Presently, Dessa had cleaned the wound down to the base of the sore and the long line of raw red flesh glared at them like an angry creature that would not leave a dream. Real, threatening, but hard to get your head around. Dessa decided that right now was not the time to inquire as to the true beginnings of this issue. It vexed her that a cut like this would be on a lady. It had been no accident, for that she was sure.

Walking over to her case, Dessa extracted a vessel about the size of the palm of her hand. It was wrapped in a brown cloth and tied with regular and unassuming sisal twine. It was probably the plainest container in the case of compounds she had carried in to tell their story.

Dessa put her fingers into the water they had been using and cleaned them as well as possible. This was not the time for any stray grains of sand or dirt to be showing up since the area to be attended to was going to be very tender anyway.

Eventually she was satisfied that her fingers were as clean as they could be, as was Glenna's injury. Dessa had also been stalling some to let the willow bark begin to perform its magic on the pain, which she knew would be acute and sharp for a short while.

Taking a deep and long breath, Dessa said, "This may sting some, but will feel better very soon."

Glenna looked at the younger girl and said, "Dear, when you are as old as I am, some stinging and some pain are just a regular part of life. And anyway, if you can make this blasted cut heal, even some, I will be eternally grateful." Glenna sighed and her shoulders slumped some indicating just how frustrated she was with the issue.

Dessa opened the sticky jar of yellow salve and dipped her index finger into the goo. A small tear shaped droplet trailed off the end; it was soft and shimmered some in the light. This she carefully applied to the wound, making sure that the groove in the long slender arm was full of salve from edge to edge with no gaps in the application.

They worked by the window where the light was better. Dessa was very intent on the work at hand and did not look up until finished. However, when she was done, the wound was perfectly covered with some of the last of Karina's special salve from top to bottom. Dessa thought, we are going to have to make more of this very soon. The large brown stoneware jug in the fruit cellar was almost half gone. And Dessa was sure that the folks at Journey would be using it judiciously as they ventured out on their spring tasks.

Dessa noted that it was just a delightful thought to consider mixing a batch of the sticky yellow stuff. She mused that she missed the kitchen and all its social bustle. The people, the smells and the genuine warmth. Journey felt very far away.

Dessa finished her memory and motioned with her head to Torrin to come over. She gave a glance to Quillan to be attentive; he nodded that he understood and put himself between the three at the window and Scraddius. To Scraddius Torrin inquired, "We also have an experimental lotion that will kill lice. This can reduce the festering of the children, especially during the winter months. Care to see the sample?"

Scraddius agreed, seeming to have lost patience with whatever was going on at the window with Glenna. The whole process was taking far too long for his taste. And the lice issue amongst the troops was a bothersome one. Much attention was lost in training due to entire squads almost dropping to their knees from the irksome itching.

Dessa looked into the face of the now very expectant Glenna who was wondering what was going on and said in a very quiet voice, "Please now just trust us; this will be very warm, but will by no means injure you. Please stay very still. Just breathe slowly and stay relaxed." Dessa smiled at Glenna and then turned her attention to Torrin.

Just as Ipi had taught them and they had done during the winter when one of the travelers at Journey had cut himself, Torrin and Dessa slid their cheeks together. With palms down and their fingers interlaced tightly they ran this assemblage together over the wound. Their hands were a whisker of a space above Glenna's arm and the nasty cut.

Glenna watched as an odd heat filled her arm and the salve that had been a thick paste, melted away to the cloth Dessa had tucked beneath.

Two and then three times, Torrin and Dessa's hands floated the length of the wound. They then slowly parted, flushed and warm, looking into each other's eyes, only as lovers do, and then they stopped all movement. Both of them looked at Glenna, and then at the wound.

Glenna's eyes followed suit and she let out a slight and almost inaudible gasp. Her arm was almost healed. She could see and feel the long line of infected skin righting itself, tightening and healing. Then at one end, the flesh came together completely, and like a graceful seam in fine linen the skin merged and healed down the length of her arm.

Yes, a fine line of a scar showed, but the infected wound was now completely gone.

Tears streamed down Glenna's face as the memory of the constant pus and the itching and the annoying issues faded to but a memory in what seemed to be, and rightly was a miracle. She slowly and carefully looked at her arm, twisting it left then right. It was hard to believe her eyes!

Dessa put a finger to her lips and said, "Please just play along. He must think it is just the salve. And the truth is, the salve alone would have healed you, it would take just a longer time."

Glenna nodded her agreement. Although not really yet understanding the need for the secret. It did not matter anyway since she was altogether not yet able to speak.

* * *

Torrin gathered himself up and walked over to where Scraddius was at his desk, busily annoying some person about cattle. Torrin just stood there patiently, waiting for the dark man with the black beady eyes to finish.

Eventually Scraddius looked up, not saying a word and just cocked his head. It was that questioning look that a cat gives you and seems to ask, "Why are you bothering me?" Torrin liked this little game; the man loved power, and anyone who loved power could be played. You just had to be careful and let them play the game one step at a time. Once they played, they lost, and sometimes never even knew it. You just had to let them think they had the upper hand while they were playing.

The truth was, people after power are usually the ones being played in the end. They are just blind to it.

"We have done our best with the wench's injury," said Torrin. "If you would, please do come and decide for yourself if the salve our team has created is worthy of investigation."

Scraddius gave a theatric sigh, and stood. He figured this would be over now and he could go find some wine and merriment to improve his mood. He sauntered over to where Glenna sat, her long naked arm extended. She and Dessa were chatting about food storage or some trivial and unimportant matter.

The man in the black robes looked. Blinked, and looked again. He then reached down, and gently picked up Glenna's arm and looked closely.

It was healed!

The implications of this were enormous.

He was sure that the greater political implications were far flung and completely lost on these medicinal peddlers. Scraddius slowly breathed through his nose. He closed his eyes and thought for a minute. Laying Glenna's arm down like it was a robin's egg, he said as quietly as he was able, "Very impressive."

With black robes swishing importantly, Scraddius reached his desk and then turned toward the group assembled before him. It was all Quillan could do to not smile, because the stress and excitement in the man's face was clearly evident. However, Scraddius tried to play it cool, as he always did.

"What you have shown me may be of interest to the king," he said all too nonchalantly. "You may retire back to your room. I will send word to you. Maybe he will see you in the morning." And with that he left the room, the door closing automatically behind him.

* * *

"How long have you been his assistant?" asked Dessa to Glenna as she packed her sample case. Dessa had sensed a tension between Scraddius and Glenna that she could not put her finger on. Since she really liked this woman, the thought of getting to know her seemed right, and she took a chance on some questions and more small talk.

Torrin, Etworth and Quillan were doing likewise, packing their cases, carefully securing their earthen jars amongst the compressed straw in their boxes. All of the compounds were in finely made brown ceramic containers.

Of course they had been crafted by Rebecca one at a time. The trick had been to fire them in the middle of winter in a place that had no kiln. Actually the oven that Torrin had built for the kitchen came to the rescue. Presently the heat from the fire that was required had driven everyone from the kitchen until the next morning. Only two of the little pots had cracked during the firing, which was lucky. And in the end, the whole lot looked very professional.

"My guess is this many winters," said Glenna holding up both hands.

Dessa did not say anything about the numbers or lack of them. She just nodded and smiled, acknowledging that this was a long time. It also told her to be careful of Glenna, that she might be more on Scraddius' side than was evident.

"Being here with him affords me some luxuries I could not otherwise obtain, such as the traders who bring me the Miswak twigs so I may keep my teeth white. They smuggle it to me, but Scraddius knows, and does not put up a fuss."

She sighed and ended with, "But I seem to put up with a lot. An awful lot," as she carefully investigated her now healed arm.

Dessa looked at the other woman and boldly said, "You are sleeping with him." It was more a statement than a question.

Glenna was not stunned by the young girl's blunt honesty at all. In fact, rightly so, Glenna figured she might feel better by sharing this odd predicament with someone. And sharing with this nomadic girl whom she would probably never see again seemed pretty harmless.

"It's complicated," said Glenna. "I guess it's always complicated in situations like this. But yes. We have our liaisons. Not too often, and always at his lodge in the woods. In fact that is where he cut me."

Dessa looked up; she has not expected that. But there it was in all its brutality. This man, no this entire kingdom, was one big monster! Did it make any sense at all? No it did not! Maybe it did, because it did not.

With these conflicting thoughts swirling in her head Dessa said, "Well I…"

And the big door Scraddius had exited by was quickly flung open with Scraddius entering the room. This time there was no theatric delay. Scraddius was purposeful in his entrance. He was followed closely by an old, mostly soiled man who seemed to be chewing something.

Scraddius said hurriedly, "May I present to you King Gaerwn."

Torrin's hand went to the back of his neck.

63.
Seren...

Most of the children were fast asleep moments after their soft little heads found pillows. They being willing victims of the excitement of the story and the drama of the whole evening. To think that not only did they themselves know more about the vaulted and wonderful couple Kaitlyn and Valterra, but to actually have met someone who knew them. Gosh! A present of knowledge that brought dreams of a gallant white horse and a tall broad shouldered hero being loved by a wonderful woman.

This would be a night of peaceful dreams that they would enjoy and remember for all their lives.

After a time, someone retrieved his lute from its leather case and began quietly strumming soft tunes. The adults were very much too excited to sleep. The energy in the room was brisk, although in a contrarian way, subdued due to its enormous intensity.

All was wonderful and normal beyond any expectation except for one wee issue.

This wee issue being Alexia.

The blonde little girl's eyes were just sparkling and mystical. You see, for as long as her little mind could remember, she and Ol' Dogger had been pals. He helped with her dolls and those wee doll people were as real for him (at least as she could see it) as they were for her. He held her when she scraped a knee. He taught her to build fires from nothing but some string and a stick and dry tinder. He taught her how to walk silently in the forest to spy on the creatures of the wood.

And so, as the lute player floated soft whimsical tunes across the room, she walked up to her pal and said with a mock sternness "Mr. Dog Ears, you are amiss!"

Ol' Dogger slowly placed the pleasantly large mug of scotches, courtesy of Miss Ipi onto the table and for the life of him could not figure out what this little sprite was talking about. "Mz Alexer (his pet name for her), whatever is ye yellow and fadn' mind speaken of?" (He would tease her that she was old and losing her memory; it was great fun.)

Alexia climbed up into his lap, stood on his knees and bent low to whisper her knowledge and tutelage into his waiting ear. With an exaggerated and very important level of whisper she said, "Dog Ears, Miss Ipi brought you a drink and you did not return the favor. It's very poor manners on your part. Look at the poor woman, just sittn' there pretending to enjoy the music, just a wishn someone would pay attention to her."

Ol' Dogger slowly brought his gaze to Ipi and noticed that everything Alexia said was true. His big strong hands wrapped gently around Alexia's waist and she found herself standing on the floor with him walking away from her.

The smile on her face was radiant.

Ol' Dogger approached Ipi without thinking. Usually talking to women caused his mouth to pucker dry and the strength to run from his muscles. But now, with her and him connecting at such a level, where she had figured out how to help him release his story, he felt the connection to be a safe one tonight.

"Mz Ipi," he said without a hesitation that surprised even him, "May I have the pleasure of procuring for ye a beverage?"

Ipi looked up, not startled, but in joyful amazement. "Why Ol' Dogger, what a pleasant surprise!" She thought for a moment and then with her head happily tilted said, "You know, I would fancy a mug of the scotches you are so fond of. They constitute a vile and obnoxious fluid, but I daresay, I do like them." And he saw her eyes twinkle in the delight of cutting lose some and letting her spirit join that of the happy crowd.

Ol' Dogger sought out a clean ceramic mug and returned with a generous portion. He delivered it with a bow and flourish of his hand. Ipi accepted the drink, and nodded her head in graceful thanks.

As soon as he had delivered his obligation he felt a tug at his hand. Looking down, he saw a beaming Alexia who with a graceful curtsy informed him that he now was required to lead her in dance.

And dance they did. Alexia and Ol' Dogger were often partners during the famous Journey parties, so this was not unusual. And they had a great time; two spirits celebrating wonder.

It did not take long for Alexia to find that her bed beckoned. So at the end of a tune, she rubbed her eyes, not wanting to sleep, but knowing that it was inevitable. She led him over to Ipi, placed his hand in Ipi's hand, and turned to find her rest. Ol' Dogger swallowed, deciding that this might not be bad. So he bowed low and swept one hand wide in an inviting arc.

Ipi, somewhat stunned, unsure of what to do, looked around. She spied Alexia standing next to the table that would serve as her bed for the night. The little girl tipped her head and slowly raised her arms, indicating stand up and dance. So Ipi did not only as Alexia instructed, but as her soul told her, it was the right thing to do.

Ipi and Ol' Dogger stood looking at each other for a moment and then Ipi indicated her head toward the area where others where dancing. She smiled as she saw Ol' Dogger's mind click back into form and lead her to the dancing area.

And dance they did. Fast. Slow. Close. Separated. And finally the lute player himself grew tired, and finished with a long slow ballad of graceful soul settling notes.

Afterward, Ipi and Ol' Dogger sat at a table near the fire and shared stories.

"I have not had someone ask me to dance in a verra verra long while," said Ipi shyly.

"It be then that the men of this worl have lost their senses on a large and depressin scale," said a mildly blushing Ol' Dogger. "Ye is a fine partner in the dance area and what's more, ye is good for the soul."

"Thank you dear," said Ipi. "But your soul is just fine. It's just that it needed some release tonight, and ye found it."

Ol' Dogger sat next to her and sighed a grateful, "Yes."

She looked at him differently for the first time tonight now. He had shaved and bathed and brought himself up to what she figured was about the highest level of civility he could muster. For a man close to three thousand years old, he actually was quite fetching.

The big room had quieted now to nothing but a few oil lamp flickers, licks of yellow firelight and mostly snoring. The two of them sat for a while, reveling in the peace.

After a time, Ipi stood, stretched her arms long and said, "For this old lady, it's time to get reacquainted with that soft mattress and pillow in my room."

Ol' Dogger looked up at her, nodding an understanding. He was bone chilling tired, but exhilarated all the same. He did not want the night to end. This had been a catharsis for him. A purification of his story. Of his past. Of what made him who he was. And they had honored him. He finished his look at her with a smile and he raised a hand to her to bid her a fond goodnight.

Ipi took his hand in hers. She squeezed it gently and said to him, "I certainly hope you plan on joining me upstairs. It's been a long time."

Ol' Dogger had not enjoyed a serendipitous moment in what seemed forever. And although his knees almost gave out, he followed with a wonderful and knowing smile.

64.
Chair

"Show me," said Gaerwn, the scruffy looking monarch. "I want to see this miracle with me own eyes. I wan te see it for real, because everybody, even my good friend Scraddius here, could be in question. And of course, if this does not work, he could very much wind up to be a dead man." And then Gaerwn turned his eyes towards Scraddius and said, "He would be a dead man, very slowly."

Scraddius, trying to keep control of things on his own terms declared, "Here it is, proof of what I told you about." He had positioned himself next to Glenna and was holding her arm. Although he was holding it like a trophy fish and it was very uncomfortable for her. Of course, neither Scraddius nor Gaerwn noticed her discomfort at all.

Scraddius began to unfold his version of a story to Gaerwn, "This maiden sustained this long and very unfortunate injury last fall. Sadly, from its length and depth, it had taken to infection, just like the bane of our soldiers in the field. It would not heal, even though the best remedies your kingdom had to offer were brought to bear. These traders of a newly developed set of medicinals applied a thin coating of a yellow ointment on the wound just before the mid-day meal. Now, you can see with your own eyes, and feel with your own hand that nothing short of a miracle is now within the confines of this room."

Gaerwn inspected the arm. He traced a darkly knurled finger down the length of Glenna's long thin white scar; a scar that was not yet hard, but fresh and bright white. He uttered not a word, but seemed lost deep in the thoughts of his wretched and scheming mind.

Scraddius glanced his eyes around the room at everyone present, clearly sending a message that no one should speak at this time. Only him. He was in control, and if you questioned that, it might be the last question you ever asked.

Eventually Gaerwn looked up and he too looked around the room. It was as if he had not noticed before now the other people standing there, being there, alive there. He actually looked somewhat surprised that other people were here.

Finally he asked to no one in particular, "Who is the party responsible for this?"

Torrin was about to speak when Scraddius firmly launched into a long stream of verbiage. "Sire, as you know, we are besieged by a constant stream of wanton traders who want nothing more than to cart off with your gold tucked firmly in their wagons. I work very diligently to filter out the chaff from those who bring real value. So I had this group prove to me the reality of what they said they offered. You are now witnessing the fruits of that exercise."

Gaerwn looked around again at the foursome and said, "Well, this may be yur lucky day. Come to the chambers to chat. I don't care at all about all this other medicinal rubbish you have that Scraddius has been scuffling on about. I will want all of this concoction that you can make. With this, I shall rule everything!"

And with those words, he turned on his heel and strode away, dark eyes gleaming with the thought of the power he could now yield.

Scraddius said to the four of them, "Bring the jar of the special yellow ointment. I shall have the rest of your wooden boxes taken back to your room. Come, come," he slapped his hands together the way a mother would as if gaining the attention of her children, "We must go now with haste; he is not a patient man."

Dessa retrieved the sticky brown wrapped container from her case and they fell in step, single file behind Scraddius.

As they followed him down long dark passages, they all wondered what the next few hours would bring. Their goal had been to secure the order for as many of the magic medicinals as possible. Then, they would be able to insert a large band of warriors within the confines of the compound. Even though Gaerwn had more soldiers, their army would attack from within, with stealth and creative disabling might. Surprise and the complete unknown of what was happening inside the castle would be on their side.

All they had to do now was procure the agreement from Gaerwn to have the shipment arrive later this summer and leave. They knew, even as they trod down the cold wet stone corridor, that the pace of building the wagons and implements of their plans at Journey was already hectic day and night.

Torrin was in the lead working to keep up with Scraddius. Etworth second with Dessa in front of Quillan. They had decided that Quillan would hold out for higher prices and Torrin would want to make a deal, especially for such a large order. The size really did not matter; they would make Gaerwn believe it was a very large and good deal with him coming out as the real winner.

They rounded a corner into a large room with interior walls that were built in what looked like a bit of a haphazard form. It took a few moments to figure out that they were now in the public chambers of the king.

There was an outer room of sorts and then behind these walls that were sorted about in a fashion were the inner chambers. It looked like it was meant to be confusing. That was exactly the idea. It was confusing.

The design had been deliberate. Gaerwn was the center of power. The outer rooms and walls were haphazard to make a stealthy approach difficult. As well as a hasty exit. Anyone trying to flee would most likely run in a circle and come back into the throne room. Gaerwn had wanted to make escape difficult.

Quillan tried to get his bearings. The outer area was dark while the inner area seemed bright with candles and warm from two large fireplaces built into the walls that seemed to spring up from the floors. He was again marveling at the engineering of the people in this land. They lived like dogs but they had displayed creative genius.

Scraddius told them to wait in a little alcove. There was much activity around. Much scurrying about. Many people, obviously very important. They were going about their business. Some were dressed in rags, some in fine linens. Others in revealing outfits of feathers and small off cuts of skins. It was all confusing, but exhilarating at the same time.

The four of them waited. Etworth thought it all very strange. Dessa mentioned that it seemed to be just a normal court for a king. Torrin had never seen a court this busy or so full of characters.

Quillan said, "The place just generally pisses me off and the sooner we leave the better."

Scraddius came to fetch them. He brought them around one of

the fireplace walls and then they were in the center of King Gaerwn's power.

Quillan immediately had a thought about the place; jesters, groveling and action, all very bright and noisy, but no substance.

Etworth thought there were a great many people to sell things to and this would be a wonderful place to stay.

Dessa was again nonplused but her inner voice said, this was a dangerous place.

Torrin on the other hand, swung his eyes across the expanse of the room, fending off the rising wrench in the back of his neck. And then he saw the lady in a chair with the black and blue face.

Actually he could see, she was tied to the chair.

And that lady was his mother.

65.
Untie

Ol' Dogger's eyes looked at Ipi like she was a fragile piece of well-crafted glass. Like she had just burst into a million pieces around him and he was barefoot. Sort of an amazed look but with a hint of danger at the same time.

Ipi closed and secured the door to the room she had been offered at the Journey Inn. Not just any room mind you. It was a room of greater proportions than most, unique in many ways and most often, even in winter; warm as a fresh pan of bread pudding.

It was perfect, except for only one small flaw; there was only one window at the far end. But she was able to look beyond that annoying little issue and enjoy the rest of its eclectic geography and charm. She also enjoyed the fact that she had some privacy and warmth. Something most anyone in this part of the world would envy.

This room was built on the big curve. The big curve that was the back of Journey's massive stone chimney. Yes, the chimney of that gigantic stone fireplace that was the center point of the big room downstairs. And by virtue of being on the chimney, this room, like Normadia's room, was warm and dry. It was like having your very own personal radiator, and she deemed it quite luxurious.

When you entered Ipi's private chamber through the well-crafted and rather large door, you were immediately presented with this broad and curving stone structure. It was amazing! Multi-colored stones, all round, of all sizes and colors made up a mosaic of no pattern other than to be quite large and almost overwhelming. Across the entire one side of the room, covering the space from floor to ceiling was this stone wall. And as your eyes followed along the massive stone edifice, you saw that the room itself curved with the stones as they rounded the corner.

At the far end stood a large wide overstuffed bed. A short set of steps actually led up to it. These were necessary since the entire frame was so high off the floor. Most men would be amazed that the top of the mattress came to the bottom of their ribcage. A bed so high off the floor that it caught the warm air of the room during the cold winter and afforded the sleeper the incredible luxury of a warm dry bed.

The room was for someone who would be staying at Journey for a while longer than most. The tall bed offered a place beneath to store the trappings of the traveler. Additionally, in the mortar holding the fireplace together, stout pegs had been burrowed into the heavy clay, mixed with sand, which made up the mortar. Here, the sojourner could hang their clothing and have it air dry as probably never before.

Just inside the door was a sturdy table that enjoyed the company of four good sized and well-built chairs. This gave any family who might be staying here a place to gather and converse. If there was no family involved, then the table was the perfect place for a long game of Tafl where there was plenty of room for the game pieces as well as the required mugs of beverage that made the long play time tolerable. Assorted small tables and stools scattered the floor plan of the room as needed. Appropriate and worthy were they of this room.

All in all, in modern terms, you might call this a suite. Ipi on the other hand looked at it as her current, and very wonderful, little slice of perfect.

Ol' Dogger sat at the table. He slowly, ever so slowly and very carefully, for no particular reason, set his mug upon its well-worn and clean top. Looking up at Ipi, you could see a longing in his eyes. A longing not for a woman, but for her.

"Dogger, you look as though you want to eat me," she laughed.

He blushed red velvet in his cheeks and said, "Sweet Ipi, I don not so much wan to eat ye, as I wan to feel the way I did when ye an me went ta sleep that night before ye took off like lightnin from a snowstorm them many winters ago."

Ipi pinched her lips. She just stopped moving and looked at him. Her eyes saw him as he was those so many, many, many nights ago. When she had spread her knees wide to make room for him as the woman she loved to be. She looked at him as the man she thought was so much more than herself. And instantly, she remembered the girl that ran from him and remembered how she had felt unworthy.

But she was different now.

As was he.

They both had been apart for so many winters. Searching for someone who was right there. Just themselves. And now, they had come back together, as two people, just as they were, but never were before.

She had transferred the scotches he had brought her to a new container; this treasured container was wrought from glass. And this particular glass was eclectic, artistic and looked like it was almost of another world. From a wide oval base that stood solidly on the table a tall and slender stem rose up to support a large well rounded bowl. Various colors flowed around and around in what looked like a never ending rainbow that just went on and on. These colors were infused into the glass and it was as if magic had taken hold of the generally clear substance. Ol' Dogger looked at it and saw that it was at the same time expressive and joyous from top to bottom.

Looking carefully at the seemingly never ending colors, Ol' Dogger asked "What is that?"

She beamed at the multicolored mystery on the table and she sat down to show him this marvel. "This is made by a new and very creative art that I understand is called glass blowing. A friend of mine brought it from a place called Mesopotamia. I have not one bit of an idea where that is, but the people there created a beauty and it's verra fragile. I had two, and one just tipped over one night and shattered into tiny slivery little pieces. And those pieces also would stick into yer skin and stay there, causing great discomfort if ye touched them wrongly.

Ol' Dogger backed off just a bit to make sure nothing from his body or near him would intrude upon this inspired craft of color.

For Ipi this was a work of treasure. A work of art that so purely expressed beauty, it made her almost giddy when she used it. And in her hands now, it was a work of fragile intimacy.

As they talked, the room became warmer. Ipi's fingers slowly slid up and down the stem of the glass, almost idly playing with the smooth hardness. Then her palm cupped the bowl, gently yet with firm grace. And continuing the motion, almost as if she were inviting it to come, let the long firmly tapered bit of art travel to her lips where she enjoyed running her tongue seductively around the edge of the bowl before consuming the inner liquid. She did this in a slow motion, never taking her eyes off of Ol' Dogger. She enjoyed the wetness that was left on her lips, and Ol' Dogger's expression upon his face.

The silence in the room thrummed in all their ears.

Ol' Dogger took a large gulp of his drink from what now seemed a very plain and dull ceramic mug. He set it down and smiled. Standing, he walked over behind Ipi and put his arms around her. His arms crossed below her neck, and in each hand he took one breast gently into his palm.

She sighed and leaned back into him. With a slow motion her head rubbed back and forth among his midsection causing him to sigh deeply.

They massaged each other without words. As time passed, they came closer and closer, letting the heat and intimacy build.

Ol' Dogger bent down and kissed her ear, played with her earlobe for a time, and then cautiously whispered, "Ye can ave me stay if ye like, as long as yer not a runnin off like las time. Ye made me heart bleed for a verra long while."

She purred and sighed and finally said quietly, "Dogger, ye brought up feelings in me last time that I could not understand and I was verra afraid. I know now you would never hurt me in any way, an these feelings are my own. But to deny them is not right. And I have missed you verra much. So no, ye will find me right next to ye in the morn."

He walked behind her and stood her up from her spot at the table where she had shown him the pretty glass piece of stemware. He turned her to face him. He worked his fingers and very slowly, never losing touch with her skin, artfully teasing and stroking, untied her dress.

As it fell to the floor, their lips reunited with the same passion and fervor of long ago.

66.
An Order

She gasped and let out her little shriek as intense color rose in her cheeks before she could control herself. If Ethelda's hands had not been tied to her thighs, she would have instinctively brought her hand to her mouth.

Torrin just stared. Blinked hard. And then turned a face toward Gaerwn that was not only murderous, but if he could, he would have spit venom.

Gaerwn had been sitting on the thickly padded throne with one leg outstretched and a big foot resting on the shoulder of some farmer who was pleading for the return of a cow. The ruddy king was dabbling with the farmer and taunting him. The brute was pushing the farmer back and forth with his big boot-covered leg shaking him like a rag doll. The man was in tears, and you could tell that this cow, or the issue around the cow, was very important. To Gaerwn it was just a chance to annoy someone and enjoy himself.

At the shriek of Ethelda, Gaerwn slid his gaze to her eyes and then followed her focus to the subject of her fright. Hmmm he thought. One of the medicine peddlers. I wonder if she knows 'em? His voice boomed orders as he kicked the farmer with the cow issue in the face and sent him sprawling, "Bring that man to me," he said pointing a knurly finger to Torrin.

Torrin's feet left the floor as two burly guards picked him up by the arms, hands firmly on his elbows. They deposited him, standing quite straight in front of Gaerwn.

The king looked Torrin up and down. As he was contemplating the young man standing in front of him, he dug a random chunk of food from between two black teeth and flicked it. This black little bit of sewage landed on Torrin's coat, sticking firmly on the fabric with a mix of spit and rot.

Torrin looked down at the small bit of disgust and did not move. He just cocked his head and returned his gaze up to the dirty brute in front of him. His heart pounded in his chest. His arms were seething to move and aid his hands at either poking out the wretch's eyes or crushing his windpipe. Torrin's whirling mind, at this point could not decide which would bring more satisfaction.

"Sweet dearest Ethelda," said Gaerwn slowly, "It would occur to meself that ye must somehow know this man?" He looked at her with disdain, "And he must mean something to ye, or ye would not have given us a very entertaining lady-like shriek?" His gaze had swung back to Torrin.

"Well?" inquired Gaerwn of the lady tied to the chair, "Are ye gonna admit to yer knowledge of this scruvuling little mutt or shall I gut him slowly right here and now and then ye can let me know?"

Breathlessly, and failing to hid her fear, Ethelda said, "I don't know him; he just reminded me of someone I knew once."

Gaerwn was now enjoying this cat and mouse game. He the cat, everyone else the mouse! "So who might that have been?" he said slowly, his eyes on Torrin, looking for some measure of fear or message from his face.

By now Ethelda had regained some of her composure, and said, almost believably, "He reminds me of our butcher's son. But it's not him." And she settled back in her chair, as much as she was able. Torrin could tell she was still reeling, breathing long slow breaths, trying to calm herself.

"Well then good," said Gaerwn. "You won't mind if I remove an ear or something really unneeded then?" he sneered at Torrin. Gaerwn smelled a rat, and he was going to flush it out.

"Suit yourself," said Ethelda. "Whatever cruelty brings ye the most pleasure."

*   *   *

In the flash of an instant Torrin found himself turned around and his throat held tightly by a large hairy and dirt ridden arm. The arm was to be expected in a situation like this, and the normal thing to do was to stamp one's heel down upon the top of your attacker's foot, trying to break as many bones as possible and drive sharp searing pain through their entire body so they had not the strength to hold you.

However, at this very instant, Torrin found the tip of a long tapered stiletto slid deeply up his nose. He pushed his head back instinctively, trying to avoid the sharp blade from entering his brain via the tender membranes inside his nostrils. But as he pushed back, the sharp knife ground against his nasal passages and he could feel and taste the blood dripping salty wetness down his lips and chin. The pain in his head began to form as a sharp point behind his eyes. His eyes too began to water and it blurred his vision.

Torrin was helpless. His reflexes behaving just as Gaerwn knew they would. Gaerwn had practiced this move hundreds of times. He had perfected it on prisoners just a few winters before.

Gaerwn, being of a mind to find new and interesting ways to keep control, had determined he needed to know and be comfortable with a way to keep ultimate control of things at any time of his choosing. Especially when a person of any sort stood before him.

To figure out a method, the big brute had ordered the transport and deposit of five prisoners each day to the throne room. Every day, just before the noonday meal he worked to refine and practice the art of his desire for the ultimate control over a person. Taking these unsuspecting prisoners by surprise one at a time, he figured out a procedure that was to his liking and amusement and then practiced it over and over.

The first part was to determine what part of the body would be his initial target. So, amongst these prisoners every day, he had plied his long sharp knife into various body parts. He decided he needed to determine what part of the body held the most surprise, because, he knew, he needed options, drama, control and not just instant death.

He found quickly that ears were just ticklish unless you buried the blade about the depth of your thumb. That did not work because they were quickly dead, and that was useless.

Next, he found that sliding the blade behind a man's eye left them completely untenable for conversation later given all the shrieking and blathering that always accompanied such an experience.

And you had to bury the blade too deep into a man's clach to get his real attention, and anyway it was too hard to find the place amongst all the clothes many people wore.

And requiring anyone to appear before him naked seemed just awkward at best.

Women were particularly difficult. Finding, let alone invading their báltaí with a knife was cumbersome. If you cut their breasts, they just looked at you like you were some sort of misguided pervert and made you feel small. Most any other place was just annoying to them and it was generally useless for controlling them at all. Women seemed tough beyond all reason.

However!

Everyone had a nose. Everyone's nose it seemed was sensitive. And, more importantly, everyone seemed to have an aversion to a long shiny sharp knife poking at the edge of their brain.

So Gaerwn had practiced and experimented with more than his share of noses. His tool of choice was his favorite stiletto that was carefully concealed in his broad belt. He had perfected just how far to dig in with the point to keep someone focused on the knife, and not on him. He knew how deep to send the blade to bring about enough blood to get his point across (pun intended) to everyone in the room. Because, there was no reason in making a stink out of something, unless you were going to create maximum impact on anyone who was within sight.

And best of all, he found that anyone with a long gleaming blade impaled up their nose was apt to agree with anything Gaerwn said. And more importantly, willing to agree with whatever was commanded. It was also a very expedient way to dispatch someone who was not complying to Gaerwn's wishes. Because a simple thrust of not only the knife, but a push on the back of their head quite plainly ended all the issues with this particular person.

And from an impact standpoint, everyone in the room got to watch this person's expression of agony, fear and death. The blood running from their nose across their face and the wretched gagging and gasping that accompanied such events were very theatrical and dramatic for Gaerwn. He was often torn between watching his victim or watching the faces in the room.

Such fun!

And the impact on the wretched lot in the room was very thorough. It seemed to settle everyone down and they all became much more agreeable. Gaerwn was known to perform his act of absolute power on unsuspecting and agreeable souls just to calm the room down.

And when you did finally extract the blade from their face, it was just easy and convenient to wipe it off on their close-by shoulder before dropping the now lifeless body to the floor. Very simple, clean, quick and most of all, very controlling from the first moment on!

* * *

So now, Torrin found himself rather cross-eyed, staring down at the glinting hilt of this stiletto dagger firmly implanted within his snout. Said dagger was grasped by a large dirty hand down which blood was now trickling in a warm small stream of crimson red. He accurately figured this blood was being let loose from within and through the front of his very captive face. This small stream of his life kept his attention that much more focused.

Gaerwn's other arm was tightly crossed in front of Torrin's throat, though not needed to control him, but there to keep him from moving and flailing or doing anything that might otherwise allow Torrin any modicum of control. However, it was pretty much not required as Torrin had decided any movement was unnecessary.

Looking back at Ethelda, Gaerwn grinned. She had a look of sheer terror on her face for she had seen this little play happen too many times before. Often with a very bad ending for the person whose nose was the focal point of the situation. Her tongue was trying to add moisture to what had become instantly dry and brittle lips. She strained at the ropes that bound her to the chair.

Gaerwn's eyes scanned the room, and not a soul moved. Not a lip moved. Not an eye was anywhere, but upon the shining blade that he, the almighty great and powerful king, had so aptly slid up this supposedly pretentious medicine man's little nose.

Gaerwn loved it.

He relished it.

He actually was physically excited and decided in a quick thought that it would take two wenches tonight to satiate his now aching desire.

He was in complete and utter control of the entire room.

Of everyone here.

Of everything.

Oh the joy of it all!

"Well my little boy," began Gaerwn. "How does it feel to be in my control again?"

Torrin sputtered a very wet and almost unintelligible response, "Again?"

Gaerwn laughed some and said, "Yes again my little tuilli. We waylaid you last spring and tossed you into the creek while studying attack approaches to that mud hut yer father called a castle. I was certain you would bleed out from the gash on yer leg. But no, ye wretched little flens. Ye came back here to haunt me. Or to let me enjoy finishing the job."

Without a word, he extracted the blade from Torrin's bloody nose and suddenly Torrin was shaken to his core. He could now see massive amounts of blood running down the front of his coat. Large rivulets of red quickly drenching his entire front. Yet he felt strangely calm. He looked down in disoriented horror at the long deep slash now open and gushing life from his arm.

And then the feelings registered.

Nothing.

He felt nothing.

Odd?

And since his nose was not imprisoned by the stiletto, he looked again, and could see why!

Gaerwn himself had deeply sliced open his very own arm. All along the fleshy part between wrist and elbow. Deep and crimson and wet with red. The blood ran freely around the raw glistening meat that was the muscle of the big man's appendage.

Torrin' body was suddenly released from the tight grip that had constricted him. He almost staggered to the floor, so heavy was his instant weight. But he did not fall. Gaining his footing, he turned toward the retched ruler. The ruler who was bleeding from his own inflicted wound who now said to the four of them, "Fix this by morning, and ye shall live. If ye don' I will ave ye burned at the stake at noon."

With that, Gaerwn sat down with a groan on the broad stone floor of his throne room and looked at the medicine peddlers in front of him. He then just laughed a roaring wicked laugh and bled upon the floor.

67.
Something

"So how long has it been since ye slept in and missed breakfast?" Ipi asked Ol' Dogger in a quiet tender voice.

"It's been quite a long time," replied Ol' Dogger in a tired but satisfied voice. He stretched himself as he had not stretched in a long time. His bones seemed to crackle in a smile all along his frame.

Rolling over towards her, he reached out a hand and slowly trailed one long finger from her head, across her face and down her long torso. Ipi closed her eyes as she let the sensation be absorbed by her skin. His finger left what seemed to be a long thin trail of passionate fire. A fire she had not felt for a long time.

He explored for quite a while, running his finger across all the nooks and crannies of his re-found lover. The only response he really received were low deep sighs of ecstasy. This seemed to work entirely well for him though.

The sun had risen much beyond the early morning hours, and the light of the day flooded their room. Eventually Ipi sighed quietly and announced that "They should get up and make themselves useful."

She looked at Ol' Dogger and their eyes met. He said, "Woman, you have thoroughly wenched me. I dunno know if I will ever stand again."

She pinched one of his nipples playfully and exited the tall bed. "It is a glorious day, and as much as I could stay with you all day long, we need to get out in the sun."

Ipi proceeded to shrug into a light shift and then headed out the door. Ol' Dogger rolled to one side and clambered out of the big bed.

He surveyed the room. What clothes they had worn were in marvelous disarray across the floor. My, he thought; tis been a long time since me clothes were strewn about for good reason. He assembled the parts and made two tidy piles. Still padding about in his altogether, he went to the window and peered out.

It was a marvelous day. The sun was shining. He could hear birds singing and the sounds of work all around echoed off the big round stones of the chimney.

Soon Ipi entered the room. She carried a pitcher of hot steamy water, a cloth and a small bar of flower pressed soap. Sitting down at a small round brown table, she washed up with the cloth.

Ol' Dogger just watched, transfixed by her grace and beauty. She knew he was watching her attend to her morning cleaning, and she moved slowly. Ipi enjoyed the thrill of having the voyeuristic, yet completely approved, attention.

Presently, she stood up and made room for him to attend to himself as she knew he would. Many winters of living experience had taught him the value of proper washing. He did not relish getting a rash that could last many a winter. So he took good care of himself.

Ol' Dogger first discarded the used water via the window. He then replenished the basin with the steamy liquid. Sitting down at the table and enjoying Ipi watching him as she tidied up, he rinsed the cloth around in a few circles and made bubbles with the soap.

He chided himself some, playing as a boy would with the water. But he thought, "She must have released some simmering spirit in me, and it's a nice feeling!"

As he brought the steamy cloth to his face, a vision appeared in the steam. In a startled voice, he said mostly to the room, "There is trouble."

68.
Repair

Hearts pounded loud drumming beats in the ears of everyone in the big throne room. Still not a soul moved.

Gaerwn looked around again, wondering if anyone was going to do anything. He continued to smile, and his big overly bushy eyebrows were raised up in question.

Quillan figured out the challenge very quickly and began barking orders. This relieved Dessa of some stress, because she knew that in this room, in this place, in this kingdom, a woman taking over would be frowned upon. In this entire community, and it was easy to see, it was controlled by the men.

Pointing at a guard, Quillan commanded, "Get me someone smart from the kitchen. Now!"

The guard disappeared beyond a wall in a quick movement, happy to be away from a scene that could still become dangerous for anyone.

Quillan continued, "Etworth, help me get his coat off and raise the arm to quench the bleedn.'" He then motioned his head to Torrin to go take care of what he needed to take care of.

Dessa just stood, restlessly waiting for orders.

As he wrestled the coat off Gaerwn with Etworth, Quillan felt a tap on his shoulder. He looked up into the very pleasant face of a smiling young lady who had a black and blue injury to her face. Quillan could see beyond the injuries to a very pretty lass. A lass who both showed peace and love and a fair amount of stress in her eyes. He was looking into the fair face of Paroish.

In a soft and unhurried voice, Paroish said to him, completely nonplussed by what was going on in the big room, "You had asked for someone from the kitchen sir?"

Quillan looked at Etworth, shrugged his shoulders and said, "See that redhead there; she will need some towels and water or something.

Her name is Gale, go talk to her."

He had not said please, or thank you, or was the least bit gracious. He was not completely sure what was going to happen here and just wanted it to be over. At least on his terms and with a positive outcome.

The young lady made her way toward Dessa and after a few moments of conversation scurried away from whence she had come.

*   *   *

Paroish stood in the middle of the kitchen, all eyes upon her. These eyes were inquisitive, thirsty for knowing; waiting to hear about what was going on in the big throne room. She swallowed hard and said, "The king has injured himself, and we are to bring a clean bucket of hot water and another of cool water along with a few clean rags to the throne room."

"Weel de ol bastar die?" croaked a wizened old lady, stooped over and grey. She had been cutting up potatoes on a big old chopping block.

"It doesn't look very serious right now," answered Paroish. "He has a long cut on his arm; his desire is to test a new medicine the people in the room are offering to sell to the kingdom for the soldiers.

"Chac," spat the old lady and she went back to cutting the potatoes.

With the news that there was nothing fatal going on at this very moment, everyone else too went back to their activities, generally muttering about something or other. It was not uncommon to hear of a sordid event going on around Gaerwn. But all this hurry up that the guard had been prattling on about seemed pretty unnecessary for right now.

As Paroish filled a bowl with cool clear water from the cistern her eyes fell upon the sticky black slime at the edge of one of the slop buckets that were dotted about the kitchen on the floor. The slithering green mass of flies crawling on top of the wastes of their cooking transfixed her for a moment. Then she remembered a conversation she had paid very close attention to with Bernabe in the stables last summer. They had been looking at the leg of a mare. The young horse was only in her second summer. She had somehow inflicted herself with a nasty gash. Bernabe showed Paroish how cleaning the wound with clear water and then wrapping it to keep the flies off seemed to help it heal faster. He had told her that it seemed either the fly and what it did to the sore or the nasty contents adhered to the feet of the fly inflamed the wound. Either way, keeping the flies away helped the horses to heal much faster.

Paroish looked through her black and blue face and reached her long arm down toward the edge of the bucket at her feet.

69.
Warm Demonstration

At Journey, the preparations were advancing well. The long boards of the frames of the wagon box had been finished and the wheelwrights were pounding away at the massive wheels. These wagons were odd shaped contraptions. Long and narrow with overly deep boxes, designed to be transporting a large quantity of freight over a rough trail.

Normadia as her normal thoughtful self had delivered mid-day nourishment and drinks for the folks who were laboring away on the four wagons. These were to become the center of their stealth attack on the dark evil (as they had come to refer to Gaerwn). The false floors in each wagon were as thin as possible to keep the weight down, but still consumed a vast amount of sawn lumber. A veritable army of cutters with long deep throated saws had been laboring since the crops had been planted to hew the long boards necessary for the ruse.

The warm sun combined with the labor kept the men and women workers very hot. Normadia was honest enough with herself to admit she enjoyed the sight of the men, shirtless and full of sweat as they pounded and sawed at their tasks. Even little Larenzque, with no shirt to cover his slight, yet taught frame showed that what he lacked in height, he made up for in rippled muscles. She sighed for the umpteenth time today. She was missing Quillan even more and the feelings inside were a void that bordered on pain. A pain that was a deep desire that needed quenching.

Larenzque approached Normadia and asked, "Would ye like a demonstration of the escape system in the wagon?"

She replied that of course she would and he seemed eager to show her the device of deception they had finally come to build in each wagon.

"Come, lie down next to me on the floor," he said, rather excitedly, pulling his shirt over his head. "We will load in ehre before we get within spying distance of Gaerwn's outer watchtowers. The front driver seat lifts off and this many (he held up six fingers, not yet having had the wisdom of Ipi's counting lessons) of us will squeeze in each wagon under the floor."

"Oh," she said, somewhat alarmed. "Seems rather tight." As they lay on their backs, their shoulders were meshed up tight together. However, her feet extended rather much farther than Larenzque's. Although, she did notice that even though his legs were not long, his boots were rather large and wide, indicating large feet. Hmmm, she wondered, almost aloud. She remembered the many discussions in the kitchen about men and the association of large feet and fingers to the other parts of their bodies. Normadia shook her head and focused on what Larenzque was telling her.

"Yes, it will be snug," he replied not following her gaze or having any idea of her thoughts. "And our legs and other body parts will be very intertwined." He grinned, "We have all tried it out, each in our own wagon, all of us full in and intermingled. All of us fully clothed and with our knives and weapons at the ready." He grimaced and chortled some and said, "We shall never be the same after this. I have never been quite this cozy together with me dearthair before. And quite honestly, I do hope this will be the last time."

She laughed and said without thinking, "Well it's not so bad being here with me is it?"

She instantly turned dark red and could feel the heat of her question burning through her cheeks as she slowly turned her eyes to meet his.

"No, lass Normy, (he had affectionately called her that nickname since they were but wee tots) not in the least."

A moment of quiet tension filled the area around them but was noisily and thankfully interrupted by two men who without warning dropped the upper floor into the wagon without so much as a word and walked away. Normadia was completely sure they had seen them there, which was confirmed by the raucous laughter she heard a few moments later.

However, now inside the wagon, with a healthy mixture of darkness and sawdust in the air, Normadia and Larenzque lay, side by side. Their shoulders touching. Their hands separated by the thickness of a hair and both their bodies generating that dazzling heat one feels when they are close to a person they would not mind being closer too.

But.

It was dark, cramped and a little frightening.

Which truly meant that it was in the end, a very exciting moment and was raising sensations that longed to be fulfilled!

Normadia had her eyes closed against the closeness of the walls in the dim light so that her mind would not escape from her head, and to protect them from the sawdust still swirling in the air. Presently she said earnestly, "Now would be a good time for ye to show me how ye plan to escape since sitting up, as an option, seems to have been removed from all possibility."

Larenzque chuckled and said, "I shall grant ye this Normy, ye is always right."

They looked at each other now, the dust having settled back to a more normal condition. They could both see the look of pleasantness on each other's face in the little bits of light that seeped in between the cracks in the boards.

Larenzque continued, "At the same time, pull yerself up on the handle above yer face and then push that big pin on the side by your hip into the wood.

Normadia did not completely grasp what was happening, but she just did what she was told, and then all of a sudden found herself sliding gently toward the ground.

What had occurred was that the floor was set to tilt to the ground at one end and the occupants would slide down to the ground and make their escape. The concealed warriors though had to release the tension on the floor for it to move, hence the handles above their heads.

"Oh my," said Normadia as she stood up and brushed herself off.

And then the clapping started and all the men who had been working on the wagons were cheering. Larenzque made a little bow, and Normadia, not to be outdone or left out, squeezed out a delicate curtsy.

And after some cajoling and more cat calling, everyone went back to work.

Normadia gathered up her serving plates, pitcher and mugs and headed back to the big building. She was still a little warm, but it had felt good to have some fun with Larenzque. And, she had thought that the wagons were quite the invention.

But oh, how she missed the touch of that devil man in her bed!

*   *   *

Inside the Journey Inn, the big room was full of women sewing the interior fabrics that would line the cases carrying the "medicinals." Even the Celsys twins had joined in. The girls were now both with child having decided to stay with the boys they had so savagely seduced at the waterfall. Their condition though seemed to suit them and they chatted and laughed with everyone.

It was a grand scene. All the sewing and laughing. And then there were the cabinet masters on one side, near the wood room, finishing up the handsome carrying cases. Rebecca loved the smell of the finished wood and the look of proud craftsmanship that each case portrayed. Inside each case, an array of glazed containers would hold the mysteries of healing – at least upon inspection at the castle gate. Only two rows of cases would hold anything. They had figured that would be enough to fool the guards. The rest would be empty.

A vast array of the glazed containers, rich in their warm brown colors, were lined along the wall. Rebecca sat at one end of the lot, feeding Macowan. His eyes were closed and his little fists moved in a gentle cadence of happiness along the smooth contours of the breast he was suckling. And her eyes were closed as well, in the pure contentment of a mother.

70.
You Represent

"Thank you," said Dessa to the pleasant blonde girl with the black and blue injuries to her face. The girl had returned to set a bowl of cool water and a steaming bucket of hot water at Dessa's side. An assortment of rags was stuffed into another bucket. They looked fairly clean, thought Dessa.

Dessa washed her hands in the hot water and then using one of the rags from the bucket proceeded to use the cool water do something that almost made her wretch up her breakfast. She began to clean the self-inflicted wound on the arm of Darius' father.

The memories of that time that seemed so long ago in her life came flooding back. She remembered the parties before the wedding. How it was all just perfect; or so she thought. But how it all fell apart when he did not need to impress her father, King Tarmon, any longer. How he was just so dirty and drunk and then so disappointing. And if it was not for this miserable wretch and how he had raised his son to be so massively horrible, that she was actually helping right now, she would be home, near her family and all would be good and...

Quillan put his hand upon her wrist and stopped her for a moment. Gaerwn did not notice. He was lying in a soft stupor now, having ordered large mugs of a clear liquid he called Aquavit, which he had consumed rather quickly.

"What is the matter?" Quillan asked her quietly.

"Just some harsh memories," answered Dessa, wanting him to let go of her arm so she could finish this vile task.

"Ye look as though ye is fighten the battle of yer life," grinned Quillan.

"How so?" said his clearly agitated sister.

Looking somewhat softer now, having realized the enormity of what she had been thinking, he said gently, "Ye has bit clear through that lip of yers."

Dessa reached up and wiped her lips with the back of her hand, and saw the red swish glistening upon her skin. Her shoulders relaxed some and she took a deep breath, calming herself. She was just about finished cleaning the wound on Gaerwn's arm, and said to Quillan, "Hand me the salve."

Carefully she filled the gap the brute had made in his arm with the yellowish sticky substance. Then, with Quillan holding Gaerwn's arm so that the sides of the gash came together, she tied five snug strips of cloth around his arm in an attempt to keep the sides of the gash touching. It should further along the healing she thought. They could not risk her and Torrin applying their heat. They would have to see what it looked like in the morning. She sighed and stood.

"Where is Torrin?" Dessa asked Quillan and then gasped as her hand went to her mouth. She looked at Gaerwn laying on the floor, a smile spread across his lips. Although, he did seem fast asleep.

Quillan nodded his head toward the side of the throne and she straightaway headed off in that direction. Quillan cleaned things up and stowed the container of salve in his bag. He found Etworth chatting with some of the guards and extracted him so they could catch up with the others.

They headed toward the throne and made their way along the side toward the back and the anteroom.

* * *

Now five of them were clustered in the anteroom of the King. This was the same room where Trebor and Ethelda had cleaned up and worked to recover some and now it seems, it is the one where Queen Ethelda was living – well at least most of the time.

Torrin was mad as a hornet. Dessa was angry, yet quiet. Ethelda was crying and pitiful, while happy at the same time because she knew, at least for the moment, Torrin was not dead. Not eaten by animals, and not a captive somewhere. Actually the last part might be untrue as of now, but anyway, she took what she could get and the ominous irony of her emotions were weighing on her.

As Quillan and Etworth closed the door behind them Torrin said loudly, "He..."

And Quillan shushed him before the second word came out and

hoarsely whispered, "I dunno if the filthy tuilli is really asleep or just a little drunk. But either way, keep yer voice down."

Torrin shot an angry look at Quillan, and then continued on, quietly, but sternly, "Do you realize that convictive little tuilli destroyed my kingdom, murdered my father in front of my mother and is now forcing himself on my mother on a regular basis? And if that is not bad enough, he is beating her in some sort of shriveled flens sport!"

Quillan could see that Torrin was breathing far too fast for good thinking. Dessa seemed somewhat stunned at all this to be doing much and Etworth was walking around the room admiring the furniture and artwork.

So Quillan said, "What do ye think the rotten sod might be afraid of?"

"What?" asked Torrin, incredulously.

Dessa realized at once the importance of these words. And Quillan could see her thinking – hard, Tallon's brutal and effective teaching rushing to her head.

Quillan turned to Torrin and said, "The only way to really beat him is by leading him somehow to run amuck. To make some sort of error, to lose control. The only way I know to have him run amuck is to find something that frightens him to his rotten core. Just like Dessa did with Chadus and the spiders."

"Oh," answered Torrin, not really understanding, but knowing it was a better plan than the one he had right now. Because right now he had no plan.

Etworth said, "Let's just somehow get out of here in one piece; we can figure this out later. Nothing is holding us here. We get to the stables and slip town." With that he opened the door to the room and two large guards with long swords just looked at him. He closed the door and said, "Or, I guess not."

Quillan said, "We still stick to our plan. His nasty arm will be mostly healed by morning. And if not tomorrow, the next day. We procure the order and leave on our merry way. Then we return and spring part two later this summer."

Ethelda, who had been pretty much quiet this whole time now spoke, "That would be all well and good; however, I have noticed a pattern in him that bothers me."

"What would that be?" asked Dessa, now a little more worried than before, and before she was plenty worried.

"He does not usually do this," continued Ethelda, "He does not usually have all these theatrics going on if the answer is straight in front of him. He smells a rat and is trying to flush it out. Something is bothering him and he cannot figure it out yet."

"Any ideas as to what?" asked Quillan.

"No," replied Ethelda, "But something is afoul in his mind."

As if on cue, the door at the other end of the room opened and servants arrived with food and drink. One of them informed the group, somewhat pleasantly, but a little like the executioner bidding their victim to have a restful evening, that they would be spending the night here. If they needed anything, to please knock on the door in the back and the guards would summon a servant.

They looked at the food, barely hungry, and silence crept into the little room and surrounded them like the cold carcass of a long dead animal.

*   *   *

It was a restless night. It was very, very late before Torrin joined Dessa on the thick rug on the floor. He and Ethelda had caught up on as much as they could. She told him he needed some rest so he could deal with whatever the brute served up to them on the morrow.

Dessa and Torrin had held each other for a long time before retiring, even stealing a few pleasant, if not rushed kisses while standing on the stone hearth of the fireplace. They relished the closeness of their hearts beating near each other, especially this one time. Knowing this could be the last and having learned never to take advantage of that warm embrace. Each had cried unabashedly. Finally they went to sleep. Dessa's head on Torrin's chest and his hand entwined in her thick red hair.

*   *   *

As dawn pierced the black sky once again, a door opened and in walked another set of servants. They removed the eating implements from the night before and deposited a light breakfast. There were a few greens from the ice caves. Warm rolls and a pitcher of lukewarm tea. A bucket of warm water and a couple of cloths were set at a table along the side for morning washing.

Dessa thought that the kitchen had maybe decided not to waste a lot of food on people who would not be needing it. The irony of it made her grin.

After they ate, they made ready to meet with Gaerwn.

And Gaerwn did what he knew worked well for anyone wanting to see him.

He made them wait.

They waited in the little room that seemed to close in as the day slid by.

They did little talking.

They did little eating.

They just sat and waited.

Gaerwn made them wait and let the tension build.

*　*　*

In a well formed line that belied any form of escape, five sturdy well armed guards finally came to fetch them. The guards were all business and it did not feel to Dessa like the second part of a very important sales call.

This was a walk to a trial.

She remembered far too well what that had felt like when she was on trial for the murder of Darius and shuddered at the memory. The guards paired up with each of the party and herded them out to the throne room.

Gaerwn was sitting upon his throne now; he was curved to the side, very casual. The blonde girl from the kitchen yesterday was gathering up her dress as she was very much naked. She then strode purposefully out of the room, her eyes throwing off daggers at them. An alarm went off in Dessa's head; she wondered what was with this girl and was she friend, foe or neither?

"I trust your evening in my most elegant guest chamber was comfortable?" Gaerwn asked with a surly tone.

"Yes," said Torrin. "We certainly appreciate your hospitality."

"Well good then, Gaerwn almost sneered. "I was hoping you would have the chance to spend some quality time?"

It was obviously a rhetorical question and Quillan said matter-of-factly, "What do you mean?"

"What I mean is," he laughed in his reply, "Is that mother and son got to catch up. Wouldn't that be right Torrin?"

The color drained from Ethworth's face.

Quillan's hands clenched tight.

Dessa wished she had her bow and arrows.

Torrin just stood and stared with a hatred so strong that it made him dizzy and suddenly the angry warning began to creep up his neck. He noticed it immediately, and wondered what had taken so long for its arrival.

Gaerwn stood and removed his big coat. The bandage on his arm was wet with the weeping of the wound. He peeled off the bandage and everyone gasped. The white stringy pus had gathered up and clung to his skin. Black areas showed around the edges.

"It does not seem to me that your medicine is working its magic," sighed Gaerwn heavily. "However, I am not worried. Although it's going to hurt like helvete, I do know that soaking this in hot salty water will clean up the mess you have created." And then he stopped, seemed to growl lowly followed by a strong announcement of, "And then I will clean up the mess that you represent to me."

Suddenly all the people who were milling about and chatting stopped dead still and were quiet. The entire room was strangely silent with the only sounds coming from the hissing of the fires and the murmurings of hundreds of huge candles that danced what seemed to be sad yellow light around the interior of the room.

71.
Firewood

Ol' Dogger watched Normadia move in graceful swaths of influence and demure friendliness all at once and with seemingly little effort. Oh, how he remembered his mum doing just that when he was but a wee lad. The room was smaller then, with the kitchen right here in the big room, amongst the travelers who would stop and rest their bones. But the warm friendliness was the same. The food just as wonderful and meticulously prepared.

Part of him actually preferred things the way they were now. With so many more people about. There was now much more color, more stories, more music and dancing. It was a great time to be here at Journey.

So in his just always friendly way, Ol' Dogger asked, "Mz Normadia, ye are just a whippoorwill here at Journey. Ye bless us all. How is ye today?"

Normadia smiled at him. Her bright white teeth sparkled against ruby red lips. Fresh color was upon her cheeks from her constant movements; this being the work she so embraced that was her everyday life. "Oh Dogger, I am as good as I might be on a wonderful day like this."

"Somehow," he said slowly, not alarmed, but quizzical. "I don' seem to be a fully believein ye. There is a catch in yer tone an I is a wondern if somethin be wrong?"

"Oh my," said the fair skinned, brown haired woman. She sat down heavily across from him on a bench and placed the tray she'd been holding to the top of the table, with a resounding thud.

He saw water at the corners of her eyes. Experience had taught him to be still, so he just looked at her, letting her decide when to speak and what to say. He had seen this before, and it was a very delicate situation to attend to. And he also knew it could be dangerous. So he wisely held his tongue and waited.

Normadia breathed out a little sigh and licked her lips. She swallowed hard and then finally, succumbing to the feelings flinging about in her head, blinked her eyes, which by now had filled to the edge with tears. As she blinked, great long drops slid down upon her cheeks and splotched on the table. She made no move to wipe them.

"I guess it is just that I miss him so terribly much," she said around a number of hastily caught breaths. "And I am fearful for him. It just seems unfair to have had him, and now be without him. It's tearen at me heart!"

Ol' Dogger reached across the table and took her soft hand into his wrinkled old one. His head tilted to one side as he searched for words of solace. Words he knew could not heal the tenderness pouring from this wonderful lass. Eventually, he bit his lip and said, "I know how ye feel. With all the winters and summers and comings and goings that I have endured and celebrated meself, I have felt for a number of ladies the way ye feel for our Quillan."

"So what did you do when they left?" Normadia asked. The question posed in a tone that sounded like a crisis.

Ol' Dogger laughed a little and said, "Well, I would cry some, and then me mum would put me to work. And I found the best thing was cutting firewood. Hot, dirty, sweaty work. Somehow the effort was cleansing."

"Does that really help?" she asked.

Ol' Dogger grinned again, saying, "Depended on the lass. For the ones I really cared about? No. But we did get a lots a firewood cut at various parts of the year."

Normadia finally smiled some. They both felt just a mite better.

72.
Final Sale

As Gaerwn sunk his damaged arm into the bucket of steaming water his face grimaced. And then just as rapidly as the grimace had come on, his face turned to normal; the color drained back to nasty and his eyes were as black as ever.

He looked up and asked in a low and wondering voice to the four standing before him, "What did you really think you were going to accomplish by coming here?"

He then extracted his damaged arm and plunged it in again, this time exhaling a loud moan that was almost erotic in nature. After a moment, he moved the wounded appendage rapidly to rinse off his own gore. He closed his eyes to let the pain subside.

Torrin looked at his mother, already tied to the chair.

Dessa looked at Quillan and he at her.

Etworth looked at his nails.

Finally Torrin spoke, staying in character, "Our goal was to enable the people in your kingdom to live a better life. Our medicinals will heal them."

Gaerwn roared with laughter. Water from the bucket splashed about and he just kept on laughing. This laughter was somewhat infectious, in a diseased sort of way. The rest of the room started to laugh too (except of course the four standing in judgment of Gaerwn).

It was not a happy laugh though; it was the laugh of pent up stress releasing from the body. A laugh that laughed at the victim, a mournful soulless happiness that said "It was not for you. It was at you." It was going to be you, the other guy to take the fall, and the bludgeoning and the pain. It was, really, an ugly laugh.

Eventually Gaerwn settled down. He extracted his arm from the bucket, wiped it off, rolled a towel around the wound and put his big coat on. Strolling down to where the four stood in line, water running from the ends of his grimy fingers, he stared boldly and angrily at each one and began to address each in turn.

Etworth looked up into the ruddy face of Gaerwn and just stood there, looking. If you knew Etworth well, you could see he was concerned. But he was also looking for a way to make the most of this. Maybe sell something or close for a future meeting; assuming he made it out alive.

Gaerwn said, "You have been here before." Etworth nodded, "You are just a peddler; I purchased things from you the previous summer?" More nodding from Etworth.

"You shall go free." Etworth's eyes grew wide. "You know many and you will tell many how the greatest trick of all could not be made on the great and powerful Gaerwn."

Etworth turned to leave, and Gaerwn grabbed him by the collar of his coat. "No little man," said the king. "You shall go free when I tell you to go. And if you do not behave, I have a gibbet cage ready for you. Although it would be somewhat small, even for your skinny little body!" And Gaerwn laughed as he pushed Etworth backwards so hard that the trader fell on his backside and slid along the cold stone floor. Etworth's eyes wide with the thought of ending his days hunched over in a too small gibbet, the rats feasting on him as dusk settled.

And as if on cue there was a loud commotion with a great amount of shouting and huffering at the back of the room. Two men, each grasping at the other's clothes came wrestling into the King's chambers. It would be described as wrestling since each was trying to control the other. And both were trying to drag the other forward and each was mad as smoked hornets in a rainstorm. Torrin recognized one of them as the farmer who had been on his knees the day before in front of Gaerwn pleading about a cow.

Everyone, including Gaerwn, stood transfixed at the pair as they slapped and kicked and screamed at each other in a vain attempt to get their point across. Each was fuming and sputtering almost incoherently about land rights and friendship and mostly about cows. It was not a cogent conversation and Torrin wondered very quickly how this sort of charade would be handled by Gaerwn.

He did not have to wait long to find out.

The big king walked over to the pair and put his hands on his hips and tried to listen for a minute to figure out what was going on.

Then Gaerwn held up his hand to tell the two to be quiet. It seemed as though even the noise from the fire fell away while Gaerwn's hand was in the air. Nary a soul breathed, let alone spoke. But the two men took no notice and kept arguing so vehemently that it looked as though they would soon be rolling on the floor exchanging blows.

Gaerwn turned toward the crowd in the back of the room, shrugged his shoulders and with purpose walked up to the throne.

Torrin noticed three women running from the room.

Next to the throne, adorning it from a large iron kettle were a variety of long straight battle pikes. It was obvious that these weapons had not seen much battle since their metal ends were shiny and bright. However, mostly, the long poles showed no sign of blood or dried on gore.

Gaerwn chose a mid-length weapon, one with a small sharpened burr about a hand length up from the gleaming razored end. He pulled its heaviness from its resting place and hefted it in his sausage sized hands. After playing with it for a moment to get the feel of it, he stopped and placed the butt, firmly and loudly upon the cold stone floor.

Neither of the men heard the sound or reacted. They were still entranced in their raucous argument.

Gaerwn gave a half hearted nod, mostly to himself (something that a person might make when they took the last cookie from a plate). He then picked up the stout pike and ran suddenly at a full fury at the back of the farmer who had been pleading the case of the cow just yesterday afternoon. As Gaerwn ran, Torrin could see the eyes of the other man grow wide. As the wide-eyed man too late raised his hand to warn his arguing comrade of the oncoming danger, the pike blew through the other man's back and then straight into the stomach of the wide-eyed newcomer.

The tearing death sounds were those that Torrin knew he would take to his grave. Both men were startled, looked down at the pole they now shared in their mid-sections and then, without fanfare, or further argument, died.

Gaerwn put a boot upon the back of the first man, the farmer. The man who had a pole deeply embedded in his back. With a mighty heave, accompanied by a loud crunching, Gaerwn removed the pike from both the men. The innards of both, and it did not matter who, accompanied the removal.

Torrin thought he would wretch.

However, before anyone, including Torrin, could react, Gaerwn launched the now wet and gruesome pike with a grand heave and sent it cleanly slicing through Etworth's chest where it made a dull 'thuk' noise and then just hung there in the air.

Etworth's eyes went wide while his heart pushed out two more beats and then he too, joined the dead on the floor.

It occurred to Torrin, as he mutely watched all this terror being played out, that he now understood why the floor was so black. He felt this an odd thought for now, and one not worthy of the disaster being played out before him, but it was a revelation. The floor was black with terrorized blood. No matter how much they cleaned it, the staining would not go away.

Gaerwn, in a mocking voice quipped toward the dead body of Etworth, "Guess your days of peddling wares to the likes of me are pretty much over. Oh dear, what a pity!"

Moving toward Quillan, acting as if nothing more terrible than a spilled glass of wine had occurred, Gaerwn now stood nose to nose with the big red man. Looking at the two of them, you might think that in an arm wrestling match neither would be the favorite. Gaerwn was older and scruffier though and you would not put it past him to toss strong drink into his competitor's eyes just to win. Quillan was not as big, but he was lean. Both right now looked mean and if you were to be afraid of either, it would be Quillan. Gaerwn was in his element; he was just nasty mean and well practiced at it. Quillan on the other hand was beginning to look like a cornered Rottweiler. And it has always been said, nothing good becomes of a cornered Rottweiler, unless of course, you are the Rottweiler.

"I want to know who you are," said Gaerwn slowly to Quillan. "You look dangerous and I like that in a man," and finally added, "If he is on my side." He finished with a sneer.

Quillan did not flinch or move. He was undecided if a show of strength at this time was wise, or backing down would be more prudent. Since he was unsure, he just kept his tongue in check and stood his ground, blood boiling and his hands clenched tight to control them.

Gaerwn's tilted head rested for a long while sizing up Quillan. Eventually he just ambled over to where Dessa stood.

He stood just too close to her. He was trying to make her uncomfortable. And it was working, but she was going to do her best to control that and not let him win at his own game. To Dessa he did not so much smell bad as he gave off a sour stomach churning stench. Small bits of something kept dislodging in his mouth and he would keep chewing unseen oddities between sentences. She found absolutely nothing about him that was not obtuse, obscure or obscene.

He looked down at her and with a gentleness that surprised even her, he slowly slid his calloused and dirty hand under her chin. He lifted her eyes up to lock with his own gaze.

Gaerwn said, "I can see what attracted him to you. But he did not look deep enough into your fiery little soul. Did he? You cannot be controlled. You are too much a free spirit. Shall we say born to be wild?" He chuckled softly.

When a person is faced with insurmountable odds that seem to provide no escape, sometimes they just go for broke. Dessa did not just feel that way yet.

"What?" she asked, as honestly as she could muster.

"Darius was my oldest. Born before his brother." Gaerwn broke his thought for a moment, "I wonder where Haphethus is?" He refocused on Dessa. "What did you do to him?"

The inside of Dessa's brain drew a long smirk, thinking, 'What have I done with both of them is what you should be asking, you insolent brute, but you will never know.' So she said, "I think you have me confused with someone else, because I have absolutely no idea what you are talking about."

Gaerwn locked his gaze with Dessa. His dark tongue rolled around unconsciously in his mouth searching for more bits of debris that were lodged always between his teeth. "I just want to know," he said coolly, "Did you murder him or was it truly an accident?"

"Who is this 'him' you keep speaking of?" she asked with a sarcasm that was cool and grated. She was in astonishment that she was alive and still bluffing her way through this.

Gaerwn looked at a man off to his right and said, "I guess now would be a good time."

Both Dessa and Torrin felt strong arms at their sides, stout smooth leather bands were firmly attached to their wrists. Their hands were tied behind them, very useless for now. Quillan felt a sharp blade point against his neck joined with an equally sharp command, "Don't move." And when those words were uttered, he felt the strong stout lengths of thick leather bindings tie his wrists behind his back. Quillan was helpless and did not like it.

Etworth would have watched in the wonderingly inquisitive way that was always his, as his eyes were faced towards Dessa. But they were sightless.

As Torrin watched helplessly with his arms securely pinned to his side, Dessa was picked up and tipped forward. Her red hair brushed the ground and she was wiggling harshly to try and take command of her situation.

Gaerwn motioned with his hand for things to continue and he

turned around, facing away from Dessa.

Dessa could feel soft hands removing her boots and petticoat and within a moment, she was bent over, butt exposed to the room, her backside completely naked.

Gaerwn, without turning around said loudly, "Does she have a dark mole, on the back of her thigh, just below her left arse cheek?"

Torrin tried to struggle free. But to no avail. The guards were strong and had a practiced and tight grip on him. A strong smack to the side of his head calmed him and helped him understand to be still.

Quillan looked away, finding no joy in viewing his sister's back side. He did notice though another pointy sword laid upon his chest. He was going nowhere.

Dessa could feel a soft hand grasping her thigh; it held her firmly and she stopped struggling, deciding she might need her strength for something yet to come. A finger slowly ran over the dark mole that she had known most of her life. And then she heard Glenna say, "Yes sire, there is a mole."

"Well now pretty lass. What do you think the chances are of two redheads having the same exact mole? Hmm?" Gaerwn said sarcastically as he turned around.

He continued on, now speaking as a teacher might speak to a pupil who needed a good sermon, "The news of your little spot came to me via the messengers who attended your wedding. It seems that Darius enjoyed the sight of your spot moving to and fro as he would make you the happy woman you were intended to be. This was one of the many tales he told around the table to his comrades while they shared stories." Gaerwn sighed and said, "Stand the little red galla back up so she can face me with her sins."

Dessa knew she had flinched at the sound of Darius' name. It was obvious that the plan they had so carefully rehearsed was falling apart. She was breathing hard as her handlers stood her back on her feet and her gaze again joined Gaerwn's. She now felt cold, as she was barefoot and naked beneath the dress.

Gaerwn motioned to the guards and a few backed away from Dessa. She stood very alone with the cold of the black stone floor achingly pushing through her feet and making her ankles throb.

He approached her, eyes hard and cold. He repeated his question in a slow word by word way that was intended to let her know it would be the last time he asked, "Did you murder him or was it truly an accident?"

Dessa closed her eyes and all the air ran out of her. She could feel her shoulders slump and the tears started to form in her eyes as well as in her heart. She was enveloped in a dark veil of sadness. She suddenly hurt from all directions in ways she had never experienced.

73.
Transition

As Dessa was feeling lost, the strong arms of the rest of the guards that had held her so tightly let go. And then, almost as if on cue, Gaerwn began to let loose a tirade of despicably slanderous fury and venomous language toward the young red haired girl. A girl who now stood very alone, bound and barefoot on the blood black floor of his throne room. One friend dead at her feet and the others bound and controlled. Helpless to assist.

"Ye miserable little cach galla," screamed Gaerwn in an piercing mocking cry. "So what if Darius had meant ta get control of yer castle from the inside? Marryn' you was torture for him. He said ye was much too nice and jus no fun. Actually, verra boring!"

The realization to Dessa that Darius had come to conquer the kingdom and really not to marry her suddenly brought sense to so many things. It was clear why he was not interested in her. He had come to wrest control as the rightful king when something happened to her father, and she was sure he would have done that before many winters had passed.

Dessa's mind continued to connect the dots; so it would make sense that she, the queen apparent, would be seen as not fit to reign. Darisu meant to tear her soul apart from the moment they were married until he stood on the throne. After all, he was a man. People would believe whatever he told them. He would position her as a confused and irresponsible wench. Angry and vengeful. Unfit. Without empathy. And it would not have taken him long to tear her apart and she would have unwittingly played the role, trying to win his black heart.

And the fact that Gaerwn himself had been scouting attack routes to Torrin's castle and Chadus scouting the valley told her the final points of the story.

Gaerwn had been planning to take over all of the northern lands.

Gaerwn was still screaming accusations at Dessa and she now listened, "Ye somehow lured my sweet boy to yer sinful wretched manipulatin' ways only to skewer him with a knife while the man was in his innocence of sleep!" Gaerwn was in a total rage; reddish purple splotches moved about his face with spittle foaming from his lips.

He continued in a now screeching voice that was sore from misuse and petrified the souls of every person in the room. "And then ye seduced me little cherub Chadus with yer alluring red curls and blasted wanton curves, only to split open his face while ye rode him like the banshee ye is!"

Dessa just stood and stared with a blank expression on her face. The rawhide bonds that now held her wrists seemed to be just a mild irritation. The image of Etworth's dead body kept creeping into her peripheral vision and she worried that Gaerwn would lose his temper and drive a long pointed spear through another heart.

She was at a loss for words. She dared not look at Quillan or Torrin. She did not want to direct the vengeful fury of this tyrant towards her brother.

Part of her wanted to laugh now.

To cry?

Spit back at him.

Tell him the truth.

The truth about Darius' lack of manhood, both size and inability to love anything but his own miserable loathing of himself.

How he was afraid of the marriage.

Commitment.

Even having any sort of respect for himself.

How all his bluster was about his shortcomings, not the least of which was in the bedchamber.

About Chadus' brutish bullying and cowardly ways and how the huge man was defeated by the innocence of a little spider. And how he was so terrified of that little spider, he did himself in, willingly and cleanly.

All these thoughts rushed through her head, jumbled and colliding. Along with the thoughts that if the team here failed, all the people, children and families of the valley were at risk. The promise of

Journey would be brutishly buried under the black hate of this monster.

So as Gaerwn screamed at Dessa, she heard the air release from her nose in a soft hiss. She had endeavored to take a deep breath that would allow her to think. Just as Tallon had taught her she must do in battle.

And then through that gentle hiss came the astonishingly soft spoken words of Ipi. Just as the spring finally emerges from winter to grace the earth in a wide loving sweep of warmth, Ipi's lexis emerged into an accepting place in her over-taxed brain. She heard Ipi say, "Remember your truth dear. Your truth will be what you are, and what you need. When you need to be yourself the most. Always be your you, because that is your real strength."

And with those thoughts bringing peace to her whole self, Dessa finally figured out what Gaerwn was afraid of.

And it took every bit of self control she had left, not to smile.

74.
Rising

How anything so cool could create so much heat was always a mystery to her. Maybe that was why she loved the dough so much?

Normadia continued to knead the heavy sticky mound with both hands. Periodically, she was forced to stop and re-lubricate with soft yellow butter to keep the creamy mixture from sticking to her long strong fingers.

It was early in the day. Brightness had not yet attached itself to the morning. As the birds shared their twerplings to greet the sunshine, Normadia greeted the day's helpers with her usual grace and ever endearing smile.

Not missing a beat in her kneading, she struck up a conversation with the baker who would in short order take the dough to its final forms for the day. He was a master at adding nuts, dried fruits and sweet spices to the doughs to keep them ever new and interesting.

She asked the Greely brother about his evening, knowing he was courting the lass Joulanne who was sweet on him. Joulanne was a quiet girl who loved to sew for days at a time. If you did not know her, you might think her shy. But just the opposite was true. She was merely very dedicated to her sewing work. And her work was creative and beautiful, sturdy and always well done.

Normadia and Greely had chatted long together, quietly by the fire, about the virtues of a woman who had dedication. It was a strength not to be dismissed, nor handled foolishly. Greely, she mused, was not just a little nervous about the courtship. He had dabbled foolishly before and now this relationship was different. Normadia marveled at the genuine caring he displayed. However she thought, why is it so hard for a man to expound his true feelings to the girl he actually craved?

Normadia knew very clearly that Joulanne was fond of the man. She sighed deeply and smiled as the heavy dough turned over again. For all their strength and might, men were just so fragile!

The washer arrived, a nice boy who was still growing and at a very awkward time of life. His arms were too long and he was growing so fast that his breeches, by the end of the summer, would be far too short for winter wear. Normadia knew that his mother was probably sewing constantly to keep up.

These were just the common issues of life though and challenges such as these were the gift of each family.

Family.

The word almost made her cringe.

Family.

The thought brought to her a familiar fear and longing that made her heart skip a beat and keep her breath short for a few moments.

Family.

Normadia had lost all hers to a fast sickness. She had been young and she still missed the arms that would hold her safe before bed and during the howling storms.

And now, most of all she missed her big red man. She missed Quillan.

She missed his size next to her that brought her a sense of safeness. She missed his kisses. She missed his full face smiles that covered her warmly as she snuggled close and used her hands to attend to those delicate and playful areas that elicited low groans of delight.

Of course she missed the firm intimate attention he paid to all her delicate parts behind the closed door of her warm room.

Oh yes, she missed all that.

But most of all, she missed all of him!

.

75.
Fiery Finish

Gaerwn suddenly just stopped his fathomless screeching and stood there; sweating rivulets of greasy moisture down his grimy face. Breathing hard. Hands clenching and unclenching. His gaze shifting to each one of them in turn. A staccato pattern of hate and loathing.

Presently, Gaerwn turned and plodded back towards the big padded throne. Sitting down heavily, he casually tossed one leg over one arm of his throne and then leaned his elbow on the other arm. He rested his big furry head upon his hand and gently closed his eyes.

After a few moments, his eyes opened and he fixed a steely gaze on Quillan."Well then, my big red man. What do you have to say for yourself?" he inquired.

Quillan slowly slid his gaze around the room, trying to catch the eyes of his friends. Neither of them though, were allowed to look at him, to give him any clues. He sadly turned his face back towards Gaerwn, and said nothing.

Quillan's lack of words, the lack of passion, the lack of feedback, just added more ice to Gaerwn's cold stare.

Gaerwn then turned his attention to Torrin. "You and I may have more in common than we know," he said quietly. "However, I cannot prove one way or the other, that you are mine." He turned his gaze toward Ethelda, uncomfortably tied to her chair. "She tends to sleep around a lot, so you never know where the screaming little chacs come from."

Ethelda just quietly lowered her head, shook it slowly left and right, and Torrin could see her shoulders slump.

Gaerwn continued talking to Torrin, "I guess if you could prove that I am your father, then you would become the Prince, and inherit all of this when I die." Gaerwn laughed uproariously, "Of course, I am never going to die, and I am never going to give you a chance to rise up over me, and take this all away!"

Finally, he returned his hateful gaze to Dessa. "You seem to be at a loss for words you pretty little galla." Gaerwn breathed a heavy sigh, "How can I forgive you, if you do not defend yourself?" Gaerwn scanned the room, knowing that everyone there would agree with anything he said. His three tormentors were making this difficult by not responding. He knew he could beat them at any game, except silence.

But then a thought occurred to him.

"Since you refuse to say anything, I can only conclude that you are guilty as charged." Gaerwn arose from his throne and began again plodding back and forth in front of the throne. Walking in lazy slow circles, his chin in his hand, thinking deeply.

Gaerwn stopped in the middle of the platform that was in front of the throne. He put both hands on his hips with his feet spread apart, in the pose of the commanding soldier.

He looked at Quillan.

He looked at Torrin.

He looked at Dessa.

Each in turn, it was a steely gaze and it was obvious his evil mind was at work.

And then said in a stately voice, "You have come here to do injury, injustice, and damage to the loving kingdom of Gaerwn. You shall burn at the stake."

"At dusk."

"Today."

And with that he walked away toward the back of the throne, dragging the chair that held Ethelda as tears streamed down her worn and weary face.

76.
Sealed

As Dessa, Torrin and Quillan were led away, the palace seemed to erupt into a state of orderly pandemonium. Just about everyone left the throne room quickly, not in a confused state, but seemingly like they had a job to do.

It occurred to Dessa that this process was not new to these people. They were practiced at murder, and were calmly performing their duties.

Having been taken out to the courtyard, each of them was put into their own small cell. Presently a couple of guards came to each of them and gave them a thin white muslin shift to wear that seemed to be cut to knee length. Each of them had to turn over their clothes to the guards, including their boots. Then their cell doors were locked securely. Just about the only thing they could see was the activity taking place in the courtyard. There were three piles of dried firewood being heaped carefully around three long charred poles that sported long black chains.

A breeze brought to them the fecund odors sporting from the area of fiery death that lay before them. Odors that seemed to reproduce in sad parade from the many souls that had perished there in indescribable agony.

As they watched, guards approached the long stout poles and slowly dumped buckets of muddy water down their length. Dessa knew that this was to keep the poles from burning. It kept the victim upright so the crowd could watch the body go through its torturous demise from start to end. And it kept the kingdom from having to replace the large thick poles very often. She had seen the routine repeated in her own kingdom a number of times.

Torrin was in the middle cell and he said, with his face against the bars and loud enough for the other two to hear, "Anyone have any ideas on what to do?"

As he finished the question, a guard smashed Torrin's very own boot that he had held in his hands into the bars of the cell where Torrin's face was pressed. Instantly blood gushed from Torrin's broken nose as the heel of the boot had found its mark.

No one said anything more.

*   *   *

The warm sunny day slowly wore on. Scattered clouds periodically brought shade and littered movement to the courtyard. Other than that, everything they could see from their cells was a sad progression of preparations for death.

Of course, no food came, no water, nothing. This kingdom which had so much to offer from an engineering and creativity standpoint, could spare no compassion or scarce resources for someone who is going to leave this evening via an agonizing, hellish demise.

The sun began to descend below the walls of the castle. As its bright yellow slowly slid behind the dark bleak stone, Quillan was sure that Gaerwn had planned it this way. He was sure that all of these executions were at dusk. This way the condemned could watch the sun slowly go down and literally feel the coolness of the earth approach their skin as all the warmth of their soul, and their life, slipped away.

As soon as the sun was out of sight beyond the bleak stone walls, a drum began to slowly pound off to one side of the courtyard. A regal progression of everyone in Gaerwn's favor proceeded out of the main building, followed by the bedraggled and now somewhat drunk ruler.

Gaerwn proceeded to come to the front and center of the three cells. He stood tall and mighty in his dirty robes. His entourage gathered around him, waiting to hear what words of valor and grace would spill from his lips. Of course, Gaerwn was a kind and benevolent ruler, and he would give the captives a chance to live. Everyone here in the kingdom knew that. He had told them he was kind. And anyone who disagreed with Gaerwn seemed to disappear.

Gaerwn had ensured that he was always right. Anyone who disagreed was gone. It was a marvelous plan.

Dessa looked at the wretch and decided that the smell of the fire pit, and the smell of decay, which was common around Gaerwn had something in common. She was not having charitable thoughts.

Gaerwn said, "Do ye have anything to say to defend yourselves?"

His steely gaze took in each one in turn, and the silence that followed almost hurt.

He then smiled an evil sneer and said, "Then we shall have some fun!"

*   *   *

The guards were obviously well practiced in this process. They led first Quillan, then Torrin, then Dessa out to the poles and piles of dried firewood and pine pitch soaked rags. Each of the three of them was securely attached to a long wet slimy pole via a strong chain that was wound around their midsection.

Young boys approached each one in turn, and drenched them with a bucket of putrid muddy water. This Dessa knew, would allow the victims to only feel pain in their feet at first. Then when the fabric around them dried, the fire would have had time to become very hot, and their skin would basically boil off of their still living bodies. It was about as gruesome as it could get.

The three of them were standing, trussed, fairly close together. It did not take long for them to find each other's hands, and they held on tightly. It was a vain attempt to give each other support, and Gaerwn knew it. He purposefully put people close together at the burning pit so they could try to console each other. What really ended up happening though was that they could see and sense each other burn and the shared terror was just so much more delightful for everyone. Everyone of course who was watching.

Gaerwn approached a large stone that was centered in front of the killing area. Three strong men approached him and picked him up so that he could stand tall on the stone. The stone was not that high; he could have easily clambered up onto it himself. It was just another show of how much he was in control and wanted attention.

Gaerwn began a little speech, "People of this great kingdom. You are here to witness today certain true and good justice towards those who would come to lie, hurt, and deceive us. These people transported illicit truths. They transported vulgar products designed to hurt you. Your great King is protecting you, as I always have done. You are safe with me; I keep you from having to fear anything!"

As Gaerwn turned toward the three, he said coldly, "I have given you every chance to defend yourself, yet you prove your guilt by your silence. The world will be a better place after you are gone!"

And with that the three large men carried Gaerwn off the rock.

In the distance, the drumming suddenly stopped. They could see a torch coming from the building, carried in stunning irony by Glenna wearing a white dress. Torrin thought it very fitting that the only person they had really helped was to light the fire. As she was just about to put her torch to the pine-pitch soaked rags at the foot of the funeral pyre Dessa said, "I have one last request."

77.

Ominous

Alexia's blonde hair was trailing behind her as she ran with her corncob doll firmly entrenched in one hand. Ol' Dogger was sitting at the table near the big fireplace, whittling away at a new whistle. He saw the little girl run into the big room through the gaping door that led to the sunshine of a warm and breezy day.

He knew instantly that something was amiss. Tears were streaming down her soft white cheeks. Her normal blazing blue eyes were red. She ran straight to the fireplace and tossed the doll into the fire. Instantly she ran over to Ol' Dogger, and buried her weeping face in his lap.

"Chil, what be the matter with ye?" inquired Ol' Dogger, very concerned and being as gentle as he could muster.

The little girl just continued to weep. Uncontrolled gasping and heaving sobs shook her whole being.

It took him a while to let her calm down, and then finally he was able to ask her again, "Chil what be the matter with ye?"

Alexia looked up at him, eyes big as Scotch ale mugs. And she whispered, as well as she could, through a clenched throat; "I'm verra scared!"

78.
Torched

At the sound of Dessa's words, Gaerwn raised a dirty and calloused hand and barked a command, "Stop!"

This caused Glenna to halt an instant before her torch touched the pine soaked rags. Glenna retreated back a few steps. She had steeled herself for this wretched duty that she had been forced to perform with two large gulps of a very strong and terrible whiskey. The effects of which were now entering her already muddled brain. She swayed a little, now completely unsure of what the right thing was to do, if anything at all. So she just stood there in the middle of everything, holding the torch.

Gaerwn crossed his arms, planted his feet firmly on the ground and contemplated the wet red-haired woman chained to his log. And said out loud in a peculiar questioning tone, to no one in particular, however mostly to himself, "Well now?"

After a few moments had passed, Gaerwn said in a strong voice, reminding everyone that he was in control, "What?"

Dessa took a deep breath, licked her lips, and in the firmest voice she could muster said, "If I am to die by your hand, I want to die with my kiss on your lips."

Dessa and Gaerwn stared at each other. She dared not look at Quillan or Torrin. She knew their mouths were probably agape in question and horror.

Gaerwn had been enjoying the view of Dessa in a thin wet muslin shift. The thought of continuing his trepid gazing for a little longer appealed to him. And, best of all, she was trussed up for his amusement. He thought for a minute, and then asked, "Why?"

Dessa pondered for a moment, and then said, "I guess I am not really sure, being terrified of what is going to happen next. But since I started my adult life with your family on my lips, I figured it was a good way to end." Then her head sagged down and her shoulders slumped signifying that she had lost the battle.

Gaerwn turned to Scraddius who was standing at his side and said, "See what little gifts nature will bring when you are good to the people?"

Gaerwn commanded the boys to drench the condemned miscreants one more time. They were drying and he wanted to make sure they were wet when the fire started. Gaerwn actually wanted to see them all close up, wet and chilled as he approached, but thought better of telling the crowd of his true intentions.

Gaerwn trudged forward, his arms raised in a triumphant salute to the victory that was now his. He picked his way amongst the wood to where the three were standing. He reached out and put both hands on either side of Dessa's face and brought his lips to hers.

Dessa let go of Quillan and Torrin's hands. Her left hand encircled Gaerwn's neck under his hair and she pulled him tight against her face. Her other hand went to Torrin's lips.

Torrin looked at the two of them. They were locked in the most terrible and confusing embrace he could ever conjure. And then he looked at her smooth white hand, held in the air under his chin.

Quillan, not able to stand it any longer sputtered in a loud voice, "Kiss 'er hand ye fool!"

Torrin grabbed the clean porcelain skin of the woman he loved, took one breath, and then with all of his might kissed her hand.

The blue hot energy that Torrin and Dessa create enveloped the three. And given the enormous theatrics and tension of the moment, the kiss that Torrin delivered on Dessa's hand created an explosive release.

Fortunately, Gaerwn had failed to bathe for a very long time. His clothes were damp with sweat. His skin greasy from body oil. Most all of him was just damp and all-around disgusting. All this grease, much of it from his diet, was also very flammable. That is, once the sweat turned to steam.

So as it was, in the blink of an eye, the damp turned to steam and the oil burned as if from a bomb. In simple terms, Gaerwn's clothes exploded off his body.

The blue sparks of electricity encircled his entire being and the hair on his body began to burn. His skin instantly blistered and bubbled and Dessa kissed on as the layer of grease and oil ignited.

When Gaerwn began to become dangerous to her, she let go of his neck and pushed his face as hard as she could backwards. And being as mad and disgusted as she was, she pushed verra hard! Gaerwn's flame engulfed self toppled backward hard.

Instantly the pine-pitch immersed rags caught fire, and the whole pile of dry wood erupted in bright hot flames.

79.
Rescue

Ol' Dogger, held Alexia's trembling body. in his lap for a long time. Eventually, the two of them settled down and she reached up and hugged his neck to her soft face.

"There is no need to really be afraid," said Ol' Dogger. "Sometimes we just need to accept what will happen. And trust that nature will take care of all the important things."

She looked up at him and said in a small trembling voice, with the purity of a child, and told him, "Yes I know, but I don't like it when bad things happen."

He watched the glint of the firelight in her eyes, and then looked at the fire. After just a moment he said with astonishment, "Alexia! Look at your doll."

Alexia looked at the doll in the fire. She jumped up, grabbed a stick and popped the doll out of the fire.

It had not burned.

80.
Adieu

Dessa was aware of the sounds and feeling of a huge bird landing in the fire behind them. Suddenly, there were the harsh crisp sounds of beating metal. Like the inside of a blacksmith shop. In just three heartbeats all three of them were loose and they escaped somehow from the pyre.

Leaving behind the cooking Gaerwn.

It did not take long for a number of teenage boys to pile more wood on top of Gaerwn. It had not taken the people there more than the time it takes to blink their eyes to know a good thing when they saw it. And they took advantage of an opportunity they never thought would arise.

They were happily attending to the disposition of their despot.

Presently, it was obvious, that the unintended victim of today's punishment, Gaerwn, would not arise. Once everyone was sure of this fact, the entire crowd adjourned to the now vacant throne room.

Scraddius, knowing that now was his time to assume his rightful place as king, immediately ascended to the platform by the throne and announced in the flicker of candles, "Subjects of the kingdom, do not fear, for you shall have great leadership to keep you safe and secure in this time of turmoil."

A powerful, firm, and steady voice answered from the middle of the crowd, "Rest be assured we will! However it will not be you."

The voice of Ethelda had rung out strong and clear. She ascended to the platform in front of the throne with all the stately manor of the Queen she had grown to be over the years. She extended her hand to Scraddius, and escorted him down a couple of steps. His black eyes were burning holes in her; however she did not flinch, or even hint of any sort of nervousness.

Returning tall to the platform, Ethelda announced again in that strong clear queenly voice, "You deserve the heir of Gaerwn. And you shall have him!"

She looked down to where Torrin, Quillan and Dessa were standing in the crowd. And she pointed.

She pointed over Torrin's shoulder to the tall, redheaded, powerfully built man that stood behind him.

The crowd instantly parted, and Accalon, the blacksmith and head armorer of the kingdom stood alone.

Ethelda continued in her sturdy, commanding and calming voice, "When I was a young girl, Gaerwn had his way with me. I bore you and you are his true heir. I cannot say that you are a child of a loving relationship, but you are a child of love. I have had to leave you here for many winters, knowing that you lived a hard life. But I had no choice." Tears were welling up in her eyes.

The story continued to pour forth. "This is why Torrin could not be the heir to Trebor's kingdom. I had born an heir of another king. However we did what we needed to do, and made the best of what we had. I love you both. And now I retire, to let you make right what has been so wrong." She wearily sat now, of her own free will on the chair next to the throne where she had been captive for the spring.

As she finished speaking and sat down, the entire crowd of people, as if on cue, knelt. They knelt before their new true king. And a man they knew would be gracious and fair.

With hands trembling, Accalon stepped up to the throne carrying the large heavy iron maul that he had used to free the captives from the fire. He gently set it aside of the big overstuffed chair. He then picked up the spears that had rested next to the throne for many winters and one by one, broke them in half. Their broken halves clattering to the floor, signifying a final end to the terrible reign of fear that was Gaerwn.

Finally, finding the words that were eluding him, Accalon addressed the people. Now his people. "I honestly had no idea. All I can tell you is this: we have endured the worst of tyranny. We have though endured. And now, free from that curse, we will make a better life for ourselves, our families and our children. I have witnessed with my own eyes the power and creative spirit you all share. The genius you have that has been forced to serve evil."

Torrin nodded and remembered the clever things he had witnessed in this large sad place. The little stove that radiated so much heat. The curtains that muffled sounds around doors. The entire system of keeping vegetables edible for the winter. These people were a bubbling cauldron of creativity. And one evil wretch had kept them from sharing their gifts with the world and each other.

Accalon concluded, "And your energy, your families, your children shall serve evil no more!" The crowd erupted into wild applause. A feeling of light gaiety that they had all but forgotten to feel for so many winters.

Scraddius began to move towards the throne eying the broken spears on the floor.

Accalon addressed him, which stopped Scraddius in his tracks, hand reaching out toward a weapon, "Scraddius I need you as my advisor."

Scraddius stopped moving, hardly believing his ears. He looked up at the new king. He looked around the room. And being smart he knew he was getting the best deal he could hope for. Scraddius simply nodded "Yes."

Accalon continued, "And if she will have me, Paroish shall be my queen."

The crowd parted and the beautiful, tall, blonde girl, now lady, approached the throne and knelt down on both her knees, tears streaming down her face. Never in all her life had she ever thought that something like this would or could happen.

For that matter, no one in the room thought any of this could ever happen.

Not now.

Not ever.

A hush descended over the room, as the whole people of the kingdom took in the incredible changes that had just occurred.

And as the quiet enveloped the room and peace reigned, Quillan said in a strong and meaningful voice, "I hope ye don't mind, but we shall leave at first light."

* * *

As you can well imagine, no one really got a lot of sleep that evening. Torrin and his mother concentrated on catching up. Dessa, Paroish and Glenna had some very frank discussions while consuming the now disposed King Gaerwn's best wine.

And of course, Dessa and Torrin took a moment to run their

clasped hands over the face of Paroish. The black and blue bruises disappeared and her radiantly soft skin returned its glow.

Quillan took the very sad form of Etworth's body outside, and he was buried with the other poor souls that had been hanging on the walls of the castle. He and the guards did not really have a "good" time, but it felt right to finally lay all of these wretched people to a calm rest in rightful graves.

One of the points that was very obvious to the three visitors who had wrought so much change was that the people in this kingdom did not know well how to celebrate. So after the cleaning up was done, Accalon opened the stores of the castle to the people. He proclaimed all the previous stores of the King to be of the common domain. And the people should rejoice.

It did not take long for the entire kingdom to figure out how to truly celebrate in a grand style!

                    *   *   *

As the dawn broke the black sky into the promise of a very new day, Torrin, Dessa and Quillan emerged from their room at the stables. Their packs and belongings followed them with the help of the attentive stable boys. And as they had figured, Bernabe had their grand steeds ready for travel.

Uta, Samoot and Calandra had been brushed almost to a shine. They greeted Dessa warmly. She told them they were in for a good ride.

A ride home.

After thanking Bernabe for taking such good care of the horses, the three of them mounted up. The big bald man was stoic, but in the clenching of his massive jaw, was a love that now could be shared with his world!

A fair-haired stable boy approached Uta's big head and he gave the huge stallion a gentle rub on the nose and then a bright shiny apple emerged from his coat. Uta said to Dessa, 'This boy has taken not only good care of all of us, he has attended to our every need and been as kind as soft summer rain on dry crops. He is a gentle soul; please thank him for me.'

With that, Uta calmly ate the apple.

To the boy, Dessa said, "We thank you for taking such fine care of these wonderful steeds. I can tell from the way he looks at you that you have been a kind soul, and he really likes you."

The lad looked up with large clear eyes to the redhead upon the grand stallion. He gently said, "Thank you ma'am."

And then, Dessa heard him say to Uta, although his lips did not move, "Ye is a fine 'orse. Lead the others safely. If ye ever return, I look forward to meeting you again. You are the grandest horse I have ever known."

Dessa's mouth was open just a bit as the boy looked at her, and she looked at him. And suddenly, for the first time, the two of them knew that they were not alone. It had never occurred to Dessa that there might be others who could talk to the animals. She sighed gently as her world just got bigger.

At that moment, as he was wont to do, Quillan took charge and decided it was time to get upon their way.

And they did.

As they began to move forward, Dessa noticed that the mud in the courtyard had begun to dry some. Windows that had been covered were open. People milled about, and they were actually talking to each other. Dessa mused that the spirit of good people would emerge quickly.

The three of them slowly trotted out of the big gate. They waved their goodbyes to people who came out of their hovels, faces alight with the new hope.

As they exited the gate they heard a thunder behind them. Five large guards on grand steeds with full saddlebags pulled up the rear.

Quillan asked, "What be the situation here?"

The lead guard answered pleasantly, "We have decided to join you for a while. We aim to spread the good news that the evil reign of terror is over." And then he added, "Thanks to you."

Quillan replied, "We are honored to have you as company."

The small company trotted slowly to the bottom of the hill. They wanted to warm the horses; they wanted to find their cadence.

Dessa said to Uta, "Are you ready?"

Uta said, "More than you know!"

And then, Uta said loud enough for all the horses to hear, "My friends, it is time for us to make thunder and go home!"

81.
Cinnamon

Quillan was oddly bothered and not sure how he ever could have gotten lost. Sure, he had left the trail to pee. By now he pondered, he should have learned to just let the others know he needed to stop and go. But they had kept sauntering forward. He remembered almost not being able to call out. Where was his voice?

Did not matter now.

He was lost.

Of course, he had stopped to enjoy a spot of tender heat from the late afternoon sun for a few moments. The bright warmth crinkly and bright in his eyes and the heat brought a smile to his face. But now the branches just keep sweeping across his face and the damnú horse keeps stopping to eat every time a nice clump of grass offered itself to his nose.

Just so damnú frustrating.

That was what was bothering him so much.

It was just so damnú frustrating!

He entered a clearing where he could stand up in the spurs and listen. He listened for any sound that would give away the others' location.

Any clue.

Any help.

Quietly and very slowly. So very slowly, he turned his head left, and then to the right.

Not a sound entered his ears.

Not one clue or inkling.

It was as if some unforeseen force had sucked every bit of nature's noise from the forest. His eyes could see the birds floating in the air; his peripheral vision sensed the squirrels busy at their late afternoon feed. Yet not one scratch of sound filled any part of his ears.

It was so quiet it almost hurt.

And then, it was there.

Just the faintest. One little bit and then gone.

He almost missed it.

And there it was again.

Just there. Just at the tip of his nose.

A sweet waif of a teasing scent. Not the sounds he had been searching for. But the most heavenly and sweetest of smells he had ever known. It filled him with a sense of peace and his mind flooded with the memories of Karina's baking. Her famous warm sticky buns, flowing with honey and chopped nuts with just the right dash of reddish brown cinnamon to turn simple baking into art. An ever present amorphous fragrance that deftly preceded her exit from the warm kitchen into the big room. The smell had a way of announcing her entrance with more panache and grace than even the loudest heralding court attendant at any royal ball.

That sweet smell of cinnamon coursed through his body, and set him at ease. His neck relaxed, his shoulders slumped down as the stress exited through the big red hands that held the reins of Calandra.

Suddenly for Quillan, all was right with the world and the stale hot air that had been trapped in his lungs flowed out with the release of the tension.

His oversized boots spurred the horse and he could feel himself chiding the animal to move forward and seek out the source of the cinnamon. Something told him that being near this place would be better than spending a cold dark lonely night in the ever damp woods.

Not far, he found emerging a home. As he approached the small dwelling, the cinnamon perfume was thicker and surrounded him, and he seemed to almost be in the fog of its essence.

A lone figure rose from what seemed to be a garden of roots. The light of the fading afternoon was darker now. The thick black wrap, glossy with forest dampness upon the figure gave not insight to the mystery of the person beneath.

Suddenly he was face-to-face with the figure. He looked down and he almost aloud wondered what sort of person would be cloaked in such a way. Alone, in the woods? Alone amongst the cinnamon?

Soft white hands of no large size swept up and removed the thick black hood. As it drifted back from the head, Quillan was held speechless by the simple beauty that stood before him.

Not one word was yet muttered. Words did not seem to have a

place here. Not much else seemed to have a place here, in this world now filled with darkening light and a simple cinnamon rule.

Quillan's speech, limbs and lips were stalled in her presence. She was not lovely. She was not beautiful. She was though, as a heart stopping simple form of art, so perfect words did just fail.

Round eyes, round face. A simple warm, broad, true and real round smile set upon pale smooth skin like sun bleached alabaster china. Dark ringlets of silky midnight black hair, speckled with sporadic white highlights adorned her radiance and lent sparkle to a quiet effervescence.

As he looked into her eyes, he was shocked to see that the whites had no lines. No red, no color. The stark contrast from her dark irises was almost unsettling. Always he had noticed with others the tiny veins that seemed to tell some sort of hidden story about a person. But here, was just pure white.

Her hand had stalled near an ear, and a ringlet of the fine black hair was wound around one of her clean white fingers. He marveled that someone who had been digging roots could have such white skin! Warmly he wrapped his hand around hers that lingered. Without a sound, she tilted her head, smiled at him and just stared in the purest sense of joy and happiness he had ever felt to wash over his entire being.

She then with what seemed no effort, began to shake his hand. He held on tightly, and as if by magic, she began to fade away, but still though shook his hand with the strength of a knight.

He then looked harder at her as the whites of her eyes melted smoothly into the darkening day and heard Dessa say, "Are ye gonna get up or shall we leave ye here to sleep?"

Quillan looked down and saw that he had a firm grasp of one hand in the other. The fingers of the hand he held were dark red. He must have been gripping verra hard. His bed roll was askew within the flittering sunlight of a new day.

He put his head back for a moment and tried desperately to remember the very vivid dream that had just passed before his mind. It had seemed so real, and was now moving with the speed of the sun away from his thoughts.

All he could think though, as he got up to join the others, was that he had just met truth in some way, some sort of truth beyond words. And was it to mean something for the future? Or now?

He shook his big red head slowly as he walked into the forest to do his morning ritual, careful to keep an eye on the path he took. So he could return.

As he stood by a tree and let the built up pressures inside from the night of sleep go back to nature, he wondered almost aloud if returning was the best answer to a question he did not yet even know. Return to where though?

And then a deeper thought emerged from within...

Why a cinnamon muse?

82.
Heading...

They all had spent a nice night in a well protected area of dense wood that provided shelter, fuel for a good fire and water.

Now upon the trail, all of them that were left in the group, thundered in great procession toward home. Clouds of dust rose from the hooves of the massive horses upon the trail.

The summer skies opened bright with warm sunshine to keep them dry and happy as they made their way toward their destiny.

Periodically, one of the guards who had accompanied the three veered off to a neighboring kingdom to tell the good news.

It was certainly a jovial pack of travelers.

Emerging at the top of a long and gentle hill, they looked upon the broad expanse of a large valley. The trail was clear, the day was bright, and their spirits were high.

They thundered on.

At the bottom of the hill, the riders reared up the horses for a short rest and a drink from a nicely travelling brook of clear water.

Dessa noticed with a great amount of amusement, that a few ducks downstream were happily quacking away. She remembered her remorseful self, before she had entered the cabin of Phlail the shepherd. The ducks in Phlail's valley had been happily taking care of each other as they welcomed the spring and warm weather. Dessa had felt like a barren sand storm since leaving her kingdom and the wretched attentive wiles of the dreaded Darius. She had envied the ducks and their ministrations to each other's needs.

Now at the brook, after the horses had drunk their fill and stopped their massive panting, it was time to go. Quillan challenged Torrin to see who could get to the top of the next rise the fastest.

And off they went.

At the top of the hill, in a dead heat, the two of them stopped. And turned around. What they saw took their breath away.

Dessa upon Uta, was now thundering to the north. A long trail of dust behind them. She had turned left at the bottom of the hill. She had not followed them. She was on her own way to a place that neither knew.

Or did they?

Quillan and Torrin looked at each other, and shrugged their shoulders. Then trotted back down the rise and followed her north. The others in the party separated from them and kept heading on to spread the joy of their news.

As Quillan and Torrin caught up with Dessa, the three were now together as one.

Again. As it should be.

Well, maybe?

83.
Issue

Of course, it is better to end a trip in the pouring rain, Dessa thought. You are so much happier to be home.

The three of them stood outside the walls of Tarmon's great castle in the wretched darkness and let the water run off their oil skins. Eventually a page of some sort had come out to ask them their business. Torrin had told the page that they were here to see the King. The Page had laughed at the good joke and told Torrin that they might be able to have a place in the stables tonight.

After a time, the small door to the side of the great entryway opened. Each of them crouched low over their steeds and entered in single file. They were covered with rain and the horses were heavy with muck from the trail.

The page with a whole squadron of heavily armed guards guided them to the stables. Once inside they dismounted.

A wizened old man slowly approached them. After regarding them for a moment, he asked them their business.

Quillan told him in no uncertain terms that they meant to spend the night and then be on their way in the morning.

The man said that they could sleep with their horses, under heavy guard. There was much unrest in the world, and very few visitors were welcome.

He lit a lamp and the three of them found empty stalls.

They had decided that when they entered Tarmon's castle, they had to be as gentle as possible. As far as they knew, Dessa was still wanted for murder and would burn at the stake if discovered. So pretty much, Dessa was hidden under her raincoat and said nothing.

After a time, the wizened old man brought them a tray of foodstuffs to share. There was clean water, meat, cheese and a few bits of dried cereal. As he walked away, a voice penetrated his mind and said, "Is there any chance you might welcome me home?"

*   *   *

The old man slowly straightened up and stopped walking. He turned to the voice that had come from under the wet black hood from the figure seated on the floor of the stall.

Slowly he walked forward. Gingerly, he grasped the front of the wet garment at the top and pulled it back. Even in the dim light you could not mistake the mass of red curls that released themselves from the confines of the wet oil cloth.

Gale gasped and fell to his frail knees. After a time he caught his breath and said, "One more day and it might have been too late."

*   *   *

Dessa entered Tarmon's bed chamber at first light. Sanura was sitting on the side of the big bed. A soft cool wet cloth in one hand and a look of concern on her face.

Sanura looked up at the intrusion and gripped the damp cloth so tightly that the moisture dripped from it onto the prone figure on the bed.

"Dessa," she gasped. "Oh Dessa, you have returned! But? Oh! Well, never mind that now." Sanura looked at the white figure of Tarmon on the bed and then returned her gaze to Dessa. She explained, "He caught a fever over the spring and it has just consumed him. There is nothing we can do." She shook her head slowly.

Dessa turned on her heel and ran from the room.

*   *   *

Gale, Torrin and Quillan were examining the hoof of a hobbled mare. She had stumbled into a gopher hole while playing tag with another horse. This mare was a fine specimen of an animal and they were considering ways to save her.

Dessa entered the stall, grabbed Torrin's hand and commanded, "Come with me."

Gale and Quillan shrugged as Dessa and Torrin sprinted away.

*   *   *

Dessa was running fast and Torrin could not get a word in to ask what was going on. Presently they came to a large door, now attended by a large gruff lady in a uniform of sorts.

She said, "Wait there you two. Ye can't be runnin' into the King's..." she caught her breath on her own words, eyes instantly wet and exclaimed, "No, it can't be!"

The cat was now going to be out of the proverbial bag. Dessa did not even consider dragging the servant into the room. She just barged in through the big door.

The fact that she was here, in the kingdom would be news everywhere in a flash. That did not matter right now.

Dessa approached the bed where Tarmon lay, withered and worn, Torrin in tow.

"Father?" she almost whispered.

Two gray eyes fluttered open and slowly peered around the room. His head did not move. Nothing else on his body moved.

As Dessa came into focus for him, color rose in his cheeks and one hand attempted to rise from the bed. The rest of his usually strong and virile body lay limp and useless.

Dessa threw herself upon the bed and hugged the first man she had ever loved. Now she was faced with losing him, before really finding him again.

Sanura stood by the window peering out to the rising of a new day. For her, it seemed that this would be the last of regular new days, with a great unknown before her. She was old enough, and wise enough to know that her future was completely out of her hands. A mug of tea was cradled in her palms and kept the morning chill that crept in from the window at bay.

Tarmon's lungs shuddered as he struggled for breath against the rising tide of fever and mucus in his chest.

Dessa pulled the covers back and tore open the top of her father's nightshirt. She motioned for Torrin to climb up on the bed.

It took him a moment to figure out what was going on and then it was clear.

They were to do it again!

Each of them used one hand to steady themselves; the other hands were attached to each other. Fingers intertwined. They lay their cheeks together, high above the dying man.

Sanura watched in amazement, not knowing, but trusting that something good was about to take place.

Back and forth their clasped hands slowly traveled across Tarmon's chest. His skin became red hot. Sanura could sense the fragrance of cooked rotten vegetables in the room.

Suddenly Tarmon sat up, and hurled himself out of the bed, knocking over Torrin in the process. He came to all fours on the floor and then proceeded to cough up and spit out great amounts of the terrible fluids that had haunted his lungs.

84.
News

All around the Journey Inn, the pounding and sawing work on the wagons had reached a frenetic staccato tempo. They had all agreed that the wagons needed to be ready to go by the summer solstice. The solstice was on the morrow.

No one really noticed the lone big horse with the tall soldier until he was very close. The noisy work just came to a slow stop as the soldier plodded into the big clearing in front of the Journey Inn.

Everyone there, whether they had a saw or hammer in their hand, knew where the soldier was from. His black and dirty uniform told them all they needed to know. This man was of Gaerwn's army. He represented the end of the world if he was the emissary to an attacking force. He could be the one asking them to surrender now, or be destroyed.

That was just the way it worked.

They all just of stared at him for a while. They knew they were helpless.

And then little Larenzque approached the man, in a somewhat cautious manner and said, "Welcome to Journey, what can we do for ye?"

The tall soldier said, "I bring news."

The other workers put down their tools, set their boards and logs upon the ground and gathered around the big man.

Something was amiss.

The soldier, whose name was Erantis, looked at the group gathered in front of him. He was instantly glad he had not come on a mission of destruction. He could easily have been the front of an assault. And with just a few words he had lured them all into a tight group. They would have been easy to slaughter. Easy prey. Not much of a sport. Anyway, none of that really mattered now.

Erantis said, "Do ye know the likes of a dark-haired man who travels with a red haired woman, a large red man and a peddler?"

The group nodded a positive reply and murmured a number of yeses. The feet of the crowd shuffled uneasily on the ground, wondering what was going on.

The soldier continued, looking a little grave, enjoying his being the center of attention when it did not involve killing anyone. "These people were captured by King Gaerwn. They were to be burned at the stake."

The group gasped audibly. But no one interrupted, waiting for what they hoped was more news. And hopefully good news.

He now waited for a few others to gather around. People were emerging out of the big building in front of him. And they seemed to be just emanating from all sorts of dark and hidden places in the woods. There were an awful lot of them. Maybe it would have taken a while to conquer this valley? Again, as he had thought before, none of that really mattered now.

Erantis continued with his story, "Just as they were being burned at the stake, the red haired woman did something to Gaerwn. It all happened so fast it was hard to see. But the real news is that the evil tyrant Gaerwn is dead."

It was a while before any person moved. The only sounds came from the goodness of nature that was all around them.

Nature, as it does from time to time, seemed to smile.

85.
Homecoming

Dessa stood before the court of law in Tarmon's kingdom. They reminded her coolly that she was still charged with the murder of Darius. They did not care who had perished at the stake that was supposed to be the end of her. Justice must still be accomplished according to the laws of the kingdom. She was alive, and it was wrong. She had not paid for her crime.

As the head justice lectured Dessa about the law in his boring monotone voice, everyone else in the courtroom stood. King Tarmon had purposefully entered the room with a number of people behind him.

An unsettled quiet descended upon the inhabitants.

The head justice stopped talking.

Tarmon motioned for everyone to sit.

And they sat, knowing that something was about to happen.

In a commandingly strong and powerful voice that surprised everyone Tarmon spoke, "My people, this has gone on long enough." He motioned for Gale, the stable master to come forward. Tarmon addressed him, "Tell this group what you know about the law."

Gale cleared his throat and began to speak. Not as they would have expected a keeper of horses to speak, but in a way that showed regal poise. "Our rule around murder came about because of the evil that Gaerwn represented. It is commonly held knowledge amongst the people of my age that once Gaerwn was no longer, we no longer needed this rule that added murder to murder. This law was enacted to keep the dangerous and fearful elements of Gaerwn's Kingdom at bay and in check when they were here, amongst our walls."

Tarmon looked around the room and asked as strongly as he could, "Who else knows about this?"

A few people in the gallery stood. Tarmon asked "Is it true?"

They all nodded their heads.

Tarmon turned toward the head Justice and said in a steely voice, "Are you finished here?"

The head justice said just one word, "Adjourned."

* * *

As was quite the opposite of Gaerwn's Kingdom, the people of Tarmon's knew exactly how a celebration should be carried out in grand style.

That evening they celebrated Dessa.

They celebrated freedom from an old law.

And they celebrated to the renewed health of their King!

During a celebration at court, there comes a time for a king to speak. When a king should make a proclamation. Tonight was to be no exception.

At the appointed time Tarmon made a sign for all to gather. He was feeling much better now, however still feeling his age. He stood as strongly as he could in the center of the floor and addressed the people of his kingdom.

"I have ruled for a long time. You are a fair and good people. You deserve the best. It is time for me to pass my crown to the person who deserves to guide you forward through the changes that now come, as peace and prosperity will make its way to this part of the world. And so, I willingly, peacefully and gracefully give this kingdom to my heir."

And with that Tarmon removed his crown, and placed it upon the head of a very unsuspecting Quillan.

* * *

As the dancing wore on, the drinks flowed, the music played and the entire people continued to rejoice. At one point, a bit tipsy Sanura led Dessa by the hand to a quiet alcove. It was time for a talk that was due now, before Dessa's departure.

Smiling smartly, Sanura began to talk while applying one long finger to Dessa's lips. This finger on the lips method was the way Sanura always kept the red-haired girl's attention. From toddler to teen. And now it still was effective.

Sanura began, "You have become a very daring and courageous woman." Her words were carefully chosen. Not slurred, just careful. "I am proud to have had a 'and in raising ye up and settin' ye on a course that seems to fit ye." And then Sanura raised a goblet to a toast.

Dessa did likewise.

They both had a long sip of their evening's beverage of choice.

And then Dessa did the most uncommon of things. She placed her finger on Sanura's lips.

The ladies looked at each other. Thin smiles of appreciation seeped to each side of their happy faces.

Dessa wanted to have a few words, "I am very grateful. You have been kind and most of all patient with me. I love you verra much."

Sanura let out a long sigh and they hugged each other for a long time. The words of their hearts now shared to each other's souls and seared upon their futures.

As Sanura turned away to reapply herself to the dance floor, she felt a strong tug at her shoulder. Turning, she looked close into Dessa's face. A bit of cloud had formed in the young girl's eyes and she said into Sanura's ear, "Was it truly an accident?"

Sanura questioned the question, "What?"

Dessa whispered slowly into Sanura's ear, "Darius. Did Darius fall on his knife by accident or was there more to it than the fate of luck?"

Sanura's eyes searched for a moment. She hesitated for just a brief moment too long, this telling a story she could never share. She smiled lightly, then purposefully shrugged her shoulders in a questioning way and left for the dance floor.

Dessa felt that little wretched piece of Darius that haunted a corner of her soul depart like dog's hot breath upon a blister. Nasty, evil and then gone.

She felt finally a wholesome peace. More than she could ever realize had been helping her all along. So much more!

*   *   *

A few days later the big gate was opened to release Torrin and Dessa for their return trip to Journey.

Before they could depart, a small band of riders appeared and entered the castle grounds. Two of the riders dismounted. A short man and a tall woman.

When the tall woman removed her hat, her long brown hair released to the air. She shook it into shape and said in a commanding voice, "My name is Normadia and I am here to find a big red man; where is he?"

They all heard a whoop of delight come from a window and then the sounds of running feet. The people saw their newly crowned king come running in a very un-kingly like fashion and sweep the tall brown- haired lass off her feet.

Both were smiling.

Torrin and Dessa did not leave until later that day.

It was a happy reunion.

86.
Headings

Both Dessa and Torrin enjoyed the leisurely trip back to Journey. The sun was warm, the forest was fresh with spring and they were in no particular hurry. Dessa rode tall upon Uta and Torrin upon Calandra.

The horses knew the trail and trotted along with ease. They were enjoying this adventure as much as the humans. There was no tenseness. No hurry. No reason to run, unless it was for fun.

Two days later they reached the large rock outcroppings above the fields of Phlial's flocks. The dark heads and white bodies of contently grazing sheep sauntered along in the distance. When the wind was right, their low bleating sounds were like nature's music upon the valley.

Dessa and Torrin with the two horses made camp in the warm noonday sun. The previous day had brought rain. Their packs, clothes and supplies had been made very damp and were in need of warm sunshine to dry.

They spread their belongings out on the large rock where Dessa had made camp and enjoyed a drying fire in front of the rock that had protected her that lonely evening so long ago. She released the two horses with instructions to not go far. They were free to roam, but must behave.

Dessa and Torrin ambled their way down to the creek where Dessa had watched the ducks frolic on her initial trip through this area. She marveled that the flowers and plants she had admired before had returned again this spring.

Stripping off each other's clothes, they used some scented soap to wash each other's skin clean and enjoy the luxury of sunshine in the meadow.

As a few bubbles floated down the stream, Dessa giggled silently to herself. Wondering if the "secret people" were looking up at the bubbles. The joy of her childhood remembrance brought more calm to her already relaxing mind.

Along with the solitude of being alone, they experienced the intense serenity of nothing around them but the mountains, trees and nature's creatures. It was nice to just be alone. Verra nice.

After washing, Torrin led Dessa up to a large flat rock that stood in stark contrast to the green grasses around it. He had laid out a bedroll on top of its flat gray surface. That bedroll was now warm and dry in the sunshine. He lifted her up onto the rock and then followed. They lay down together, arms entwined letting their damp naked bodies release moisture to the warm air.

After they were dry and the heat from the rock had warmed them, they explored.

They explored each other.

Carefully and slowly they attended to all the little bits of each other that are keenly sensitive to explore in your lover. Fingers flitted and tugged at delicate places. Lips moved slowly over warm skin that responded sometimes with goose bumps and sometimes with accompanied low moans of pleasure.

Dessa was always amazed how her attention could give rise to such changes in Torrin's parts. She enjoyed how his fullness filled her hands as she stroked him in alternating attentions of fast and slow. The feel of his heavy denseness was a delectable delight to her as she used tongue, lips and the softness of her face to edge him on toward greater and greater anticipations.

Torrin found himself lost in her curves and softness. He ran tongue and fingers from her toes to her ears. Nibbling and playfully biting just enough to drink into his soul the various alternating states of her skin. She was delicately soft everywhere, but in some places her skin held more thickness and he could feel the soft porcelain smoothness of her between his lips. As he explored the soft mound of redness that adorned where she and all women were cleft, he could tell from both wetness and the low throaty sounds she was uttering that he was performing the right magic.

Before long they could feel the heat of their passion forming almost dangerous temperatures upon the rock, and so Torrin tossed the bedroll into the grass to keep it from catching fire. Their bodies now lay on the smooth surface of the uncovered stone. Dessa grabbed his hair with both her hands and guided his lips to hers. They were able to share a deep passionate and long kiss. One they had not been able to do for quite a long time. The sparks and heat danced on the rock. The sparks danced in the sunshine for the world at large to enjoy.

Presently they both lay back enjoying the brightness of noonday upon their naked bodies. After the peace of being together had descended upon them, that peace left, and new urges entered. Torrin turned toward Dessa; her head was cradled in one hand. He slowly drew two fingers down her forehead, across either side of her nose, outlined her lips followed by a slow descending over her chin.

His hand outlined the curvature of her breast and gently stroked the soft underside before paying gentle attention to her sensitive nipples. Eventually his mouth and tongue followed lower where his hand had been and he explored that very tender part of her warm body in the sunshine, for a verra long time.

To Dessa it had seemed that her entire body had levitated off the top of the rock at that point in time where Torrin had created that incredibly hot magic. That magic that was completely indescribable, which happened between them and delightfully to her. It was a magic most often created by him with a careful coordination of his fingers and tongue. He had succeeded in warming her before, and now, he had set her as if on fire.

After catching her breath and letting the lightning that had seemed to course through her dissipate, she took control. Dessa lay him down, and spent time with her lips creating groans and signs from his very sensitive and happily well responding parts. Soon, she straddled him and slowly performed her own magic. As he completely filled her up, her now long red curls danced upon his chest, tickling his nipples. This was just the way she liked it. The tall dark-haired man now sported a smile that would not stop. As did she.

That night, two very satisfied lovers slept entwined in each other's bed rolls. The rocks in front were warmed by a hot fire. For the first time in a long time, after making love and attending to their every need, there was nothing but the stars to keep them company.

* * *

Dessa noticed as they rode away the next morning, that the ducks were still happy. Quacking away at each other, just as before when she travelled this way.

However, this time she shared that happiness.

* * *

It took almost the rest of the day to traverse Phlial's long valley. They stopped and spent a wonderful evening with the shepard and his sons. The boys had grown larger and wiser. Phlail was strong and happy. He was amazed at the lack of scars on Dessa's skin and told and retold the story of Dessa's heroics to save his entire family from the attack of the wolves. Torrin sat with his mouth agape as he listened.

The next day they encountered Tallon, who greeted them as long lost souls and of course they feasted on chicken. Tallon was interested to know that Quillan was now the King in Tarmon's kingdom. After just a few moments Tallon announced that he would be setting off to the kingdom. Maybe as early as tomorrow to check on his brother, and most importantly visit with his mother.

As Torrin and Dessa's journey continued, they passed the creek where Dessa had dispatched Haphethus. Not one sign of the evil man's presence on the Earth was about. They moved on, not needing to spend any energy in this place. Although, the forest had seemed to have regained equilibrium with the place.

It seemed peaceful.

As they rode, they longed for home. But they also longed for a warm bath in a secluded place. So they detoured some and headed for Bartoly and Rebecca's cabin.

They planned to repeat their evening in the shallow pond near the cabin. Celebrating the successful end of one adventure and preparing for another.

Attending to the needs of, and running the Journey Inn.

Dessa seemed to tingle as she rode. She had never experienced so many days in a row with such peace in a long while.

Torrin grinned a lot and seemed to never slow down.

87.

Transitions

As the two approached the little cabin in the woods, Torrin had thoughts of both adventure and peace. Bartoly and Rebecca lived free and pursued their passions with earnest. Both were always sought out to fulfill the needs someone had. Bartoly was the most innovative and clever smithy known to anyone. Rebecca could make just about anything out of clay that anyone needed.

Rebecca and Bartoly rejoiced in their arrival. Chores were quickly finished, especially with help from the two arrivals. Torrin enjoyed milking Jacqualde. Dessa relished close and unfettered time with little baby MacGowan.

They planned a great feast for the evening as they caught up on so many things that had engendered good in their respective recent past.

Rebecca demonstrated new colors and art forms that were finding their way into larger and more elegant fine pieces of kitchen ware.

Bartoly explained how adding various other bits of ore to his smelting was giving him harder and harder steel to work with. The new strength was amazing and he could craft lighter and stronger tools for his customers.

Of course Torrin and Dessa told their story of freeing Gaerwn's kingdom. He figured it was one he would have to become good at telling over the course of time.

Presently the day lent itself toward the darkness and the little pond beckoned.

Rebecca retired to the bedroom area to feed little MacGowan. The rest of the group cleared the feast of smoked turkey they had been sharing at the grand table near their hearth. And then Dessa excused herself to the privy.

Walking back, she found herself at the top of the valley's path that led up to Rebecca and Bartoly's cabin. She was right near the place where Ailis the Fergal and the horse had left with Chadus' dead body upon it to return it to Gaerwn.

The evening was settling upon the valley. A bit of lightness still adorned the darkening sky, and it outlined the tall mountains in the far distance. It was as if someone had drawn a jagged line across the sky in some sort of huge mural of nature.

Dessa sat down in the tall grass and just marveled at the site before her. One by one small stars began to appear in the distant horizon as the blackness slowly enveloped everything around her.

She more sensed then heard the footsteps behind her. She was not afraid nor surprised that they had come to see her. She was a little surprised that they had come together.

To her right the long large and shaggy gray body of Praritor settled in gently against her hip. She could feel the warmth of the day emerging from his thick fur. He put his big head upon his paws and seemed to be looking at the sky with her.

To her left, Ailis the Fergal settled in gently against her other hip. She felt him relax, and he also settled his head upon his large paws and looked at the sky.

Dessa said, "Although I am certainly happy to see both of you, something tells me you are here for some important reason."

Both Ailis and Praritor said nothing for a long while. She could hear their deep breathing and sense the rhythmic beat of their respective loving hearts.

Soon Praritor's deep slow bass voice broke the stillness, "We come primarily, no more or less than to bid you well."

Ailis said, "Yes that, and to let you know that the evil cat Sgail perished in the attack on Bartoly and Rebecca along the trail. You need not fear him any longer."

Praritor's head turned towards her; she could feel a bit of sadness in his eyes and then he said, "Many did not believe you could do what you have done. You have brought a peace to this forest that is something we have missed for many winters."

Ailis concluded, "I do not often say this, but it has been a pleasure serving you."

Both of these huge, stately and heroic animals stood together. They walked down the hill a few paces and then turned around to face Dessa. They stood shoulder to shoulder, neither much different in size than the other. Their steely gaze seemed to bore into her soul.

As Dessa was about to tell them a deepest thank you from her heart, a shooting star blazed across the valley. The light of it blinded her for a moment. And when her sight returned the two powerful creatures in front of her looked at her oddly.

Ailis let out a bloodcurdling screech that only a large cougar can produce and Praritor released a wolf howl toward the trees that told all of the small animals he was there.

Dessa asked, "What is it?"

Yet no response came. The two animals looked at each other as if they were surprised to be there, in each other's presence.

There was no response to Dessa as they both disappeared into the blackness of the forest from whence they had come.

Dessa felt like she had lost two wonderful friends. Their seeming lack of response to her question left her heart cold and at a loss.

She knew something was different.

   * * *

Torrin found her sitting in the grasses in the settling darkness.

He asked her what was going on?

She mumbled something about animals and nature and moving on. He was not quite sure what she was talking about.

Then she led him to the pond.

She needed a release.

Or something. She was not sure what. But she was sure it did not involve any clothing.

* * *

After the experience with Ailis and Praritor, Dessa was almost in no mood for a romantic bath. However as Torrin lit some candles and removed his clothes she remembered all of the tortures they had recently suffered. She decided that a little more play time was in order and she relaxed as her skin came in contact with the cool night air and she tossed her clothes onto the dry ground.

The water was chilly as the both stepped naked into its cleansing movement.

Wrapping their arms around each other they shared a deep passionate kiss. This was both for warming the water and for warming their mood.

The kiss warmed them as it always did. However no blue sparks and no extra heat was to be found anywhere.

Another transition.

88.

Home

Dessa and Torrin both knew that by the end of the day they would be back within the tall warm embrace of the thick walls of the Journey Inn. They had left Rebecca and Bartoly's cabin the day before and made good time on the trail.

Around them the landscape became more familiar, and the trail wider from heavier use. They picked up speed and conjured up the energy that would take them to their destination.

As always, the adventure of a trip is wonderful, but the warm embrace of your own bed, your own friends, and your own home are even better. "Beginnings and endings," thought Dessa, "bring such memories to all these adventures!"

As they trotted at a fast pace, Torrin wondered how Normadia had left the help in the kitchen, and what things would be like without her. It occurred to him that he was hungry for a good dinner in front of the broad, wide fireplace. His boots off and drying, feet up on a bench and fun people around him.

Dessa and Torrin turned the corner from the thick forest to the big field surrounding the Journey Inn. All at once, everything from the past month on the trail changed, and was at once, the same.

They were home!

Of course, as is the way of the forest, word had gone ahead that the two of them were thundering back home. And their world welcomed them back with gracious and open arms.

Children surrounded them as approached, offering to take care of Uta and Calandra. It was a distinct honor to be brushing down one of the grand steeds that helped to reduce evil to ashes.

Dessa decided that this much brushing might be a bit much. So it would be best to let the horses decide on their fate. So she asked them their preference. She was somewhat taken aback by the wisdom of the oddly long answer.

Uta said, "These folks have a need to pay tribute to the fate ye kept from tearing them apart. Tell the children that each shall have a turn. For the steeds would appreciate a brushing every day until all has had a fair turn."

After Dessa delivered the message, it dawned on her the irony of it. Uta had just guaranteed himself and Calandra special attention for many days. She looked at Uta and she could have sworn he smiled a silly grin.

But then all she heard was a horse's whinny. And the words they had shared so importantly were now lost. Dessa could feel sadness touch her soul. For she knew that the gift of chatter with Uta was now gone. Gone like the lost soothing warm bass of the words of Praritor. Gone as the wisdom and tight wit of the cougar Ailis the Fergal.

Dessa hoped for more, so she said to Calandra, "How was the trip for you?"

The only reply was a snort of air from Calandra's wet nose and a shake of her head to remove flies from her ears. Calandra's big eyes just took in the world as they came to a halt in front of the grand stables of the Journey Inn.

Dessa wondered how many more transitions would occur.

* * *

Dessa and Torrin dismounted. Instantly, the crowd gathered around and pressed in upon all of them, people and horses included. Questions and hugs flying to and from everybody. The jubilant turmoil was refreshing and seemed to be a good conclusion to a long series of mysteries and adventures.

After some time passed, Torrin ascended upon a large rock and addressed the gathered crowd. It was nice to see shining and smiling faces.

Faces of people he knew.

Faces covered with the dirt of the field or the dust of wood cutting.

Faces that kept track of energetic children.

Faces that would greet family members and friends warmly at the end of another day at the Journey Inn and in the valley.

At once, the words Torrin intended to proclaim stuck in his throat as the emotions in his heart almost burst in happiness. A happiness that brought tears to the edges of his trail weary eyes.

These good people had believed in a future together. They trusted him and their plans to be safe from the tyranny of Gaerwn. And now their happy throng, safe children and cheerful welcome overcame him like cool spring water on a hot day of work. Quenching, satisfying and clearly a gift itself.

After a few deep breaths, Torrin cleared himself of the choking joy in his throat enough to say, "Tis good! Nay great, to be back. Ye all are like shelter in a storm and yer greeting just makes our hearts a patter with joy."

Cheers and smiles, as well as raised strong arms and heads shaking in agreement, greeted his words.

Torrin continued, now with Dessa beside him, "But this happy occasion is somethin to really celebrate, and is cause for a good ol' fashioned party, Journey style!"

The crowd erupted. Ol' Dogger danced a happy jig with Ipi's hand in one of his.

Suddenly the eyes of the crowd grew wide, looking at a scene behind Torrin and Dessa. The two turned to see Larenzque with two other men supporting the longest alpenhorn Torrin and Dessa had ever witnessed. The three were sharing something from a small cask and wetting the mouthpiece of the horn. Obviously preparing it for use. Larenzque held a small black bag in his hand.

Torrin remembered the admonishing from Kamale last fall when the danger had been so acute. The words were still clear in his head:

> *"You need not worry. When you blow that horn, and you'll know the time to do it, we will be there. Every blasted one of us will be armed to the teeth and ready to destroy anything that gets in the way of who we are: our families, our children, our farms and our future."*

Suddenly Torrin was terrified. He instantly feared that Larenzque and his sturdy friends would blow the horn and the valley would erupt in a fighting frenzy.

Torrin shouted, "No, we are not in danger!"

Larenzque grinned mischievously and walked over to where his two heroes stood upon the rock. Smiling as only the powerful little man could he said, "We blow this many times for trouble," he held up two fingers.

Turning to the crowd, Larenzque shouted the question, "And how many times do we blow it for a party?"

As one, the entire assemblage raised one hand each and pointed three fingers skyward while shouting a loud, "Hurrah!"

As if by magic, all eyes were instantly on Ipi, and she said loudly, "That would be three."

And they all, as one, erupted in a chorus of "Three."

Torrin and Dessa looked at each other. It dawned on them how new they really were to this odd place of the earth. But they knew the right thing to do and they both held three fingers skyward.

With no further delay, one of the men who had been at Larenzque's side took in a great chest-full of air. When it seemed as though he would burst, he blew into the mouthpiece of the monstrous horn.

The sound was unlike any Dessa or Torrin had ever heard. Or for that matter, felt. The deep bass reverberations were as much a sense of variegated vibrations that pressed on their skin from the air, as one of sound that pressed upon their ears.

The billowing reverberations started a little slow. It actually started with a bit of a shrill. And then the bass of the horn took over and the bleat was one that would travel over hills, across forest paths and through the thick woods for a very long way.

When the first man was empty of air, the second man took over. The same sound and feeling erupted from the large end of the horn setting firmly upon the ground.

Very much the same sound.

Very much identical to the first in pitch and length of time.

Then the first man, now refilled with air, blew the third time.

This process was repeated two more times.

The next part of this wonderful little act of communication was just as amazing as the first. Because, Torrin and Dessa would find that the magic had now just started.

The most amazing series of events occurred.

All faces looked toward the distant mountains.

The clouds seemed to stop.

The chirplings of the birds were silent.

Not a creature in the woods stirred or made a sound.

The air itself seemed to hold its breath and be still.

A few minutes passed, as did the expected echoes from the far away mountains. And then in the distance, it began. Horns began to blow in answer to the great resonance and message of the Journey Inn's horn.

One

Two

Three times each blew.

Each with a slight variation of sound. Unique to its owner. Unique in length of time. But unmistakably, three each.

After a few minutes of blowing, the crowd turned to look at Larenzque. Their faces awash with question.

What Torrin and Dessa had not noticed was that with each response, Larenzque had taken a stone from a circle of stones he had quickly and carefully arranged on the ground. One by one, the stones had disappeared back to the small black bag. This was an indication that all the messages had been heard and answered.

However, one stone was still left.

Quiet mutterings ensued.

Eyes scanned the horizon.

Wondering.

Waiting.

Nothing.

Almost dejected, the group began to disperse. The party atmosphere still glad upon all their faces. But concern for the possibly lost soul weighing heavy on their hearts.

As always, the realities of the harshness of life, the work and their toil, and of the time they shared would remind them of the frailties of their very existence. Life would remind them to take with grace the blessings they could manage.

Then the shrill shriek of a child pierced the air. And as one, they all heard the distinct voice proclaim "Momma!"

A little blonde ragamuffin, shoeless and dirty, had screeched the word and was now pointing to the tree tops. Her face almost bursting in anxiousness.

And then, as only the spirit of a little girl could have felt it first, it came for the rest of them.

Low and mournful. A little short in length. But nevertheless. Three blasts from far, far away.

The mutual "Hooray" of the throng almost bowled Dessa and Torrin off the rock.

It was truly now time for a great celebration!

*   *   *

Anyone who could make this special party arrived within three days. Some had to stay back and attend to animals on farms. But anyone who could traveled the distance. And they arrived in good stead.

Loud, raucous music filled the air. Dancing by massively glowing bonfires was great fun for everyone. And of course, sharing what whiskeys and distilled forms of art everyone was brewing was a good order of business. Some of the batches of brew were still young, it being spring and all. But after the first few mouthfuls, it all worked!

The wagons that had been built for the sneak attack were used as lodging for some, and admired by all. A few of the folks who had worked on the wagons decided to add a wagon shop to the side of the great stables at Journey. They meant to start a business of selling these to folks who needed sturdy transport.

Grand storytelling to beat grand storytelling was almost a contest many participated in, but few cared to win, since winning did not matter here. Torrin and Dessa were telling stories of their time at the great dark castle when the topic of Etworth's demise arose.

After a great many toasts to the strange and tepid man's departed soul, someone asked about Kalmar. Where was it? What was it?

Ipi, who had been heading to Kalmar in order to head south before being trapped by the blizzard, entreated all who cared to listen about the great city on the sea. She talked of tall ships loaded with cargo. Huge sails billowing in the wind that bore these ships to and from the docks.

She talked of strange and wonderful people who were so different. So different, yet full of life. She told stories of distant lands. She talked of art and powerful kings. Astonishingly large castles beyond the size any in the north had ever dreamed of. She immersed all their ears on the realities of the harshness of life under these kings and their lords.

Ipi went on for a while. As usual, she was a great storyteller and could paint the picture of magic and mystery with her inspiring and colorful words.

Before the last bit of music for the evening was played, Torrin was directed to ascend a large boulder and make a speech.

He had been concerned for this request, and was not at all sure what to say. As he clambered up, he still was at a loss to bring forth words that could express the happiness and joy that surrounded them all.

At last he stood and faced the happy throng. Firelight danced on their faces and happiness in their eyes.

After a thought, he motioned and the tall redhead who was now obviously his companion for life joined him. They stood side by side. Hip to hip and very inseparable.

Torrin lifted his mug in the air and shouted, "To us all!"

That was all he needed to say, and all anyone needed to hear.

*   *   *

And life in the warming days of spring continued now as it was meant to at the Journey Inn. Warmth and color were in full blossom along with the activities that added so much variety and spirit to the days. Travelers, kauppasaksa, visitors and the regular lot were busy at work. Some stayed inside. Some outside in wagons or tents. New and wonderfully colorful kauppasaksa from far away displayed wares never seen before.

News of the demise of Gaerwn had spread. The threat of his tyranny no longer haunted travelers. No longer haunted the adventurous souls who brought niceties such as salt and silk to the hard working people of the northern lands. It was said that the ships of Kalmar were unloading all their wares to many more kauppasaksa who were now willing to travel north.

Dessa and Torrin had never witnessed such an array of goods and frivolities before. Glass in many forms, such as mugs and windows. Journey had some glass windows, but none that were clear and they lacked a prism from every angle. These were fine pieces of artistry from a place called the Espanola.

Knives, daggers and swords of all sizes and shapes filled one wagon. These were as fine as any work Bartoly could produce. At once, Torrin was concerned for his friend's ability to compete. That was until he found out that the kauppasaksa needed more stock and were looking for a good smithy.

Ipi was carefully scrounging about for rare items. She needed vanilla and saffron. Both of which were in abundance, but the kauppasaksa seemed to be asking so much more than Ipi cared to part with.

Dessa found blue velvet. Fine, soft and wide. It was of perfect creation. She walked away with enough to create a new gown to replace the old one she had brought along with the good wishes of Gale. She had pretty much worn it out and it was time for something new.

All in all, it did not take Dessa and Torrin long to get back into the cadence that was so much a part of the Journey Inn. They knew that summers were short, and they needed to make the most of the warm days that were offered to them.

A few nights after returning, they both collapsed into the soft sand of their clamshell bed. They did not need to lower the top down any longer since the mystery of the blue sparks had seemed to elude them for now. This was just fine for the summer, since it was very warm upstairs in their room anyway. The sand however felt cool against their naked bodies.

Dessa just now finally got around to telling Torrin about how sad she was to no longer have the ability to speak with the animals. She missed the great gray shaggy wolf Praritor and the cougar Ailis the Fergal. She missed knowing that they were looking out for her.

Torrin mused that it seemed to go hand-in-hand with their loss of blue sparks when they kissed. And then he suddenly became quiet and thoughtful.

Torrin said, "Harold told me when he and Karina left, that we might be surprised. Surprised at how the world around us would rise up to help us. Help us protect the promise. He said we needed to relax and accept it."

Dessa replied gently, "I guess when I think about it, talking with the animals is a pretty incredible thing. It seemed so natural at the time. I'm certainly glad all that was there when we needed it!" And the memories of her friends flashed through her mind.

She sighed a little and moved closer towards Torrin. Taking his big strong hand in hers she knew she was holding onto something that was real.

As they let peace settle upon themselves Torrin let out a gentle "Oh," and then quietly asked, "And I ave been meanin to ask ye. Did ye ever figure out what Gaerwn was afraid of?"

Dessa purred some as a kitten would when snuggling with a child. She stretched her legs some, relaxed and then said in a voice that was as smooth as fresh cream, "Nothing more than his true self."

Torrin said, "I am verra sorry, but my sweet lady, that does make no sense ta me."

Dessa took some moments to choose other words to explain, "He was afraid of accepting himself for who he was. That kept him from accepting anyone else. Because he did not love himself, he could not love his world. So he kept piling up things and people and kingdoms and armies to find happiness and peace. But it could never work, because he never could love himself."

She looked up at him in the dim light of the candles, the round top of the clamshell bed was up for now, since they did to have to worry about sparks. Her round eyes told him that she hoped he would understand, and then it hit him like a horse kick. The words Karina had used, "he's here." As if they really had been expecting him. He had been there, but it took the summer for him to really find himself. And when he did and accepted it, things started to fall into place.

And he looked down at Dessa. This wonderful, smart, warm and charming woman was now part of his life.

This place!

Things were not as he would have expected, but some things were beyond his reach. His control. But things were in so many ways right. And his heart settled some to more peace than he had ever expected to feel.

It had been a long day in the sun of farming and digging and the heavy chores that come with summer. After a warm kiss they both settled in for a long, well deserved sleep.

Torrin fell into a deep sleep after two breaths. She could feel him head into a deep slumber.

Dessa's tired mind searched for sleep. However, the possible new question inside her body that had arisen the other day for her stole her peacefulness. The profoundness of it took far too much energy and kept her mind swirling for her to find rest. She decided to ask the midwife Kneafsey about it in the morning. Once she had settled her mind on that goal, she relaxed.

Finally she was fast asleep.

     *   *   *

It was very dark.

Torrin felt his head graze the edge of the top of the clamshell as he quickly sat up in bed.

Something was wrong!

Smoke!

As he ran down the hall toward the stairs that led down to the big room, the doorway exploded toward him…

The End…

       Well, maybe not…

Epilogue...

Kneafsey looked at the half burned mug in her hand. Its contents were stale and on the verge of spoiling. She hoped some new casks would be ready by the morrow and water could be brought from the falls. Her legs were too tired to walk the path for clean water, so she drank what was there.

The beverage was evil, but evil seemed to go with the mood.

The sun was setting and cast strange shadows from the forest across the flickering flames of their small cooking fire.

Kneafsey said to Ipi, "It's one thing to ave em die in your hand when they is jus a wee thing. It's another ta ave 'em scream in pain all grown."

Ipi nodded and drained the putrid contents of the stained and chipped black ceramic mug held in her own bandaged hand. "Eye, it's all just foul."

Their eyes looked again at the corpses. It was as if they could not look away. The burned bodies, lined up to be put to the earth in the morning.

They would stand guard tonight to keep the animals away.

Journey
Part III of III

1.

~~Tough~~ Pure Love

And from the depths and mysteries of the deep and broad forest, to the ruins of the Journey Inn, the people returned.

They all returned.

Just as flowers emerge in the spring from what was frozen winter ground, they all emerged from the forest.

As leaves will fill the trees of the forest when the warmth and daylight conquer the cold black of winter; they all filled the field around the Journey Inn.

Many more people in number than the crowds attending and playing in the regular summer festival. Even more than the celebration that had just brought such happiness to them all. More in number than the good folk that seemed to wander to and away from the Journey Inn all during the warm days of summer, did they appear.

Hammers, saws, axes, pitchforks and shovels were their choice of weapons. Small forges upon carts pulled by strong steeds were already fired in the morning light, ready to build, bend and create.

Together with eager faces and strong arms, prepared to work did they stand. They stood side by side, ready to beat back the evil that had taken what they loved.

And they would take it back together.

* * *

Torrin clambered up and stood tall on the large rock that not long ago had been the center of the great party. His eyes scanned the crowd. The sheer magnitude of the number of people astounded him. He was instantly humbled that so many folk would drop their work, put their home on hold and come to help.

Unbidden.

Unasked.

Unpaid.

Dessa reached up a hand and he held it. He held it for just a moment, and then brought her up to stand beside him. It was clear to him now, more than ever, that she was with him. That they stood together.

Never ever really alone.

His gaze turned over his shoulder at the black ruins of the Journey Inn. Hot flashes of the memory of their narrow escape were still seared in his mind.

The door that exploded out at him in the hall had saved him. Saved him from being cooked by the flashback of flames that shot out of the stairwell and for an instant covered the space and ceiling above him. If he had been standing in the hallway, he would have been gone in that violent moment of explosive flame and scalding heat.

After that instant of unstable flashback fire had subsided, Dessa dragged him back to their room, while banging on the doors to the rooms in the hallway. She made sure everyone that was on the second floor was following them. One by one, they quickly escaped a fiery death via one of the large windows in that special room Torrin and Dessa shared. Safety was but a quick run across the roof of the stables and a short jump to the ground.

Some twisted ankles and one broken arm had resulted from this second story escape. No one was terribly injured though and all were entirely grateful.

The same could not be said for many other poor souls. Poor souls who had been sleeping in the dark of night in the big room downstairs.

The big room that had been their safe haven, until it turned to turmoil and death.

Journey had escape windows. But as with any fire, for anyone in it, their world was dark, smoky and turbulent. These escape windows were hard to find in the ensuing panic and confusion. Yes, these windows had been a savior for some. For others, a goal that was never achieved.

Two other doors had been built for just this sort of event. But unfortunately, as is often the case, some people had stood up as they ran from the room. These unlucky folks were instantly suffocated by the heat and smoke. They fell in the doorways, blocking others' escape.

For the rest of the dark night, Dessa and Torrin had used their healing powers on as many as they could. They saved many. Cured many wounds.

There were limitations. They could not rush the process. And it drained them quickly of their own energy.

As the sun rose to illuminate the devastation, their eyes saw their worst fears. And then Dessa became very sick. She retreated to the forest for a while to let the nausea calm. She knew the nasty feelings would pass, as they had done for a few days now. She and Rebecca had talked about and even shared a bit of a laugh at the cross they had to sometimes bear. A cross that gave them but the greatest gift of all.

Torrin was worried for her, but she assured him that she would be fine, after a fashion. She hugged him gently and told him that she was the least of his worries right now.

* * *

Standing on the rock, Torrin shook these memories away and returned to look at the crowd. Just as this crowd had looked for guidance and assurance when they heard the news of the Gaerwn's intent. They looked now for the next step.

But they looked for more. More that they could not have, and he would not promise. For what they needed, was much deeper than what they wanted.

Torrin and Dessa had discussed this at the waterfall the day after the fire. Many people were gathered there. Washing what they could. Nursing wounds. Supporting each other.

Mourning.

Resetting.

The talk around the water had been of rebuilding. Of creating the new Journey Inn. Of a bigger, better, safer and longer lasting building. One that would last for more eternities than the original.

This talk engendered back the spirit of these damaged people. This talking was what they needed right now. The needed to build some hope.

He and Dessa had quietly together disagreed with the talk. They agreed between the two of them that something more was needed. Simply rebuilding the structure was not what was needed deep in the hearts and souls of the people here in the valley.

After consideration, they took counsel with Ipi. They knew they needed her deep thinking.

They found Ipi seated on the ground, her back against a wagon wheel. She was cradling Ol' Dogger's head in her lap. Dogger had lost a hand saving Alexia from the inferno. Dessa and Torrin had been able to heal the wound, but his hand was gone.

Dogger looked haggard and old.

Ipi looked haggard and old.

Dessa and Torrin explained their feelings to Ipi. Their feeling that simply rebuilding the Journey Inn was not what was needed. That there was a larger opportunity. An opportunity to deliver the destiny that had been worked on and so carefully preserved for so long.

Ipi sat with lips pressed together for a while. She was deep in thought as she stroked the singed hair on Ol' Dogger's head.

Then after a time, Ipi agreed with them. Yes, there was something more, and something less that was needed. She spoke just a few words, that solidified Dessa and Torrin's decision. "Yes, in times of loss, people strive to go back to the way they knew. The old way. They see it as the safe way. But to do so is not possible. To truly beat a loss, one must grow and create the new."

And with those words, Ipi fell into a much needed sleep from which there would be no disturbing.

*   *   *

Now, standing upon the rock, facing the people and after a long deep breath, Torrin began to speak. He tried his best to choose his words carefully and he held tight to the hand of Dessa. "We have suffered a great and mighty loss. We must mourn and honor those whom we lost and what we lost."

His eyes scanned the faces. Hardly an eye blinked in the bright sunshine.

"We are all sad. I am sad. I cannot put into words just now how I really feel. It is too difficult. But what I feel about the loss, is nothing compared to how I feel about this." And he waved his hand across the crowd, indicating the assembled group.

He continued, "Look around you. Look at what you are. You are bigger than this and you know it. You always have been and it's time that the Journey Inn became as big as you!"

The crowd murmured their agreement.

Torrin continued, "You must rebuild the Journey Inn. You must make it better and stronger and a place for the future. A place where you will teach. A place where you will love. A place where the very souls of every traveler and searcher of truth is welcomed with open arms. Just as you have done in service for eons before."

Loud applause and cheers rose up from the crowd. And then quickly died out as the very subtle nature of the words Torrin had uttered sank in.

Questioning murmurs now emanated from the group. People glanced around, questioning looks dawning on their faces.

And Torrin removed the subtly of the message.

"To truly love something is to build it and use it in service to others. We have accomplished that over many winters here at Journey." He paused to let the words sink in for a moment and then said, "But we have only accomplished that here."

Torrin breathed deeply and bared his soul with these words, "For us to spread the truth of the promise, to let others experience what we know as good and right, we must take it to the rest of the world. And when we do that, the rest of the world will prosper as never before. You and I both know, in our hearts, in our dreams and in our very souls; the only way to build a better world for our children, our families and our neighbors, is to live in a world that is free for all people."

A stunned silence descended over the crowd. The true power and uniqueness of what they had here in the valley had never really occurred to them as a group before.

Sure! Why not let others live free? Why not even out the power so that not only the kings and queens lived well, but all people? It worked here! It could work anywhere.

But to take it to the world?

Wow!

Torrin concluded, "We leave you in the very good hands of Larenzque to guide the rebuilding down at the waterfall. A place where running water will keep the new Journey Inn as fresh as the promise of this valley." Torrin nodded to Larenzque and was greeted with a confirming nod.

Someone shouted, "What if others won't listen? What if you fail?"

Torrin replied, "Then too many will suffer needlessly. Which is what will happen, if we do not take the chance to do what Valterra, Kaitlyn, Harold and Karina strived so hard to save."

"How will you do it?" another shouted.

Torrin smiled at Dessa and said, "Of that, you may be rest assured, we have no idea."

* * *

Since the fire they all had been living in the wagons that had been fashioned for the sneak attack on Gaerwn. It had not been easy, but was not terrible. They had stayed dry and off the ground. But of course, sleeping with four others around you every night did get old.

Torrin and Dessa agreed that some quiet time alone was sorely needed. They had both concluded that having a quiet and unhurried time to repeat the intimacy they had shared on the rock above Phlial's cabin was in order and overdue.

It was mid-summer before Dessa and Torrin were ready to make their way south toward the great port city of Kalmar. This trek would begin their journey of taking the promise that had left the sacked city of Troy thousands of years ago back to the populations of the world. And in doing so, they would face all the power hungry 'Gaerwns' of their time.

They packed their meager possessions, but really did not want for anything vital. The people of the valley had been very generous in resupplying their needs for their journey. And from what they had been told, it was only three days by a good trail.

The new Journey Inn was rising in good stead above the pool near the falls. More and more massive timbers cut straight and clean, greeted each day. It was construction of incredible proportions and great engineering.

The people of the valley had sent word to Gaerwn's old kingdom; they were looking for ideas on how to rebuild. Smart and practical engineers, craftsmen and artists of all kinds appeared to help. It was amazing how creative and innovative these folks were in the art of putting together a large structure. These people were joyful to be able to share ideas and innovations. Such as an ice cellar for the storage of fresh foods as the valley people had never seen before.

All of it, coming together and very exciting!

Torrin and Dessa were sorry to miss the completion of the new Journey Inn. They did promise to return and report on what they learned. They also promised to fill everyone in on their plans before leaving for any long period. If they decided to travel off the port to distant lands on one of the huge ships with the billowing sails, they would return for goodbyes. And, both Dessa and Torrin had some very important farewells to make to friends and relatives scattered about the vagaries of the beautiful lands of the north before going far.

In both their minds, they felt that the immensity of what they were embarking on was not yet clear. So they had decided that just maybe, this first foray was to see what the world had to offer. And to offer the world some new ideas, and gauge its reactions to these ideas.

As they trotted off down the trail, the sun was early in the day, but with a promise of warmth. Dessa sat tall upon Uta, she was still comfortable in the saddle. Although, she knew those days were not many. Memories of a large Rebecca on the horse with her after the rescue on the trail wandered through her mind. Dessa was already feeling a little full and somehow blossoming. It felt good.

Torrin rode Samoot as was usual. The mare had grown fond of his riding style and she always behaved. They paired well.

Calandra took again the role of pack horse. It suited her.

Dessa said to no one in particular, but loud enough for Torrin to hear, "I do declare, these horses still smell like a smoky fire."

And then surprisingly, she heard, "Maybe we need a bit of a bath."

Dessa was stunned to have again heard Uta's voice in her head. All she could muster in reply was, "Really?"

Uta said in a very matter of fact way, "Seems you are going to need our help."

Questions that need answers in Journey, Part III of III:

- Can the Journey Inn continue to thrive without people who have the gift?
- What does Uta mean?
- What reception will Dessa and Torrin receive in Kalmar?
- What really is Dessa's condition and how does that change their plans?
- Faith in what you believe is one thing. The culture of a city and the rest of the world can be very much another. How long will it take?

Answers to these questions and many more will be provided as we ride to the incredible conclusion of

The Love Story of the Century

Recipe for
Karina's Salve

For anyone curious, here is a natural recipe for Karina's salve.

I am not promoting its use at all. And it may be wonderful, or a complete failure for you. But the ingredients do make ya think. And, when you think about it, the nasty bugs that our friends had to battle with five thousand years ago, were not as nasty as they are today.

This concoction came from this website:

http://www.mrshappyhomemaker.com/2012/11/healing-boo-boo-salve-a-k-a-homemade-natural-neosporin

- 1/2 cup coconut oil (proven to help heal burns - plus it's anti-microbial, anti-bacterial, and a great moisturizer – read more here)
- 1/2 cup extra virgin olive oil (full of vitamins and a great moisturizer – read more here)
- 1/4 cup dried comfrey (a herb for healing wounds – read more here)
- 1/4 cup dried calendula (a herb for healing wounds and skin irritations – read more here)
- 2oz beeswax (equals out to 2 of the 1oz bars or 4 tablespoons – *you can also use beeswax pellets so you don't have to worry about slicing through it*)
- 2 tablespoons of honey (natural moisturizer with anti-microbial properties – read more here)
- 10 drops lavender essential oil (anti-bacterial, anti-microbial, and analgesic – read more here) (*optional*)

About the Author...

Catlan Samuels lives near Lake Ontario in upstate NY in the Finger Lakes wine region. The view from his writing desk is a dense forest through which runs a strong flowing creek. He seems to have found favor with a large family of chipmunks who enjoy the tops of his usual morning strawberries and inhabit the earth underneath his deck.

Friends say he can see over the horizon at a future for others that is often good, if they are willing to make the trek and stay to the true trail. Straying can find one in the company of a viciousness that has a bad lasting effect.

He and his sons share some passions. The youngest races things with motors and Catlan has been known to strap on a vehicle and take it for a spin around the track at stupid speeds. The older son and Catlan share a love for outrageous scotch and an annual Christmas tradition is to find the wildest one around for each other. One bottle, recreated from the Endurance expedition, sits carefully in a wooden box in the cabinet (look it up, simply amazing stuff!).

Hiking the NY Adirondack high peaks left a lasting impression on Catlan as a young man and continues to be a passion today. His love of the forest is clearly evident in his stories. He is passionate about the power of people working together and the everlasting quest for finding true love and freedom dominates a large part of his somewhat oddly wound brain.

To find out more and to keep in touch...

- Google Search: Journey Catlan Samuels
- Amazon: Amazon.com/dp/B009WBJAO0
- Barnes & Noble: Shows up in Google search – Nook version
- Web site & video: TreborArthurPublishing.com
- Facebook: Catlan Samuels
- Twitter   @CatlanSamuels
- Email: catlansamuels@gmail.com

Made in the USA
Columbia, SC
04 March 2021